PAGE *from a*
TENNESSEE
JOURNAL

PAGE *from a*
TENNESSEE
JOURNAL

FRANCINE
THOMAS HOWARD

PUBLISHED BY   PRODUCED BY

amazon encore   MELCHER
                     MEDIA

Text copyright © 2010 Francine T. Howard

Printed in the United States of America
10 11 12 13 14 15 16 / 10 9 8 7 6 5 4 3 2

This book was originally published in hardback by AmazonEncore in 2010.

Published by AmazonEncore
P.O. Box 400818
Las Vegas, NV 89140

Originally produced by Melcher Media, Inc.
124 West 13th Street
New York, NY 10011
www.melcher.com

Library of Congress Cataloging-in-Publication Data
2011907788
ISBN-13: 9781612181301
ISBN-10: 1612181309

Cover design by Laura Klynstra
Interior design by Jessi Rymill
Cover photographs: (top) © Vintage Collection/arcangel-images.com;
(bottom left) © Natural History Museum of London/Alamy;
(bottom right) courtesy of the Library of Congress

SOMETIMES I THINK YOU WHISPERED YOUR SECRET
INTO MY EARS WHEN I WAS STILL IN MY CRIB
BECAUSE YOU COULDN'T TELL ANYONE ELSE.
I PRAY THAT I'VE DONE YOU JUSTICE.

Thank you, Miz Mabry.

CHAPTER ONE

Annalaura Welles stirred out of her fitful sleep to the certainty of two things. Husband John was gone for good this time, and even with the help of her four young children, she would be unable to bring in the tobacco harvest by the end of August. Though this was coming up the second year she'd sharecropped the McNaughton mid-forty, she still wasn't used to living in the converted upper reaches of a barn.

The sky loomed dark through the small window cut at the foot of her sleeping alcove. She owned no clock, but her tired bones told her it was about a half-hour 'til sun rising, and she laid a tentative hand on daughter Lottie's bobtailed braids as the five-year-old slept soundly beside her. Almost drowning out the child's soft sighs were the snorts of the three pigs on the bottom level, fifteen feet below. The smell of their fresh dung made its way up through the openings in the floorboards. The cows hadn't lowed their own good mornings yet, and she wanted her Cleveland to get a little more rest.

She had to work him like a man, but Annalaura was always mindful that her oldest boy was not yet twelve years old. She fretted just as much over Doug and little Henry. All four of her children would have to step into the world way too soon if she couldn't sort out this mess John had left her. A moonbeam flooded through the open crack in the roof that McNaughton had neglected to repair during last winter's snows and she realized she had awakened too early again.

The first two weeks after John left in early June hadn't been too bad. She knew going into her wedding thirteen years ago that no man as good-looking as John Welles was going to stay faithful for long to a woman plain as a corn-bread skillet. But now it was mid-August with harvest time closer than she wanted. In all his wanderings, John had never been away from her, or his children, more than two weeks. She reached an arm over her head to locate the splintery rafter beam to guide her as she eased herself to sitting. She had knocked herself in the head too many times to attempt getting up quickly in these tight quarters. She knew colored still lived in some bad conditions in Tennessee, but after all, this was Our Lord's year of 1913. Even in slavery times, her Aunt Becky and her own grandma Charity had lived better than this.

She shifted her feet onto the rough, knot-pitted floorboards and raised her body upright with just the merest rustling of the corn husks that made up the mattress John had given her as a wedding gift. Before she stood, she checked again on Lottie, who had barely stirred in her sleep. Annalaura had no intention of awakening her children before sunup, knowing they would get no rest and precious little food until way past sundown. Lottie had squirmed most of the night in the heat of the barn. Sometimes Annalaura could swear that the pigs and the cows below were choking all the air out of her children for their own breathing. Standing, she bunched her nightdress in her hand. The thin fabric felt wringing-wet damp with her sweat. Barefoot and stepping carefully from the planked box McNaughton had built to serve as a bed for his tenant farmers, she avoided all the familiar squeaks and creaks in the wide-apart floorboards as she checked on the remnants of last night's supper, which would soon serve as today's breakfast. Annalaura lifted the cracked saucer she'd laid over the remains to ward off the mosquitoes and the mice. She poked at the four hardened biscuits. Though her three-year-old, Henry, had reached for a second, she had to take the crusty bread from his hand and divide it between her two older boys. No amount of explaining that she had flour enough for only ten biscuits a day, and that had to serve the five of them for two meals, could comfort a wailing Henry.

As she walked across the floor to the clothes nail hanging on the wall above middle son Doug and baby Henry's little pallet of a bed, she remembered how John had described the place when he first saw it. "This room ain't big enough to hold three six-foot-high men laid head to foot in either direction." Then, she had to laugh to keep from crying at how low they lived. Now she was terrified that soon even this sty of a place wouldn't be theirs.

In the dimness, Annalaura shimmied her nightdress over her hips and reached for the nail that held her work outfit. As she lifted the gown over her head, her hand brushed her breast. For a second she wondered what John would think of her body now. He had always pretended that her middling height frame was "just right ... not beanpole skinny nor so fat your bottom fill up two seats on the church pew."

With food being stretched like it was, Annalaura knew she had lost weight. She put a quick hand underneath her breast and gave it a little boost. Hadn't changed all that much she thought. Her husband had told her that she had tight tits, and she guessed that was still so. Sometimes, when he didn't know she was watching, she'd catch a gleam in his eye like he believed she had the best-looking female shape in all of Montgomery County. But what did she care what John Welles thought about her body? She couldn't put any stock in the words of a man who had probably laid down with a dozen women before he ever met her and two dozen afterward.

Annalaura reached for her work shirt with its two missing top buttons. Waiting to earn enough money for a new spool of thread, she had saved them in the old snuff tin she'd believed she had hidden so well in the smoke house. Never mind, she thought, as she stepped into her ankle-slapping skirt, the waist band twisting on her narrowed body. There'd be no one who mattered to see that her blouse wasn't properly fastened under her chin. She patted her chemise and drawers, which lay on the shelf above the nail hooks. She only had one set, and they were for Sunday. Besides, there was no need to put on drawers and a chemise on a scorcher of an August day like this one promised to be. Not when she would be in the fields from just past breakfast 'til sunset. With her work brogans laced on her feet, Annalaura climbed down the ladder leading to the bottom floor, hitching up her skirt as she moved. She held her breath as she walked by the three sows and the two milk cows. She didn't know why. They were no more smelly when she stood close to them than they were when they sent their special aromas drifting upward to the barn rafters and her family.

Several feet outside the barn sat the chicken coop. Just beyond, stood the brick smoke house that McNaughton allowed the family to use for the preparation of its meals. That is, when Annalaura had food enough to prepare a meal. Inside the makeshift kitchen, Annalaura checked the larder. With half a barrel of flour left, she figured she had enough to last 'til the harvest in mid-September. She had a jar of dried butter beans, and used with care, the contents could be stretched into next month. The only slab of bacon John left her had run out two weeks ago, but she still had half a can of bacon fat. The cornmeal was low, but she reckoned she had enough of that for bread once a week 'til harvest. The garden had very little left in it. A few pinched-in tomatoes, one row of tired green onions, and the last of the pole beans were all that were left standing. In normal times, she would have put in the turnips and her other fall vegetables, but there had been no money for the seed—not after John had cleaned out her snuff tin of all but two dollars back in June. She hefted the weight of the salt container and the baking soda. Both were too light to the touch. Annalaura had been taught to be a good manager, and she suspected that was the real reason John Welles picked her over all those other females who swarmed over him like a hog going to slop.

She had been seventeen when twenty-two-year-old John came parading his wares in front of her. To say that she was surprised was to put the lie to the sun coming up in the east. Yet, when he asked, she had nodded her slow yes. Even back then she wasn't really sure about John as a husband, and now she had the hard times to back up her earlier doubt.

To announce the arrival of the sun, the rooster began strutting his stuff and greeted the day with a piercing crow. The dark silhouettes of the tobacco plants came marching up at her like short children. And that was the problem. Would the plants be tall enough for harvest in two weeks?

As much as she wanted, she couldn't put off facing the truth much longer. She carried a pat of lard for the breakfast biscuits as she climbed back up the ladder. The cows mooed their discomfort.

"Ma, I can start the fire in the smoke house." Cleveland's voice came out of the gloom of the second platform bed on the opposite side of their living space.

Annalaura stepped off the top rung to see young Henry stretched out on the straw pallet he shared with Doug. Lottie had already climbed down from their platform bed to sit herself on one of the two backless crates at the table.

"Never you mind, Cleveland, I put the fire on. Lottie, I put some butter beans on the back of the stove for supper. I want you to watch them." Annalaura set the chipped cup with the bacon drippings on the table. Little Henry jumped from his perch and raced his middle brother, Doug, for the same crate chair. Doug won, and Henry set up a howl.

"Come sit with me, Henry, and hush up that noise. Cleveland and Doug, we've got a hard day ahead of us."

"Momma, cain't we have somethin' else besides biscuits and bacon fat for breakfast?" Lottie dropped her head on the table for an instant. Brightening, the five-year old's cocoa-brown face broke into a wide grin. "Let's have eggs. I'll go fetch them." The little girl thundered to the ladder.

Annalaura shook her head.

"Doug will help you put them on to boil, but they ain't fo' breakfast. They gonna be our noonday dinner." She reached for one of Henry's shoes and tried to jam his foot into the tight-fitting high top.

"Momma, I'm hungry now. I want eggs now." Lottie poked out her lower lip and gave Annalaura her best "po' chile" pout.

"Eggs now. Eggs now." Henry clapped his hands. The grin spread over his face as he celebrated his sister's misery.

"Hush up, both of you." It pained Annalaura to let her voice sound as sharp as it did. Too roughly, she shoved the shoe onto Henry's protesting foot. Ignoring his screams as best she could, she eased him to the floor as she tried to compose herself. Annalaura couldn't let the children see how bad off things really were. At least, not until she could come up with a plan. She got her voice under control. "No mo' than four eggs now. I don't think them old hens is laying much any mo'."

"Then, can we have that old one for supper tonight? Ain't had chicken in ever so long." Doug's voice sounded chipper, though at nine, he should already have known the answer.

If not, Cleveland was there to supply it to him.

"No, you jackass. If we keep eatin' the laying hens, we won't have no eggs at all." Cleveland dodged Doug's slap at his head only to be met by Annalaura's backhand to his shoulder.

"Ain't I told you 'bout no swearin'? 'Specially in front of ladies and children." Annalaura looked down at Henry, still on the ground protesting the offending shoes.

"Papa swears sometimes." Cleveland folded his arms across his chest and wagged his head, looking so much like John that it gave Annalaura a startle.

"Your papa ain't never swore at me nor you children not nary a time and you know it. Decent folks don't use those kind of words." Annalaura clamped her eyes shut for an instant as her head swirled her world around her. She couldn't take out her fear on her children. "It's just a hard day comin' up, is all." She watched her eldest drop his hands to the table and look over at her.

"Every day is hard for us, Momma." Cleveland's voice dripped the sound of a weary old man.

Annalaura sucked in her lip. It wasn't right for children to have to pay for the sins of the father. While Henry bellowed his discomfort and Doug and Lottie scampered down the ladder, Annalaura stood to get the kitchen knife. It was time to cut the sole from the leather on Henry's shoes. Cleveland followed her with his eyes.

"You think Papa will be back befo' the harvest?" For all his manly cares, there was still something of the little boy in her firstborn, and Annalaura was glad that all his childhood hadn't been taken from him. He still had hope.

"Yo' papa be back in due time. He left us here 'cause he knew we'd be all right." She pulled off the vexing shoes. Annalaura didn't like telling lies to her children, but she had just come upon the idea herself that her husband was gone for good.

"You think Papa's gone to Clarksville?" Cleveland's doubting voice showed more than budding growing-up lows and highs.

"Clarksville's not but five miles away." Annalaura knew that if John were in that close-knit colored community, she would surely know about it. "I reckon you could be right. Yo' papa's sure to walk through that do' just about any time now." With the shoe sliced open to allow Henry's toes wiggle room, she swept the boy back onto her lap.

As Annalaura slipped the shoes onto her toddler's feet, Lottie and Doug bounded up the top rung of the ladder.

"Did you get them cows milked, Doug?" She sat a now-pacified Henry back on the floor as Cleveland headed down the ladder.

"Ain't much milk, Momma." Doug held out the half-full pail of still foamy white liquid. Henry grabbed a cracked cup from the table and banged its side.

"Why'd old man McNaughton take that calf last month, Momma?" Doug asked.

"Ain't nobody know the ways of white folks. I heard tell he sold it." She guided Henry's hand into the pail and helped him fill his mug to brimming.

Lottie, grabbing the only other cup the family owned, dipped it into the bucket, splashing a few drops of milk onto Henry's face. Doug stood staring with unseeing eyes at the two young ones. Annalaura scowled. Her Doug was not a patient child.

"Lottie, let Doug have a sip of yo' milk," she commanded a protesting Lottie.

Her second son looked up at her, one bare foot behind the opposite knee.

"Momma, you think I can go to school after harvest?" Doug looked back at her with the face she thought looked most like her own.

They shared the same copper-shaded brown skin and the same wide-set amber-colored eyes. She didn't know how to answer this brightest of her children.

"You said I could go to school when the tobacco got in."

"Lord, boy. Why are you botherin' me with school? We got us nothin' but work aplenty to get that tobacco in." She put an extra sharp edge to her words to hide her own growing misery. She'd find a way to fix this mess. She always had.

"I got to go to school after last harvest. Didn't have to quit 'til spring plowin' neither." Defiance crept into her boy's voice, and she knew what was coming next. "Papa would let me go."

Annalaura dug her nails into her palms to keep from screaming out the truth to this child. "Get yo' boots on and get on out to the field. If we can get this tobacco sticked by September, I'll make sure yo' papa lets you go to school."

The smile on her boy's face was worth the lie.

CHAPTER TWO

Alexander McNaughton looked over the food wife Eula Mae spread before him. It was the same breakfast she had prepared nearly every day of their twenty-year marriage. His eyes swept over the green, flower-printed oilcloth covering the kitchen table. Everything looked like it was there. A mess of eggs—she usually scrambled four for him—the four thick slices of bacon cut from the slab kept in the smoke house, the porridge bowl brimming to the top with grits, the potatoes cut into chunks and cooked in lard, the basket of fresh-baked biscuits in the center of the table, his big mug of black coffee were all there. Yet, something was missing. He glanced over at Eula standing at the stove tossing the tops of the green onions into the grease sizzling in the big cast-iron skillet. He watched her finish off the second helping of potatoes she knows he will want. Without a look in his direction that he could detect, Alex watched his wife pick up the crock of butter, turn, and walk toward him. She set the butter down on the table within easy reach. He gave her a barely perceptible nod as he picked up his fork.

Eula was good that way. Alex didn't have to waste time telling her the same things over and over. She just knew what had to be done around the place and got right to it. Unlike most women,

Eula didn't spend her time yammering over nothing. If it hadn't been for the rare, late delivery of the butter this morning, Alexander wouldn't have given his wife even this much considering. Sometimes, a thought entered his head that he should tell Eula how much she meant to him, but loving words had never come easy for him. Besides, speeches full of sugar could turn a good woman's head and spoil her. He shot a second quick glance at his wife. What Eula lacked in looks, she more than made up for in hard work. With her tall, sturdy frame and arms almost as big around as his own, Alex never doubted that he had chosen the right woman all those years ago.

Not that he had much choice, mind you. Lawnover never did have a belle in all the forty-three years of his life. The closest claim to a beauty came from the neighboring Thornton place—Eula's younger sister, Bessie. Now, that girl had potential. Much smaller-framed than Eula, with high, pointed tits, and hair the color of corn tassels, Alex had thought about sparking her even though the Thornton clan stood more than two notches above his own in what passed for Lawnover society. But, before he could act, some rich dandy from Kentucky swept her away. With his hundred and sixty acres of hardscrabble tobacco land, Alex couldn't compare to a man with three hundred and sixty acres of good Kentucky bottom.

After Bessie Thornton, no respectable, single white women were left in Lawnover except for two widows, and they both had children. Alex did not fancy raising another man's get. Since his place had to be farmed, he needed a no-nonsense woman who didn't need a lot of petting or pretty words. He took his chances with Eula. Though she was a Thornton, her homely, round face and big-boned body had already made her a spinster. When her father said yes and Eula didn't object, they married.

Eula took her seat opposite him at the table just as Alex mopped up the last of the bacon grease with a biscuit. She set the fresh bowl of fried potatoes down. He signaled that he wanted no more. He spotted the look of mild surprise on her face.

"Got to go check on the mid-forty this morning." He was not in the habit of telling his wife his comings and goings but today was an especially busy one. "That friend of Ben Roy's is comin' by to leave the rest of the money for the calf. Tell him to put it on the bench in the smoke house."

Running his hand through his still thick, pale yellow hair, Alexander moved to his feet, sloshing a bit of coffee onto the table. He caught Eula looking at the top of his head. At least he hadn't gone bald like almost all of Eula Mae's male Thornton kin. As she wiped up his coffee spill with a clean dishrag, she worked her mouth to speak.

"Did I hear that the colored man on the mid-forty run off?" Eula didn't usually start a conversation with him.

Alex had already moved toward the door when he turned back to the sound of his wife's voice.

"Something like that." He took in her look as she worked her skinny lips to say something more.

Lucky for her that she had never been pretty because time hadn't done too much more damage except for the gray streaking her field-mouse-colored hair. Her sun-reddened skin had long ago taken on the look of badly tanned leather, pockmarked with pea-pod-size brown dots. Alex knew that was the way of it with white farm women.

"Isn't he the same colored man that brought in the big money last year on that po' piece of land you rented him?" She held her eyes at the collar of his shirt.

It didn't pain him much to give Eula her due when it came to managing the household money. There was none better in all of Lawnover, but no woman needed to know all of her husband's business. He didn't like discussing money with a woman, but Eula was right. He had let the sharecropper family farm his worst forty acres last year, and they had made him three thousand dollars, more than twice as much as any other tenant farmer he ever had, black or white.

"I remember when they come here asking to farm the place. The man…what was his name…he said he could make some money for you." Eula turned her eyes directly on him.

"I recollect him saying some words like that, but all niggers pretend they can bring in a bumper crop. You can't set no store by what a nigger says." Alex remembered the man. "Name of John, I recall. Said he was John Welles." Then, he remembered the woman. She was part of the colored family that had lived on Thornton land since way before the War of Secession.

"He looked strappin' big enough to do the job, and that oldest boy looked like he could be a pretty good help too." Eula looked him straight in the eye as she spoke. "Ben Roy says he hasn't seen him around in a month of Sundays." Eula walked back over to the sink and pumped water over the dirtied dishrag.

Alex frowned. Why was Eula's older brother meddling in his business?

"Ain't the first time that nigger's run off. Usually stays a week or two. I reckon I know the ways of my hands better than your brother." Alex glared at his wife. She knew as well as he that the tenant farmers were his business, not hers, and especially not Ben Roy Thornton's.

"It's just that I had a feeling early on about that man." She wrung out the dishcloth as she turned toward him, her eyes searching for a spot somewhere between his collar and chin. "Did it seem to you that the man was a bit too forward? Not uppity, mind you, just a little…" Eula's voice trailed down low.

Alex read respectful apology in both her words and her eyes. Though he had every right to be upset at his wife's indiscretion, he nodded his head. She was only a female. Even so, Eula did seem to have a good head for sorting out people. Most times, she had the good sense to know that it had to be the husband who decided these things. Still, there had been something about the sharecropper that caught Alex's eye two years ago. Maybe Eula was right. The fellow had skirted too close to uppity.

"It's not but two weeks 'til harvest." Eula's voice strained out of her throat. "If the man is gone, who you gonna get to bring in the tobacco?" The quick flash of worry that crossed his wife's face was dashed away almost before he could see it.

"I reckon I can sort that out without either you or Ben Roy telling me how," Alex snapped as he scowled his displeasure.

What had gotten into Eula? Had his wife talked around the barn to get to what was really bothering her—the tobacco harvest? Yes, it would hit him in the pocketbook in a tight year if the nigger actually had run off, but money worries were not for women. Eula knew that. Talk of money around any of the Thorntons always started that rumble in his stomach. Most of the time Alex felt just fine with the clothes, food, and furniture he'd provided for Eula in their twenty years together. But, every now and again, something came along to remind him that he had married a Thornton girl, raised with taffeta dresses, real china plates, and a half dozen colored cooks and maids. He'd never had a harvest big enough to provide his wife with even one full-time cleaning woman. Not that Eula had complained about his ability to support her. At least, not that Alex had noticed.

Eula dropped her head and stared at the well-scrubbed floorboards. Both reddened hands went to her bosom. He watched her suck in and then poke out her lower lip like she wanted to say her sorrys. Instead, she walked to their black wood stove and stirred the peaches he finally sniffed bubbling in the big pot.

"You canning more preserves?" He tried to soften his criticism. Eula had meant no disrespect, he was certain. "I'll bring you back some mash, and you can make peach brandy."

Without looking behind him, he stepped out of the door. Alexander had to fix this mess on the mid-forty. He couldn't afford to lose three thousand dollars and a chance to get Eula a little help with the cleaning. If the man was really gone, he'd have to throw the woman and her get off the place and find another nigger soon.

CHAPTER THREE

At only ten in the morning the sun had already blazed through the long sleeves of Annalaura's shirt. Perspiration cascaded down her forehead and arms as she swung her hoe at the offending weeds. Standing upright, she wiped the sweat off her face as she glared at the trespassing foliage. The weeds were keeping the tobacco plants low. She lifted an arm again and planted it across her forehead, wishing that the threadbare cotton of her work shirt could sop up some of the sweat coming faster than she could wipe it away.

Annalaura tapped the hoe to the ground. 'Cropping had always been tough work, but last year, with John, Cleveland, and even Doug, the family had stayed on top of the job. Without John...she pushed the thought of her missing husband from her head. She glanced over at Henry, who had dropped to his knees in the next row. The child had mounded a pile of dirt scooped from around the rugged root of one weed. He wielded the stalk of a particularly low-growing tobacco plant to push a small pebble over his newly constructed "hill." The boy had given voice to each piece in his play.

"Henry," Annalaura shouted. "Stop that playactin', and get on up ahead to find me another patch of weeds." She watched a reluctant Henry stop his game.

Untying the bandanna from her head to wipe at more sweat, Annalaura sighted Lottie over her shoulder. She had assigned her daughter's weed-pulling duties close to the path that separated the barn and smoke house from the field. That way, Lottie could run in and check on the supper butter beans every hour or so. But Lottie was neither checking on supper nor pulling weeds. The girl skipped between two rows of tobacco, singing her made-up song. Annalaura shook her head. Unscrewing the lid from a Mason jar full of fresh drawn well water, she motioned Henry toward her. Seeing the water, the boy ran to his mother and reached for the container. Annalaura guided the rim to his lips. She called over her shoulder to Lottie without looking at her daughter.

"Stop that skippin'. Take yourself a draw of water and get on back to work." She nodded her head in the general direction of a second Mason jar laying on the ground near the smoke house.

With Henry squatting on the dirt watching the antics of an earthworm, Annalaura took a swig of liquid from her own jar. She wet her palm with a few drops and rubbed her hands over her cheeks. So much heat sprang from her legs that she felt they had been wrapped tight in a feather quilt. She flapped her long skirt to stir up a bit of air. The relief was short-lived. Sucking in her lower lip, she bent down and grabbed the back hem of her skirt. She brought the cloth forward through her legs and up to her waist. Annalaura snatched up the wide sides and tied the whole thing into a knot at her middle. While the briars might prick at her bare legs, at least from ankle to mid-thigh, her legs would get some relief from the suffocating skirt. Rolling up her shirtsleeves and flapping her arms in the air, Annalaura tried to stir up another breeze while her eyes scanned the acres for Cleveland. The boy was nowhere to be seen.

Ever since John disappeared, Cleveland had taken on the toughest jobs without being told. Annalaura reckoned he must have been working the fence line dividing McNaughton's mid-forty from his back acreage. She knew the tenant farmers on that piece had a better spot of land than she and John had been given to farm. At her colored church on Sunday mornings, she spotted the family as newcomers to Lawnover. While the woman was round and pudgy, the man was of good size and their two sons looked almost grown. The family hadn't said more than a polite "howdy do" to the old-time Lawnover colored. Still, even with all their back-forty hands, it had been the Welles family who brought in the most, and the best quality, tobacco of all the McNaughton acres last year.

The new family was on the back acres again this harvest. Like everyone else in Lawnover, they would know of her troubles. Annalaura realized they believed they could best the Welles family in 'cropping now that John was gone. She tried to swallow away a lump that came into her dry throat. If only she could say a good, out-loud cuss word against her missing husband. She shook the notion away. Annalaura didn't have the energy to waste on a man as stuck on himself as John Welles.

When the dandy of Lawnover came courting, nobody had been more surprised than she. Annalaura even told her Aunt Becky she wasn't sure about this caller. Didn't folks call him a "sportin' man?" But Becky said John had more than gambling, drinking, and woman-chasing in his head. With his good sense and fine looks, he was the colored catch of the county. Annalaura had never wanted a "catch." She just wanted a man who would work alongside her—a man who wanted more than to sharecrop some white man's acres for the rest of his life. John Welles was not only discontent to tenant farm, he also wasn't happy staying true to just one woman. Annalaura tossed her head to clear it. She had no more time for a man who would leave his wife and children in such a fix.

She dropped to a squat and pulled at a particularly bothersome weed. From her spot, she looked up at the sky to see nothing but an uncommon blue. Almost all the rest of Montgomery County was praying against rain this close to harvest, but not her. Annalaura needed those shoots to grow bigger, and she needed that spurt right away.

A twitch shot through the right side of her back. She unwound her knees and hips and arched herself to her feet. Raising her hands over her head to stretch out a threatening kink, she looked down at Henry. Still spread-legged on the ground some ten yards distant, the boy played both parts in a make-believe puppet show using two weeds to act out the parts. Annalaura shook her head. She had no further words for either of her youngsters. She could only drive them so far. As she swung around toward Lottie, two crows on the fence post separating the main lane from the rough path leading to the barn and smoke house took sudden flight. Annalaura shaded her eyes with a hand. Her heart did a two-step as she stared down the path at a horse and rider trotting toward the barn and her.

"Henry, get over here, now." She had no time to cajole her son with soft-sounding words. Even a three-year-old had to recognize the sound of danger in a mother's voice. Without moving her head as the rider approached, Annalaura hissed at Lottie with lips moving as little as she could manage.

"Quit those weeds, and come over here slow." Annalaura's whispered, no-nonsense command caught the girl openmouthed.

Fright replaced surprise on the child's face as she instantly dropped her fresh-pulled weed, bent double, and walk-ran to her mother. Annalaura's eyes remained on the horse and rider.

The visitor could only be a white man because no colored would be out riding the lanes when it was harvest time. Besides, no colored could afford a horse like the gray Annalaura saw approaching her. Dread as heavy as the Tennessee heat landed on her bare head. With her hands on the shoulders of both Henry and Lottie, she pushed them further behind her skirt. Without moving her head, she slid her eyes from side to side in a frantic attempt to locate Doug and Cleveland. She thought she spotted swaying in the tobacco stalks some fifteen rows distant. She prayed that both her boys would stay quiet and out of sight. Just before the rider slowed his horse enough to see her face, Annalaura dropped her eyes to a spot at the middle bricks of the smoke house. As the man reined in the gray some twenty yards from where she stood with the two children, she shifted her eyes to the horse's foreleg.

"You doin' any good out there?" Already, the voice was harsh and accusing her of the worst.

Just as she feared, the rider was the owner of the acres her family tenant farmed—Alexander McNaughton. She gave Henry and Lottie securing pats as she raised her head in line with the horse's flank. It was a carefully practiced motion that let her lift her eyes up to the rider's trunk so she could, at least, read his body movements with him unaware that she was watching.

"I'm doing right fine, suh." She kept her voice low with just the right amount of practiced servility in it. She saw McNaughton's brown-booted foot, covered by his faded work pants, stiffen in the saddle. She gauged him looking over the acres. She kept her neck bent and her eyes busy as she waited minutes for him to speak again.

"Don't look right fine to me." The suspicion in his voice came as no surprise to Annalaura.

She stilled her shaking shoulders. It was now her job to tell this white man that summer sun couldn't stop a determined colored woman from doing what she had to do, man or no man.

"Yas, suh." She made sure he heard the contriteness in her voice that she had been found out in a little white lie. "We's workin' hard at it, suh." She drew out his title in one long bowing-and-scraping breath. "Gonna bring it in for you, suh. Just like last year."

There. She had opened her battle plan. Remind him of the bumper crop her family had given him at the last harvest.

"Last year ain't this year, now is it, woman?" He shot her his first warning.

But, warning or no, Annalaura had too much to lose not to fight back.

"No, suh. It surely ain't."

McNaughton twisted in the saddle to scan the acres on the other side of the smoke house. She took the opportunity to raise her eyes a fraction of an inch while she still kept her neck bent low. When she watched the middle of his blue work shirt swivel back around in her direction, she saw his trunk incline slightly in the saddle toward her.

"These shoots ain't nowhere near tall enough." He let the accusation hang in the air for her ears to take in.

She knew this was not the time to answer. Suddenly, McNaughton's face came within line of her lowered vision as he bent over in the saddle to rest a forearm on his knee. Her racing heart picked up a pace, and she squeezed Henry and Lottie's faces into the folds of her hiked-up skirt. Little Henry coughed and she eased up just enough so the child could breathe. This white man was staring at her and her children.

"Those the only pickaninnies you got with you?" The words coming out of McNaughton's mouth lacked the same bite as the earlier ones, and to white ears, may have been heard as soothing.

But not to Annalaura. Without calculating the impact of her every word, she lifted her chin, and for a brief instant, looked directly into this white man's face. Her own inside warning system pounded through her ears, but her words came out faster than she could listen.

"I have four children, sir." Even though talking proper to a white man could earn her a good beating for being "uppity," she made sure he heard every syllable of her carefully enunciated sentence. She let every bit of the teaching she had received that one winter from the colored teacher down from Fisk University linger in each word. Her children deserved to hear from their momma's own lips that they were more than a white man's insults.

She dropped her eyes to just above McNaughton's belt buckle praying that he hadn't caught her twin infractions—raising her eyes to his face and speaking like colored could be educated the same as whites. She watched him sit upright in the saddle as his left hand jerked on the reins. Then he slid his forearm to his knee again. Barely aware, Annalaura dug her fingers hard into Lottie's shoulder as she fought not to look into this man's face a second time. She heard little Lottie's soft whimper of pain, and Annalaura began rubbing the sore spot.

"Tell me then, woman, where are your other two children?" His words and his sound didn't match, and Annalaura had to catch herself from looking directly at him.

He had called her a "woman." Coming out of the mouth of a white man addressing a black female, the word meant little more than hussy or worse—a woman ready to be led to a man's bed. If that's what he thought, she had to make quick amends. But the sound of him had suddenly softened, and that worried Annalaura even more.

"My older boys is workin' the far field, suh. One is almost fo'teen and the other jest about twelve." She knew the Lord would forgive her the lie.

With the greatest care, she eased her head up so she could see McNaughton's mouth. He was pursing his lips like he was thinking over some weighty issue.

"That would make 'em big enough to do some work." His tone sounded promising.

Annalaura couldn't help letting her eyes flash on his whole face. The top half of his head was shaded by his wide-brimmed straw hat, which kept her from reading his eyes. The lower half of his face was not as red from the sun as she expected. He turned his head slightly, and the light caught his deep blue eyes fixed on her.

With dawning horror, Annalaura realized that McNaughton had locked his eyes onto her bare legs. Thoughts tumbled in her head as her hands spasmodically opened and closed on the shoulders of her children. She wanted to loosen the knot at her middle and drop her hem to the ground. But nothing in God's Tennessee would allow her that modesty. No colored woman could ever show a white man that she believed he could be thinking those kinds of thoughts about a field hand. The heat and the worry made her head go light, and she felt herself sway.

"Ain't your man John Welles?" McNaughton eased the horse to the edge of the tobacco rows.

More to keep herself from falling, Annalaura's head came up. She fixed her eyes on his shoulders hoping that her offense would not be too great. Though she tried, her dry throat would not let her answer.

"Or do you have a man at all?" He didn't bother hiding the smirk in his voice.

She sensed his eyes scanning her thighs. One hand slipped from Henry's shoulder and almost went to the tie at her middle. She willed it back in place.

"Yas, suh. My husband is John Welles. He's gone up to Hopkinsville to see 'bout his folks. They doin' better now. My John should be back just about any hour now." She knew better than to ramble on like this with white folks, man or woman, but she had to let this man know that she was not an unattached colored woman. A colored woman without a man was fair game for every white man in Montgomery County.

"Hopkinsville is it?" McNaughton straightened in the saddle.

Annalaura kept her eyes on his shirt.

"What's Welles doin' in Hopkinsville?"

That he was about to catch her in a trap was draped over every word he uttered. McNaughton would want to know why John had taken off for Kentucky when he had forty acres of white man's tobacco to harvest in the next two weeks. Annalaura dropped her head lower. Hitched up skirt or no, she had to let him think that her husband knew his duty to white folks, to his family, and to his wife.

"My husband's family ain't from around here. They is from Kentucky. His auntie took bad off sick, but sick or well, my husband will be back to get in your tobacco." She jerked her head up quickly to indicate the acres in back of her.

She gave his face a quick read before she dropped her eyes again. He laid his forearm on his knee. With her eyes lifted as far as the lower half of his face, she watched him drop his head to the tops of her boots as he slowly slid his stare up her legs. She sensed his eyes come to rest just under the knot tied at her middle. A rash of prickly heat raised up on her lower abdomen.

"Woman, Hopkinsville or no, husband or no, you've got two weeks to get me my tobacco." She watched him straighten in the saddle. He pulled on the reins and headed the horse back up the path toward the lane. "Remember. Two weeks. 'Til the first of September, or you and your get are off this place."

She watched him dig his heels into the horse's side and set the animal trotting up the path and away from her.

CHAPTER FOUR

With little guidance from Alexander, the gray trotted up the path and turned right onto the lane bisecting his acres. He let the horse have his head as he fought the urge to look back. He didn't need a second glance to tell him what he already knew about the mid-forty. The tobacco stalks were too short, and he was middling uncertain if they could be brought in on time even if the woman did have a man on the place. He knew as well as she that the tobacco had to be in no later than mid-September, and that meant cut, stacked, and hung in the barn to dry. He hadn't dared hope that Welles could duplicate last year's profits, but getting nothing when he had hoped for at least fifteen hundred dollars would definitely be a blow. Determined as she was, that slip of a woman couldn't do the job, not even with the two older boys she'd lied about. No, it wasn't the tobacco that made him yearn to turn his head for one more look.

Rocking in the saddle as the gray moved down the two-buggy-wide lane to his back-forty, Alex let his mind wander to the woman. She didn't look like a good wind could blow her over, but neither was she built for work like most field hands. Eula had her beat by far in the husky department. Yet, he could see that she wasn't soft. One look at those tight, coppery-bronze thighs glistening in the mid-morning sun told him that. The way the rays caught the color of those bare legs made his mind wonder what other pleasures she had under that hiked-up dress.

Alex slowed the horse to a walk as the gray approached a leafy canopy of alders. This close to noon, they both needed a cooldown. He ran his shirtsleeve across his forehead trying to dismiss the growing pressure in his groin. McNaughton forced his thoughts onto the new family on the back-forty. What there was of tobacco on their plot was taller than the Welles's acres. But that family was never going to earn him three thousand dollars. He supposed they put their backs into the work, but they were not John Welles. As the gray continued its loping pace, Alex squirmed in the saddle. He couldn't keep the thoughts away. He remembered the first time he had seen the Welles woman.

Most of the tenant families looking to farm came in the fall to see if they could work the last few weeks of the harvest, hoping that the owner would then feed and shelter them all winter. He should have known then that there was something different about John Welles. The man had tapped on his back door in April, just at the time when the hard winter ground was breaking up and the best farmers wanted to start their plowing. Most tenants didn't want to work then. White man had to drive them to the fields, but not so for John Welles.

There the nigger stood, hat in hand, big and strapping, looking like he could do the job. Welles had done most of the talking with his woman and children standing behind him. Alex had to concede that John Welles had been as smooth as corn silk with his words, saying all the things a tobacco farmer wanted to hear from a prospective tenant. Even then he thought Welles had sounded almost too good. Now, Alex realized that just as the new applicant came close to crossing the line into uppity, his woman spoke up and reeled him back. Today, he remembered his first look at the wife.

Those amber eyes, with their slight upward tilt, had come up just a fraction of an inch too much whenever she spoke. Her words came soft and low, just like they did today, but they always took the edge off whatever her husband had just said. As soon as she got her piece out, she stopped and let her man speak until he skirted close to the line again, and there she was, smoothing over his too-glib words.

Alex couldn't put his finger on what was so different about her. He hadn't thought her uncommonly pretty back then, but he hadn't yet stared at the soft oval curves of her face, nor those full lips that looked just right for a man to suck into his mouth. He hadn't taken in the whole look of her until today. Back then, it had been more in the way she stood erect behind her man. Even in that shapeless flour sack of a dress she'd worn, he could still guess at the outlines of her slender figure. The gray cleared the welcoming shade. Alex flicked the reins again as he spotted the next set of trees in the distance. It was getting harder and harder to ignore the stiffening in his pants. He took off his straw hat and fanned his face as he shifted in the saddle. Lord knows he couldn't remember the last time a hardening had come on unbidden with Eula. In their first year of marriage, he recalled hankering after her in that way. After she lost the baby, he supposed her interest in him waned, and so did his in her. It wasn't that he didn't need a woman, and most of the time, it was Eula he bedded. Unlike other men down at the back room of the Lawnover store, he had no need to complain about Eula not being willing. That was another way in which she was good. His Eula never refused him like some men said their wives did. Even Eula's brother, Ben Roy, had complained against his Fedora. Alex never had that sort of trouble with Eula. As far as he could tell, she seemed all right with whatever he wanted. Come to think of it, she never troubled him by what she might have wanted or not wanted. She knew as well as he, that a woman was there to do a man's bidding in the bed-room, and the timing was his call. After twenty years of marriage, he only needed to come to her every two weeks. Of course, that didn't mean a man didn't need some variety every now and again.

An oriole swept down from the upper branches of an oak tree and swooped in front of the gray's eyes. The horse broke stride a second before Alex could steady it as horse and rider cleared the second stand of trees. Now that he'd seen her again, he guessed that the Welles woman had never gone all the way from his mind. No wonder. Blackberry juice kept a man young. Every white man in Montgomery County knew that.

Scrunching his brow, Alex reckoned that the last nigger woman he'd bedded was about six months back. He'd gotten to her first after he learned that her husband had been killed on the railroad down in Nashville. She'd been good for a few rounds, and like always, he knew the change would keep him faithful to Eula. It had never crossed his mind to be unfaithful to his wife. Unlike his Thornton in-laws, he didn't keep going back to the same nigger women year after year. Once or twice a year with a new woman each time was good enough for him.

Alexander rounded the slight bend in the lane and spotted the fence with the missing rail that separated his back-forty from the Thornton place. He reminded himself to get after that new man to get it fixed as soon as harvest ended. As the horse neared the path leading to the old log-hewn cabin, he wondered if the Welles woman really had a husband who was coming back "any hour now." If she did, she was off-limits. No white man in these parts went with a nigger who had a man around the place. Made no economic sense. Husband was sure to get surly and slow down the work, wrecking things for both himself and the farm owner. It was smart business to only mess with nigger women who had no man around, like the widow woman he had last winter.

As his gray turned onto the narrow path and started toward the new family working in the field, the hardening in his pants rubbed against the saddle. McNaughton knew the truth of it and so did the Welles woman. No matter what she said, the sharecropper's wife, with those legs ready and more than able to straddle a man, had no full-time husband about the place.

Alex trotted up the lane to his own barn after riding his acres. What to do about the mid-forty still hung in his mind. He gauged the time at nearly three in the afternoon. The sun reigned at its August hottest with the sky showing no sign of rain in the foreseeable future. Without rain, there was small chance the stalks would grow much taller, even with all the weeding the Welles woman was doing. Patting down the gray, he resolved to give more thought to the mid-forty after he'd eaten the midday meal Eula was holding for him. He stopped at the pump at his closed-in back porch to wash his hands.

Stepping through the rear porch door into the kitchen, he barely nodded a greeting to Eula, who moved quickly to her feet as soon as he appeared. Except for the clear space in front of his chair, the kitchen table was cluttered with dozens of Mason jars, some empty, some capped, and others filled with peach preserves. Alex pulled out the mash from the Lawnover store he had visited after making his rounds and laid it on the table next to Eula's account journal.

His wife scurried to the stove and began ladling string beans and fried corn onto his plate. She topped it with two deep-fried pork chops and set the plate, mounded with his dinner, before him. He watched Eula move to the safe to pull out a fork just before he discovered its absence on the table. On her way back, she stopped at the stove to cut off a hunk of corn bread. As his wife bent over to lay his bread on the oilcloth, Alex caught the strong aroma of vinegar.

"You wash your hair?" He didn't bother to hide the touch of surprise in his voice as he ran the date through his head.

He slid his eyes toward the almanac calendar hanging on the inside of the open pantry door. Today was Friday, but was it that Friday? He spotted the galvanized bathing tub sitting on the floor of the pantry. Normally, it would hang from its hook on the back porch. Eula had washed her hair and bathed.

"Uh huh" was her only sound as she pushed aside her journal and set down her own plate.

Did she expect him to remember these things? Every other Friday he took Eula to bed. It was a routine that had worked well for them for nearly seven years. What was the cause of the washed hair he wondered? She only did that about four times a year. But he had no time to probe the whys of Eula's actions. He would be ready for her tonight.

A light knock on the back door caught a forkful of string beans on their way to his mouth. He gave Eula an accusatory look. She knew better than to have visitors come when he was eating his meal. With "I'm sorry" written across her face, Eula left her own plate untouched as she pushed open the kitchen screen door and walked across the porch to the back door. Whoever it was, Alex trusted Eula to get rid of them as fast as possible. He was surprised when she returned and stood over him without starting her own meal.

"Some colored man's at the door." Her voice sounded apologetic.

"What colored man?" Alex wanted to hear none of this. Couldn't Eula see that he had just started his dinner? It was her house, and she was responsible for keeping niggers or anybody else away who would disturb him.

Still, she stood.

"New to Lawnover. Says his name is Isaiah Harris." When Eula made no motion to sit, Alex put down his fork and stared at her.

"Wants to know if he can farm for you next year?" The tail end of her voice ended in a question.

The mid-forty, never entirely off his mind all day, flooded Alex's thoughts.

"It's harvest time. Lots of tenants want to work two or three weeks at harvest and then coast off me for the next six months." Alex pushed back from the table, though he did not stand. He ran the possibilities through his mind.

"Maybe he could help out on the mid-forty?" Eula did not meet his eyes when his face trained on hers.

"Can't this nigger come back tomorrow?" Annoyed at the disturbance, still Alex wasn't at all sure the mid-forty could wait until tomorrow.

Before Eula could bob her head yea or nay, Alex got to his feet, almost knocking over the chair. "I'll get this over with now."

The man who greeted him outside the porch door, stood with his head bowed, waiting respectfully for Alex to begin his greeting. Alex took his time looking over the fellow. At first glance, the man looked able enough. Almost as tall but not nearly as muscular as John Welles, this one verged on the skinny.

"What's that name again?" Alex estimated the fellow to be in his early thirties.

A man in his thirties was usually a decent worker, while young bucks in their twenties were nothing but trouble. Alex searched his farmyard for the man's family.

"It's Isaiah, suh. Isaiah Harris." The man busied his fingers turning the brim of his hat over in his hands.

The lane to Lawnover swept right by his barnyard, and there was no sign of Harris's wife or children. Alex shifted his weight and stared at the applicant.

"Well, Isaiah, how old are you?" Alex folded his arms over his chest in growing unease. A man in his thirties should be fairly settled in his ways. Where was his woman?

"I'm thirty-one, suh." Isaiah kept his eyes properly on the ground, and Alex liked the way he stooped his shoulders. John Welles had stood a little too tall for his own good.

"How many in your family?" Alex asked with Eula standing right behind him.

"Ain't got none, suh." The man kept his eyes on the bottom stoop of the step where Alex stood.

"Ain't got no what? Don't have no family or don't have no wife?" Alex's face drooped into a frown. "A man old as you ought to have a family unless he's a sportin' man. You a sportin' man, Isaiah?" He could smell the vinegar in Eula's hair assaulting his nose.

"Naw, suh. I ain't no sportin' man. Jest ain't got me enough money to get me a wife right now." Isaiah twirled the hat in his hands faster.

"How you gonna bring in forty acres of tobacco all by yourself?" Alex's frown deepened.

A single man most often brought a ruckus with him. Women helped settle a man—black or white. Something in his gut felt uneasy about the idea of an unmarried man on the mid-forty. Alex had just about made up his mind about Isaiah Harris when Eula whispered in his ear.

"He won't be by himself. That missing man's wife and her older boys can pitch in." The sound of her voice startled him and he half-turned toward her. "As soon as the crop is in, you can send them all on their way."

Though getting rid of a sharecropper who ran off whenever the notion took him felt like a good idea in Alex's head, Eula knew better than to bring up business matters to him, even if it was only in front of a nigger. He wondered if his wife had taken sick with her strange behavior.

"Isaiah, I'm goin' to think on it and let you know day after tomorrow. In the meantime, you think about gettin' yo'self a woman to keep you through the winter." He heard Eula gasp at his suggestion of unmarried cohabitation.

He smiled. Hell, they were just niggers. The Bible didn't say nothing about niggers not sleeping together before they were married. His mind flashed on Eula's brother, Ben Roy Thornton. What would the Bible say about him? Married to Fedora for almost twenty-five years, he'd kept the same nigger woman for almost six of them. As he closed the door on Isaiah, Alex decided that Ben Roy had committed no sin. After all, his brother-in-law wasn't keeping company with a white woman.

That night after Eula dried and put up the last of the supper dishes, he lay in bed waiting for her. When she slipped in beside him wearing her summer cotton nightshirt that covered her from neck to ankles, he turned off the lamp. No need to waste oil on seeing a sight that he had looked upon for twenty years. Though she had never had much in the way of curves and highs and lows, it was still better to remember her the way she used to be rather than the thick flabbiness he touched nowadays. Some Fridays he felt like he was laying his body across one of his downed alder trees after a spring flood. It was thoughts of the alone nigger woman on the mid-forty that hardened him enough to put it to Eula Mae this night.

CHAPTER FIVE

Though she never regretted her marriage to Alexander McNaughton and the stepped-down life it brought her, Eula still took great comfort standing in the oversize Thornton kitchen where her mother had directed the preparation of so many family meals. Back in Momma's time, one day during the last two weeks of August had always been set aside for the preserving and storing of the fruits of the garden and the arbor. Momma had a full-time colored cook and a cook's helper, but this special day was the time when all the Thornton women, blood and in-laws alike, gathered to peel, core, boil, and jar for the barren winter months. These days, there were about half a dozen more female Thornton kin than back in Momma's time. Still, the job took a whole day.

While Alex was off riding the fields, Eula had gotten up when it was still dark to gather and feed the chickens and hogs. She had milked all three cows before she readied herself to get into the buckboard Alex had hitched up for her. The ride to her childhood home on the neighboring farm had taken no longer than fifteen minutes.

Standing at the new six-eye, coal-burning stove Ben Roy had just bought for his Fedora, Eula alternated sampling from the five big iron kettles, all in various stages of cooking. She delighted in the routine of sameness, and through the years of this mass production had developed an efficient process to get the job done on the allotted day. Now, with six burners, she could keep five pots simmering, instead of three, with the sixth eye available for the cooling. That would cut off about three hours of sweat-pouring work. In the years since she took over the job as main canning-day cook from her dead mother, Eula had learned to block out the Thornton women's chatter and lose herself in her own memories of girlhood.

Although there were four Thornton sons, Eula and Bessie had been the only girls. She and her sister could not have been more dissimilar. Bessie, five years younger and half a head shorter, had taken more after their curvaceous mother in height and build, but she was her father's spitting image in coloring. Bessie's hair had definite yellows and light browns to it, while Alexander had once described Eula's hair color as "neither this nor that... more like the color of house dust..." Eula knew in her heart that he hadn't meant to hurt, so she never held the remark against him. But Old Ben had clearly favored his younger daughter with her creamy complexion, pinched-in waist, high bosom, and light brown eyes. Old Ben had said Eula's eyes reminded him of the burned underside of a cook pot. Her father had meant to hurt, and Eula did hold it against him.

Her father had just about cried when that Kentucky man came down and asked for Bessie's hand though she was only sixteen. It had taken Momma Thornton a lot of breath to convince her husband that the marriage would be a very profitable one for Bessie. But the old man had still been reluctant to bestow his blessings on the union until Momma reminded him that Eula would never make such a good marriage. In fact, their oldest daughter stood an excellent chance of being an old maid. In that case, it would be up to Bessie to take in her sister. Unable to deny the wisdom of his wife's reasoning, Old Ben bid a sorrowful good-bye to his favorite daughter.

"Eula Mae, are those peaches 'bout ready?" Cora Lee, one of the Thornton cousins, jarred Eula out of her musings as she stuffed a tea towel into a Mason jar to complete its drying. Ignoring the annoying Cora Lee, Eula bent over a pot of dark cherries just coming to a boil. She lowered her long-handled wooden spoon into a second kettle on a back burner. Filling it only a quarter full and raising it to her lips, she blew on the hot peaches to cool them before she stuck out a tongue to sample.

"I declare, Aunt Eula, I don't know how you can stand there over all those cooking pots in this heat." Tillie, Ben Roy and Fedora's just-married twenty-one-year-old daughter, patted the kitchen table, which was nearly covered with bowls of cherries, pits, peaches, cored apples, plums, sugar, flour, glass jars, lids, and sealing wax. Tillie's hand came to rest on her aunt's account journal. Flipping to the back cover, the newlywed began to tear at the last page.

Without thinking, Eula tapped the wooden spoon on the edge of the iron pot holding the cherries.

"Tillie, your momma's got a fan in the kitchen safe. Use it, not one of my journal pages." Eula gave her niece an apologetic smile.

"Eula Mae, you still writin' down everything in that journal of yours? How many jars of this and how many cans of that? I declare, all that figurin' would drive me crazy." Fedora waved the paring knife in the air while she held a half-cored apple in the other hand. "I can't be bothered. I just use stuff 'til I run out. If I need more, Ben Roy will buy it off'n somebody." Finished with the cored apple, Fedora handed it over to Cora Lee.

With a few quick strokes of her butcher knife, Cora cubed the apple into six parts.

"I just like to know how much I have so I can pace myself." Eula really wanted to tell Fedora that her Thornton mother-in-law had insisted that the mark of a good homemaker was how well she kept her farm books.

Mother Thornton had been a master at managing the household accounts on the large farm, and while Bessie was the prime target of her instruction, Eula had been a keen observer.

Right after her sister left for Kentucky, Alexander came courting Eula, if courting was the right word. There had been no long buggy rides in the country, nor any chaperoned picnics under the elms with Alex. He sat with her one time at the church social and the next she knew, Old Ben told her that a McNaughton had asked for her hand. She really didn't need her mother's constant reminders of how lucky she was to have escaped spinsterhood, especially since her twenty-second birthday was just six months away. Eula needed no prodding. She knew she was fortunate that a good-looking man had wanted her. Though the McNaughtons were just a notch above piss-poor, Alexander was more mannerable than her brothers. Better still, she had quickly understood the rules of their marriage from the outset.

Her husband had needed a good manager for his farm, and she had provided that and more. It took her no time to anticipate his every need before the thought came into his head. Even when she knew his decisions were wrong-headed, like the time he bought a lame racehorse with most of their year's tobacco money only to have to destroy the animal four months later, Eula held her tongue and stretched the two months' worth of winter supplies into four. Since she never talked back to Alex, nor disobeyed his orders, he had never raised a hand against her like Eula was sure Ben Roy had done to Fedora. She would love Alexander McNaughton forever, no matter what might come between them, because he had shown her his tender side when he held her in his arms all night after their baby girl had been born dead.

If there had been any problems between herself and Alexander, Eula would never discuss them with Fedora, though Ben Roy's wife was the closest in age and sibling order to herself. Even though Fedora always did act more Thornton than the blood Thorntons, and commanded the other females to confide in her, Eula never dared chance that discussion. She admired her sister-in-law for many things, but she never liked to confront her on anything because the outspoken woman always had to have the last say.

"Eula, how 'bout those peaches?" Jenny, a cousin on Eula's father's side, asked as she took two dried Mason jars from Eula's young niece. "Tillie, get over there and check on your aunt and them peaches."

"Hey, Jenny," Fedora's sharp voice snapped through the kitchen. "You ought to know by now that Eula is the best cook in the Thornton family. Because she don't have a hired girl, she's got more practice than the rest of us put together." Fedora kept her eyes on the apple in her hand. "Them peaches will be ready when Eula says they are. If you want to get yo'self out of here before the chickens go to roost, we'd all better stick to our own jobs."

In some ways Fedora had the kind of manner that Eula envied. Her older brother's wife said what she thought when she thought it, and she never bothered to put a sugar coating on it. Eula remembered how pleased her father had been when Ben Roy announced, proud as a fightin' cock, that Fedora had agreed to marry him. The bride-elect had been fair-to-middling pretty with her straight, dark brown hair and eyes that slanted just a bit like an Indian's. Fedora was low to the ground, though you would never know it by the way she bossed every Thornton woman, and half the Thornton men. Ben Roy bragged on catching Fedora, but

Eula always thought it should have been the other way around. Her brother, by himself, inherited half of their father's six hundred and forty acres.

"Tillie, take these apples on over to your aunt." Belle Thornton, wife of Eula's younger brother, Jessie Roy, commanded her niece.

Eula dipped the spoon back into the low-simmering pot of peaches for a second sampling. She held out the spoon to offer Tillie a taste only to see her niece's eyes grow wide and the recent bride's face blanch white. Grabbing at her stomach, Tillie turned and ran through the kitchen and disappeared beyond the dining room door.

"If you asked me," Belle slid the rubber seal around the necks of the Mason jars as they came at her in assembly-line fashion, "I'd say she's in a family way. Wasn't that wedding in June?"

Eula buried her gasp in the steaming pot of cubed apples. Cora cleared her throat. It didn't take long for Fedora to pounce.

"Are you counting the months since my girl's wedding, Belle Thornton?" Fedora's eyes flamed.

"I ain't sayin' nothing bad 'bout your Tillie." After fifteen years as a Thornton, Belle still hadn't learned not to bait Fedora. "I know it's been two months since she walked down the aisle in that tight-fittin' dress. All I'm saying is that it's about time for a baby."

"Don't you think I'd know if my own daughter was expectin'?" Fedora bristled.

Although the warmth from the stove and the smothering outside heat creeping through the open kitchen windows made her woozy, Eula bent her head closer to the steam from the cherry pot. As her own sweat dripped into the kettle, she could hear the other women squirm in their chairs.

"Maybe she don't know herself," Jenny interjected.

"That's right, I sure didn't know," answered Belle. "All that marryin' business is just so overpowerin' anyway. That first year, a woman don't know if she's comin' or goin'." Belle pounded the edge of her knife against the table.

Eula set her mouth in a firm line to stop the forming frown. On the morning of her wedding, she had fidgeted while Mother Thornton instructed her on the ways of the wedding night. "He's a man," Momma had said. "Let him have his way with nary a complaint nor a whine. You just lay there and it'll be over quick. Whatever you do, don't give him no encouragement."

Abruptly, Eula dropped her wooden spoon into the pot of just-put-on plums and walked over to the kitchen table to retrieve her journal. Pulling a pencil from her apron pocket, she picked up her account book and neatly marked a three besides the peaches column and a four next to the column lettered "cherries." Belle, Jenny, and Cora gave her only cursory glances while Fedora continued with the apple coring. Tillie slowly made her way back into the room, her face showing dampness from the water she must have splashed over it.

"I saw yo' husband, Wiley George, at the Lawnover store the other day," Jenny spoke out as Eula slipped her journal back to the table and made her way over to the stove. "He looked like a happy bridegroom to me."

"Tillie, when did you last have your rags washed out?" Fedora plunged the paring knife deep into a half-cored apple.

"Momma." She whispered in a voice heard by every woman in the room.

"I checked your rags myself about two weeks before you married Wiley George." Fedora frowned as though her mind was clicking off the months. "That was back in the first part of June. Well, have you dirtied any rags since then?"

"Momma" was all Tillie managed a second time.

"Fedora, it's as plain as the nose on your face that she's expectin'." Belle announced airily.

"Tillie, get over here." Fedora rose to her feet as Tillie made her way slowly around the table toward her mother. As the girl approached, Fedora laid her hand across her daughter's belly and leaned an ear close. Sitting back down, Fedora looked right past Cora and turned to Eula.

"It's a baby all right," Fedora announced as Cora nodded her head.

"A baby? Momma, I can't have no baby. Not now. I just got married." Tillie's voice held the distinct sound of encroaching hysteria.

"Fedora, didn't you tell this girl where babies come from?" Belle could barely eke out the words through her laughter.

At the stove, Eula turned her back to the women. Suddenly, the steam from the pots and the hundred-degree kitchen heat almost overwhelmed her. She leaned against the handle on the oven door. Closing her eyes, Eula tried to steel herself against more talk of babies.

"Momma, I could die givin' birth." Tillie sank into a vacant chair.

"It's nineteen-thirteen, missy, and I reckon old Doc Starter knows enough to get that baby safe out of you." Fedora, like mothers before her, dismissed Tillie's fears.

"And you can't use that excuse to get out of your duty to Wiley George, neither." Cora Lee snickered.

"Every woman here knows about a wife's duty to her husband, Cora Lee." Fedora had just about reached her own boiling point. "We don't need you to remind us."

Eula's own pregnancy had started off like Tillie's with some-time sickness in the mornings, but that had been slight and she had worked the farm alongside Alex. As for her wifely duties, despite what her mother had said, after the first few times, she hadn't minded at all. Through the years, if she let herself, she found her duties downright enjoyable. It was becoming increasingly harder to follow her mother's advice and "just lay there." Many a night, especially now that Alex was only coming to her every other Friday, she wanted to put her arms around his neck and run her hands down his back. Sometimes she wanted to push him so deep inside her that he would have to fight to catch his breath for love of her. But if she did any of those things, he would think she was an easy woman just as her mother predicted. "It's the way of a husband. Don't act like you enjoy it. He'll think you learned those things from some other man." Eula often wondered what "those things" were and how did her mother know about them, anyway?

"You are as strong as an ox, Tillie Thornton Jamison," Fedora pronounced. "You will have this baby and keep Wiley George happy too. That's just the way of it." Fedora ended the discussion.

"Well, I'm not like one of the colored women. I just can't go dropping me a baby in the morning and go back to the field right after dinner." Tillie shifted in her chair while Fedora gave her a "watch your mouth" look.

Eula took the cooling pot of peaches to the table to Jenny who began ladling them into the washed-out Mason jars.

"That puts me in mind of that colored wench on the Bredge place." Belle's choice of words always did border on the bawdy, and Eula wondered again why her younger brother had chosen a woman just a step away from white trash to marry. "I saw the wench at the store in Clarksville last planting time. She had these two springy-haired yella' children with her and her belly swoll out to here, again." To watch Belle's hand draw pictures of the woman in the air, the observer would have believed the poor creature's stomach was bigger than a bushel basket. "Now, she is as dark as dirt and her man is as black as midnight. Where did those yella'-skinned pickaninnies come from?" Belle shook her head for emphasis.

"Well, if I was forced to say, I'd specify that it was between that white sharecropper Jim Bredge hired on three years back and that squatter family down by the railroad station." The deliberate sound of Cora Lee clucking her tongue did not escape Eula's ears.

"Nobody's forcing you to say nothin', Cora Lee." Belle poured the sealing wax over a jar of just-filled plums. "Besides, I don't think it's that white trash squatter family. That man's got about eight of his own young 'uns crammed into that one-room shed already."

"That man's almost sixty." Tillie sat with her hand rubbing her belly.

"Age just makes them all the more randy." Jenny shot a look at Tillie that brought titters from Belle.

"By my reckoning, I'd speculate on that sharecropper." Belle swiped the outside of a Mason jar with a wet cloth. "Don't he crop the forty acres right next to that nigger woman with her own high-yella kids?"

Eula flinched when she heard Belle's "nigger" epithet flung into the kitchen. Mother Thornton had taught her girls that a lady used that word only when strongly provoked. It was a term reserved for men. Only low-class white women uttered it away from the sanctity of their own homes. Coming out of the mouth of an in-law, the sound of it felt like fingers rubbing the wrong way against a blackboard.

"Why do you all think it has to be shiftless white trash? Hettie, on Papa's side-forty, has two yellow-skinned girls already, and her husband is as black as that stove Aunt Eula's standing at." Tillie spoke with a "case closed" attitude so like Fedora's. "I believe those women sell themselves when they get over to Clarksville."

"What do you know about a woman selling herself, missy?" Cora Lee asked. "If the truth be told, I'd say Jim Bredge hisself wasn't out of the woods."

A sudden quiet, deep as a pond in January, wrapped itself over the kitchen. Only the sound of the bubbling fruit in the kettles broke the silence. Eula held her spoon suspended in midair, afraid to lay it against anything, lest the sound rock the room like a rifle shot. She was quite aware that Fedora had not uttered a word in over five minutes. With her back still to the women, Eula heard someone clear her throat.

"Lord, here we are going on and on about babies. Eula please pay us no mind. We get to talkin' silly sometimes." The sound of Cora's nervous giggling brought Eula up from the kettle.

Before she turned toward the group, Eula set the muscles of her face into a mask and sealed them in the steam of the kettles. Every woman in that room, except Tillie, knew who fathered Hettie's three children, and it wasn't her long-gone stove-black husband, or the white trash squatter, or Jim Bredge. But no self-respecting white woman would ever dare utter the name of the father in the presence of his wife, not even when she was sitting no more than two feet away.

"I'm sorry, Aunt Eula," Tillie waved a hand around to include the other offending women in the room. "I forgot that you and Uncle Alex did have a baby once."

With her masklike face in place, Eula managed to give her niece a slight nod of her head. Fedora, concentrating on apple peels more than Eula had ever seen, lifted her head slightly as she sidled her eyes in Tillie's direction. Eula watched the younger woman's own eyes grow wider as she grabbed at the waist of her dress.

"If there is a baby in here, Aunt Eula, do you think I might lose it like you did?" Fedora's arm moved with such speed that Eula swore she only saw a white blur as her sister-in-law whacked Tillie near the elbow with an unpeeled apple.

"Will you stop your nonsense? You ain't about to lose Wiley George's baby." Fedora glowered at her daughter.

"I don't really know the story, Aunt Eula." Stubborn Tillie rubbed at her arm but kept her eyes on Eula. "I only know that you and Uncle Alex had a baby that died. Was it the whooping cough?"

The scraping sound of Fedora's chair as the woman jumped to her feet brought Eula's eyes hard around to her sister-in-law. Faster than a blink of an eye, Fedora reached across the table and snatched the spoon from the cooling pot of plums. Wielding the implement like a sword, she struck her daughter hard on the shoulder.

"I taught you better." Fedora's face had gone red. "You leave your aunt be. Not everybody wants to talk about what pains them like you do girl." Fedora held the spoon ready for a follow-up blow as Tillie shifted her hand to her shoulder.

"I ain't pryin', Ma. I just want to know what happened to Aunt Eula's baby."

The other women worked at a pace that Eula hadn't seen all day, but she knew every ear was turned up as keen as a hunting hound to hear her answer.

"She died abornin'." Eula's lips felt like they were moving through hardened clay. She tried to clear her throat. "Do we have another case of Mason jars?" Sweeping past Belle and Cora Lee, Eula stepped as slowly as she thought seemly out onto the back porch and the pump.

She bit into her lip. As she primed the pump handle, she wanted to shout out. Damn Jenny and Belle and Cora Lee. Why did their silly conversation have to drag her into it? Babies, yellow babies, coming babies, dead babies. Was it better to hurt her or Fedora? As the water started its trickle out of the pump, she cupped her shaking hand to gather a fistful and splash it over her face.

CHAPTER SIX

"Henry, run these sticks over to the barn." Without looking at her son, Annalaura took two crooked branches off the pile of stripped tree limbs accumulating from Lottie's run between Doug and the mound at Annalaura's feet.

The little girl, drenched in sweat, dropped eight more sticks atop the slow-growing pile before she collapsed between two rows of tobacco.

"Momma, I'm hungry." Little Henry plopped on the dirt across from his sister and let the sticks in his hand fall in different directions.

Annalaura reached down for the water jug on the ground, unscrewed its top, and offered it to Henry, while she glowered at Lottie.

"Girl, get up from there. Don't you know that it's September and we've got to get these sticks sharpened for spearing the tobacco? Mr. McNaughton wants his tobacco now."

"I don't care 'bout no ole tobacco. Momma, I'm hot." Lottie crawled over to Henry, who held the water bottle to his lips.

Before her daughter could lay her hands on it, Annalaura slapped the child's wrist.

"You'd better care 'bout some old tobacco, and you'd better be glad you're feelin' some heat on your back right now. Store it up. If we don't get this harvest in, come winter, you'll feel nothin' but cold snow on your behind." Annalaura looked up at the sky. She was grateful that early September had brought cooler weather, although, with the work they all were doing, she knew the fires of Hades couldn't feel much hotter. "Henry," she commanded, "give your sister some water, and get those sticks over to the barn so Cleveland can sharpen them for the staking."

Annalaura took a menacing step toward her son. The child scrambled to his feet, grabbed at the sticks, and ran them to the barn. Lottie, her back to her mother, climbed to her feet and started a slow walk back toward Doug. Before the child disappeared between the rows of still-growing tobacco, she called out to Annalaura in a singsong.

"I'm still hot and I'm still hungry. Hot and hungry." The child took off running. Annalaura had no intention of chasing her daughter. A flash of anger fought with a shade of regret for just an instant as mother looked after her fleeing child.

John Welles had left them in this predicament. She was working her children worse than what Aunt Becky told her the overseers had done in the days of slavery. With her sleeves rolled up past her elbows, Annalaura brushed a bare arm across her eyes. Only some of the dampness clinging there was from her sweat. She swallowed hard. Blubbering was not going to help any of them. John had left her without a word, either angry or peaceful, and that was that. There was no one else in this world to save her children from certain disaster other than herself. She clamped down on her lower lip. Maybe that pain would stop her from feeling sorry for herself. After all, the Lord had answered part of her prayers.

She looked up at a sky streaked in white clouds. None of them bore any resemblance to rain. Two weeks earlier, she had prayed mightily for rain that never came. Now she knew she had prayed for the wrong thing. It might have been all the hoeing and weed pulling that did it rather than her prayers, but the tobacco had miraculously stretched itself above the ground to a just pass-able height for spearing. This would be no bumper crop, but if she, Cleveland, Douglas, Lottie, and even little Henry worked fourteen-hour days, maybe they could bring in half of McNaughton's forty acres. If she had the time, she would drop to her knees and pray like she had Sunday last. She wouldn't pray for rain this time. Rain would be a disaster. All she wanted was another miracle.

Henry came walking in slow motion back to the pile of sticks that needed to be sharpened. Out of the corner of her eye, Annalaura saw the little boy's toes poking out way beyond the sole of his sliced shoe. She raised up from stacking the sticks to look at her youngest. He was only three years old, but already, he walked like an old man. From this distance, she swore she could see frown lines etching themselves into her baby's forehead. As he approached his mother, the tot began to sway. Annalaura dropped the sticks in her hands, swept up her skirt, and caught the child before he toppled into a tobacco plant.

"Momma, can I have some soup?" Henry whispered.

Annalaura tried to gauge the heat coming from the sun. She knew it couldn't have been over eighty degrees—a fairly cool September day. It wasn't the heat that made her baby swoon. Picking up Henry, she cradled him in her arms and carried him to the barn. There, in the stifling air of a building smelling of cows and pigs, Cleveland sat surrounded by two stacks of sticks.

"How many more you reckon we need of these, Ma?" Cleveland pointed to the shorter pile as Annalaura laid Henry on a slim bundle of hay.

At least the cows had food for their supper.

"That pile there," Annalaura pointed to the already sharpened sticks, "is enough to spear about five acres. Cleveland, we've got to bring in at least twenty so we can stay on this place this winter."

Her boy looked at her with the certainty of impossibility on his face.

"I'll get Doug to help with the sticks while you get the rafters ready to string up the tobacco once it's speared." She lifted her head to the top of the barn.

McNaughton had built their lodgings to take up less than a third of the rafter space. The rest was to be used for the hanging and curing of the tobacco.

"Doug don't like to work in the barn. That dryin' tobacco gives him the wheezin' attack," Cleveland reminded her, though Annalaura needed no help remembering her second son gasping for breath when he had a bout of what John called the "asthma."

If she had any other way, she would spare Doug the frightening experience. Hell, if she had any other way, she would spare all her children this misery. She turned toward Henry who lay still and ashen with his eyes closed. She had to feed her children. Stepping outside of the barn she called to Lottie.

"Come on up for dinner." As she let the words come out of her mouth, she fumbled in her pocket for the four eggs boiled this morning.

She moved to the smoke house and the low-simmering pot on the back burner. Filled to the brim with water, it contained less than a cup of dandelion greens. Annalaura looked over at the spot between barn and smoke house where she had gardened so well last year. Except for the brown tops of two scraggly onions, the garden plot was bare. There had been no time to tend it and, worse, no seed money to start it. She didn't dare ask McNaughton to advance her the seed like most of the other owners would do, because she knew she wouldn't be able to pay the farmer back. As Lottie headed from the field with Doug trailing behind her, Annalaura checked the sun. She had fed all four of her children with the next to last cup of cornmeal way before sunup, and now it was close to two o'clock and their dinner would be a boiled egg and a pot of water seasoned with no more than the look of a green dandelion. She wiped her forearm over her eyes again. She refused to let them see her cry.

It took her children less than five minutes to gobble down their egg and skimpy cup of dandelion water. When the little ones turned their faces to her, she saw the futility of asking for more in their eyes. She allowed all four to rest for another twenty minutes, though Cleveland had tried to argue that he was ready to go back to the sticks. She insisted that he lie down on his cot. She put Henry on her lap, and with the hem of her skirt, wiped his dusty toes and tried to push the top of his shoes over them.

"Cleveland, watch after the others, I'm taking Henry with me to Aunt Becky's."

"But, Momma, the tobacco…" Cleveland tried to protest before Annalaura silenced him with a hand.

"I'll be back way befo' dark to work on the sticks." She saw the question in Lottie's eyes but silenced her daughter before it could be asked.

If she'd had a buckboard, she could have made the ride to the Thornton back-forty in under fifteen minutes, but with walking and carrying an exhausted Henry, it had taken her close to an hour. He had fallen asleep and his three-year-old weight felt like thirty pounds of unbroken rock. Just as she spotted the cabin in the distance, she shifted the child to her other hip. She hoped the sight of him would keep Aunt Becky from asking too many questions. Annalaura loved her aunt, but the woman had the all-seeing eye of her Cherokee mother. She would know what the trouble was before Annalaura could get out a good word. Annalaura nudged Henry awake as she turned up the path to the old mud-chinked cabin where Aunt Becky had been born a slave on Thornton land sixty years earlier. After the War, she had married a man who called himself Murdock, though Becky never used his name, nor did she ever move away to live with him. Rebecca Murdock had always lived on Thornton land, and she had always been far more than an aunt to Annalaura.

Geneva Thornton Robbins had been just twenty-nine, and Annalaura four, when the galloping consumption separated mother from daughter. Steps from the gray, weathered front door of the old slave cabin with its iron ring for a knocker, Annalaura rummaged in her head for a memory of that day. Her mother's face was less than a blur these twenty-five years later. Not even her smell lingered in the adult Annalaura. What was clear as a pond after a springtime thaw was the remembrance of how the four-year-old had begged to be allowed to live with her pipe-smoking grandmother after her mother's death.

Grandma Charity's lap had always been inviting even when Annalaura's mother was alive. The woman with the strong nose, straight, still-black hair, and cinnamon-colored skin had rocked young Annalaura to sleep many a time. As a youngster, she nestled into her grandmother's ample bosom and let her drowsy mind take in the stories of the old woman's own girlhood.

Charity was just nine when the soldiers marched her entire village out of their North Carolina home. The woman had repeated the story so often that Annalaura could almost see the Cherokee cabins. Grandma had always insisted to her doubting granddaughter that the Indian cabins had been much finer

than the ones the white men built for their slaves. The Cherokee had always lived in houses of wood that kept a body warm
and snug in the winter with fireplaces that were built right in the
center.

Annalaura set the half-asleep Henry on his feet as they paused
outside Becky's front door. The unhappy-looking child set up a
wail that sounded just like the one Charity used to imitate all the
crying that occurred on that long walk out of North Carolina.

"That walk to Oklahoma was from sunup to way past sundown, with the soldiers on their tall horses poking their fire sticks
into the backs of anyone who lagged." The old woman had always
begun the tale the same way, as her bare and calloused feet set the
old rocker in motion.

"That piece of a trail was just about washed away in Cherokee
tears." Grandma Charity creaked the chair.

Henry stamped his feet in time to his wailing as he reached
his impatient arms up to Annalaura. The cabin door creaked
open on its rusty hinges, and Aunt Becky peeped her head out
of the gloom. She looked her visitors up and down, and as usual,
Annalaura could not read her impassive face.

"You feedin' that chile?" All Cherokee women had the knowl-
edge of the herbs, and most had at least a smattering of the gift of
second sight. Aunt Becky always told her that. Rebecca Thornton
Murdock was only half-Cherokee and that should have slowed
her down, but the speed with which the old woman could read
anybody's intentions both annoyed and amazed Annalaura.

"Just had dinner." Even if Becky was close to knowing why she
had come to her cabin, Annalaura couldn't just blurt out that her
children were so close to starving that it seemed an actual fact.

Becky still held the door open only a crack. She turned that eye
on Annalaura again. When the earthen-skinned woman finally
did open the door, it was to grin a gap-toothed smile at Henry.

"Come on in here, chile. Auntie's got a treat fo' you." Becky slid a thin, calico-clad arm around the back of Henry's head and guided him into the interior.

Though the sun still showed promise of another good three hours of bright daylight, the kerosene lamp in the center of the old wood-blocked table that Annalaura remembered so well from her own girlhood remained the main source of light within the long room. The open-spaced cabin boasted one window, but Becky kept the lamp-oil-smudged window glass covered with particularly heavy burlap curtains. The heat from the lamp made the room even more suffocating than normal. Annalaura pulled out one of the two table chairs only to discover that a leg had loosened from its seat. Without a word of caution, Becky pulled out the other chair and pointed Henry in its direction. The old Cherokee disappeared into the semi-gloom of a corner where Annalaura knew the food safe, with its supplies, stood. After Rebecca twisted off a lid from a nearly empty jar, she reached for a spoon from the table. Scraping the sides and bottom, Becky came up with a tablespoon of peach preserves and held it out to Henry. The child beamed at the treat.

"Jest had dinner, did he?" Becky spoke without laying her eyes on Annalaura. "What you gonna feed him fo' supper?"

Annalaura knew her aunt was indicting her for not being able to feed her own children. "Times is a little bit hard these days, is all." She bent down to knock the wooden peg back into the chair leg.

"Uh huh." Becky had the weary sound of a woman who knew all about hard times.

Times had gotten even harder after Geneva died. The good-as-orphaned Annalaura had never understood why her mother's older sister had insisted upon keeping her at the cabin instead of letting her live with her grandmother. Her aunt would never say more than it had been a promise made to the dying Geneva.

"Raise my girl. Don't let her ever go to Momma." But, when Anna-laura got up to some size, she deviled the other colored children in the neighborhood until they whispered in her ear when they were sure her aunt wasn't around. "There's bad blood between yo' Grandma Charity and yo' Aunt Becky." If they knew more, Anna-laura couldn't even beat it out of them.

"Come on over here, baby." Becky, her back bent from fifty-five years stooped over the tobacco plants, beckoned Henry who was playing with the spoon in his mouth.

The boy licked at the long-gone taste of peach preserves. The wraith of a woman walked the child back into the gloom of the cabin and pulled out a small square of corn bread from the food safe.

"Take that outside, baby, so you don't get crumbs on Aunt Becky's clean flo'." She left the door open a crack as Henry sat on the stoop stuffing the corn bread into his mouth.

Rebecca walked back over to Annalaura and took over the one sound chair. One bony arm reached out for her pipe. She put it in her mouth unlit.

"When you last heard from that sportin' man husban' of your'n?" Becky tapped at the bowl of her pipe. Her eyes had not yet settled on Annalaura.

"I reckon he's too busy to send word," Annalaura lied.

"Uh huh." Becky took a draw on the dry pipe.

Annalaura stiffened. Her aunt always had a way of dragging out the torment when she wanted to lay into Annalaura. "I 'spect he'll be back right before the end of the harvest."

"Thorntons brought in the last of their tobacco day befo' yes-tiddy." Becky finally let her eyes light on Annalaura's face. "Yours ain't barely ready to spear yet. You need a man to help."

Annalaura steeled herself against those Cherokee eyes that always made her squirm. "No good not keepin' yo' man satisfied in bed," Becky pronounced.

Annalaura felt the blood rush to her face.

"You need the conjure woman."

"I don't need no conjure woman." Annalaura wanted to take back the rise in her voice, but not the words. "I need a speck of food to feed my children until the tobacco is sold."

"A woman who can keep her man happy don't need to be searchin' fo' scraps of food." Becky took another draw on the cold pipe and took her time pointing it at Annalaura. "I'll say this fo' you. Keepin' a sportin' man under one set of covers ain't easy for no woman, 'specially one as strong-headed as you."

"I don't care if John Welles is satisfied or not. I need to feed my children." She caught a glimpse of Henry coming back through the partially opened door.

With an upward tilt of her head, Becky shooed Henry back outside.

"Now, you talkin' nothin' but foolishness girl. A man ain't good fo' much, but a woman needs one around to lessen this world's misery." Rebecca frowned at her. "What you need is some extra special strong herbs from the conjure woman."

"Aunt Becky, if I could kindly borrow some meal, a dab of flour, and maybe some jars of greens, I will pay you back double when my harvest money comes in. I don't need no conjure woman to make me up no love potions. A man will only double my misery." Annalaura looked back at her aunt, who held her cold pipe at arm's length like a rifle aimed at her niece's face.

She slowly let it circle in the air.

"I could never settle my mind on why a fast-thinkin' man like John Welles wanted to marry up with a fresh gal like you. You got a comely shape, right 'nough. God's truth, men can act the fool over a plumped-out behind and a big pushed-up bosom. But you got yo' shortcomin's. Ain't many a man wantin' a woman with a troublesome quick tongue." Becky clamped the pipe stem between her teeth and kept her lips drawn back. "Gal, you better bless yo'self twice that John Welles ain't minded layin' in a bed with a woman with a keen reckonin' head."

"I wouldn't want John Welles in my bed even if he was still around here," Annalaura flared. "I wanted to leave that man right after I had me Cleveland." She had heard John speak his, "I'm doin' this fo' our family, darlin'," at least two dozen times too many. Even if her quick-thinking husband won more than he lost at gambling, she still hated the thought that he could lose her babies' hard-come-by school money.

"What foolishness is you talkin' now, gal?" Surprise slipped out of Becky's mouth.

"John Welles hid my letter from Grandma Charity. The one she wrote tellin' me where she was and invitin' me to come live with her in Oklahoma."

Annalaura nearly jumped from her rickety chair as Becky slammed her hand on the wooden block of the table with such force that Annalaura wondered if the old woman had broken an arm.

"It ain't fittin' for a married woman to speak such talk. Letter or no letter, you got no business running off to Oklahoma." Becky's voice came out of her mouth like a snake spitting venom. "John Welles may have his gamblin' ways, but you married him. It's up to you to lay in his bed, lumpy as it may be, let him do what he's got to do, and act as happy as if you'd gotten your gold heaven crown right now." The sturdy table shook a second time as Becky pounded it.

"Hell, Aunt Becky, I can't lay in a bed with a man that is always laying up in some other woman's bed." Annalaura had barely gotten the words out of her mouth when she felt the stinging slap across her cheek.

Becky had knocked over the good chair as she reached across the table to deliver the blow.

"I learned you better than to cuss, gal. A good woman can always find 'nother word to say what she means. 'Sides, a man don't want to hear a decent woman sayin' a cuss word." Rebecca, who had been a woman of a fair size in her young days, had shrunk down to just a little bit above Annalaura's nose. But right now she towered over her like Goliath gloating over David. "Get that runnin' off foolishness out of yo' head. When that man does come back, you gonna keep him so tuckered out, he ain't never gonna stray no further than yo' front do' without him tellin' you first."

Becky moved to the corner safe and returned with a half jar of cornmeal and a tin of flour. She held out a bloodied parcel wrapped in tobacco leaves. Annalaura held her hand to her cheek.

"Take this here rabbit. It's just the front quarters. Ben Roy brought it to me this morning."

Annalaura knew that Becky lived alone in the cabin and had long ago passed her work usefulness on the farm. Still the Thorntons kept her fed and clothed with a few supplies every month.

"I'm right sorry, Aunt Becky." She held out her hand for the bloody package. "My babies haven't had meat since Independence Day. John only left us one slab of bacon and we just finished that up." She bit her tongue when the hard look threatened to come back into Becky's eyes for criticizing John.

"Here's some meal and flour. I'll fetch you some salt and baking soda, and I've got the last of the pole beans in the garden. You can have some of them fo' your children." Her voice had softened. "When he gets back here, yo' man don't want to hear that his woman couldn't keep his children fed. Now get on back home."

The walk back to the barn took even longer because Annalaura couldn't carry both the supplies and Henry. The boy took ample opportunity to protest his fatigue by sitting down at every other rut in the much-rutted road. It was nearing dark when she guided her youngest up the ladder. Even before Henry reached the top rung, she knew something was wrong.

"Momma, Cleveland hurt his leg." Lottie shoved Henry aside before Annalaura's head had even cleared the opening.

"What do you mean, hurt his leg?" Before she could gaze in the direction of Cleveland's cot, Doug's desperate wheeze for breath caught her attention.

She dropped to the pallet on the floor where the young boy hung his face over a bowl of lukewarm water and frantically waved both hands to bring up the nonexistent steam.

"I heated the water myself, Momma." Lottie's note of pride was lost on Annalaura who had a sudden vision of her five-year-old aflame around the cantankerous stove McNaughton had rigged up in the smoke house.

"I told you not to go by that stove unless I was near." The sharpness in Annalaura's words was at counterpoint to the panic rapidly taking over her mind. She heard Cleveland groan a greeting to her.

"It's all right, Momma. Doug took sick before I had my fall. I was in the barn when Lottie was boilin' the water." Cleveland's wail sounded his hurt.

Another grunt came from the cot as Annalaura jumped to her feet and ran over to her eldest. The boy was laying in his alcove, the side of his face badly scraped.

"Lottie, get me some water from the basin there," she commanded the girl, as Henry ran to comply.

"Lottie already done give me a rag, Momma. It's my leg." Cleveland nodded his head in the direction of his left leg, and the effort brought forth another grunt.

She watched her rock of a son dissolve into tears.

"My Lord, Cleveland. What done happened?" The left pant leg of her son's one pair of work britches hung in bloody shreds around his knee.

The skin over the shinbone, between knee and calf, had doubled in size, and a deep scratch ran across the area. Annalaura grabbed the wet cloth from Henry and laid it gently across the wound. She knew the bone was broken. She only prayed it was a clean break.

"I was in the rafters, Momma. Gettin' things ready for tomorrow, so we could start to hang the tobacco. One of the beams broke and I fell. I'm sorry, Momma." Cleveland's voice dissolved into a howl that chilled Annalaura's heart.

"Don't you fret none 'bout that tobacco. Aunt Becky's heard word that yo' papa might be comin' back just in time." The lie came quick off her tongue as she took a second wet rag from Lottie and patted Cleveland's face with it.

She wanted to take her firstborn into her arms, hold him close, and take away all the grown-up worries that had no business on the shoulders of a twelve-year-old. Instead, she hugged Lottie and smoothed her daughter's hair.

"You done a real good job. Now go fetch me that broom handle in the corner. Henry, get the sacking off the bed. Doug, once I get Cleveland's leg tied up, I'm gonna heat you up another big bowl of water to get that ol' wheezin' gone." She spoke as though she had everything under control.

Only those older than twelve would know that the truth was the exact opposite.

CHAPTER SEVEN

Alex hadn't needed to look at the calendar hanging on Eula's pantry door to tell him that two weeks had passed since he last visited the mid-forty. He had trotted the gray down the lane that bisected his acres every day since he spoke to the nigger woman on the place in mid-August, but he hadn't wanted to look too close at the tobacco.

As he slowed his horse this morning, what he had to do was clear. No lone woman, with four pickaninnies way too young to be of any use, could bring in what a full-grown man couldn't. He'd have to shoo her off the place and do what he could to get at least some of his acres in before first frost. Fifteen hundred dollars was a lot to lose. As he snapped the reins to the right to guide the gray up the path toward the barn on the mid-forty, memories of the woman's bare thighs fought to push aside his good sense. He shifted his weight in the saddle hoping against everything reasonable that the woman's husband hadn't yet returned home. Slowing the horse to a leisurely pace, he let his eyes drift over to the fields. With the barn still some two hundred yards up the path, he stopped the gray and slid to the ground.

Alex walked over to the tobacco stalks lining the path. Damn, if at least some of them didn't look just about passable for spearing. Remounting, he scanned the acres on the other side. Sure, the tops of the stalks were uneven, and without much of a look, he could see that all the plants hadn't reached harvest-ready yet, but the woman had done more than a middling good job. McNaughton galloped the horse to the barn and dismounted.

The September sky dawned a mild pink with the promise of good working weather. A wren chirped a greeting in this second hour past dawn. Pushing up the wide brim of his straw hat, Alex looked over the fields again. Strange, he didn't see the woman or her children. They should have been hard at work in the fields by now. He smelled the hogs at their slop and peered over toward the other side of the barn. Although he couldn't catch a good look inside the dark interior, he heard the cows grunting as they chewed their hay. They had been milked, for sure. Three scrawny chickens sauntered in front of him. He was certain that they, too, had already laid, and their eggs taken. The woman had been up, but where was she now?

He spotted the opened door of the smoke house and walked over to it. Inside, Alex felt the heat from the coal-fired oven. The whiff of baking biscuits greeted him. Walking closer, he looked into a cast-iron kettle and saw nothing but water dotted with blobs of grease. Where was breakfast? McNaughton looked around the walls of the smoke house. Even though it was September, and summer supplies were bound to be low, still there should have been at least one slab of bacon left on the hanging hook. And, where were the woman's winter preserves?

Alex stepped outside to glance at the garden plot between smoke house and barn. Last year he remembered the abundance of vegetables and noted to himself that his newest tenants had the gumption to tend their own food and bring him in a bumper tobacco crop to boot. These were niggers worth keeping. Now, the plot showed only bare reddish-brown Tennessee dirt. Not even the withered top of one green onion was left standing.

The slurping of the sows struck his ears as he neared the barn. Shaking his head, Alex no longer had any doubt that the slowest moving of the creatures had long passed her piglet days. He'd slaughter her for the fall and advance some of her meat to the tenants against their tobacco shares. Then Alex remembered. The harvest on the mid-forty promised to be a mighty iffy thing at best this year. Just inside the barn, the two cows were busy at work on their short stack of feed. He reminded himself to bring in more hay for the coming fall. That, too, could be held against any profits the Welleses might claim. The ladder to the living quarters above lay in place. He moved toward it, but before he could call out his halloo, the sound of someone struggling for breath in the upstairs living space caught his attention. It was the sound of a child. As Alex moved closer, the woman's voice, marshaling her children into order, floated down through the square opening.

"Hey, you up there," Alex shouted out. "When you comin' to the fields?" With his booted foot on the bottom rung of the ladder, he looked up to see the woman's young girl looking down at him, her eyes wide in surprise. Before he could negotiate the first two ladder rungs, the swirl of a skirt thrust the child aside. Two worn work boots and a flash of two milk-chocolate colored ankles confronted him.

"I'm comin' right down, suh." The woman dropped to her knees in a thud as she bent over the opening to look down at him. The top of her shirtwaist lay open and both breasts fell hard against the cloth, almost overflowing it. Colored like first-tapped maple syrup stirred with a cinnamon stick, they were three shades lighter than her sun-drenched face.

Alex stopped his climb to stare. The woman scrambled to her feet, turned, and began to back down the ladder with her skirt pulled tight over her buttocks. He stepped off the ladder, his eyes never off the rounded shape above him. His hands gripped the side rails as his eyes told him that he wanted to reach up and touch that rounded firmness coming straight at him. This was nothing like the vanilla pudding flabbiness Eula presented him every fortnight.

"I'm fixin' my children breakfast. I'll be with yo' tobacco directly, suh." On the ground, the woman turned toward him, her eyes flitting like a hummingbird between his shirt pocket and his face.

"It's past sunup. Ain't you a bit late gettin' to my tobacco?" He had the uneasy feeling that there was more to this woman's late start than she was telling.

Had the husband come home? Was that why her shirt fell open just enough to offer him a teasing glimpse at the top swell of one breast? He felt the heat starting in his britches again. He tried to push the thought away, then reconsidered. Why couldn't he have business and pleasure, too?

"Yes, suh. It's just that my oldest boy had a fall yesterday." She bobbed her head toward one of the rafters.

Alex followed her glance and spotted the place where a beam had given way. He turned toward the small pile of spearing cuttings.

"You ain't got enough sticks to spear more than five acres. There's forty that need to be brought in." He looked back toward her.

The woman's eyes flickered up to his face.

"You surely are right, suh, but my middle boy will be down in a minute to sharpen some more." Her eyes drifted down to his shirt pocket. "By tomorrow dawn, I'll have that first acre in for you."

"Your middle boy—is he the one I heard wheezin' upstairs?" Alex sucked in a breath.

This woman was a good talker. She couldn't possibly bring in an acre of harvested tobacco by tomorrow, not with nearly two good hours of this day already gone.

"The wheezin' sickness only takes him when he's with dryin' tobacco. I'm gonna have him sit outside to do the sharpening." Up went her eyes to his face for just an instant. "He'll do just fine."

"Is this the boy you told me was no more than twelve years old?" He had to hand it to her. She could move her words around with surprising quickness.

"He strong like a mule, suh, and my girl will fetch and carry the sticks. I'll do the spearin' myself." The eyes met his for the whisper of a second before he watched her drop them to the fourth button on his shirt.

"Woman, are you tellin' me that you and your three picka..." he remembered her admonition of two weeks earlier "...children are going to bring in an acre of tobacco by nightfall? What about tomorrow? Where is your man, anyway?" It was his turn to give her the hard look.

Quick as a flighty bird, she brushed past him and stepped out into the breaking day. Alex walked to catch up with her.

"No, suh. I don't reckon I can get an acre in by nightfall, but I can surely do it befo' midnight." This time the eyes met his and lingered long enough for him to look into their velvety bronze softness.

This woman had pools in her deeper than well water. What would it feel like to dip into those depths?

"My children and I will work from sunup to sundown spearin' the tobacco. After I put them to bed, I will sharpen the sticks 'til my oldest boy can do the job in two or three days." The eyes were up again, searching his.

He stared back at her until a look of remembrance crossed her face and she quickly dropped her eyes to his boot tops.

Alex moved away from her to survey the fields a third time. When he turned back, the woman had stepped inside the smoke house. He followed.

"How do you expect to work your children like grown-up field hands if you ain't feedin' them?"

The woman bent over the open oven door, a tin pan of four hot biscuits in her cloth-shielded hand. Surprised at the speed with which she straightened to her full height, Alex paused.

"I will get yo' tobacco in for you, Mr. McNaughton, suh." She drew out his name.

This woman had more sass in her than was good for any female, black or white. A good slap would remind her of her place, but he hesitated. Holding the hot tin in front of her, she moved to the door of the smoke house. Alex stopped her.

"I don't believe you can bring in my tobacco for me."

The right side of his body brushed her left shoulder. His left arm stretched across the door frame directly in front of her chest, his long shirtsleeve no more than inches away from her shirtwaist with its open top button.

"I've put on a hired man to help you," Alex made the decision as he spoke, "but the cost will be high."

She looked up at him, the cooling tin of biscuits in her hand, puzzlement on her face. "What can you give me to pay for the extra help?" He watched the woman's slow shake of her head as her eyes blinked the dawning understanding of what he was asking.

Her mouth, with those full kissable lips, opened and closed twice.

"Sir, please forgive my forgetfulness." The words came out slow. "You asked about my husband. He has been delayed in Kentucky—his auntie and all—but he left me a message for you." Each word came out as exact as a tobacco-weighing scale.

Did she think that sounding like a proper-talking Nashville colored schoolteacher was going to keep him away? He didn't appreciate uppity-talkin' niggers.

"My husband, John Welles…" she let the name linger on her lips, "wants to beg yo' pardon about the delay. He knows I can bring in twenty acres all by myself in the next two weeks. He also know he owe you forty and would like to make up for it in the winter."

No nigger, male or female, had ever gathered the nerve to try and bargain with him or any other white man. He should take a stick to this woman and beat her back to remembering her place. Instead, he let his hand slip down the front of her dress, stopping at the second buttonhole just at the rise of her breast. He listened to her soft intake of breath and waited while she failed to let it out. Her eyes remained on his face. He knew she dare not push his hand away.

"Suh, my husban' may not be home for a few days but he comin' back. I am a married woman."

Alex made sure his nod was neither a yes nor a no. This woman had more than crossed the line of disrespect.

"Your get needs some bacon and fresh meat. Maybe some greens and preserves. I'll be back tonight with all of that." He knew she was deserving of a good thrashing if for nothing more than raising her eyes to him.

But instead of laying into her, he wanted to drop his hand down into her shirt and discover what firmness awaited him there. Hell, he wanted to park his manhood within her right then and there, but in those eyes swimming with life, he didn't yet see compliance. He'd never forced a woman, and he especially didn't want to force this one. She stood stock still. As close as he was, he couldn't be sure that she had let out a breath.

"A few chickens wouldn't hurt none either," he added as he watched the biscuit tin jiggle in her hand for the flash of a second.

Alex did some quick reckoning, and the warning signs jumped into place. A woman who could think quick like this one was a dangerous thing. But the longer he stood close to her, the more certain he was that this was one danger he wanted to embrace. He steadied himself for patience. With a mind like hers, she would soon see that her options with him were none. He gave her a slow nod to make sure his meaning had registered before he turned and headed for the gray.

"I'll be back tonight," Alex repeated as he reached for the reins. Behind him, he heard her fight a grunt in her throat.

"I thank you kindly, suh, but no."

Did the wench say no? Why, even his wife had never hinted at refusing him. Not that he cared enough to press his case with Eula Mae. He turned back toward the woman, damning the hardening in his pants. Her eyes never left the dirty and scuffed toes of her own shoes. He took a step toward her. He could order this woman to do anything he wanted. Alex knew it and she knew it. He could have her on her knees with his manhood in her mouth within one minute if he wanted. Alex took another step closer and fumbled louder than he needed with his belt buckle. Though she fought hard to conceal it, he saw her cringe as she heard the rough, scraping sound of leather against metal.

Alex stepped close enough to brush her stomach with the leather end of his belt. He dropped it just below her belly button and let it slowly search for the outline of her drawers. He could feel his lungs searching for more air, but only by a close look at her chest could he see the woman flinch. Her eyes remained on the ground, her breasts poked full against the thin, much-washed fabric of her shirt. Alex suspected she hadn't taken a breath in many long seconds. He wanted to throw her to the ground and hike her skirt to her hips. He wanted to feel for the drawers he was certain weren't there. He moved his chest against her breast.

"Suh," her voice was no more than a whisper as she tried to push the cooling biscuit pan between herself and Alex, "my husban' would like to know if you would consider just one mo' thing."

The eyes were still respectfully down, but she had just turned the key that she knew would push him back, if even for an instant. This woman had more smarts than any colored needed. She was worth far more than a quick roll around on the smoke house floor. The throbbing in his pants moved to his chest. He wanted this woman right now, but he thrilled at the excitement that would come when she fell into his arms all on her own.

"Depends on what the one more thing is." His breath brushed her ear, but she held both her body and eyes steady.

"John Welles," she drew the name out in the warming morning air as though her husband deserved all the respect of a preacher, black or white. "John Welles know he wronged you." The eyes came up level with the lower part of the barn.

Alex watched her chest rise and fall as she finally took in little gulps of air.

"You been most generous to let us farm your land." The eyes moved to the mid-planks of the barn as she eased her body slowly around toward him, the pan of biscuits sliding across his shirt.

One breast brushed his chest as she pivoted. He laid his hand on her arm, stroked it from elbow to wrist, and flicked the pan of biscuits to the ground. He felt the recoil and quick recovery of her body.

"Last year, you let us keep 'most half of what we brought in to you." Without so much as a look at the fallen bread, she laid her now empty hand across her stomach like it was a metal shield.

Alex dismissed the move and did quick mental calculations. Of the three thousand dollars brought in last year, technically the Welleses were entitled to forty percent according to the terms of their original deal.

"Less advances I made to you, of course." He blurted the words out as he watched her resume her slow turn until she faced him directly.

Alex laid an arm back across the door frame. Her right shoulder touched his wrist. Her eyes stayed at pocket level.

"That was most generous of you, suh." The woman's eyes lifted to his face with all the speed of a snail on a tomato vine. "This year, my husband would like to ask if you would take two out of every three parts of what we bring in to you?" She had succeeded in making her face resemble an innocent angel, but she hadn't succeeded in masking her good sense.

This woman could do figures in her head as good or better than Eula who had all of her eighth grade education.

"Less advances." He spoke again, wanting to bite his tongue. A white man didn't bargain with a nigger, especially a woman.

But, then, if the miracle came and she brought in fifteen hundred dollars this year, she would be entitled to only five hundred instead of the contracted six. He had already advanced her that much. If he took the deal, he would get to keep the entire year's sale in exchange for letting her stay in the barn for the winter. Now, he had to convince her to give him a little something extra.

"Yes, suh. I would take it kindly if you would allow me seed money for my fall vegetables and for a new sow and maybe a dozen or so more chickens." Her eyes locked onto his.

Alex breathed hard. A young sow alone was worth almost sixty dollars. Where had a woman learned to figure like a man?

"Woman," his voice was hoarse, "I've told you before. I've got me a man who wants to farm this place right now. I know your man will be back, but if the God's truth be told, even you don't know when. You and those kids need food so you can work the harvest proper. Without it, there's no reason for me to let you stay, now is there?" Though he had dropped in his own bargaining chip, he had also just given a colored woman a power over her fate that he hadn't given even to Eula Mae.

CHAPTER EIGHT

"John Welles, John Welles. Open this do'. I know you is in there." If the sound of the afternoon train rumbling down from Chicago hadn't been enough to wake him from his sleep, the rusty-razor voice of his landlady more than finished the job.

John put the rolled-up rag he used for a pillow over his head to block out the sound. He had no need to hide his eyes from the light in the crowded, windowless storeroom. The thin stretch of daylight that did make its way miraculously under Miz Sarah Lou Brown's storeroom door was all that he ever saw of brightness when he finally was lucky enough to fall asleep on the pee-stained mattress after his thirteen-hour workday.

"It's the first Friday in September, and you ain't gittin' out of here this day 'til you pays me my rent." Miz Brown's fist pounding on the door matched the voice in grating on his nerves.

John peeked out from the makeshift pillow. The little dab of daylight that had been there disappeared, covered over by Miz Brown's more than ample body. He knew she would either stand there all day or put a shoulder to the door and break through it like a cardboard oatmeal box. John rolled to his hands and knees and pushed his tired body to standing. Without the sun to guide him, he depended upon the three p.m. train heading to Florida from

Chicago to give him his time bearings. Wearing only his summer drawers, John stepped over a crate of corn and two tins of lard to reach down to the floorboards he had first pried open right after he moved in to the two-story clapboard house. Squatting on the floor, he pulled the loose board up and lifted out the blue bandanna that held his money. Fumbling in the darkness, he retrieved four quarters, seven dimes, and sixteen nickels. Damn. He had hoped to have enough in change so that he wouldn't have to break one of his silver dollars. They were too hard to come by. For the flash of a second, Annalaura's disapproving face flicked into his mind. He pushed the vision away. He loved that woman more than he could show, but she had more mouth on her than he had time to deal.

"John Welles, I got no time to fool with you. I've got me people lined up 'round the block to take this here place. Country boys comin' into Nashville, fifteen, twenty a day. I don't need none of yo' foolishness." Sarah Lou's voice just about shook the storeroom door off the hinges.

That the old biddy was right riled John the most. So many men from out in the country got the same idea in their heads. No colored was ever going to amount to anything if he kept sharecropping for the white man.

"Let me get my britches on Miz Brown, ma'am, and I'll hand yo' money right to you." Even if he could have afforded better, there were too few rooms to rent for all the colored who were pouring in to the city.

Too few places to lay his head, too few jobs to make the rent, that's what a country man could expect if he decided to risk everything on Nashville. John pulled on his overalls and reached for his shirt as he walked over to the door, only stubbing his toe once on a forgotten box that sat near his mattress.

"Here's yo' money, Miz Brown, the whole of it." He opened the door wide enough for the space to frame his six-foot-tall body. John laid two silver dollars and the four quarters into his landlady's hand.

Her fingers snapped closed over the money as she tried to look around him and into the room.

"How much they pay you down there at that smithy shop?" Her wig, that looked more like the tail off a red squirrel, had been put on even more crooked than usual today.

"I've got me 'nuff money to keep the rent up. You don't need to worry none, Miz Brown."

"You don't work nothin' but fo' hours a day down at the smithy shop, but you out every night." The plump face frowned up worse than a prune. "I told you I don't allow no gamblin' peoples to live in my place. I runs a respectable boardinghouse. Why, I got two colored schoolteachers living right here. They..."

"Miz Brown, ma'am. I works six mornings a week, six o'clock to ten o'clock, cleanin' up horse sh...horse dumpin's...at the blacksmith shop. He pays me fifty cents a day. That's my room and board, and yo' rent right there."

This woman, who liked to set herself front and center in the second-best church pew at the Nashville colored Baptist church every Sunday, didn't need to know much more than that. John could see that her frown had only deepened. To keep her face from caving upon itself, he decided to give just a little bit more.

"I gets me a little extra money by running grocery deliveries." He doled out a hint of one of his patented smiles.

She didn't need to know the full truth. Six days a week, from five in the afternoon until one o'clock in the morning, John Welles ran hams, chickens, sides of beef, and just about every other fancy food a colored man could dream of to a certain Nashville address. At the same time, he also ran gin, bourbon, whiskey, and good branch water to Miz Zeola's whorehouse. For each of his eight- or nine-hour days, he got paid seventy-five cents. Altogether, he earned seven dollars and fifty cents a week.

"You just keep on bringin' me my rent every Friday, and you and me will get along just fine." Miz Brown almost had a smile on her face as she turned toward the three wooden steps that led to the back door and her kitchen.

Seven-plus dollars a week was a hell of a lot more than John ever earned in Lawnover. By the time that cracker McNaughton got through with his "advances" last year, John had only a three-hundred-dollar share to last him the whole of the next year. And this despite the bumper crop he and Annalaura had brought McNaughton. John and Annalaura had gone over the figuring together, but his wife had been the one to ask, in her most respectful way, for an accounting. McNaughton, thinking the two of them too dumb to understand figures, had rattled off bloated costs for rent, milk from the two cows, meat from one pig, garden seed, clothes, and a little starting food. His "advances" came to almost nine hundred dollars. Hell, the man on the back-forty had only brought in half the tobacco he and Annalaura had gathered, and that family's share had been two hundred and fifty dollars. That was when John knew he had to leave.

Closing the door behind him, he slipped in the big padlock that Miz Brown hated, and turned the key. Welles didn't want that woman snooping around. She wouldn't bother his money, there was way too little of it for her anyway, but she might put her hands on the pistol that he kept hidden behind a chink in the wall up near the ceiling.

Now that Miz Brown had awakened him with her rent nonsense, he decided to head off early to his brothel job. In the two months he'd worked there, he'd taken every opportunity to get in the face of the owner. Miz Zeola's whorehouse was just about the best in Nashville that serviced the workingman colored. Oh, John knew about the fanciest brothel in town with its curly-haired, high-yella gals, but they only serviced the colored doctors, lawyers, businessmen, and it was said in the quarter, more than a few of the richest white faces showed up there, too. But it was Miz Zeola who had the market cornered for the workingman with a decent paying job. And she treated her customers just fine.

To make up for the lack of looks in her women, Miz Zeola saw to it that her male guests had an extra fine dinner for just a fraction of the cost at a regular restaurant. She laid out her tables with white cloths, and in the summertime, even put sweet-smelling night-blooming jasmine in glass jars right there in the center. And it wasn't like Miz Zeola's girls were mud-duck ugly. While most of them didn't have the bright color and light eyes, her brown-skinned girls were more than fair-to-middling pretty. The madam trained them to keep a man in ecstasy longer than any other whorehouse in all of Nashville. John was sure of that by all those pleased moans and grunts he heard coming from the rooms upstairs when he went to the pantry door to pick up the dirty dishes. John had known better than to sample his employer's wares—that had gotten many a country boy fired right quick—so he wasn't sure what the women looked like under their fancy dresses, but he guessed their stuff couldn't have been any finer than his Annalaura's.

A ride on the horse-drawn trolley cost five cents. Since a nickel was hard come by, John opted to walk to Miz Zeola's. The twelve blocks gave him plenty of time to think about his wife. She hadn't been his pick right off, of course. At twenty-two, he was still too wild. He hadn't reached full-grown manhood when he first discovered the effect he had on women. Working the tobacco like he did had given him the muscles to fill out his tall frame. His older brother, who sheltered him after the death of their parents, always told him that he was far better with words than was safe for a black man. And when that first married woman started batting her eyes in his direction when he turned on his smile, he went straight home and got out the broken bit of that looking glass his sister-in-law used for her own primping. He practiced showing those teeth for hours.

When he used his "Yes, ma'ams," and "No, ma'ams," together with his well-practiced smile, along with those words that came easy to him, just about every colored woman in Lawnover fell all over herself trying to make nice. He was more than happy to accommodate, though he had never been a fool. John Welles wasn't about to get shot for messing with another man's woman. He poured on the charm for the ladies but always knew where to stop the dime. Trouble was, it didn't taken him long to go through most of the eligible women, old or young, in Lawnover. Soon, he stepped on over to Clarksville and the "sportin' houses." Now, there was action. The whorehouses in that town were about as rough as the back end of a barn compared to Miz Zeola's, but those old rusty country girls had taught him many a new trick in the back room of those juke joints. And then he'd met Annalaura.

Met wasn't exactly the right word since he'd watched her grow up. She was seventeen and still living on the Thornton place with her Aunt Becky when he finally took serious notice of her. There she stood in her Sunday best with those buttons across the front of her dress ready to pop. She was the only woman in the room who wasn't falling all over him. He'd taken her a long way since those days. After they married, he'd even shared a few of his whorehouse secrets with Annalaura. Of course, he had sense enough not to tell her where he'd learned those things, but that was easy since she'd come to the marriage bed with no idea of what to do with a man. At first, he thought he could talk her into anything. He smiled at the remembrance of her frowned-up face when he reminded her that all wives were expected to do what their husbands wanted in bed. She'd gone along with most of it, but hardheaded Annalaura had drawn a quick and deep line in the dirt over some of what he asked. Neither the devil nor her husband could make her cross over it. The grin on his face was wide as he reached the brothel's screened-in back porch.

He knocked on the big oak kitchen door at Miz Zeola's. Most folks who had heavy front doors with fancy carvings and curlicues all over them had knotty pine, skinny-as-a-stick back doors. Not Miz Zeola. She always kept her kitchen door locked and insisted that it be made of two-inch solid oak with strong brass hinges. She let everybody know that she didn't want any-body coming through her doors, either front or back, without her knowing exactly who he or she might be.

"Yokel, ain't you early?" Big Red, Miz Zeola's head cook, was already elbow deep in flour and lard making the crusts for the pies when he undid the lock.

By the smell of it, at least two peach cobblers, heavy with cin-namon and nutmeg, were baking away. Big Red mounded up a pile of dough and slapped it on his wooden work board as he turned to stir the big kettle of cut-up sweet potatoes, sending their syrupy scent throughout the kitchen. On the eye next to the kettle stood a second pot full of turnip greens mixed with ham hocks bubbling their heavy promise into the air.

"Thought I'd get me an early start today." John didn't take kindly to Big Red.

All three hundred pounds of the red-boned man sneered down at Nashville newcomers, especially those who had share-cropped for the white farmers. Those, he thought, were too dumb to ever make it at big city living. To Big Red, John Welles was just one of about five "yokels" working for Miz Zeola this summer.

"Uh huh. You one slick country boy all right." Big Red gave him a quick look before he started rattling off the supplies needed for that night's supper.

Red never gave him a written list, and John was convinced the cook could neither read nor write.

"Six loaves of light bread, fo' hams, a peck of sweet potatoes, and half a bushel of black-eyed peas," John repeated the list back to Big Red in his most conciliatory voice. He had no time for an argument with this man.

When he first arrived in July, John watched the other yokels go the rounds with Big Red only to be fired in rapid order. Welles had spent his first month in Nashville eating only one meal a day trying to stretch the money he had taken from Annalaura until he could get himself a job. Losing both job and money after a few days to a big red-skinned cook who had no real power did not interest him. John would shuffle like Massa's best nigger until he could get his chance with Miz Zeola.

"Ain't I jest told you 'bout the liquor? We needs twelve mo' bottles of bourbon whiskey, three jars of good branch water, and fifteen mo' of gin." Red turned from the greens and glared at John.

"Ain't no need of you comin' 'round here early to get in yo' good licks with Miz Zeola. She eat country boys like you fo' breakfast." Spittle from Big Red's mouth found its way into the greens pot. "I see you flashin' them teeth at every woman come 'round here. I hear them words, smooth as rum, that you po' over Miz Zeola's head. I'm here to tell you, it ain't gonna work." Big Red gave the side of the greens kettle a loud whack with the wooden spoon.

"I hears every word you say, and I surely will take it to heart. But I think you gots me wrong. I'm headin' back to my family as soon as I put a little something away for the winter." John spread his lips but made sure his white-on-white teeth didn't show.

"Every country boy 'round here is runnin' from the tobacca. Ain't September harvest time out in tobacca country?" Red's eyes were narrow slits when he turned toward John.

Welles saw more of the Indian in the cook than he did in his wife.

"That it surely is, but my woman got kinfolk to help bring in the harvest." He let his words drip just a hint of apology as he lied to Big Red.

It wasn't that he hadn't thought of Annalaura in the three months he'd been gone. She was never really off of his mind. Of all the women he'd ever met, she was the cream on the milk. Sometimes, he'd fix his mouth to tell her how much she meant to him, but every husband knows that sweet-talkin' words can be the ruination of a good wife. When he left her after the two of them put the seed in the ground in late May, he had every intention of getting back to her bed way before the September harvest. But that thirty-two-dollar pot he won playing poker up in Clarksville seemed like a message straight from the Lord. It had Nashville written all over it. And there was no time to dance with Annalaura. Even though his wife had more sense than all the other females put together, still she was a woman and would never understand that it hurt a man to the middle of his soul to do no better by his family than to have them live in a white man's barn sleeping with the hogs.

"You jest make sure you don't git too big for them country overalls of your'n." Big Red liked to guffaw at his own jokes.

John had wasted enough time with this man who acted enormously satisfied with his role as chief cook in a whorehouse. John had grander plans. He hadn't slipped into the smoke house and pried open the locked metal box where Annalaura kept their savings for naught. He counted out over ten dollars that his wife had saved for school shoes for Cleveland and Doug. He had promised his sons that they could both go to school right after harvest. Doug, in particular, had been excited. Though his second boy was coming up fast on ten, the child hadn't had more than a year's schooling all put together. Yet, Doug could both read and write a little.

John was determined to do better by all his children. Even little Lottie would have her chance at school. He took only eight of the dollars and left Annalaura a little bit over two. A woman as clever as his wife would find a way to make it stretch. Of the two slabs of bacon hanging in the smoke house, John took only one though he did take most of what was left of last fall's preserves. He knew he was leaving his family in a tight spot, but he had every intention of being back in Montgomery County no later than mid-August. He had no idea that Nashville was going to hold him this long, but he was too close to satisfaction to go back home with nothing. For sure, he'd be back by Christmastime. By December, he would send both his boys off to school in fine style and he would put a fancy yellow, ruffled pinafore on Annalaura.

"Thank you for the words and the list. I'm jest gonna check to see if we have enough clean dinner dishes in the dining room safe." Before Big Red could mount a protest, John, his deferential half-smile in place, backed out through the swinging door that divided kitchen and pantry from the dining room.

This time of day, and with any luck, he might find Miz Zeola herself. He had wasted enough time with a colored man who was going nowhere in this world. John hadn't left the best thing in his life for nothing.

Miz Zeola's dining room cabinet was built into the wall, but you wouldn't know it because of all the mahogany surrounding the massive piece on the sides and even up to its nine-foot-high top. The safe was almost the length of the twenty-eight-foot room. Behind its four sets of leaded glass doors, Miz Zeola must have kept six different china patterns of twelve settings each, not to mention the matching crystal and silver. Though it wasn't part of John's job to check on the china, it was the only way an outside man could ever get into the main-floor rooms of the bordello. It was the job of the hired girls to keep the contents of the safe clean. They did the polishing of the silver 'sticks that sat four thick and stood three feet tall on the dining room table that sat twelve. At the entry, with the kitchen swinging door at his back, John scraped his boots clean on the rag rug Miz Zeola kept there for just that purpose. He wanted no telltale signs of dirt when he tipped across the burgundy-red carpet to peek into the small private hideaways Miz Zeola had set up for her best customers.

On the opposite side of the room from the china safe, the madam had carved out three little rooms, each no bigger than six feet by seven. Their doors were papered in the same wall covering as the rest of the room. The brass doorknobs held flowers that seemed to melt into the wallpaper. Three mirrors, each no bigger than two feet square, separated the doors. Miz Zeola wanted no outsider looking into her business. To the uninitiated, the doors looked like part of an elaborately paneled room. Inside, small tables were set for two, and a little kerosene lamp gave out the only light in the windowless rooms. If a person took a notion to peer close enough in the dimness, the outlines of a settee draped in satin sheeting could be seen. John smiled at the finery.

After he had plucked the money he needed from Nashville, he would drape satin sheets over a big four-poster bed and wallow all over it with Annalaura's tight, fine body wrapped in his arms. What his wife's face may have lacked in great beauty, that body of hers more than made up, with those curves and dips that made a man just about holler to the skies at their perfection. Of course, none of this could he tell her. Women didn't need to get their heads puffed out. A swish of air startled him out of his thoughts.

"You gittin' yo' eye fill of my rooms? Lessen you can pay, I don't want no country boy in this part of the house. What you doin' in here anyway?" The clock had not yet sounded five, and Miz Zeola hadn't quite finished her evening toilette.

Her usual perfume, which she declared came straight from New Orleans and always preceded her arrival by at least two rooms, had yet to be applied. John had neither smelled nor heard her approach and turned quickly around, closing the private door behind him. He whipped on his best sheepish, got-to-forgive-the-boy smile.

"I am mightily sorry, Miz Zeola. I had a little bit of extra time, and I jest wanted to make sure everything was at the ready." He kept his eyes on the dressing-gown belt around his employer's considerable middle while he let her absorb his words. He had learned, early on, that women loved it when a man gave them a chance to talk.

"If you got that much extra time, then maybe I needs to cut back on yo' hours." The satin of her purple dressing robe rustled as she stepped toward him.

He felt her eyes climb all over him more than once. He was used to that from women. Zeola was no different.

"Where you from again, country boy?" Those words on any-body's lips, male or female, were beginning to wear on his nerves almost as bad as when the white Lawnover farmers called him "boy," though he was thirty-four years old.

"Montgomery County, ma'am." He lifted his eyes to face her, leaving only the slightest trace of a smile.

"John, ain't it? How long you been with me?" She turned her face into the feathered boa at her dressing-gown collar and fluffed it with her long scarlet-painted fingernails.

"Yes'm, it's John. John Welles. And I'm pleased to say I've been working for you fo' almost three months." He let the smile flash for just an instant before he dropped his eyes back to the loosely knotted belt.

"Let me tell you one damn thing, John Welles. If you want to keep on workin' fo' me, you will stay where I put you." She poked one plump hand at him, as the curling rags in her hair wagged with each word she punched into the air. "You will come and go where and when I say you can, and you will not step foot into any place I say you cain't."

John snapped his eyes to her face. He couldn't recall when a woman had laid into him like this unless it was Annalaura when she fumed over his gambling ways.

"You got a woman?" She shot the question at him like she was accusing him of stealing her candlesticks right off her table.

"Yes'm." John had to think quick like he sometimes had to do with his wife.

"Chil'ren?"

"Yes'm." He let that answer hang in the air while he sized up this woman.

"But they ain't here in Nashville, is they?" She folded her arms over her big bosom.

"No'm. They's with her family in Montgomery County." What business of this woman's was his family?

"John Welles, yo' country boy games ain't gonna work on me. I knows you is in Nashville to make yo'self a killin' so you can get back to that fine gal you left on some white man's farm." Reaching into the pocket of her gown, she dragged out a long cigarette holder. Plunging a hand deep into the other pocket, she pulled out a cigarette and stuck it in the holder. "For all yo' shuckin' ways, you ain't stupid, John Welles, tho' you would have me believe you was close to simple-minded." She walked to the safe, pulled open a drawer, and withdrew a box of matches.

"No, ma'am. I don't reckon I am stupid. I'm in Nashville to earn enough money to bring up my family." He raised his head and eased his back up straight to give himself more than a head advantage over the stocky woman. Still, Zeola had a way of making a man feel just a little bit smaller than he actually was.

"Tell that pretty story to somebody else. Nashville runs thin real fast on country boys. Livin's too quick here. What you boys really want is big money in lightning time so's you can git back home and buy yo' own place." Zeola turned those hard-as-glass eyes on him, the just lit cigarette dangling from its holder in her hand. "Now, tell me, John Welles, if I ain't spoke the truth?"

John didn't even think Annalaura could read him this well, and she was damn good.

"I'm not braggin' on myself, Miz Zeola, ma'am, but I surely will make me enough money to buy my own farm." He'd given his wife credit for being able to see inside him like no other because of her Cherokee grandmother. "I already got my eye on twenty acres down near Lawnover. Me and my wife could make that work real well."

Everybody knew some Indian women had the second sight. That was why he'd taken off for Nashville without a word to Annalaura. If he'd stayed to argue the point, she would have known he was itching to go and would have tried to talk him out of leaving. She was hardheaded that way. She'd never understood that a wife was supposed to shut up and let the husband do what he knew to be right for the family, even if it meant a few sacrifices here and there. Even a blind man with one leg could see that 'cropping was never going to make a way for a colored man. When she saw all that money he was going to lay at her feet when he returned home, maybe that hard head of hers might soften into forgiveness.

Zeola circled him, looking him up and down just the way she did when a new girl came in for a job. She wouldn't take the applicant if she was too homely, too sickly, or looked too broke down. She preferred scared and ruined country girls who had been done in by no more than two men. John wondered what price she was setting on him?

"You 'surely will' make you enough money here in Nashville, is it? You know how many country boys tell me the same thing? They cain't last six months in this town." As she spoke, her hips swayed in time to her words. "What makes you think you won't be back in yo' Lawnover right after first snowfall?"

"Miz Zeola, I am truly sorry to hear 'bout them other men, but ma'am, ain't none of them me." He could feel himself looking down upon her from his full six feet. "Beggin' yo' pardon, ma'am, this job may not last as long as I'd like, but there's other ways fo' a man to earn good money here in Nashville." He kept his smile inside.

"Uh huh. Some of them ways will get you into the white man's jail quicker than I can yell po-lice." Her eyes had squinted down so far that a body couldn't tell if their color was gray or brown. "Believe me, John Welles, you don't want no parts of a Nashville jail." The mound of purple shimmered as she wagged her head. "A man with a strong back but a little mind may wish fo' Nashville all he wants, but you is right, wishin' ain't gettin'."

"And a man with a strong back, strong mind, and quick hands is a natural in Nashville." He put his full stare into her eyes.

She gave it back to him and then some.

"A natural, is it, John Welles? How much gamblin' you done?" The red-painted fingers splayed themselves under two of her considerable chins.

"It was gamblin' money that got me this far." This was the chance he'd waited for, but he knew he had to let this woman think she was drawing the truth out of him.

"I don't allow no lyin', no cheatin', and no liftin' of my money. Country boy, believe me, I'll know if one nickel of my money is missin'." The eyes opened a bit. She pointed one finger at his temple.

"Ma'am?" John faced her, puzzled.

"I needs me a country boy who's smart enough to act dumb so as to be taken fo' honest at my poker games. I want you to hold the pot. If even one dime is gone, it won't take me to kill you, the players in the game will do it fo' me. And more than one of my gentleman callers is handy with both a knife and a pistol. Do you take my meanin'?"

"Yes ma'am. My head figurin' is right good." John's heart picked up a beat. A thousand dollars would buy him a farm in Lawnover and all the stock that went with it.

"My rules is simple. You play it straight at my tables, take account of every nickel, and I gives you five dollars flat up out of every pot. To see if you can work it, I'll let you sit in on two of my weekday games. That'll give you ten extra dollars a week. Do right by me and I might sweeten that deal considerable." Zeola strutted to the sideboard, opened one of the doors, and pulled out a bottle of bourbon and a shot glass.

"Monday's yo' slowest day, Miz Zeola. I'd be pleased to start then." He thought he saw her flash a quick gold-toothed smile at him.

"Two mo' things. You treat my high rollers like they was Gawd Almighty, and once a week, I'll have one of my girls service you for free. You can have Sally. She close to thirty-five and I'm gonna have to let her go soon, but she'll show you enough new stuff to keep you satisfied fo' a mighty long time. Now git on back to yo' regular job." With the back of her hand, she waved him off.

CHAPTER NINE

Eula slapped the pork chop on the floured board, gave the pepper holder a shake, reached her hand into the salt jar, and spread a pinch over the meat. She flipped the chop over and repeated the process before she dropped it into the hot grease sizzling in her skillet. She counted the chops as she blew a stray strand of hair out of her eyes. Three in the skillet cooking and six on the platter already done.

"Oh," she jumped back as a particularly large splatter of grease landed on her bare forearm. She dabbed at the burning place with a dry kitchen rag, draped the cloth near the stove edge, and hurried to lift the heavy lid off the potatoes bubbling in their own skillet. She reached into her apron pocket and pulled out two green onions. With the knife she'd yanked from her spice rack, Eula sliced the green tops into the potatoes.

Eula chanced a glimpse at her husband. Alex, sitting at the table with a cup of coffee, gave no notice that he'd paid attention to any of her hurried activities. Coffee at night? Fresh-cooked pork chops at supper? This was more like breakfast or dinner rather than the last meal of the day. True, Alex had spent a heavy week finishing up the harvest. All but the mid-forty were in the barns and hanging on the drying poles. It was still just the first week of September. Maybe that accounted for her husband having her cook up enough food to feed the entire Lawnover Joseph-the-Shepherd Baptist Church on a Friday night.

"How much of that chicken we got left from dinner?" Alex stood and walked over to the stove to stare at the skillet.

In twenty years, her husband had never watched her cook, nor questioned her portions. The surprise of it all had just about taken every word out of Eula's mouth.

"We got a whole one left. I'm going to warm it for breakfast," she managed.

Alex barely escaped a second grease splatter.

"Where's the butcher paper?" He paced from the stove to the table to the porch door and back again.

Eula watched him walk the same path a second time and forgot to turn over a pork chop. Was her husband walking in circles?

"Butcher paper?" She ventured a tentative response.

"Yeah. The butcher paper." More than a trace of annoyance shot out of Alex's mouth.

Startled at a husband who almost never raised his voice to her, she neglected to remove one of the chops from the skillet.

"It's rolled up in a corner in the pantry." She watched Alex brush past her and head into the back room off the kitchen.

Eula inventoried the day to see what might have addled her husband into such a frenzy. Breakfast had been as usual and dinner had been hearty enough. Surely, he couldn't be this hungry. There had been nothing untoward with the chores. Yes, Alex had milked the cows when, technically, that was a wife's job. In fact, he had done the milking the last two mornings. But she hadn't paid much mind to that. In their marriage, the two of them had worked out most things in a way that didn't require talking. Each could just see what outside chores needed to be done and head

straight to it. Whichever one happened to be in the barn at milking time just did the milking. Alex liked it that way.

But this Friday night puzzled her. Perhaps the lagging harvest on the mid-forty worried her husband more than he let on,
though Eula prided herself on being able to read Alex better
and faster than he could read himself. She bit down on her lip as
her husband came back into the kitchen with a torn-off strip of
butcher paper in his hands and three jars of her peach preserves.
Laying them all on the table, Alex walked over to the food safe
and removed tomorrow's breakfast chicken. The smoky smell of
burning cloth finally told Eula she had dropped her dry kitchen
rag too close to the fire.

"My Lord," she shouted as she began to beat out the flame
with her hands.

"Here." Alex reached her in two strides and poured his coffee
over the rag. "How much longer for those chops?"

Eula pulled at the collar of her dress. It was too tight in the
heat of tonight's kitchen.

"They'll be ready by the time I heat up your pole beans and
corn bread. Do you want buttermilk or sweet milk for supper?"
When had her husband last acted like this?

"I'll take the pole beans in a jar. Where's the corn bread?" He
had moved back to the kitchen table, the four cooked pork chops
dripping grease over his hands. He scrunched the brown paper
over the meat.

Eula stood stock-still. In the back of her mind, somewhere,
the scent of burning meat registered, but, for the life of her, she
couldn't match up the smell with anything she was supposed to
do about it.

"Take with you? You're takin' the food out of here? I thought
you wanted a big supper tonight—the harvest being over and all."

The grease popping all around her sounded like firecrackers on the Fourth of July.

Only the sight of Alex's shocked face brought her back to herself. Realizing too late that she had walked dangerously close to the line of wifely impropriety, she turned to the skillet and pulled out the last of the singed pork chops. Her head down, she scurried to the safe and reached for a clean rag. She busied herself with scrubbing the grease splatters off the stove and her wall as though her life depended upon it. Eula had stunned her husband and herself with her questions.

"I'm droppin' some food off for that old woman over on the Thornton place." Alex had slowed his pace as he moved to the stove to retrieve the remaining pork chops. He turned to the china cabinet, reached to the top shelf, and pulled down her biggest bowl, with its blue sprig of flowers and thin strip of silver around the base.

Eula stood openmouthed. That oval-shaped piece of china was her only "silver" piece and her pride. In twenty years, she had never actually put anything in her favorite wedding gift. A hundred questions marched themselves into her mind. She worked her mouth hard to get them out, but her mind worked even harder to keep them in. Her mouth won the battle.

"Ben Roy's place? Old woman? Surely, you're not talkin' about Rebecca usin' my weddin' present bowl?" Eula wanted to drive her teeth through her tongue when she saw the quick flash of anger on her husband's face.

"Yeah. Rebecca. Ain't you always tellin' me she's a Thornton responsibility? Well, you're a Thornton. I don't want your brother thinkin' we're too hard up to do our share." He walked into the pantry and returned with two big jars of pole beans and a Mason jar full of honey.

"Is it the mid-forty?" Eula's mind reeled. She didn't dare chance a look at Alex.

Her husband appreciated a woman who had her own mind, but he appreciated the female even more when that woman kept it to herself and didn't bother him with it. Despite all the warnings shooting through her head, Eula had to sort this one out.

"I thought that colored man you hired was goin' to start on Monday. Two weeks or more 'til a cold snap." Though she held her head down, the flashes from Alex's eyes pierced right down to her belly. If she didn't look at him, she could finish her words. "That should give him time aplenty to get in most of the forty."

Alex's face flamed the color of over-ripe cherries.

"I don't want to hear you fret over the mid-forty again. That's all taken care of." His voice sounded like the hiss of a snake in her ears.

"Name's Rebecca Murdock, you know. She don't ever use that name, but she was a married woman once. Married a colored man from outside of Lawnover. Still likes to call herself a Thornton even though she's not really one. Just one of our colored from before the War." Eula prayed that what Alex called "mindless woman's chatter" would guide his own mind away from her wifely slip.

She could bear his annoyance much easier than his anger. Scooping up the corn bread, he added it to the other wrapped parcels and headed out the kitchen door.

"You reckon she's still up this late at night?" Eula fought hard to make her voice sound everyday.

Alex was already at the porch door when he stopped and turned back to her. Behind him the last of the September sunlight had gone thirty minutes earlier, and the moon had already gained supremacy in the sky.

"I told you I'm takin' some of this food over to that nigger woman on your brother's place, then I'm takin' the rest to the tavern for a poker game. Don't stay awake." The spring in the screen door was a strong one, and when Alex let it close on its own, the sound of it snapping back into place reminded Eula of a rifle shot.

Moving quickly to the kitchen door, she called after him. "Won't Ben Roy be there? Fedora usually packs up the food for those poker games when Bobby Lee's busy." She tried to put the picture of Alex bringing food to the Lawnover store into her mind. It wouldn't fit.

Alex reached the barn and his horse. He gave no sign that he'd heard her call. Eula turned around to stare at the shambles of her kitchen. It wasn't that her husband had never gone out after supper before, nor that he had never gone to play poker at Bobby Lee's General Store, but he had never been the one to bring the food. Pouring the hot grease into a tin can, Eula caught herself talking out loud.

"Like Alex always says, this is just women's silliness. Some foolishness I can't even put a name to." Eula scrubbed at the pork chop skillet hard enough to scrape a knuckle. "Alex and Ben Roy just got into it again. Taking food to old Becky must be Alex's way of getting back at my brother." Hearing her own words did not soothe her worries. She walked over to the safe and pulled out her journal. Alex had surely made a dent in her supplies tonight, but, like always, she would find a way to manage.

Climbing into bed, Eula touched her husband's empty pillow. Alex wasn't much of a gambling man. She hoped he and Ben Roy could work out whatever their fuss was about. With the moon at half-mast, a thought that the problem lay somewhere on the mid-forty fought its way into Eula's mind. She pushed it back into the darkness where it belonged. Just woman's foolishness. She and her husband had had other iffy harvests, and they always made out just fine. As she turned down the wick on the bedside lamp, that churning feeling in her stomach that wouldn't settle down told her that sleep would come hard this night.

CHAPTER TEN

The moon had already launched its transit across the sky when Alex saw the lantern light shining through the small window at the top of the barn. It was the first thing he spotted as he turned off the lane and onto the path leading toward the living quarters on the mid-forty. Somehow, he had supposed the place would already be in darkness. He gave the gray a little kick in the side. The horse reached the barn in a few quick strides. There, standing just inside the partially opened barn door and wrapped in a frayed quilt, was the woman.

Though it was nearly nine o'clock, and the September evenings were cooling down, Alex didn't believe it was quilt weather just yet. Her boots from the morning peeked from underneath the heavy cover. What was she wearing underneath that quilt? Breasts, hips, and those bare thighs—pictures of her nakedness rumbled through his mind. He didn't bother to push back his grin as he scrambled down from the horse. Alex kept his eyes on the woman as he fumbled with the parcels slung across the saddle. The warmth moving up his body heightened his anticipation as he walked toward her. She stood, unmoving, with her head bowed. Alex had almost reached her when the ruckus from the living quarters dashed down upon him.

Loud crying from the woman's youngest child competed heavily with shouts from the shrill voice of her girl, and the running feet of he knew not who. Alex stopped several yards from the woman and pointed upward. Didn't she know to be ready for him?

"Why ain't your children asleep?" He didn't want an audience of children.

"They'll be asleep soon enough, suh."

He had to strain to catch her words and wondered why. She certainly spoke her wants loud enough this morning. Now, it was too late for her to back out of their bargain. Shifting the pouch to his shoulder, Alex reached toward the woman. His hands reached to loosen the tight grip she kept on the edge of the quilt. Just as his hand touched hers, she turned and moved toward the barn, the quilt sliding halfway down her back. Alex saw that she still wore the same dress from the morning.

As he stepped inside, the lure of fresh-cut tobacco that should have signaled an early September greeting at his entrance was noticeably absent. As his eyes adjusted to the gloom, he watched the woman walk past the cows bedded for the night. All was quiet on the lower floor of the barn. The chickens had tucked in their wings for sleep. Outside in their pens, the three hogs had gone silent. He watched his tenant gather the quilt over one arm as she stopped near a small stack of spearing sticks. Behind her, the last few bales of hay lay mounded in a short pile topped with the pitchfork. Bits of straw covered the barn floor. He looked at the woman with her head still dropped. Did she want to tumble him right there? His back was too stiff to roll around on the hard boards of a barn floor.

The light shining down from the small opening of the living quarters framed the woman. Headed toward the ladder, he made out the curves of her body, even under that shapeless dress she wore. Moving after her, he watched the sway of those rounded hips, her skirt hitched just above her knees.

"Momma?" A boy of about nine stared at Alex as he cleared the top rung of the ladder. Dropping the quilt to the floor, the woman stooped to pick up her suddenly quiet toddler. The young girl stood barefoot near an alcove that held an older child with his leg tied to a broomstick. The girl's mouth lay open, and Alex could see that she still had most of her baby teeth. The boy in the alcove pushed himself to sitting as he grabbed his sister by the arm and yanked her toward him. The boy's shocked face matched the girl's.

"Evenin'." Alex gave a half nod in the general direction of the children as he laid open the leather pouch on the small wooden table.

He wanted them fed and out of the way as soon as possible. Hell, he'd send them down to sleep with the cows if this took much longer. Pulling out the jars of spring beans, he noticed the two barrels lined up at the table. Then he remembered he had given two of his own cast-off chairs to the tenants on the back-forty when he furnished their quarters. He made a mental note to look for real chairs for the woman. Alex's hand smeared with grease as he unwrapped the pork chops. He thought he heard a quick intake of breath from the woman when he pulled out the bowl of smothered potatoes. He laid out one of the jars of peach preserves along with several squares of Eula's corn bread. As he looked around for plates, Alex caught the eye of the toddler in the woman's arms. The child's arm suddenly jutted toward a pork chop. Squirming to be released, the toddler ducked his head inches from the rough table edge.

"Henry." Embarrassment shadowed the woman's voice. "You ain't been asked yet."

The boy gave a quick look at Alex and buried his head in his mother's shoulder, setting up a soft whine. The woman bounced the child gently in her arms.

"Where's your plates?" Alex asked.

"Lottie, go get the tins." The woman nodded toward her girl.

The little girl started to move but her older brother's grip held tight on her arm.

"Momma, can I be asked, too?" The girl wrestled her arm free as her eyes darted from the food-laden table to Alex and back again.

"Lottie, ain't I taught you to wait 'til you're spoken to?" The woman's rebuke pleased Alex.

She was raising this get right.

"And, drop your head." The woman's audible whisper landed on the girl, who ran to a corner of the room and retrieved four tin plates, which she placed on one of the crates since the table was full.

The child scurried behind her mother's skirt and dropped her head. Alex gave a halfhearted try at suppressing his smile. If the truth be told, this get had some pleasing ways, but they were definitely posing a problem. He stepped back to look for hanging hooks on the wall only to brush into the woman's middle boy. Stepping quickly to avoid knocking over the child, Alex caught his heel in a large opening in the floorboard.

"Momma, that man don't know to stay away from the knot-holes." Little Henry's tears turned to howls of glee as he pointed at Alex.

The woman looked as though she wanted to squeeze herself down through the two-inch round hole and disappear. Instead, she pushed her son's head deep into her shoulder. Alex could hear the child's muffled pleas for air. The woman kept her hand tight on the back of the boy's head. Wordlessly, she bobbed her apologies toward Alex. He backed up and started to walk toward the wall opposite the oldest boy's alcove of a bed.

"Suh, be careful. There's holes all over these floors." The middle boy pointed a finger at the next opening less than eighteen inches from where Alex stood.

"Doug." The woman's rebuke to her child was mixed with sharpness, embarrassment, and clear confusion.

Alex followed Doug's pointing hand and saw no fewer than four knotholes that could definitely cause damage to a small child's foot. He turned to look at Henry, his buried face finally released by his mother though she held her hand over his mouth. The little boy shook his head vehemently trying to push away his mother's hand.

"Why don't you feed your get and tell me where the clothesline is." Alex had barely gotten the words out of his mouth when Lottie shot past him and grabbed a pork chop.

It took her mother one stride to reach the girl and remove the chop before it reached the child's mouth.

"Lottie Welles, you got mo' manners than that. You turn yo'self around and thank Mr. McNaughton for his kindness. You, too, Doug and Henry." As her mother delivered the message, the little girl turned and dropped a quick curtsy to Alex and mouthed a barely heard thank-you.

The toddler finally succeeded in freeing himself from his mother's arms and grinned his thanks.

"Thank you, suh," came from Doug, who sidled up to the table but waited until his mother started to fill the plates.

The woman turned to Alex.

"The hooks is in the wall on either side of the sleepin' corner, and the line is hangin' from the far one." She spoke to his shirt pocket while her two youngest children shifted their eagerness from one foot to the other.

Despite the obvious hunger of her children, the woman did not hurry her words. She waited until Alex gave her a nod before she returned to ladling food onto the plates.

As the woman busied herself, Alex maneuvered his way around the porous floor. A fresh dropped cow pie shot its fragrance up to him through one of the openings as he neared the sleeping alcove. He didn't remember the floorboards being this full of knots when he hurriedly built the tenant quarters four years ago. Of course, the wood had been salvage. Holding his breath, he spotted the thin wire clothesline hanging from one hook, its mass bunched up on the floor near the space the woman called the "sleepin' corner." Alex frowned when he looked at what passed for her bed space. Hadn't he given his tenants a proper bed? This was an area barely six feet long and four feet wide. For his six-foot frame, this would be a tight fit. Worse, instead of a bed, a thin mattress lay on top of a built-in box of wood. The mattress was bare.

"Where's the sheets?" Alex spoke out quickly without remembering that the children were within earshot.

He grimaced at his error as he glanced across the room to the opposite alcove and the woman's oldest son.

"Sorry, suh. I had to shred it up yesterday when my Cleveland fell from the rafters. I think his leg is broke. I used the sheet to tie the leg to the broomstick." She pointed a filled food tin at Cleveland.

Watching for more knotholes, Alex walked to the woman and took the tin from her. The quiet in the room felt steep. He handed the plate to the woman's eldest while he stared at the broomstick-trussed leg. He ran a hand over the skinny extremity, careful not to increase the pain. He stopped at mid-shin, bent down, and placed his other hand behind the boy's leg at mid-calf. With a quick jerk, he moved his hands in opposing directions.

"Uhh." The child yelped. Tears splashed his cheeks, the plate of food trembling in his hand.

Before Alex could reach for one of the torn sheet strips, the woman was at her son's side. The look of a mother tigress protecting her cub flashed out of her face. Alex spoke up as he retied the strips of cloth.

"Break ain't bad. Just had to set it proper. You did a good job tying it up. Have the boy eat his supper." Alex moved to his feet, grazing his head on the low sloping roof.

The woman lifted a hand to touch the forming lump, and just as fast, withdrew it.

"I thank you kindly, suh." It was the softest tone he'd heard from her yet.

With the clothesline strung, Alex retrieved the dropped quilt and hung it across the wire to fashion a semi-private bedroom. He sat on the formless mattress and made another note to himself to find a better cast-off. Behind the makeshift screen, he heard the woman stack the tin plates and put away the extra food. Alex took off his boots and willed her to hurry.

"Doug. You sleep with Cleveland tonight. Lottie will take yo' place with Henry on the pallet." As much as the woman's arrangements signaled progress to Alex, the protests of her children foretold more delay.

Behind the quilt, Alex unbuttoned his shirt.

"Why cain't I sleep with you like always, Momma?" It was the whine of little Lottie.

"You'll sleep where I tell you, and I don't want another word about it. I need Doug to sleep with Cleveland in case he needs help in the night."

Behind the quilt, Alex heard the woman drop to her knees.

"Shh. Henry's already asleep. Momma will give you a good-night kiss and you go on to sleep yo'self."

Alex strained his ears to catch the sound of the woman's lips on flesh. He undid the top button of his trousers when he heard her footsteps coming toward him. He watched the quilt slide back a few inches.

"I thank you most kindly fo' the food, suh. My little ones is tired from their long day. They'll be asleep in a minute, but my Cleveland is in some pain." Only her face showed through the quilt. Her eyes rested on the bottom of the windowsill next to Alex. "If it pleases you, suh, now that they've got some food in their bellies, I will have my children asleep right at dark tomorrow night. Would you care to come back then?" Her eyes sidled from the sill to the top of his head.

Despite himself, Alex had to admire this woman. Here she was still trying to bargain with him when the deal was long closed. He reached for a small metal flask in his pants pocket. Unscrewing the cap, he leveled it toward her.

"Give him this. It'll cut the pain." He didn't bother to suppress the little smile that kept coming to his lips. His excitement for this woman was growing by the minute.

"Suh?" She looked puzzled, confused.

"It's whiskey. Give him a tablespoon and take one for yourself." Alex pushed the flask at her.

"My babies don't take no strong drink, suh, and neither do I." Her eyes went directly to his own. Her head bobbed her no thanks.

Alex's smile broadened. "It will cut the pain. Give it to him." Alex moved toward her. She took a half step backward, almost pulling down the quilt. He pressed the flask into her hand.

Her eyes looked at him, wide apart. Alex smiled as he reached for the second button of his trousers. The woman stumbled away from the quilt. Alex nearly laughed out loud. Sitting on the corn husk mattress, he removed his boots.

Thank goodness the living quarters were small enough for him to almost make out the sound of sleeping children despite the muffling of the quilt. Unlike adults, they didn't snore and it was hard to figure out their sleep-breathing. He was certain the two youngest had been out for nearly twenty minutes and the middle boy's—Doug was his name—asthma-wracked breathing showed that he had soon followed. Alex just wasn't sure about the one the woman called Cleveland. He'd heard her administer the whiskey and the boy's reaction to the burn as it went down his throat. That had been nearly fifteen minutes ago. Behind the quilt, Alex took off his shirt.

Finally, he heard the woman stirring. He listened to her footsteps as she walked around the room and paused. He guessed she was making sure each child was asleep. He pulled his trousers over his feet. The woman's footsteps slowed as she neared the quilt. She stopped right on the other side. He heard a long-drawn intake of breath as she eased herself around to his side of the blanket. Wearing only his summer drawers, Alex stood to greet her. Her hand went to the makeshift partition, almost pulling it down again. He steadied it as he pulled her toward him.

"It'll be cold tonight without that blanket." The woman pointed to the askew quilt. "Sorry, suh, I don't have another." She held her crossed hands over her chest.

Her gaze must have been on some faraway star she spotted out of the small window above the sleeping alcove, because they sure weren't on him. She nodded toward the temporary wall.

"If you want, it might be best to do this tomorrow. I can borrow a quilt from my Aunt Becky by then." She couldn't quite disguise the note of desperate hopefulness that fleshed out her words.

Alex sucked in his lips to dampen his smile. She was running out of excuses, and Lord knows, she'd tried just about every one. Soon, she'd concede defeat and come to him willingly. He put his hand under her chin and lifted her face to his. She lowered her eyes.

"What do they call you, woman?" He turned her chin to look at the planes of her face. Even with her wide-set eyes held nearly closed, he liked their look. But they came in second to those pouty lips. He ran his thumb from her lower lip to chin. Alex's breath came in hot spurts.

"Annalaura. Annalaura Welles. My husband is John Welles."

Just when he thought she was ready to give in to him on his own terms, she fired back with her little reminder. No husband foolish enough to leave such a woman was coming back tonight, and tonight was all he needed.

"No, no. Anna was my momma's name, and it ain't my momma I want to think about tonight. I'll call you Laura." He pulled her closer, feeling the crush of her breasts against his chest.

Alex slid his body sideways against their firmness. When he pushed her back, his voice was almost a whisper in his own ears.

"And, tonight, Laura, I can guarantee that you won't get cold without that quilt." He bent to kiss her only to find her lips pressed tight together like he was trying to feed her castor oil.

Her whole body trembled under his touch. He could feel those shaking shoulders move to push him away, tense up in mid-motion, and stop. Her body was fighting him. He released her to reach down for the whiskey flask.

"Take a swig of this." He removed the cap and held the metal bottle in front of her.

She nodded her no, blinked the remembrance of her place, and answered in a voice that held almost no sound.

"Thank you no, suh."

Alex took a drink from the container and put it to her lips.

"You need a drink." He tipped the flask to her closed mouth.

She barely parted her lips. He was certain that almost none of the liquid made its way into her throat. Alex pulled her back toward him and let his lips glide slowly over hers. He felt her body go limp. Suddenly afraid that she might pass out, he slipped an arm around her back. He'd never heard of a colored woman fainting. He'd always been told that colored women were strong enough to take anything. Alex pulled back from her and watched her face closely. Laura's eyes were now tightly closed. He put a hand over the spout of the flask and poured a bit more of the liquid over his hand. Though she clenched her jaw as tight as a wood vise, he managed to part her lips with his fingers. She shook even more as he took her into his arms again. Alex tapped his liquor-soaked finger over her lower lip, rubbing little circles over its fleshy softness as he moved his hand from left to right. Even in the dim light, Laura's lip glistened like a juicy plum as he leaned over and drew it into his own mouth. The taste of spiced honey and ripe, fresh-picked strawberries filled his throat and went straight to his head faster than any whiskey he'd ever drunk. The scent of her was like a sandalwood platter he had once smelled on the back of a peddler's cart. It was from Africa, the peddler declared, and cost five dollars. Alex hadn't spent the money. Kissing her again, he sucked in her upper lip, drawing it out long and slow into his own mouth. He let his tongue probe inside Laura's mouth, but there was no answering response. In his embrace, he let his hands run down the sleeve of her blouse. She held her arms stiff at her side.

"Put your arms around me," he whispered in his half-voice.

Slow like a herky-jerky at a carnival, Laura reached her arms to his shoulders and stopped. They lay there like two leaves of untied tobacco. Shining through the window, the silver light from the moon laid a streak across the back of Laura's blouse. Alex stepped away and put a hand at the open band collar of her top. He felt the tension in her increase. He knew she wanted to slap his hand away. In the dimness he felt her hands on his shoulders open and close as though she were pleading with them to complete Alex's bidding. She was still fighting the battle to push him away, but soon, she would acknowledge their bargain.

Slowly he undid the four remaining fasteners on her blouse. Laying the garment open he was surprised to see a chemise underneath. It hadn't been there this morning. Fingering the thin cotton, he could tell it was her Sunday best. Had she put it on to please him, or to hide herself from him? With great care, he unfastened the buttons.

"We can lay our heads on this." He slipped off her blouse and tossed it on the skinny mattress.

The woman's eyes still hadn't opened. Alex slid his hand from her waist up between the open chemise as he pushed the garment off her body. Threads of silvery moonlight shone across her breasts. Alex struggled to catch his breath. Her nipples looked like lumps of nutmeg ready for the Christmas baking sitting atop a high-mounded cinnamon bun. His own fingers began to tremble as he encircled each nipple, letting his fingers explore in ever-widening circles. He tried to cup each breast, but the fullness overflowed even his large hands. He felt Laura's shaking increase with each breath she took, pushing her breasts even more firmly into his hands.

Alex sat heavily onto the corn husk mattress, his thoughts refusing to marshal themselves into coherent order. He managed to lay his hand against the waistband of her skirt. He fumbled for the button and let the garment drop to the floor. Underneath, Laura wore her summer drawers. He was certain they hadn't been there this morning, either. He let his hands slide to the side to undo their ties. The woman dropped one hand from her breasts to grab at the top of her falling drawers. Alex brushed her hand away as the pantaloons drifted slowly down on top of her skirt. He felt her body sway away from him, and he pulled her closer.

Laying his head on her bare stomach, he let his tongue slide from her belly button up to the beginning roundness of her breasts. With his hands on those firm hips, he pulled her down toward him and sucked one nipple into his mouth. A long ago memory of fresh-cut raw cane sugar flooded his throat, and he felt he was about to float away into a river of delirium. He slid his tongue across her chest and drew in the other nipple. He felt her knees soften under him, and Laura grabbed at his shoulders to steady herself. He glanced up at her face. The moonlight had captured the top half in a glow that reminded him of a sepia-toned Bible picture. He let his tongue linger as he traced it down her belly again. He moved his mouth lower, exploring her stomach until he reached her spirally haired triangle. Breaths were getting harder for him to take. He turned her to the mattress. She sat with a loud rustle of the husks. Her eyes, which had been closed tighter than a new-trussed pig for many long minutes, opened wide at the sound.

"My babies will wake up, suh. Maybe you could come back tomorrow?" The trembling in her body had reached her voice, and she could barely get out the words.

Alex pushed her gently down on the mattress. Her shaking rattled the corn husks even louder. She lay straight-legged on the bed with one arm wrapped over her breasts and the other stretching to cover that triangle of hair. He rolled on top of her and bent down to kiss her just as she turned her head slightly. His lips caught the corner of her mouth. He used the strength of his legs to spread her thighs. She held them together like an unheated piece of iron at the smithy shop.

"Bend your knees." His voice was almost as gone as hers. He felt her falter in her effort to respond. Alex slipped his hands under her hips. Her legs felt like lead as he guided them upward. He moved his fingers to the spirally haired triangle to explore the depths of the wetness within. The woman arched her back and almost convulsed for breath as he pushed his manhood into what felt like the golden portals of heaven.

The moon shining in his eyes stirred Alex from sleep. He immediately knew where he lay. The satisfaction in his body hadn't gone away. He knew she was still there. Alex lay on his side with his knees bent. The woman, Laura, lay with her body curved spoonlike inside his. Her skirt was thrown over them both from waist down. Her blouse, which had earlier covered them, had slipped to the floor. His hand lay across her belly holding her close to him, her bare bottom firm against his manhood. Alex let his hand travel up to one breast. He squeezed it again, still pleasured by the rounded firmness. When he took hold, he knew there was more than soft cotton mush in his hand. Laura stirred.

"I'd best be gettin' to the smoke house." Her voice was weak as she tried to scoot toward the edge of the mattress.

He pulled her back knowing she could feel his growing manhood.

"You don't need the smoke house at this time of night." He let his hand drop back to the triangle.

Laura pointed at the window.

"Moon says it must be close to midnight. I reckon you'll want to be gettin' back home before much longer." She made another attempt to rise when Alex rolled her onto her back. She looked startled. "Suh, it's late." Her earlier fright had dissolved into alarm.

"I want you to put your arms around me and hold me like I'm the man who's goin' to take you north and pour sandalwood perfume all over you." Alex kissed her face, breasts, belly in quick succession.

Slowly, she laid her arms around his neck.

"Now squeeze tight," he commanded as he entered her for the second time that night.

The light from the moon now shining past its zenith made her skin glow copper like a new penny. He couldn't tell which he enjoyed more—the first or the second time. He knew he was more than up to a third go with Laura. He glanced over at her and was sure she hadn't slept at all. Her breathing was still too fast for that. He guessed she'd lain without moving the entire time he'd been asleep. Alex leaned over and kissed her on the ear.

"Honey, I do have to go now." He let his hand stroke down her breast one last time as he moved her to sitting.

She half turned toward him, a quizzical look on her face. If he had misspoken, it was understandable. He hadn't made love a second time since the earliest days of his marriage, and this had been so much sweeter. He reached for his drawers as Laura stepped into her skirt.

"You don't have to get up. I can find my way down the ladder in the dark." He touched her hand as she buttoned the skirt.

"I've got to go to the smoke house to wash out that pretty bowl you brought the potatoes in." She reached for her blouse.

He grabbed her wrists.

"Let me look at you just a minute longer." He pulled her between his bare thighs.

She laid her hands against his shoulders. This time, there was no trembling.

"Suh, thank you for the food fo' my children, but I reckon you don't want the sunshine to catch you here." Even her voice sounded stronger.

Alex released her as he stepped into his trousers. Laura started to move beyond the curtain.

"Wait," he whispered to her as he tossed the shirt he'd just retrieved back onto the floor. "I want to kiss you again."

Slowly she turned, but she didn't step toward him. He pulled her closer and began fumbling with the newly buttoned blouse. She pushed him away.

"Suh" was all she uttered as she walked beyond the quilt to the table and the bowl. Alex dropped to the mattress to put on his shirt and boots. Hearing her ready herself to descend the ladder, he pulled down the quilt.

"No need to hurry with that bowl. I'll be back in a couple of nights to pick it up." He didn't have to wait long for her response.

Laura stood with Eula's bowl in her hands, blinking non-understanding back at him. He walked over to the table and took the hand-painted container, with its streak of silver, from her hand, setting it on the table. Alex gathered her in a tight embrace and kissed her lips. He released her to reach into his trouser pockets. He retrieved something and dropped it into the bowl. A thin shaft of moonlight caught the coin. Alex watched her face when the value of the silver dollar registered. It pleased him greatly to see that wide-eyed look of confusion on this most satisfying woman. As he headed down the ladder, Alex felt her stares into his back and sensed her confusion. He had just given her a whole day's wages for a working white man. As he reached the barn floor, he knew this woman was more than worth it.

CHAPTER ELEVEN

John's new brown and tan houndstooth coat was stronger on looks than it was on warmth. Still, he had no cause to complain since he had given just one silver dollar for it to a man over from Davidson County who couldn't take Nashville anymore and lit out for home. A coat warm enough for the late November weather would cost John two dollars, and since it had to look good as well as offer warmth, the price could come closer to three. As John stepped through the back door of Zeola's, he didn't bother recounting his money situation. He already had the rent for December, and that wasn't due until a week from tomorrow.

"Close that do'. You born in a barn?" Big Red slid his bone-handled butcher knife sideways into the just-cooked Thanksgiving turkey.

Two pecan and two sweet potato pies cooled on the sideboard, and, by the smell of the cinnamon in the air, two apple pies were about to come out of the oven.

Reaching behind him, John absentmindedly pulled the door closed as he gave a quick nod to the cook. Big Red, with his no-manners self, was no longer of any interest to John.

"I sees you got yo'self a new checkered coat for the occasion." Big Red made short work of both turkey legs and now started on the breast.

With only a quick head shake in the cook's direction, John walked toward the connecting pantry door into the dining room. "Well, slick, you ain't as good as you thinks you is. I sees she's got you sittin' the first pot. How many mens you think is gonna leave the family table and come on over to Zeola's on Thanksgivin' evenin'?" The knife in Big Red's hand swayed in the air like a leaf on a flimsy branch.

John stopped short and turned to the cook.

"Red, you save me that there juicy thigh and I'll give you fifty cents from tonight's pot." John walked through the swinging door with Big Red staring after him.

While the cook mostly talked nonsense, the thought of the amount of cash in the holiday pot had crossed John's mind. In early November, Zeola had moved him from holding two poker pots a week to four. Now, Monday through Thursday, John Welles was the pot man for all the early poker games at the whorehouse.

He opened the door into a dining room in mid-Thanksgiving meal. Not wanting to disturb the diners, John nodded a slight greeting in their direction and eased himself around behind the chairs holding six of Miz Zeola's girls. Miz Zeola sat at the head of the table with the elderly and widowed Mr. Jackson who, according to the girls, couldn't really lay a woman—though on more than one occasion, he had just about died trying. This was the early shift. Zeola fed her girls and got them ready to take in any walk-off-the-streets. She figured that on a holiday, some lone man might hanker for female company. Zeola didn't count on getting more than a dollar a girl for these quickies. Mr. Jackson was a charity case. He paid three dollars once a week, come summer or winter, just to spend two hours staring at one of Zeola's buck-naked, less-than-prized girls.

The real money didn't usually come until after eight o'clock, when the wives of all the regulars had fallen asleep, dog-tired from their Thanksgiving efforts. Miz Zeola included a whiskey-laced pecan pie, bought her ladies new finery, and gave her regulars a dollar off the usual price, all in the spirit of the holiday. The liquor flowed free on Thanksgiving and Christmas. Zeola figured if she could just get the men to come in, relax 'em with good booze and cheap women, they would be more than happy to sit in at a high-stakes poker game.

John just hoped her plan would work now that he was holding the pot. He'd heard tales that on some past holidays, there'd been so many players lined up that Zeola had to run three or four games instead of the usual two. It was hinted that for her best customers, Zeola even held the pot herself.

"I hope you had a bite to eat already, John Welles." Zeola unthreaded the watch chain from her thickly powdered bosom and pulled out the timepiece. "I got two men sittin' in the room already and two mo' just stepped into the house." She tilted her head and squinted one eye to get a better look at the watch. "Them last two gonna play first and lay later."

Everybody at the table, including Mr. Jackson, who almost popped out his false teeth, let out a howl.

"Big Red will be savin' me a plate, Miz Zeola. I'm gonna see that you have a bang-up first pot to help you celebrate yo' Thanksgivin'." John turned down the wattage of his smile as he left the dining room and walked across the empty hall into the parlor.

Miz Zeola's parlor was the biggest room in the house. She'd had some colored carpenter come over and put up four floor-to-ceiling pillars, although they did no earthly good at holding up anything. In front of each one, she'd set two velvet-cushioned chairs, but what made the space special, were the tall potted plants she placed on the side opposite the chairs. She fixed them in such a way that the big leaves just about covered whoever was sitting there. With the candlelight scattered just so, and those bushy plants, Zeola hoped that nervous newcomers, and the Nashville law that sometimes sniffed around on official business, would be too busy looking to see who was hiding behind those palms to pay much notice to the two doors that looked like skinny five-foot-tall amateur painted pictures. They weren't as well hidden as the little rooms off the dining area, but it would take somebody who'd stepped through them before to know where on the picture frame to push at the hidden handle to get them to open into the poker rooms.

Of course, the piano man was also part of Madame Zeola's plan. This afternoon, the parlor was empty except for A.C. playing the blues down low. Miz Zeola always patted herself on the back at her find of the piano man and paid him well to stay at her establishment. In that rough voice of his, he could sing as well as play. The only thing Zeola didn't like about A.C.'s playing was his choice of the blues. She absolutely banished it from her parlor during business hours. She only wanted to hear that new music coming up from New Orleans, jazz she called it. The madam said it made her customers want to tap their feet and move their bodies and that's what she wanted—men to keep moving their dollars out of their pockets into hers.

A.C. looked up as John walked toward the concealed doors but didn't break a chord in his rendition of the Memphis blues. As good as the piano man was, John sided with Miz Zeola. Tonight he didn't want his poker players crying into their bourbons-and-branch over some woman gone to another man. He wanted their minds fixed on straights, full houses, and aces over queens.

"Game's 'bout to start." John leaned over the top of the upright. "Can you give us a little bit of that jazz music?"

A.C. stopped and pulled down his lit cigarette from the top of the piano. He narrowed his already small eyes at John and went back to playing the blues. John gave a half-smile and pushed open the picture-frame concealed door and walked into the smaller of the two smoke-filled poker rooms.

He took a quick survey of the occupants while nodding his polite good evenings. Two men looked up from the liquor Miz Zeola had so generously poured for their wait.

"You here to play?" The dark-skinned speaker, dressed in a plaid shirt and striped pants, had obviously spruced himself up for the evening.

"Miz Zeola's wants to know if you needs yo' drinks freshened? Two mo' players will be here directly. I'm the pot man." John took in the look of the other player without letting him see his eyes shift in the man's direction.

While the fellow had on a starched white collar and the beginnings of a suit, the second player didn't look much more prosperous than the first. Since John's promotion three weeks ago, his cut of the cash put in the gamblers' pot had gone from a straight five dollars to a dollar per player and ten cents on every dollar in the pot. The trouble was he was still assigned to the small games where a big pot might be forty dollars with a top of six players. That gave him ten dollars a game, but in the three weeks since Zeola had changed the rules, games like that had been hard to come by. Still, his newfound wealth was enough to move him out of the storeroom and up to the second-best room on the top floor of Miz Brown's rooming house.

Without waiting for an answer, John walked over to the small round table set up as a makeshift bar and picked up the opened bottle of bourbon and the branch water sitting nearby. He splashed the dark liquid into the men's glasses, three quarters full. He topped each off with just a few drops of the branch. Both players nodded their approval, and the one in the starched collar slapped John on the back, just as the trick door pulled open.

"Whoo whee, look at that purty checkered suit the pot man's got on." Pete, one of Zeola's long-standing regulars, stepped into the room.

When he wasn't building fake columns in the whorehouse parlor, Pete did carpenter work for the white folks who lived on the outskirts of Nashville. Pistol Pete, as he ordered the girls to call him, came in about every two weeks for servicing and a poker game. He was a loud talker but a small-time player. John nodded his good evenings to the newcomers.

"I brought me a friend from Memphis. Git him one of them drinks, pot man, and don't skimp on the liquor." Pete pulled out one of Zeola's straight-backed chairs as he pointed to the new man.

John reached down deep to pull out his best meek expression as he lifted two glasses off the liquor table and poured each almost to the top with bourbon.

"Pot man, here, is from the country. Way out in the country, the girls tell me." Pete swigged down half the glass in one gulp.

John guessed this was not his first drink of the evening.

"This here's Bubba." Pete started to slur his words.

"Pleased to meet you, Mr.... er." John held out a hand to the newcomer who reached to shake it to loud laughter from Pistol Pete.

"Whoo whee. That's how you know they is from the country. Manners fallin' all over theyself." Pete finished off the glass and handed it to John.

The first two players exchanged nervous looks as Bubba sat down. John was certain he saw the starched-collared one pat at the pocket where he kept his watch.

"Let's get this game on." Bubba's liquor glass remained untouched. "Name's Johnson. Who's dealin? Anybody but Pete."

All eyes at the table swung toward Bubba Johnson. With his thick November coat and porkpie hat, Mr. Johnson looked like

Miz Zeola had mistakenly sent him to the wrong poker game. This one looked and sounded like he meant business. Maybe John would get a decent cut tonight, after all.

"It's up to you all." John remembered the drill.

Zeola had insisted that her pot men give the appearance of being absolutely neutral. That's what made a man good at the job, she offered. The players had to trust the man guarding the dollars they'd anted up for the play. And a good pot man could show no favorites. He not only had to look well fed, but he had to be dressed in Nashville's latest to show the players that their money didn't mean a thing to him.

"How long did it take you to get that hayseed out of yo' head? Even a conk in yo' nappy hair ain't gonna make you look like you from the city." Pistol Pete's meanness grew with each passing minute. "A country boy is a country boy and they ain't no two ways 'bout that."

The man with the starched collar gave out a quick, nervous laugh then, just as fast, washed it away with a hardy swallow of bourbon. John watched Bubba cut his eyes at Pete.

"Like a lot of folks, I started out in the country." John pulled out the fifth chair and sat down, setting the bottles next to him. "And I ain't learned it all, that's for sure, but I do know my way around a big city poker table, and that's all that matters tonight." John peeled the tape off the card box and pushed the unopened carton to the center of the table.

Mr. Plaid Shirt, sitting next to John, took in a deep breath. Bubba slapped his hand on the table as he squinted approval at John.

"I can deal," the plaid-shirted man responded as he pulled the cards from the carton and began to shuffle.

The starched-collared one was the first to lay his dollar on the table. The dealer added a second as did Bubba. Pistol Pete tossed in two. John made sure that nobody could see it, but his smile almost broke out wide all over his face. This Thanksgiving could be his first truly thankful one in a long time.

"That's it for me." The fellow in the starched collar pushed back from the table and pulled out his pocket watch from his make-shift suit. "It's 'bout nine o'clock. I been here for close to fo' hours. I'd best be headin' home."

"I'm goin' upstairs and lay me a woman. Pot man, I'm co-min' later to get my money back. Come on, Bubba." Pistol Pete knocked over his chair as he stood and glowered at the plaid-shirted dealer. "Pot man, this ho house got any new gals fresh from the country?"

Bubba leaned over to John, ignoring his friend. "See if you can get me into a bigger game when I come back downstairs." Bubba spoke low as he reached into his pocket and pulled out a silver dollar. He slid the coin across the table toward John.

Nodding his thanks, John smelled the perfume before the wearer pushed open the hidden door.

"Evenin' gentlemen." Zeola, and her favorite fragrance, al-most overpowered the small room.

Even Pistol Pete, with all of his senses drowned in alcohol, reeled backward.

"Woman, I wants yo' best gal tonight and I wants her fo' two hours." Pete scowled at Zeola who didn't break her smile as she nudged him in the side.

"All my girls never stop talkin' 'bout Mr. Pistol Pete. I got one set aside special just fo' you." She leaned in close to his ear, but her whisper came out as loud as a rooster crowing at dawn. "And I'm gonna give her to you fo' two hours for only three dollars, and I guarantee she won't disappoint." Dismissing Pete, Ze-ola swirled her chiffons toward Bubba. "I do hope you enjoyed the evenin', Mr. Johnson." She held out her hand.

"I'll enjoy it even more in about forty-five minutes." He reached into his jacket pocket and pulled out a billfold. He laid a five-dollar gold piece in Zeola's palm. "I wants yo' next game." He winked at her as he helped a very drunk Pistol Pete through the door.

"Well, who's the big pot winner, tonight?" Zeola stuffed the gold piece into her bosom.

"That would be me, ma'am." The plaid-shirted dealer finally lifted his eyes from the pot.

"Ain't you the one." Zeola sounded impressed as she turned to John. "Pot man, how big is it?"

"Sixty-six dollars and fifty cents, Miz Zeola." John had already run the figures through his head. He would be getting over eleven dollars, counting Bubba's tip.

Zeola made quick work of counting up the pot, but she slowly and carefully placed each of the coins and bills into the winner's hands. With the two remaining players watching, she fanned out six one-dollar bills and laid one five-dollar gold piece into John's hands.

"That extra forty-five cents is from the house cut." She turned to the plaid-suited fellow. "Since this is yo' first time here, I want you to enjoy Miz Zeola's hospitality. I'll charge you only a dollar for one of my best girls." She reached over to the bourbon bot-tle and filled up the winner's glass and handed it to him as she walked him to the door.

John clutched his twelve dollars. If the pots continued to be this good, he could be home by Christmas with enough money to make the day very merry indeed for Annalaura and the children.

"Don't put that money in yo' pocket just yet, John Welles." Zeola closed the door behind the last two players. She kept both hands behind her back, holding the knob shut tight.

"How much of that money you sending home to yo' wife?" Her fake eyelashes swept her face like big black cobwebs as she reached a hand toward him.

Startled, John swung his eyes toward her.

"Yeah, I know you country boys leave yo' women at home when you come over here to Nashville." She turned her palm upward and rubbed her fingers together.

"Beggin' yo' pardon, ma'am, but I know how to take care of my family." John pulled out his special grin, the one he always used when it was especially important to put the charm on a woman getting too big for her drawers.

Zeola dropped her hand and walked a slow circle around him. At his back, he could feel her eyes boring into him.

"Looky here, Johnny-boy, I don't need you makin' eyes at me. I been in this business since befo' you ever laid yo' first woman." She stood flat-footed in front of him. "Now, I likes you well enough to see that you don't mess up."

"No, ma'am. I ain't got no intentions of messing up." John clamped down on his tongue to control himself. He wasn't used to not speaking his mind with a woman unless it was Annalaura. He knew an argument with her was useless.

"You ain't my first country boy, you know. I seen a lot of them come and go. Some get so full of theyselves that they go outta here feet first with a Texas jacknife stuck in their gut. Others try to shuck and jive me, and I show them the do' fast." Zeola waved her chiffon sleeves in the air. The scent of her perfume attached itself to John's new coat. "You may think it, but I'm not meddling in yo' business. But, if you don't know that a good-lookin' country boy—who thinks he's the smartest thing to ever hit

Nashville—and his money is soon parted, then you ain't nothin' but a fool."

"Yes'm. I do understand but there's no need for you to worry 'bout my family. I'm gonna take care of them just fine." His grin came so automatically when he tried to fool the women that he now had to work hard to keep Zeola from seeing it.

"I'm proud to hear it, but I'm takin' five dollars a week outta yo' pots to save for yo' woman whether you likes it or not." Her hands went to her hips, and all of her chins waggled when she shook her head for emphasis.

John seethed as he let the smallest of smiles cross his face. He'd done without a mother since he was six years old. With more than twenty dollars already stashed in the floorboard box back at Miz Brown's, he knew what he was doing.

"'Tending no offense, Miz Zeola, but I'm used to taking care of my wife myself."

"Man, how long you been in this town? You been at my place fo' months. How long you think any woman on a cracker's farm, sharecroppin', can take care of herself on her own?"

"She ain't on her own, Miz Zeola. She's got her people to go to." It wasn't quite a lie.

"You done good tonight." Zeola nodded.

"Now I'm gonna cut yo' rate on my Sally 'cause she done got herself in a family way. You can have her fo' a dollar, but it betta be after business hours."

John swallowed twice before he trusted his voice. "That's most kind of you, Miz Zeola, but ain't Sally too old to have a baby?"

The idea of paying for a woman had never set well with John. He had always been surrounded by women who had been more than willing to give him anything he wanted for free, and now Zeola wanted him to pay for one of her girls as some kind of bonus for his loyalty. He knew he should think of it as just another part of goin'-along-to-get-along just like at the sporting houses, but this one didn't set right with him. He held nothing against the whore, but he wanted no part of another man's leavings, business or no business.

"If you got yo' eyes set on one of my chambermaids, you can get yo'self ready to step on out my back do' and don't never look back." Zeola's face looked like the aftermath of the battle of Clarksville.

"No, ma'am. I don't want yo' hired girls, nor Sally neither. I don't needs to pay fo' no woman." The words had slipped out before he could snap them back.

The darkest, most dreary winter's day couldn't compare to Miz Zeola's face. "Too good to pay, is you? Just stay away from my chambermaids."

"Miz Zeola, ma'am, I'd feel real bad showin' disrespect to a woman 'bout to have a baby. But, if you say she wouldn't mind, it would pleasure me to take you up on yo' kind offer of a dollar fo' her time." He hoped he'd found the right angle to bend his neck in apology.

"Hmm. Don't let Sally be none of yo' worry. She ain't but six months anyway." In a flurry of chiffon, she huffed through the door.

Alone, John pulled out his new, squared-off handkerchief. He mopped his forehead before he began tidying the game room. He had risked too much to ever slip like that again. Zeola was nosy, and he had already told this woman more of his business than she needed to know, but he was learning quick that she was not a woman to wink at and forget. John had to have her on his side. The idea bounced in his head that his wife and his boss were both women who took more than a shuck and a grin to satisfy.

At the rate he was going, he would have plenty of money to make a big splash next month at Christmas. But, a big splash would not be enough to ward off Annalaura's anger. John needed far more than toys, pinafores, and satin sheets to warm up his wife. That made her all the more priceless. He had to get enough money to buy a place of his own, and he needed Zeola to hand him those late-night pots. Big Red had said the second game pots sometimes got up to two hundred dollars with eight men playing two decks. That was the kind of money he had to have to make all this worthwhile.

John put the dirty shot glasses in the basin Zeola kept under the little table. The room had no mirrors—bad for poker playing—but he made an attempt to pat his hair in place. Cut short, John knew he didn't need a greasy-style conk to make him attractive to the ladies. After he'd fulfilled his obligations to Sally, so she could rave about him to Zeola, he would head back to the boardinghouse and his two new housemates. One or even both of the colored schoolteachers could help him pass the time away from his wife. When he got home in the next couple of months, he knew not to tell Annalaura about this part of his adventure. In that one way, she was just like all other women. A man gone from home a long time on family business got lonely. Paying for a woman was no substitute. The companionship of the school-teachers would make the time away from Annalaura tolerable. Even if his wife could never accept it, a man had to be a man, and what the wife didn't know couldn't hurt her none.

CHAPTER TWELVE

Eula tugged at her shawl to see if it would fit around her a second time to ward off the mid-January cold in the smoke house. Even the closed door didn't stop the wind that had whistled at her window most of the night from creeping into the room through the unplastered walls of the outbuilding. With fingers frigid from the weather, she held up the lantern to the shelf she reserved for her canned vegetables. Normally, she checked her stock every Monday, but not until after breakfast. Today, she'd gotten an early start because Wiley George planned to drop off Tillie for a few hours while he and Alex went over to Lawnover. As she held the light higher to read the labels on her Mason jars, the frown in her forehead deepened.

With her lamp held close, she counted the jars of canned tomatoes a third time, but the number still came up thirty-five. She lowered the lamp to the worktable where her journal lay open to the page marked "vegetables." She traced one rapidly numbing finger across the rows. There it was—tomatoes—and the number beside it read fifty. Since Alex enjoyed her tomato preserves and she included them on his plate at least twice a week, she was quite certain of the accuracy of her count. Fifteen Mason jars of tomatoes were missing. She drew her fingers down the other

columns. Turnips, collard greens, carrots, pole beans, and butter beans all came up short in the recount. There were no errors.
Eula pulled her fringed shawl closer as she lowered the lamp to
the fruit shelf below. Mason jars of peaches, pears, plums, cherries, and strawberries were missing with no accounting. Even
more perplexing than the vacant spaces on her shelves was the
clear evidence that the shortage was increasing each week. She
glanced over at the hams and hog sides hanging on the hooks.
Their numbers were also down, but Alex had explained their
decrease. Back in December, she watched him box up a particularly large package of just-cured bacon and two whole hams that
he said were destined for his sister in Kentucky. Eula remembered being so stunned by this unusual generosity that she forgot
to conceal the surprise in her voice. When she mentioned that
his sister had always appeared too well-off to need food from
them, Alex flashed a quick torrent of angry words that doubly
baffled her.

Holding the lamp in front of her, Eula put the closed journal in the crook of her arm and stepped out of the smoke house,
latching the door behind her. She glanced around to see if the sun
was preparing its appearance. The ground was still hard with frost
and the night smells still lingered in the darkness. With caution,
she stepped up the gravel path to her porch door and into the
kitchen. Sitting at the table, Eula opened her account book and
carefully lined out the old numbers. In her square handwriting,
she wrote in the new. The missing jars both puzzled and annoyed
her, though she was keenly aware that annoyance had to be banished from her mind as unworthy of a good wife.

Her irritation stemmed from her pride. Eula didn't need
Reverend Hawkins to remind her that pride was a sin almost as
bad as bearing false witness or coveting thy neighbor's ox. But, if
pride hadn't been strictly forbidden to the righteous, Eula knew

she could hold her head higher than any other white woman in all of Lawnover when it came to farm managing. That the food stocks were dwindling and she couldn't explain the loss gnawed at the one talent where she knew she was the best. Still, such a boast was prideful and she tried to push the sinful thought out of her mind. Eula tapped her pencil on one of the open journal pages. The assault on her pride did nag at her, and tonight on her knees, she would have to pray extra hard for forgiveness. But another worry, far more serious than missing tomatoes, clouded her mind, and she wasn't quite sure how she should address that particular subject to the Lord.

Dropping her pencil on the table, Eula stood and walked to the corner behind the stove and lifted the poker. She jabbed it into the coal box to stir up the fire in the cook stove. The kitchen remained too cold for her to remove her shawl. Most mornings when Alex got up first, he stoked the fire, but not this morning. She took a corner of her shawl and rubbed clear a little spot on the kitchen window. A pale white glimmer of a January day shone back at her, and still no sign of Alex. Eula dropped to her chair and wrapped her arms under the shawl as she started a slow rock. Maybe she should offer up a prayer right now and get these unreligious thoughts out of her head.

The wind had been fierce last night, and sleep had been hard to come by. Though she never, on purpose, touched Alex unless he asked, Eula didn't have to feel the cold sheets on his side of the bed to know that her husband had been away all night. And she didn't need the whistling wind to remind her that it wasn't the first time her husband had stayed away from their bed. Some years, his nights away had been as many as four or five. Those times, he had casually mentioned, were spent playing cards with Ben Roy at the Lawnover tavern. Last evening, Alex had made no mention of a game nor of the tavern.

Returning the poker to its corner, Eula went back to the table and stared at the columns and numbers in her journal. She needed no written record to recall that her husband hadn't been close to her more than three times since September. She required no jog to her memory to wonder if something, or someone, other than a game of cards was the cause.

The first time Alex passed over their Friday together, she paid scant attention. He hadn't joined her at bedtime, and he had been beside her in the morning. When that second September Friday slid by, she admitted to a fleeting moment of curiosity, but that passed when she attributed her husband's lovemaking absence to the hard work and long hours he'd spent bringing in that troublesome mid-forty. After he returned to her bed right after full moon in October, she dismissed her earlier fretting. Her relief was short-lived. After his two quick visits in November, the last of which she had carefully maneuvered herself, there had been nothing. That was when her impure thoughts began.

Momma Thornton had never said it outright, but Eula had pieced together enough information in her growing-up years to know that men, long married, sometimes acted like Alex. When she was fifteen, she caught her mother in a back bedroom rouging her cheeks and puffing a white powder all over her face and down the front of her open shirtwaist. She had never seen the frown lines etched so deep in her mother's face before, nor had those eyes looked as though they'd seen more than they wanted.

Eula's mother had promised her a new set of hair ribbons if she wouldn't tell her father that his wife's newfound attractiveness was anything but natural, glowing beauty. The next morning, her mother came out of her room smiling, with the rouge long gone from her cheeks. Momma had winked at her and whispered, "It's a wife's job to keep her man happy." Eula got red, blue, and green ribbons the very next time Momma went to town. And she learned that a less than vigilant wife could cause a husband to stray.

After twenty years of marriage, had she forgotten that early lesson? Though she loathed the thought of rubbing her face in white powder and painting on red cheeks and lips, she knew a wife's responsibilities. It had taken careful planning, since a trip to the Lawnover store was out of the question. A description of everything she bought there would have gone straight to Alex's ear. Instead, she managed to catch a ride to Clarksville with Ben Roy when Fedora was over visiting Tillie. While her impatient brother took care of his own business, she hurried over to the mercantile store. She bought a bar of a sweet-smelling soap—the clerk called it lavender. She wasn't at all sure how Alex would take to soap that smelled like a flower rather than good old homemade rendered tallow. In case the lavender didn't work, she bought a bottle of rose water. Back home, she splashed half the bottle of roses into the galvanized tin wash tub and scrubbed her skin raw with soap that smelled more like the bark of the tree rather than the purple flower. Even so, it had worked. When Alex came in from the fields that Tuesday night, he took her to bed. That had been in late November and no amount of scrubbing and soaking had worked again.

The kitchen had not only warmed up, it had become fiery hot. Eula dropped her shawl from her shoulders and let it fall to the floor. She reached for her journal and used it as a fan. There were images flying around her head that no good wife should entertain. Sin and sinful thoughts were the province of Reverend Hawkins, but she would never dare discuss such things with him. Over the past few weeks, she'd nearly rubbed the print off some of the pages of her Bible looking for the precise chapter and verse that said distrust of a husband outranked pride as a major sin. With two hands, Eula batted at the air with the journal. God help her, despite weeks of effort, she could not banish the thought of Alex with another woman. If he had strayed, and she couldn't accept that he had, it must have been her fault.

Though Momma Thornton had been very strong on telling her eldest daughter about her shortcomings, she had never been much at sharing talk about the bed habits of men. Eula got most of her information on the ways of men and women at quilting bees, canning parties, and even at church socials when she sometimes overheard snatches of conversation. Fedora had hinted that husbands lost "the feeling" after a number of years of marriage. And her sister-in-law had made it clear to the ladies that it wasn't the fault of the wife. Eula wished it were so. If she could ask Fedora how a husband lost such a thing and what a wife could do to help him retrieve it, she would do everything within her power to keep Alex home with her.

Alone in her kitchen with dawn finally breaking full and pale this January morning, Eula failed in her efforts to put flesh and bone to the other woman. If such a person existed, who could she be? Surely, no one Eula knew. None of the women at the ladies' quilting bee or the church socials had ever paid Alex more than a passing glance in twenty years, despite his good looks. Eula slammed her journal to the table.

As she stood to start breakfast, she was certain Alex was out riding the acres. Perhaps a fence had blown down in last night's wind. Still, the missing food, her husband's decreasing interest in her as a wife, and the early risings had all happened about the same time. Gripping her pencil, she suspended it over the margin of her journal. Pressing the pencil down hard to stop the wavering lines her shaking hand might make, she wrote down question marks next to the columns of missing foodstuff. In the margin she lettered, "Must ask Alex," and changed her mind. As she drew her pencil over and over the words, a gnawing sensation, worse than a mouse at the corn barrel, grew in her belly. She didn't know how or why, but her stomach told her that somehow the mid-forty was part of the answer to her quandary.

CHAPTER THIRTEEN

It was the sound of another blast of wind rattling the barn window rather than the sliver of pale light creeping through the shutter that finally forced Alex to open his eyes. Even without looking, he knew the ground outside would be frosty this January morning, but under two quilts with Laura's soft body spooned inside his, he felt bathed in warmth. He awakened with his arm over the roundness of her belly. He let his hand slide even lower. She stirred and he leaned to kiss her ear. She swiveled her head toward him and peered at the slender shaft of light from above.

"It's morning," she murmured as she turned back and started to scoot to the edge of the sheet-covered mattress.

He moved his hand to her waist and held her even tighter. In the last four months he had worked on training himself to awaken just at daybreak. That way he could be in his own barn starting chores in twenty minutes. But when the weather turned cold and he put up the new shutter over the barn window, too little light entered the sleeping alcove he now shared with Laura to alert him to the breaking dawn.

"Morning can wait." He stroked her shoulder.

It was getting more and more difficult to leave her. She put her hand over his and broke his hold as she squirmed to face him.

"Daylight just about here. It's best you get back home." She pulled away and sat on the edge of the mattress as she reached between the two quilts for the new flannel nightgown he had given her.

He let his fingers run down her bare back. She didn't resist. In the past few months, he was almost sure he detected a softening in her behavior toward his embraces and kisses. Now, she followed his lead without being instructed, and sometimes, he could almost swear, he felt her lips responding to his. He knew she no longer trembled when he caressed her. More than once he heard her sharp intake of breath when he thrust inside her. He was almost certain her moan came from pleasure. Alex knew it pleased him to wait several seconds for her reaction, and when he sensed her letting go of her resistance, he plunged even deeper. Then, there were the times he felt her fingernails gently rake his back. He was convinced that Laura was fighting, and losing, the battle against the passion she didn't want him to see.

"I'll put your coffee on." She slipped the gown over her hips in the small cubicle Alex had constructed for their privacy.

Where once the quilt had been the only thing separating them from the children in the barn loft, he had built a wood-slatted wall with a narrow opening for a doorway, which he covered with a heavy burlap curtain.

"Watch yo' head when you get up." Laura pointed to the sloped roof that allowed just enough headroom for her to stand upright at its highest point in the new little bedroom but caused Alex to stoop at all times. She pushed aside the curtain and walked out into the main room.

Despite her best efforts to get him up, Alex pulled the bottom quilt under his chin to compensate for the loss of Laura's body heat. It was getting harder and harder to be without her embrace.

After his first visit in September, he knew he'd soon return to the barn and Laura's arms, but he told himself he would come no more than one or two times a month. Before September ended, he was already riding up the lane three times a week and found the gray wanting to turn onto the path into the mid-forty even more often. Now it was a daily battle. He found himself on those acres at least once each day even if it was just to check on Laura to make sure that neither she nor the children wanted for anything.

When Alex first recognized his dilemma, he tried to solve the problem of his frequent nights away from his house, and Eula, by vowing to leave right after the lovemaking. That had always been difficult. And, though it had been slow in coming, Laura was beginning to respond. Alex could not leave her now.

This half hour before dawn had become his enemy. Most mornings he tried to wake up even earlier so he could make love to her before leaving for his own home. This morning's late awakening denied him that pleasure. He pushed both quilts away and sat on the side of the bed, his feet resting on one of the cotton rugs he'd supplied next to each of the sleeping areas. He didn't really need Laura's warning. He had spent so many nights in the little cubicle that he had become expert at judging the slope of the roof. He hadn't bumped his head since before Christmas. If he sat upright on the edge of the mattress he still had almost two inches of clearance. As Alex leaned over in the semi-darkness to retrieve his pants from the floor, the light from the low-burning kerosene lamp flickered a path from the kitchen table where it sat, to the floor and to his trousers. Following the path of light through the opened burlap curtain, he watched Laura busy herself at the little potbellied stove he'd installed. Vented to the outside by a stovepipe, and with a small brick hearth set on the repaired floorboards, the stove gave off just enough heat to warm water and coffee, and take the worst of the chill off Laura and the children.

Slipping on his pants, he watched her stretch an arm for the coal shovel to replenish the fire. As she opened the door of the little stove, a welcoming burst of heat drifted into the chilly room.

Shirtless, Alex walked through the narrow doorway to finish buttoning his pants. As he slipped belt into buckle, he glimpsed Laura pulling her flannel gown tight around her middle to keep it away from the open flame. While his hands mechanically pulled his belt tighter, his eyes trained on Laura. Something was different about her movements this morning. He wasn't aware of how deep his frown had furrowed as he let his eyes roam over her. Replacing the shovel, she gave him only a quick look as she turned to reach for a rag to lift the hot coffeepot from the embers.

The slenderness of Laura's body made those places where it curved and poked up and out all the more appreciated and pronounced. For the past four months Alex had explored every contour of that body and had thrilled at every in and out and every up and down. This morning, for the first time, he saw a new fullness. Even in the gloom, only partially relieved by the kerosene lamp, he noted that her breasts still bounced under the flannel of her gown. That always pleased him. As the dimness in the main room gave way to the breaking dawn, and to the lamp that Laura had deliberately trimmed low, he could see that the roundness of her hips still filled out the lower half of her gown. But looking closely at her now, he wondered how he had missed this new plumpness. As he rummaged his mind over the past few weeks, he was certain he had felt the changes, but until right now he hadn't really given any thought to the cause of that little protuberance at Laura's belly. His eyes on her stomach, he walked toward her. Busy pouring coffee into a mug, she gave him another quick glance. He waited while she topped off the mug and handed it to him.

"Careful. It's hot." Laura turned the cup, handle-side, toward him.

He took it from her as he reached to turn up the kerosene lamp. She started to move away, stopped, and pointed to his mug.

"I can cool it if you want." Her voice sounded unsure, questioning.

Alex set the mug on the table as she reached for it.

"Leave it." He couldn't move his eyes away from her middle.

"What?" She sounded confused.

"Come back to bed." He moved his eyes to her face as the storms of protest began to mount.

Before she could voice her refusal, a look of dawning awareness that he wanted something more than lovemaking reflected out of her eyes. Alex took her arm and led her back through the bedroom opening. He turned and bent his head as he backed through the door frame and sat down on the mattress. He pulled her between his spread legs. She looked puzzled. Reaching behind her, she slid the burlap curtain closed while Alex kept his hands tight around her waist. Looking at her face, he pushed the gown up to her waist, showing her triangle and belly. She grabbed at the flannel with one hand as she rested the other on his shoulder. He let one hand glide gently over her stomach from just below her breasts to the triangle, then across her belly from side to side. He heard her take in a breath and hold it for several long seconds. He laid the side of his face against her belly and listened to her racing heart.

"Laurie, what's this?" He watched her hand fly to her stomach before she could win her usual battle to restrain it. He could hear little gurgling sounds in her throat as she tried to answer.

"I'm getting a little fat on your food, is all." Her voice sounded strained and false.

This time he let his fingertips circle her stomach. He could feel the trembling in her whole body. He took the palm of his hand and pushed in on the swelling. She trembled.

"Laurie, is that a baby in there?" Alex fought the huskiness in his voice.

The slim shaft of light from the shuttered window above them came in brighter as the fullness of dawn broke. The light caught the lower half of Laura's face in its white grip. He watched her mouth open and close, her lips turn up to a smile and then down to a frown. He heard little bubbling sounds in her throat and watched her swallow two, three times. He had never known her not to have a quick answer for everything.

"You would tell me if there's a baby in there, wouldn't you?" Before her movements registered fully in his head, she dropped to her knees, forcing her body between his legs.

Faster than he could respond, she lifted the flannel gown over her head, showing her nakedness. As she leaned forward brushing her breasts against his pant leg, he saw for the first time, a playful smile on her face. Her hands reached for his belt buckle. As she unbuttoned his trousers, that funny little smile that seemed to fade and revive itself only to repeat the cycle within the blink of his eyes was accompanied by a sassy little twitch of her shoulders. Too surprised to react, Alex followed her lead as she lifted her body and leaned her naked breasts hard into his bare chest and pushed him back onto the bed. With the light from the shuttered window glowing behind her like an old painting, he watched her climb onto the mattress beside him. While he lay there, she pulled his trousers over his hips and off his legs. Torn between surprise and extreme pleasure, Alex fought to keep his eyes open. He'd waited too long to miss even one delicious moment of Laura's real feelings for him.

Naked, he watched her face move down his chest to his own tuft of hair. His eyes slid closed against his will when he felt her wet kisses just above his manhood. An involuntary shudder rocked him as he sensed Laura's mouth moving up his body. Her legs straddled him, pushing her thighs against his body. His own heart pounded in his ears louder than any blacksmith's hammer on an anvil.

Alex forced his eyes open when her lips reached his chin. She stopped and raised her nutmeg-ripe breasts level with his eyes. With a gentle sway to the side, she pushed one nipple into his open mouth. Alex sucked on the honeyed taste, his eyes shut, his mind floating, his body quivering. He felt the kisses planted on his forehead, on his hair. He squinted open his eyes just as she took his two hands in hers and guided each to her breasts and she bent down again to find his lips. Her tongue searched inside his mouth and caressed his own. The taste was sweeter than Christmas oranges. The feel of silken threads covered his body and stroked every inch of him. Somewhere, rummaging in his mind, was the thought of a baby, but it faded away when Laura lifted her body just enough to guide his manhood into her with her own hand.

"At last," thundered out of him as his mind drank in Laura's passion.

CHAPTER FOURTEEN

"They say some colored women eat the starch right out of the walls. Dig their nails right into it, pull it out, and pop it straight into their mouths." At seven months pregnant, Tillie squirmed on one of Eula's hard-bottomed kitchen chairs.

Standing at the washbasin rinsing the last of the breakfast dishes, Eula paid scant attention to her niece's chatter. As she reached for a drying towel, her mind pondered on that non-seeing look in Alex's eyes when he finally wandered into the kitchen hours after the sun woke up.

"What?" Eula forced her eyes to focus on her niece, but her head insisted upon returning to the recollection of Alex.

It had been more than an hour after the break of dawn when her husband walked through the back door. Except for the eggs and the last of the bacon, his breakfast had already been cooked. Eula cracked the just-laid eggs into a bowl, and she braced herself for some words, any words, from her husband that would tell her where he had passed the night. Already dressed for Tillie's upcoming visit, Eula stood at the stove, the fork pressing down hard on the bacon in the cast-iron skillet, making sure that it browned evenly just the way Alex liked it. Careful not to utter a word, she made certain that the look she carved on her face showed her husband neither approval nor disapproval, simply that she was ready to accept whatever answer he gave her.

The bacon sizzled its doneness. Eula kept her face toward him. But as she stood there waiting for him to break the cold human silence of the kitchen, she realized that she might be there all day rooted like a stalk of harvest-ready tobacco waiting for a hired hand to wander by and spear it. If the truth be told, she couldn't be sure that Alex had actually noticed her in the kitchen at all this morning.

To him, she might have been a great, gray blob that blended in with the gray of her kitchen walls. If he was inclined to pay any mind to her, it would have been when she set his coffee mug down and his hand brushed hers as he pushed the hot coffee aside. Surprised, she said nothing. As she set his breakfast before him, she gave him a close look out of the corner of her eye. There was a tiredness about her husband like none other she had seen. It was not like he had plowed five acres without a mule and every muscle in his body had ached him into immobility. No, his fatigue was covered all over with an air of supreme satisfaction.

As she watched him slice into his eggs, she noticed a little smile that kept coming and going across his face. She got the feeling that her husband wanted to laugh out loud like he had just brought in the biggest and best tobacco crop in all of Montgomery County.

He had eaten his breakfast as if he were the only person in the house. The first words she heard from him all morning were when Wiley George hallooed at the door right after Alex pushed away his empty breakfast plate. There had been no "good morning," no "hello," no "Eula, pass the salt." There had been nothing between them except that look on his face and in his eyes that definitely put him in some place other than in the McNaughton kitchen.

"You got to watch 'em when they're working in your house." Tillie labored to turn in her chair to face her aunt.

Eula jolted at the sound of her niece's voice and nearly jabbed the fork she was drying into her hand. Tillie's short grabs for air between every two or three words finally worked their way into Eula's ears and shook her out of her reverie.

"What are you talkin' about? What starch?" Eula sat down heavily, only half paying attention to Tillie, who looked miserable with discomfort.

Her mind started to drift back to the morning and Alex. Knowing that the pictures of him flooding her head would do her no good, she decided to hang on to every word Ben Roy's silliest child spoke this morning.

"Momma's new hired girl told me that her sister's husband's cousin does it. She says that the walls of the cousin's cabin are filled with big holes, all from eating the starch right out of them." Tillie grimaced as she grabbed at her stomach.

The gasps were becoming deeper and more frequent. A shaft of concern flickered in Eula's mind. Though she never wanted to remember those days, had she panted like Tillie right before she lost Alex's baby?

"Aunt Eula, I've had myself these pains for the last week. If I can't have my own hired girl, maybe the starch will help. The girl says it might."

All the old worries bubbled in Eula's mind. There had been no early pains, no warning, really. But, there had been the weight. She reckoned she had put on fifty pounds. She stared at Tillie's midsection. Sitting out front like a watermelon, the baby didn't seem to take up much more than twenty pounds. Maybe it had been Eula's extra weight.

"Did you speak to your momma or Wiley George?"

"I told Momma, and she says pains are natural." Tillie blushed and looked down at the floor. "'Course, I didn't tell Wiley George.

But, Aunt Eula, I don't think pains are natural. If I don't eat me some starch, I could lose this baby." Tillie's wide-opened eyes stared at her.

"Hush, girl. You're not about to lose Wiley George's baby." At this moment, it was 1893 and Eula was a twenty-two-year-old mother-to-be. She closed her eyes to gather strength before she gave Tillie a reassuring nod.

"But, how do I know that? Did you know that your baby was gonna be born dead?" Tillie's hand flew to her mouth almost before the words squeaked out. "Aunt Eula, I didn't mean it. It's just that I'm so worried."

Moving like a woman twice her age, Eula's leaden feet dragged across the floor to the other side of the table and Tillie. She pressed the girl's head against her chest.

"No, I didn't have no warning that the baby wasn't going to live." Eula clung to Tillie. Her disembodied hand stroked Tillie's hair. "I didn't have no pains and my breathing came easy."

"I know you did all you could to have Uncle Alex's baby." Tillie hung on so tight that Eula couldn't catch her breath.

"That was twenty years ago." Eula fought one hand free and reached for the back of the chair to steady herself.

"I know Uncle Alex don't hold it against you. Even Momma says he don't." Tears spilled. "Twenty years? Didn't you and Uncle Alex try to have another baby?"

An eerie silence draped over Eula's kitchen as the sadness that she could never fully lock away—those precious moments waiting for her baby to take that first breath that never came—pushed out.

"Of course we did, sugar. The good Lord just didn't see fit to send us another." Eula dropped to the chair. She reached for her niece's hand. "I'll ask Alex to speak to Wiley George. He'll hire on your own girl."

After those first months, she and Alex had never mentioned the baby again. Even the cradle her husband had fashioned himself was covered with heavy burlap and stashed in the back of the pantry. She'd never before asked a real favor of Alex, but she knew that at the mention of a baby, he would do what she asked. She patted Tillie's hand. "By March, you will have you a fine, healthy child."

CHAPTER FIFTEEN

"You can't go to school today." Annalaura stirred the egg in the cast-iron skillet with one of the new forks Alex had given her.

Declaring it done, she reached for the bread she had already sliced and covered with two strips of bacon. Hurriedly, she slid the scrambled egg onto the bread and reached for a second piece to lay on top. She paid scant attention to Cleveland sitting on the edge of his mattress, rustling the corn husks as he rocked on his bed in his little alcove.

"Why not, Momma? You're makin' lunch for Doug. You're lettin' him go to school today. Why can't I? You know my leg is as good as new." The petulance that should have shadowed her eldest boy's voice was absent—replaced with a knowing resignation.

Annalaura wrapped the sandwich in butcher paper and placed it in the pocket of Doug's oversize hand-me-down, but serviceable, corduroy coat. Sitting on one of their two new kitchen chairs, Doug finished lacing up his winter boots. With her mind refining every word of the pleas she was going to have to make, she barely noticed any of her children.

"'Cause I said so, that's all." Her voice snapped in the frosty air.

The silence from Cleveland's corner, when there should have been great protest, finally pushed aside her carefully practiced speech. She turned toward her boy. A sudden shaft of remorse brought her up short.

"'Sides, I need you to look after Lottie and Henry. You can go to school tomorrow." Cleveland sat in his nightshirt watching Doug slip into his new jacket. The middle boy patted the pocket where Laura had put his dinner as he bounded across the floor toward the ladder.

"You goin' somewhere, Momma?" Cleveland asked, moving to his feet to grab Henry's arm as the youngster skidded too close to the ladder opening in his attempt to follow Doug.

Lottie, sitting in front of the hearth of the potbellied stove, ignored the ruckus as she played with her Christmas porcelain-faced doll. Annalaura poked her tongue into her cheek while she watched Cleveland. A chill ran down her back in the mildly warm quarters. She feared her almost twelve-year-old knew more than he should.

"I'm goin' to Aunt Becky's. Nothin' for you to fret over. Just watch after the youngsters, and I'll be back in time to start supper. There's plenty to eat for dinner in the cupboard." She gathered the breakfast dishes into a basket and readied herself to take them down to the smoke house. "Have Lottie wash these." She looked at her daughter, who did not let on that she had heard a word her mother said.

As Annalaura turned to back down the ladder with the basket over one arm and a handful of skirt in the other, she hoped that Alex would not drop by before she could return. Better yet, she prayed that he wouldn't come at all. If she could hold him off just a while longer, this nightmare might be over. She had made a desperate effort this morning to keep him from knowing.

The usual trek took Annalaura almost an hour as she carefully picked her way down the frost-covered dirt lane. Water puddled in the deep ruts, some of them deceptively icy in the January morning, making the journey all the more treacherous. If it didn't also mean a broken neck, she would have welcomed a fall. Maybe that would be the best thing after all. As she walked those last few yards past Aunt Becky's dead, snow-covered garden, even the blue wool coat Alex had given her could not keep away the chill sweeping over her body.

Shaking from more than the weather on this white sky day, she tapped at the door of the old cabin on Ben Roy Thornton's place. Her first few knocks were soft and unsure. She knew what she had to face inside, and it was a coward's way not to get to it. She knocked harder. With her ear to the door, she listened for Becky's slow shuffle.

"Aunt Becky, open the door. It's me. Annalaura." She fought to keep the fright out of her words.

Slowly, the door opened a crack, and Annalaura stumbled into a murky interior made no brighter by the low-burning fire in the old fireplace. Rebecca Murdock, at sixty-one, was still spry enough to step out of her niece's way. The smell of black-eyed peas, but without the soul-warming scent of ham hocks, came from the big iron kettle setting on the fireplace grate.

"Whoa, girl. What you doin' rushin' in here like the night riders is after you, and here it is broad daylight?" Becky shut the door, dipping the long, low-ceiling room into even more dimness.

The old woman waved an arm in the direction of her wrought-iron bed while she made her way toward the oak-wood table. Annalaura headed for the four-poster, the nicest piece of furniture in the room by far. Weary from more than her walk, she let herself sink into the bed's feathery softness. Across the room, Becky seemed to lose quick interest in her visitor as she picked up her pipe from the table and tore a sheet of paper. Her back to Annalaura, Becky stepped toward the fireplace and held the rolled-up paper to the flame. She brought the lit strip to the bowl of her cob pipe. Drawing in a heavy breath to ignite the tobacco, Becky walked back to her chair and finally trained her eyes on her niece.

Annalaura swallowed hard, worked her mouth to start the stream of words she knew she had to get out. Just as she started to speak, Becky raised a palm toward her. Annalaura remembered. It was the same "wait" sign she recalled Grandma Charity making when the old Cherokee wanted to ready herself for bad news. If waiting helped bring on the second sight, Annalaura wanted it to pass quickly. Her courage was rapidly waning.

"Aunt Becky, I need to see that conjure woman." Her mouth was so dry she could only hope that her aunt's hearing was still good enough to catch her words.

She hadn't given much thought to it before, and maybe it was because Rebecca was getting older, but the resemblance between her Aunt Becky and her Grandmother Charity was startling. Becky's nose had a decided bent to it, and her skin had settled into a clearly defined copper undertone. Becky's hair, still mostly black, was twisted into one long braid that hung over her left shoulder. It was almost as straight as Grandma Charity's. While Annalaura's hands fumbled with a corner of the feather quilt, Becky took another long draw on her pipe, letting the smoke rise in the air. Becky's narrowed eyes looked at her without blinking. Annalaura pulled the coat tighter. Her body shook with chills, but her face was almost as warm as the fire in Becky's fireplace. How much longer was this Cherokee second sight going to last? Perhaps Aunt Becky was going deaf. Maybe she hadn't heard after all. Could Annalaura get those words out again?

"I can pay her something, but I need to see her quick." Annalaura rocked on the feather bed.

"When's he comin' back?" The sound of the voice that had chewed and spit snuff for over forty years rattled off every wall in the one-room cabin, as Becky took a third draw on her pipe.

Though she turned her face away from the fireplace, Annalaura still felt its heat blasting her from chin to forehead. Was it true? Could these old Indian women really read minds?

"That's just it. I don't want him back. I've got to find me a way to keep him from knowing." She bit her lip.

She had let too much slip to a woman who already knew what she was thinking. Creak, creak went the old rocker. It was the same one Grandma Charity had sat in when she rocked Annalaura to sleep all those years ago. Becky, with those eyes narrowed to pinpoints, said nothing. Annalaura wrapped both arms around her middle and squeezed her eyes shut.

"Just tell me where I can find her, and I'll walk all the way there tonight." Annalaura let the pleading in her soul whisper in her voice.

"You got money to pay?" The sound of the old woman's rocker hadn't broken stride.

"Yes, ma'am, I do." Annalaura moved to the edge of the feather mattress as she tried to get the sound of the rocker out of her head.

"You takin' yo' babies' food money for this conjure woman?" It was a cross between a question and an accusation coming out of Becky's mouth.

Annalaura opened her eyes and trained them on the low-burning embers in the fireplace.

"No, Auntie, I got money to feed my babies and seed money to plant the summer vegetables come April." She gave her head a vigorous nod for emphasis.

She had to find the key that would unlock the secret of the conjure woman from her cantankerous aunt. Maybe it was money. If Becky believed she had enough to pay, perhaps she would not guard the woman's name like it was the secret to the Holy Grail. Becky took another draw on the pipe, and Annalaura watched the smoke encircle the woman's head. The quiet in the cabin was broken only by the snap of a log in the fireplace and the hiss of the peas boiling in the pot.

"Let me see, gal. You do have food fo' your chil'ren." Those eyes trained on her niece. "You got money fo' spring seed." Those eyes didn't blink. "You got you a warm new winter coat." Becky smacked her lips on the pipe stem, but her eyes bored into Annalaura. "You don't want 'him' back, whoever 'him' may be." The word came out of Rebecca's mouth like she was the hangin' judge pronouncing Annalaura "guilty." "And you tell me you needs a conjure woman." If there had been a wall clock, Becky would have marked off a good five minutes of puffing on her pipe as her rocker kept up its unceasing creaking. The old woman finally leveled the worn pipe like it was a firing pistol. She aimed it straight at her niece's stomach.

"Who's the daddy?"

Annalaura felt her body leap from the mattress and her feet propel her to the rocker without her willing them.

"I've got to see the conjure woman, Auntie, please help me." All the morning's planning on the exact words and tone to use to gain Becky's assistance left her. She stood at the rocker before her aunt, her whole body shaking.

"I said who's the daddy, and don't hover over me, gal. Set down." Becky's accusing voice had always sounded like an ax splitting a chunk of wood.

She stumbled into the chair by the table. Words tumbled over themselves trying to get out of her mouth.

"The hired man that helped me bring in the tobacco last fall." Annalaura let the lie slide out on short bursts of air.

"Uh huh." Creak, creak went the rocker.

"Me and him got real close during those tough times." She prayed Becky would believe her long enough to give up the name.

"He the one give you that coat and the money for the conjure woman?" Creak, creak.

"Yes'm."

"He the one give you food fo' yo' chil'ren?" Creak, creak.

"Yes'm." She couldn't prod her brain into action fast enough to keep up with the circle thinking of a Cherokee woman.

"He the one tie up that gray hoss of his in yo' barn three, fo' nights outta the week since September?"

A tornado could have swept up the old cabin, but neither the pace of Becky's creaking rocker nor the puffs on her pipe would have changed one bit. The aroma from the meatless black-eyed peas melted into the gray pipe smoke and collided with the din in Annalaura's ears.

"He the one name of Alexander McNaughton?" Creak, creak.

Somewhere in Annalaura's head a long, low, keen moan crowded out the sound of the rocker. Some thing whirling in the core of her being forced her feet out from under her. A woman's voice that sounded like it might once have belonged to herself screamed at the roof beams.

"Gawd help me. I don't want it. I don't want it." Annalaura dropped to her knees with no control over her legs, but she felt no pain.

Like a puppet pulled by a string, her neck arched back, bringing her face up toward the rafters. She slapped her hands together in prayer. "Please, Lord Jesus, take this thing outta me. I don't want it." That other woman's voice had not dropped one octave.

The tears flooding out of her own eyes stopped her from seeing anything except the soot-black cabin roof, but the touch of still-strong hands around her shoulders guided her to her feet. Some great force from behind propelled her to the chair. She didn't know how long she sat there listening to the strange woman's moans, but something hot and steamy touched her trembling lips. Work-worn, cinnamon-brown hands passed before her eyes as they came to rest over her own. Together, they tipped the container to Annalaura's lips.

"How far gone is you, chile?" Becky's voice sounded like Sister Muriel in the church choir singing "Sweet Chariot." But the funeral song "Precious Memories" better matched how she felt.

Again, Becky pushed the cup of thick black-eyed-pea soup to her mouth. Her aunt's hand pushed down on the back of her head, forcing her to take in sips of the soothing soup.

"I think he hit right off. September. I think I'm four months." The words came slow and hard between sobs. With the hot soup and her own shame, the room filled with heat. Annalaura shook her arms out of the coat and let it lie across her shoulders.

"Why didn't you come to me right off, girl?" Becky turned the pipe upside down on a pottery plate as she lifted Annalaura's head to face her. "I'd been able to fix you up some special herb tea then."

"I kept thinking it couldn't be so." The shaking in her body continued, but now it came inside a room that seemed warmer than the hottest mid-August day. "He don't have no other children. I thought, maybe, he couldn't have none. At least, I wouldn't have to worry 'bout that."

Only Becky's steadying hand kept her from splashing soup on the table. Sucking in her lips until they disappeared into her mouth, Annalaura dropped her head.

"I haven't had me no word from John since he took off in June." She took another gulp of the hot soup. Becky's hands were still over hers as she tipped the cup.

"And you ain't thought that I'd know what to do? That I wouldn't understand?" The chastising sound in Becky's voice was unmistakable.

The tears stopped on Annalaura's face as she remembered Johnny.

"I was 'shamed, Auntie." She whispered the words as her chin dropped down to rest on the blue serge coat. "I'm a married woman. Now, everyone in this whole county will know that I've been with another man." The tears started again and spilled down her cheeks as she finally faced her aunt, her hand covering her mouth. She spoke through barely split fingers. "Don't matter none that John is off cattin' around again. That he ain't never comin' back to me. Aunt Becky, I'm a married woman." That other woman's voice threatened to take over her own again.

"And what do you think you could have done about it?" Becky's voice was soft as she tightened her grip on Annalaura's arm.

Annalaura dropped her eyes again. She wanted to pull the collar up around her ears. She wanted to climb back inside that coat so deep that nobody in this world could ever look upon her again.

"You think yo' husband would go easier on you if he thought it was a colored man's chile?"

"Colored or not, it's my fault," she whispered into the coat. "If I had just told him no when he brought all that food. If I hadn't hitched up my dress that day. If I had just kept my mouth shut. If…" The sobs racked her body.

"If you'd let yo' babies go hungry, if you had yo'self on two crinolines and three chemises under yo' dress and that coat, if you'd looked cold and dead…" Becky's strong hands raised

Annalaura's head from her chest. "Ain't none of them ifs would have made a damn bit of difference."

Annalaura's eyes widened. She had never heard her aunt speak a cuss word in all the years she had known Rebecca Thornton Murdock.

"But somethin' I did or said must have made him look at me. Made him think I wouldn't fuss too much if he came to my bed...if he touched my body," Annalaura stammered.

Becky sat back in the kitchen chair with the wobbly leg. Her hand tapped at the bowl of her pipe.

"If a Tennessee white man comes ridin' along and spots an apple orchard and decides he wants him an apple, ain't nothin' that apple can do to make him pick a different one. It can't hope that a breeze will come up and knock it to the ground. It can't pray that a bird will peck a piece out of its side so it won't look so good. A colored woman in Tennessee is just like that apple. Ain't never been a brown-skinned woman who had any say over what a Tennessee white man can do with her body." Becky's voice trailed off as if she had been suddenly transported to another world.

Annalaura clung to the mug as though it were her lifeline.

"I was only fifteen when Old Ben Thornton came sniffin' 'round me. It was slavery times, but when it comes to a white man wantin' a black woman, slavery or no, it's all the same in Tennessee." The pain in Aunt Becky's voice edged deeper, and for the first time, the agony of it filled Annalaura's soul.

"Cousin Johnny." She didn't have to work hard to let her tone sound reverential.

The name on her niece's lips seemed to shake Aunt Becky out of her growing morass.

"I'll give you the herbs, but I can't get you no conjure woman." Becky's voice sounded gruff.

Was it about Johnny?

"I don't want this child, Aunt Becky. The conjure woman can ream it out of me. I've heard of it workin' on others." She lowered her voice though the two were the only people in the lone cabin in the middle of forty acres.

"You hear tell of those 'others' dyin' from the conjure woman, did you?" Becky sat back in the chair, careful of its one shored-up leg, the pipe clenched between her teeth.

"I know some die, but I've already had me fo' babies. I'm strong enough for her to do her business." Strength was eking its slow way back into Annalaura as she nodded her head for emphasis.

Becky took a long draw on her pipe. She let the smoke curl in the space between them.

"You know 'bout yo momma and the conjure woman?" Aunt Becky rocked slightly in the broken chair.

"No'm." Annalaura feared her aunt would crash to the floor.

"You 'member yo' momma dying?" Becky kept the pipe between her teeth without taking another draw.

Annalaura shivered. "I can barely remember." She peeled back her own memory curtains.

"'Cose you can't. I shooed you out into the rain when I brought yo' momma back from the conjure woman." Becky let her eyes slowly drift across Annalaura's face.

Annalaura read in those eyes that her aunt believed she was speaking the truth.

"Yo' momma was about as fur gone as you. Too late for the herbs. Happened 'bout this time of year, too."

Annalaura tried to bring the mug to her dry throat. "Auntie, Momma died of the gallopin' consumption. Remember?" She let each word come out slow to bring her aunt gently back from the depths of time.

"'Cose I remember, girl." Becky's eyes looked at her hard as glass. "It's you who don't remember." Aunt Becky tried to suck another draw on her pipe, but it had gone dead. She got up and relit it from the fireplace. She settled back into the rocker.

Annalaura swiveled her chair around to face Becky.

"This old cabin was here in slavery days." The old woman sounded of the long-ago. "It's where me and yo' momma was born. But, when yo' momma married yo' daddy, she moved off of Thornton land. Still, every Sunday she would come by here to visit yo' grandma Charity." She took a deep draw on the relit pipe. "Yo' grandma Charity had herself a man caller by the name of Jessie. Much younger than yo' grandma. I swear to goodness, that grandma of your'n was a high stepper."

Becky had slipped back in time. Suppose Annalaura couldn't bring her aunt back in time to help?

"I ain't gonna dwell on it." Becky slumped back in the chair. "Jessie forced yo' momma and she come up with a baby she didn't want to tell yo' daddy about."

"Forced her? Forced her to do wh…" Dawning shock stopped the word in Annalaura's mouth. "You mean he…like…you?"

"No. Not like us. Jessie wasn't white. He knew better'n to take what wasn't his. Yo' momma was married to yo' daddy just like you is married to John Welles. A black man should know to respect that. Yo' momma was powerful 'shamed and didn't tell nobody 'til it was too late. Just like you. Ain't none of us knowed it 'til the conjure woman come up and told us Geneva was near 'bout dead. I fetched me a wagon off of young Ben Thornton and lit out for the conjure woman's house. Got yo' momma back home."

Annalaura almost lost her perch on the chair. "Auntie, what are you saying?" The words cut her throat. "Momma died of the consumption."

"I tell you like it was. Yo' momma died befo' the rooster crowed that next mornin'. Died with Jessie's baby still half in her." Rebecca clamped her eyes shut.

"Momma died with a conjure woman? Died because of a baby?" Annalaura shook her head. "Daddy? What about my daddy? Did he know? Did he kill the man?"

"Jessie lit out of here even befo' yo' grandma left for Oklahoma, and don't nobody know where he went."

"I'll fix you some herbs that'll help yo' baby's color come in darker." Becky's regular voice returned. "Best when a white man's chile come out tan. Less trouble that way. Chile can be passed off as a throwback. My Johnny came out white." Aunt Becky drifted off into that other place where her Johnny still lived.

Annalaura could see by the rheumy stare in her aunt's eyes that she wasn't coming back this day.

Annalaura pushed herself up from the chair and headed for the door. "I thank you kindly for the soup."

"You got fo' chil'ren. I'm too old to raise another dead woman's young 'uns. No conjure woman." Aunt Becky shut her eyes and folded her arms across her chest. The creaking rocker sped up.

No conjure woman. That's what Aunt Becky had said. The sun had passed its height two hours ago. The sky threatened snow again. Annalaura made every step she took on the long walk home a slow one. Iced-over rutted ponds did not bother her this time. She needed every precious moment of this trip to plan out a way to keep Alex from knowing that this baby was his. There was no need to congratulate herself on her morning efforts. She had tried every lovemaking trick John had ever shown her, and some others that just popped into her head when she lay with Alex. This morning, every frisky move kept the man's mind off babies, but in a few weeks, all of Lawnover would know of her pregnancy. She would give it her best efforts, but she couldn't be sure if a repeat performance would keep Alex's mind occupied on her, and off his baby. John Welles was a different story.

She'd felt it in her marrow ever since August, but sometimes that little flicker of hope that John might find his way back to his children jumped into her head. But when her husband let Christmas pass without a sign, she knew she'd been right all along. John Welles was gone. Even so, word of the baby would get to him wherever he was, and as certain as colored would always tend tobacco, he would divorce her. Annalaura stopped by the side of the lane, standing no more than two feet away from an iced-over puddle. She waited to catch her breath from the flip-flopping of her heart. She clutched the coat to her chest. Despite his cattin' around with every flirting colored woman in Lawnover and his gambling ways, John had his loving side.

But every time she thought she could feel real love for John Welles, he would up and disappear for weeks at a time.

Hard as it was, she could manage the loss of her husband at her side because she never really had all of him anyway. But divorce was a cold, final thing. The Lawnover colored Baptist church would ban her as a Jezebel. Fresh tears began their frigid roll down her cheeks. She swiped them away with a mittened hand. There was no need to cry over a man who had left her over seven months ago, not when she had to put all her smarts into Alex McNaughton. His was the immediate threat.

What would Alex do if he learned this baby was his? Annalaura plodded past an oak tree. Would he treat her the way most Montgomery County white men did when they tired of their colored women? Would he just move on to his next one and drop by with an occasional silver dollar, or a ham, or a suit of hand-me-down clothes for his yellow child?

There were many such women and children in Lawnover, and if the baby didn't look too white, people could pretend that the father was some strange colored man from down county. If the woman was lucky enough, and the baby came out looking tan with dark eyes and frizzy hair, then maybe she could find a man who would take her to wife. Annalaura brightened for the first time that day. If Aunt Becky's herbs really worked, perhaps one day, she could find a toothless, old, widowed colored man to take her and her children into his house. The flash of encouragement that quickened her step along the lane faded as fast as it had come. Even such a man wouldn't want a woman carrying the sin of divorce.

Annalaura looked up the lane to see the barn in the distance. Each step felt as though she pulled fifty pounds of tobacco behind her. She had to make sure Alex tired of her.

In the beginning, she was sure her amateur ways would run him away in a few days, but he had stayed and she wondered why. She had steeled herself for quick and rough, even hurting, lovemaking. Instead, he had been considerate, tender, gentle, and especially passionate. His caresses were soft and warm. His kisses long and lingering. And when she didn't respond in kind, there had never been an explosive blow, or an angry word. He talked to her like he cared what she felt, and on some things, he even listened to her answers. And after lovemaking, he always held her close.

Sometimes, the kindness he showed to her and her children almost made her forget that she should hate this man. Still, if the state of Tennessee gave her the right to say no to him, she would use it. A woman ought to be able to say yea or nay to any man who wanted to come into her body. Yet, if Alex had been colored...well then, maybe her answer to him would be y... She pushed that thought deep into a box in her mind. There could be not even a little love with a white man.

Maybe Alex would treat her the way Ben Roy Thornton treated his Hettie. Together, those two had two-and-a-half yellow-skinned children living right there on the Thornton side-forty. Right under Fedora's nose. Of course, Ben Roy's wife, like all the other white wives in the county, had to pretend that those babies got dropped off at the side-forty by a passing peddler cart. Mr. Ben Roy had fed, housed, and clothed Hettie and his children for the past five years. Everybody in Lawnover, black or white, knew the parents of those children. The path leading to her barn was just a hundred yards away. She stopped again and jammed her hands into the pockets of the coat.

No matter how sweet his ways, it would be far worse for her if Alex treated her like Hettie. Being a white man's "other family" was almost as bad as being divorced. Annalaura started the final few yards to her turnoff thinking the words in her head so loud that she burst them out in the air.

"God, don't let me be Hettie. Don't make this man want to stay." With the path looming before her, she dropped her eyes to the ground. She had one more choice.

The hired man. Aunt Becky hadn't believed her, but if she could convince Alex that the tenant farmer who helped bring in the harvest in September was the father, he would leave her. And, with any luck, Alex might beat the baby out of her. She prayed that he wouldn't kill her only because her four children needed her alive. Turning onto the pathway, she kept her head down, trying to build her courage. For the sake of them all, she had to convince Alex McNaughton that he was not the father of this baby.

CHAPTER SIXTEEN

Alex pitched the last of the hay bale to the cows for their after-noon feed. He glanced over at the remaining hay loosely piled un-der the ladder near the back wall. That should be enough to last the animals through the winter. He had already mucked out the barn, and that completed the last of Cleveland's afternoon chores. It was nearly three o'clock, and Doug had just climbed the ladder after coming home from school. Upstairs, Alex could hear the boy practicing his reading. Cleveland had spent the day looking after Lottie and little Henry. Laura wasn't home, and Cleveland had been close-lipped about his mother's whereabouts, telling Alex only that his mother had gone to her aunt's house. The young-ster couldn't say why. Alex hadn't pressed, but he hoped that his taking over Cleveland's afternoon chores would loosen the boy's tongue. He had unfinished business with the mother.

The delicious memory of the morning had made him barely able to concentrate on his own morning chores. When he came in for breakfast he vaguely recalled Eula saying something to him but little of it registered. Whatever it was must have been fairly important to his wife, because she never bothered him with talk unless it was of some urgency. He did recall that her journal lay spread in front of her, and she may have asked him something about peach preserves and hams. He only knew that he rushed through his farm jobs with his mind nowhere on his duties. Alex couldn't focus on anything, or anybody, other than Laura. Her unexpected display of feelings for him, and that plumpness in her belly, crowded out everything else. He rushed back to the mid-forty right after he'd managed to rid himself of Wiley George in Lawnover.

Alex had returned to the mid-forty about one in the afternoon only to find Laura gone. He waited over two hours for her return. Where was she? His mind whirled back to the one thought that had driven him since morning. Could there really be a baby? Putting the pitchfork back against the wall, Alex walked to the doorway and looked down the path toward the lane. The wind had started to kick up and the sky threatened snow. If Laura was actually pregnant, he couldn't have her out in this. He took in several deep breaths. Could he believe what his senses were telling him?

He and Eula had made a baby, but just that once, and at twenty-four, he hadn't paid much attention to either Eula or what his senses told him about her changing body. They'd been married almost a year when she told him a baby was on the way. Back then, he thought that was the way of a marriage, and he gave neither Eula nor the coming baby any further thought until his child's birthday also became her death day.

The doctor hadn't said one way or another if Eula could ever have more children. She just hadn't. Mostly, he felt it was a weakness in his wife that kept him from becoming a father and there was no need to worry a good woman on her failing.

Although some men gave their women a lot of grief because of it, Eula deserved better. But, every now and again, as the years passed with no other babies from any of the four or five women he'd been with besides Eula, he fretted that maybe the fault did not all belong to his wife. Sometimes he thought that maybe there was a weakness in his family line. His own pa had sired only Alex and his sister, though he had lived with their mother more than thirty years. Was Laura about to change all that?

Standing in the shadows of the barn door opening, he watched her walk up the path long before she saw him. He had told her the coat was a cast-off from the church. In truth, he had bought it brand-new in Clarksville. Alex had purchased two, one blue and the other black. Neither had been very expensive, but both were warm. The black had tortoiseshell buttons, and he had given that one to Eula. He hadn't realized until he read her surprised face and heard her shocked comment that he had never given his wife a just-for-nothing gift in all of their married years. But it was the blue coat with its extra-thick lining that had really caught his eye. And today, with the snow clouds forming in the afternoon sky, Laura needed its warmth. As she passed the smoke house, it was no wonder she still hadn't seen him. Her head was bent down and the collar of the coat turned up almost to her eyes. As she closed in on the barn, he stepped out into the pale sun. He didn't dare risk taking her by surprise. Not now.

"Your Aunt Becky lives 'most a mile down the road. You shouldn't be walking that far in weather like this." Alex watched her stop in the path just beyond the smoke house.

The startled look on her face told him he had just brought her back from some distant place. Alex closed the space between them and touched her shoulder. He was surprised when she jumped.

"You're cold and it's about to snow." He began rubbing her shoulders to warm her.

Alex felt her body stiffen like their first days together. He frowned and pulled her to him in a tight embrace. Her arms hung at her sides.

"Is your Aunt Becky sick?"

She trembled in his arms again.

"No. Not sick." Her words muffled into his shoulder.

Alex led her into the barn and away from the drafty door. They stopped in front of the cows still chewing on their hay.

"Let's warm you up." He slid his hand to the middle button on her coat and slipped it open.

Alex laid his hand across her midsection. He felt her stiffen again. Annalaura's eyes stared at the barn floor. The beginnings of concern set up in his mind. Despite this morning's passion, Laura was keeping something from him. He rubbed his hand slowly around her belly.

"Are you sure there's no baby in there?"

Her head jerked up to face his before she turned around to stare at the feeding cows, but not before he glimpsed her look of panic.

"Laura?" He waited for an answer.

"No. Ain't no baby."

"Let's go upstairs." She was keeping the truth from him, but why? He pulled her toward the ladder. "I'm gonna get me a good look at your belly in the daylight. I'm gonna take off your clothes." Alex felt her feet dig into the barn floor like she was one of the planting mules.

"No," Laura almost shouted at him.

Startled, and with one hand on the ladder rail, he stopped and turned toward her. With those amber eyes opened wider than he'd ever seen them, he knew she couldn't miss the look of puzzlement on his face.

"What?" Alex hadn't meant his question to sound as harsh as it did.

Laura began a frantic shake of her head. "I mean...my children...you can't...sorry." Laura's skin was a beautiful chestnut brown, but it always had red undertones. Right now, her face looked like a ripe cherry. "Tonight. Please do it tonight. It's only afternoon. My children will see."

To his ears, her voice carried the sound of fear. A new sensation of worry rushed at him.

"I'll send them downstairs. Won't take but thirty minutes. I need a good look." He tightened his grip on her arm and started up the ladder.

"Mr. Alex, please wait. I'll tell you."

Laura hadn't addressed him with such formality since early October. In this fresh wave of surprise, he released her arm and she scurried around the ladder. He followed. Annalaura stood with her back to the pile of hay. Even though her head was down, Alex could see the tears falling. His own heart quickened.

"Tell it, then." He could barely catch his breath as he watched Laura slowly lift her face to his.

"Yes, suh. There is a baby." She stood with her eyes closed, her hands fisted at her side, just like those first days in September.

Alex wanted to smile his pleasure at news of a baby, but that strange look on Laura's face stopped any budding pride from building within him. He watched her swallow two, three times before her eyes slowly opened.

"Mr. Alex, suh, I has to tell you the truth."

He heard her words, but the pounding in his chest, loud as hailstones during a bad downpour, drowned out their meaning.

"If you've got a baby in there, Laura, why didn't you tell me before?" He placed his hands to her shoulders to steady her.

"Because I know you is goin' to kill me." She swayed under his hands.

Alex shook his head trying to let some understanding enter his mind. No words came from his mouth.

"This baby, suh, ain't yours. It's the hired man's from harvest time." Her eyes clamped shut.

"The hired man?" He could feel her tense for the first blow she knew was coming. "You talkin' about Isaiah?"

"Yes, suh. Isaiah Harris. He this baby's daddy."

Alex watched Laura reach down deep to get the breath to whisper out the name. Her hands lifted to her belly as though she thought he would send a blow in that direction first.

For long seconds, Alex couldn't find the words to speak. He remembered Isaiah Harris perfectly. The tan-skinned man had come to his place in early September to ask for a harvest job. He, Alex, Laura, Cleveland, Doug, and little Lottie had all worked fourteen-hour days to bring in the tobacco. Even Henry had helped by ferrying water from the pump outside the smoke house to the barn where Cleveland, Laura, and Lottie hung the tobacco. With Harris's help, the two men had been able to spear the tobacco on all forty acres. Even though it was far from prime, the crop had fetched a little over sixteen hundred dollars, not as much as last year but still a hundred dollars better than the tenants on his back-forty. Alex had thought it a miracle. All during those two weeks, he had kept close tabs on Isaiah Harris.

A man, any man, black or white, knows to mark out his territory. And, he had no doubt, Harris understood that Alex had marked out Laura as his own. Sometimes, the two men finished their spearing way after supper. Isaiah offered to sleep on the floor of the smoke house to get an even earlier start the next day. Alex would have none of it. He put Harris in the back of Eula's buckboard and drove him back to the main barn each and every night. He stashed the gray's saddle on the porch, and he seriously doubted that Isaiah Harris would walk all the way to the mid-forty at midnight only to come back again at four o'clock in the morning. No man, including Isaiah, would be fool enough to take another man's woman when she had been clearly spoken for. Laura was lying, but why?

"What makes you think Isaiah is the father? I was with you before he ever stepped foot on the mid-forty." He watched her eyes open and blink, although the shaft of sunlight coming through the barn door fell nowhere near the stack of hay.

"I...I just do." His head shook its confusion. "A woman knows these things."

Alex hadn't paid much attention to what Eula knew or didn't know, and maybe a woman did feel more when she was pregnant, but he doubted it. He pulled Laura into his arms and kissed her. He felt her body push into his as her lips responded for the wisp of an instant before she pulled away. He tightened his grip on her shoulders and he knew the truth.

"This baby is mine and ain't nothin' you say can make me think different." He pushed her down to the pile of hay and dropped beside her.

The rungs of the ladder lay angled above them. He saw her hand clutch at a piece of hay as he finished unbuttoning her coat. She turned her head to look at the bits of straw in her outstretched hand while he shifted her skirt to her waist. She brought a fistful of straw to his shoulder as he untied the string to her winter drawers and lowered them to just above her triangle. He put his face lightly to her stomach. Brushing her belly with his cheek, he was certain he felt something inside her move.

"Alex," she sounded almost out of breath as she let the straw trickle across his back. "If this baby frets you too much, I understands." Her voice grew stronger. "Sometimes a baby with the wrong woman can be bothersome to a man." Her breathing came easier and she let her eyes rest full on him. "It ain't too late if you don't want it. It would pain me to bring a world of trouble with yo' family down on yo' head." Her voice carried a strange mixture of fear and hope.

What did she mean? What possible difference could it make to Eula if he had an outside child with a colored woman as long as he looked after the farm and clothed and fed his wife? He could see Laura was just about bowed down with fear. He rubbed his hand over her belly as he raised up to look at her face. She looked as though she were willing him to say some particular words she wanted to hear. But what?

"Laurie, quit your worryin'." He brushed her forehead with his lips. He tasted the dampness of sweat, although the barn was just about cold enough to freeze the water in the pails by the cows. "I'm gonna take care of this baby. You don't need to worry about no midwife. I'll get the best colored doctor in all of Clarksville out here." Did he feel her shudder?

When she didn't respond, he stroked the side of her face with his fingertips. Didn't she understand that a man can't really call himself a man until he can show the world the living proof of his manhood?

"I'll send this child all the way to the eighth grade if you want." He leaned over to kiss her again.

Annalaura turned her head just as his lips approached her face, and he caught the corner of her mouth. Her breathing was coming in harder again. He reached down to pull off her drawers. Her hand stopped him.

"If you really want this chile, we can't be together so often." Her voice came soft, low, and filled with worry.

"What do you mean? Have I hurt you?" Twenty-one years peeled away in the flash of a second.

Had he been the cause of Eula's lost baby? His hand reflexively left Laura's stomach.

"No, no. You ain't hurt me." She turned her face back toward him, and a hint of alarm flashed quickly in those eyes. She dropped her head, and the cherry-red color returned to her cheeks. "You, ah, you been very good to me. It's just that you, ah, yo' love come on strong. Maybe too strong fo' the baby." She let her eyes flicker a second on him before she firmly placed them back on the pile of hay. In the fading afternoon light in the barn, they looked soft, even loving. "Don't come back tonight. Best if you come over no mo' than one or two times a week."

This time Alex thought he heard hope etched in her voice.

"If you think that'll be good for the baby." Before he could sort out her request, she sat up against the hay piled against the side wall and slipped her arms around his neck.

She pulled him close. He felt her fingers run down his neck and up into his hair as her tongue probed into his mouth. He pushed her back down onto the hay.

"After today, I won't bother you more than three times a week. I promise I will be careful."

"No more'n once a week," she whispered as she led his hand to the top of her winter drawers.

CHAPTER SEVENTEEN

The sound reminded him of a woodpecker worrying a tree somewhere far off in the distance. Knock, knock. He wasn't ready to come out of his sleep just yet though there was nary a dream in it. The woodpecker kept up his work until a fantasy burst on him full grown. He was in the middle of the Clarksville battlefield and the Union cannon were bombarding the Clarksville rebels. With bullets flying from both directions, he didn't know which way to run.

"Welles, John Welles. Is you in there? Miz Zeola wants you." The knock thundered into his bedroom like a cannonball had fallen onto the pillow next to him.

He jumped bolt upright, flinging his arms up to ward off the next attack, only to come into hard contact with Savannah's nose. The grade-school teacher had lifted her head off the pillow beside him just as he reacted to Big Red's voice. He looked over at his lovemaking partner of a half hour ago. Her mouse-brown eyes stared big at the door. Her face looked like she expected the whole Confederate army to storm though and drag her off into slavery. Knock, knock. Big Red was getting even louder. John reached for a corner of the blanket on the double bed to cover himself.

"Oh, my Lawd." Ignoring the accidental blow, Savannah, the older of the two schoolteacher sisters living next door in Miz Brown's best room, snatched the blanket from his grasp, pulling it completely off the bed. She wrapped the heavy cotton coverlet around her ample body as she jumped to the floor.

Now naked in the room lit by late afternoon sun, John watched the woman turn in circles with his blanket snug around her as she sought a place to hide. One of her breasts escaped the swathing and drooped nearly to her waist. Savannah was five years younger than his Annalaura, but the schoolteacher had a body that looked more like a middle-aged Zeola than a young woman who had never birthed a baby.

"John Welles, Miz Zeola wants you and she wants you now. I ain't standin' here foolin' with you no mo'." Big Red's voice oozed its own particular charm as John motioned Savannah to stand behind the door.

"Hold on, Red. Let me git my britches on." John took his time donning his trousers.

He wished Savannah would stop bending and straightening her knees. Each time she did it, he could feel the floor shake. John pulled on the knob and opened the door into Miz Brown's second floor hallway. Big Red crowded out what sunlight shone through the hallway window at the front of the house. The cook's substantially sized feet, planted firmly on the floor, blocked out the garish red roses stitched into his landlady's carpet.

"My shift don't start 'til eight o'clock. Ain't but fo' now. What Zeola want?"

"It ain't fo' you to ask what Miz Zeola wants. It's fo' you to come when she calls." Big Red turned and rumbled down the staircase muttering all the way.

Before John shut the door, he peered over at the hallway window. Though he had the second-best room in the entire board-inghouse, and he paid a pretty four dollars a week for it too, his only view was of the brown clapboard siding of the house next door. Through the hall window he could see the limbs of the crape myrtle tree in the front yard bending under a gusty March wind. Tiny buds lumped out all over its branches, and he could see more brown dirt than snow on the ground surrounding it. As he looked through the second floor window, it was clear that spring was just about to make its full appearance. A jumble of images flooded his head. Pictures he didn't want to see. As Christmas gave way to Easter, sometimes he'd imagine Annalaura struggling to put food on the table. It was all he could do not to throw away Nashville and rush back to Lawnover. But if he gave up now, his family would always lead a life of nothing.

"Close the door," Savannah hissed. "You know I can't be seen in a man's room. The school board would fire me for sure." Savannah pounded on his arm as she moved her girth against the back of the door.

John slid his hand away just in time to avoid a broken finger in the quick-slamming door.

"Red ain't seen a thing. You got nothin' to worry 'bout, but you better get yo'self dressed and back to yo' room before yo' sister gets back." He watched her move toward the trail of clothes scattered along the thin carpet on the floor.

Savannah scurried into her chemise and tugged her winter drawers to just below her waist. She reached for, and then tossed on the rumpled bed, the corset he'd had so much trouble unlac-ing. As he grabbed at his own shirt, he took another look at the woman he'd been bedding ever since Sally got too big to entertain and Zeola sent her off to do the ironing for the other girls.

"Oh, my Lawd. I been on this job seven years. I sure don't want to lose it." Savannah pushed an arm through her white shirt-waist.

"It's Sunday. Ain't no school board members gonna be 'round to look in on you in yo' own house." John was pleased to be with Savannah though she was about the plainest woman he had ever bedded.

But if she hadn't been hovering over downright homely, she never would have risked her schoolmarm reputation to sleep with him. She was a smart woman, and at twenty-six, she knew she was already far gone into spinsterhood. She carried about a hundred extra pounds, mostly from chin to knee, Still, she was a kind-hearted woman, and she understood when he told her right up front that he couldn't do no serious courting. She nodded her head and admitted that her only marrying prospect was a sixty-year-old widowed Baptist deacon with four teenage children who told her plain that they didn't want another momma. Although he hadn't been Savannah's first, she wanted to find out what this lovemaking stuff was really all about before she got saddled with a man known to be tight with a nickel and quick with the hell-fire and damnation, especially when it came to girl children and women.

"My sister won't be back for another hour." She stepped into her skirt and tugged hard at the too-tight waistband to get it fas-tened.

John sat on the edge of the bed to pull on his high-buttoned shoes. He looked over at Savannah as she tried to lift a leg to buck-le her own shoe.

"I'll be on my way now." With one shoe still unfastened, and holding on to the offending corset with its strings dangling in all directions, Savannah cracked the door open a peep and looked both ways before she opened it barely enough to squeeze herself through.

"I'll see you next Sunday," he called after her back.

The schoolteacher didn't acknowledge him as she quietly closed the door behind her. On most Sunday afternoons, ever since January, he had slipped Savannah into his room while her younger sister was out courting. The plaid-shirted poker player from Miz Zeola's had taken a liking to the sister, though John thought he was far more interested in a teacher's first-of-the-month payday than he was in the charms of a rather ordinary looking woman. Still, it had kept Savannah free for nearly three hours every Sunday afternoon when the sister went off with her suitor to church socials and buggy rides chaperoned by the preacher's wife. That was just fine with John since Savannah didn't ask anything more of him than two hours in bed once a week. And being with a woman who didn't expect courting meant he was being true to Annalaura.

In all their married years, John had never been unfaithful to his wife. The women at the ho houses and the sportin' houses didn't count, and neither did Savannah. Just before he stepped out of the door, he patted at his pockets remembering to take some cash from his hidden savings box with him. What did Zeola want now?

The dining room was empty when he arrived some thirty minutes later. He walked right past Big Red, who, from the smell of it, was boiling cabbage to go along with the corned beef John spotted in the big kettle on the back of the stove. Red had mumbled and raved in turn, but John hadn't bothered to even glance in his direction as he pushed through the pantry door. Although no one sat at the dining room table, John knew to stand and wait until invited to sit. He walked over to the parlor. It, too, was empty though he noticed that the door to the main poker room was open. He went back to the dining room.

"I tole you to be here thirty minutes ago." Zeola stormed into the room in a flowered day wrapper that was untied.

John was sure that bunched-up bulge underneath her wrapper was her nightgown though the time showed close to five o'clock in the afternoon.

"Yes, ma'am. As soon as Big Red tole me, I walked here on the double." He let his face show concern he did not feel. What was so all important?

"Walk? Hell, man. Ain't you got a nickel fo' the trolley? I got me troubles here." Her nightcap sat askew atop her head, and half her curling rags were still tangled in her hair.

"Miz Zeola. Tell me what I can do to help you out." He watched her walk over to the safe and pull out the bourbon and a glass.

She shoved the branch water to the side as she poured the dark brown liquid nearly to the top. Zeola turned around and squinted one eye at him as she downed the liquor in two swallows.

"How much money you got saved in yo' poke, John Welles?" She belched.

What had gotten her into such a snit, he wondered? The woman hadn't even bothered to stick a wig on her head, let alone lay on that pound of rouge and powder she wore every night. Here she was, asking him about his personal business. Ever since November, and his four pots a week, he'd been able to save up nearly two hundred dollars to take back home. When he lit out the first of April, he would have close to three hundred if Zeola was true to her word and handed over the money she was holding for him. Of course, that wouldn't be enough to buy those twenty acres he had his eye on down in Lawnover, but he had no more time to wait.

"I gots me enough to take real good care of my family, Miz Zeola." The half smile on his face began to hurt as his jaw locked into place.

"I got no time to play with you, John Welles." She put the glass back to her lips, grimaced when she found it empty and stalked back to the safe. "Now, how much money you got saved?"

"I been able to save enough to keep my family fo' most of a year." He figured he was close to the truth. Three hundred dollars could keep a family alive if they had a place to stay and went hungry a little bit. He lifted his eyes to her face, but he was careful not to paste on a smile.

"You saved any mo' than two hundred dollars?" She pulled out the box of matches from the safe drawer.

John had to make this job last only another three weeks until April and his return home. If he was really careful or really lucky with the pots, he could bring home another forty-five dollars. He couldn't afford to anger Zeola right now.

"A little more than that, ma'am." He watched his boss dig into the pocket of her wrapper and pull out a cigarette.

She held it, unlit between her fingers. Why was she hell-bent on finding out how much money he had saved?

"Three hundred dollars won't let that woman of yours live in no kind of style." She bowed her head as she lit the cigarette, looking at him through the curling smoke.

"How long you plannin' on stayin' with me, John Welles?"

The question came at him like a sledgehammer.

"As long as you needs me, Miz Zeola." He watched her toss her head like she knew a lie when she heard one.

"I got a deal for you, but I ain't havin' you up and leave 'til I say so. You understand?" She pointed the cigarette at him as she slowly walked across the room and planted herself in front of the door leading to her parlor.

John could see the open door of the big pot room just behind her. "Ma'am, I'm here as long as you needs me."

"I tole you befo' not to mess with me. I knows you tryin' to lay up money to get back to tobacco country, and I knows it's plowin' time. You'll be outta here lickety-split as soon as you get five hundred dollars in yo' poke." She took two quick puffs on the cigarette, then let an ash fall on her fringed rug. She looked at him like she was daring him to call her a liar.

"I ain't got but a little over two hundred, Miz Zeola. And I ain't 'bout to leave you 'cause I..." He didn't know that a woman her size could flash around a table and four chairs to stand within six inches of him quicker than he could finish his words.

"I don't give a damn 'bout the lie you gettin' ready to tell me, country boy. I want to make you a deal." In addition to her no powder and no wig, Zeola hadn't taken the time to clean her teeth. The smell of onions from last night's smothered pork chops blasted at him.

"What you offerin', Miz Zeola?"

"The big pots." She took a step back, and John let out a breath.

"What you mean, the big pots? Alfred sits the big pots." He didn't like it when women talked in circles.

"I wants you to hold the big pots. Leastwise 'til I can get me somebody else. You take over the weekends, Fridays through Sundays. That's three of 'em." She sucked in on her cigarette.

"And Alfred? What pots will he sit?" It would be best to proceed slowly until Zeola could start talking like a woman with at least some of her wits about her.

"I see Red did keep that loud mouth of his shut and ain't tole you a thing. Alfred took off with Sally. He the father of Sally's baby. They both left me high and dry, and I got Bubba Johnson and seven other high rollers comin' in at ten o'clock." She jerked her head toward the secret door to the big gaming room off her parlor. "Take it myself, but I got me the police chief comin' in tonight. I got to make sure everythin' goes jest right. I gots my hands full. He wants that new young gal I took in last week, and she ain't nowhere near ready enough to entertain a white man." Zeola turned around in a swish of wrapper.

"Whoa, Miz Zeola." John held up a hand. For a woman used to being close-mouthed, Zeola was pouring a whole barrel of words over him. "You tellin' me that Alfred ain't sittin' pots no mo'? That he took off with Sally?" John flashed on all the nights he'd spent with the far gone pregnant Sally knowing her baby wasn't his. "What kind of money we talkin' 'bout, Zeola?"

She stopped her puffing and her pacing. "Pots with Bubba Johnson playin' been runnin' to almost three hundred a night." Zeola's voice steadied.

"Three hundred dollars?" The figures he ran in his head were working wonders to calm him. "You say there's eight players tonight? What do I get fo' holdin' the big pots?"

"Twenty dollars out of every pot and a dollar a man at the table." Zeola was settling into her old self again.

"Make it forty and five dollars a man." John leveled his eyes at his boss.

Zeola let out a laugh so deep that it rolled right up her spacious belly to the front of her nightgown.

"Well, Johnny, I guess you ain't much of a country boy no mo'. You sure you wanna go back to plantin' tobacca?" Her laugh came so hard that he could barely catch her words.

"What 'bout my fo'ty dollars?" He had no intention of her joshing him off target.

As fast as her laughter came, it dried in her throat.

"You may not be a country boy no mo', but you ain't quite slick enough to git one over on Miz Zeola. I'll give you thirty out of every pot and two dollars a head. That'll give you over a hundred dollars a weekend just fo' yo'self. Take it or leave it." All of her earlier panic had evaporated.

"And I keeps my little pot games durin' the week." He made sure it sounded more like a foregone conclusion than the question he knew it should be.

A little smile flickered over Zeola's lips.

"You do both pot jobs." She motioned him to step across the hall and into her parlor. She pointed to the gaming room where the serious poker players sat.

As John moved to squeeze past her, she clamped her hand over his shoulder. He felt like he was being held in a red-hot blacksmith's vise.

"You give me two mo' months, and you will have enough money to buy them twenty acres in tobacca country. No mo' plantin' fo' the white man. Come this here June, the ground you put that seed in will be yo' own." She dug her nails deep into his shoulder.

He felt the blood oozing under his work shirt.

"You cross me, country boy, and Big Red will do mo' than wake you up from whorin' with that schoolteacher."

CHAPTER EIGHTEEN

The Thornton farmhouse, sitting in the middle of Old Ben Thornton's six hundred and forty acres like it did, had always been the natural place to host the annual first day of planting dinner and prayer for the Thornton clan. Though the four Thornton boys each received unequal portions as their inheritance, with eldest son Ben Roy getting the biggest and the best, all the kin agreed to gather at the family home to share in the big meal and pray in a successful tobacco season. Farmers all over Montgomery County were doing much the same during mid-May. Throughout the county, farmers would group together on the first day of planting, stand side by side with their local preachers, and pray for warm skies and the proper amount of rain.

On that sun-filled, wind-free day when Ben Roy declared it planting time, Fedora had twenty-four hours to arrange for all the Thornton women to bring together the meal that would be served after the men had set their tenants to sowing seed. Because Reverend Hawkins had to cover fifteen farms in two days, he wouldn't get to the Thorntons 'til close to two o'clock this day.

While most of the Thornton women spent their time complaining at the short notice that came regular every year, Eula always had her stores in place. She could tell far better than her brother when the sky and the moisture in the earth teamed up to tell all farmers that the ground was ripe for seeding. When the first of May dawned, she went to her smoke house and got out one of the few remaining slabs of bacon to flavor the pole beans canned late last summer. Every May morning during those first couple of weeks, as she walked by the chicken coop, she set her eyes on the pullets that would make the best fryers and gave them extra feed. A day or two before she knew Fedora would come frantically knocking on her door, she began her cooking. She baked her chess pie and shoofly cakes, fried up her chicken, opened her Mason jars of beans, greens, and turnips, and when they were ready, put them all away in a cool place on the porch by the pump.

Sure enough, as the third week of May dawned, Fedora lashed her buckboard over to the McNaughtons and issued her breathless command to come join Cora Lee, Tillie, Belle, Jenny, and all the other Thornton women for the prayer dinner to wish for an easy plant, good growing weather, and a profitable harvest.

"My greens ain't nowhere big enough to pick, and I've got none canned." Belle, as disorganized as ever, made the same complaint Eula had heard for fifteen years now. She ignored her sister-in-law and continued to spread the red-checkered tablecloth over the last of the three tables Fedora had set out in the big yard behind the house. With close to thirty-five Thorntons showing up, Fedora always held the prayer dinners outside since Ben Roy had guaranteed perfect weather by his selection of the planting day.

"What did you bring then, Belle?" Cora Lee asked, as she spread out a flowered tablecloth on a second table set closer to the house.

"I had my girl fry up some chicken and make a sweet-potato pie." Belle stood to the side, acting, for all the Thornton world to see, like she was supervising the other women. Fedora's colored

cook gave Belle a quick glare as the longtime servant started laying platters of smothered pork chops and preserved lima beans
onto the first table, which was already set with its white cloth.
Cora Lee stood up straight and whispered over her shoulder to
Eula.

"I think your brother must have seen somethin' else in that
one to marry her besides her cookin'." Cora took a platter of corn
bread from Fedora's cook and set it on her table. Whatever her
youngest brother saw in the ill-mannered Belle escaped Eula.
Her table covered, she walked past Cora Lee without answering and headed into the kitchen to retrieve her own platter of
chicken and bowl of greens. Let Belle and Cora Lee fight it out on
their own.

"Cousin Eula, where do you want me to set this chess pie and
cake?" Jenny balanced both in her hands as Eula entered Fedora's
kitchen. She gestured to the red-checkered table just as she heard
Belle's voice call through the open kitchen door.

"Eula, when you bring out your plates, would you grab some
for my table, too?" Belle may have been an ongoing irritant for
Cora Lee, but Eula had long ago gotten used to the ways of her
sister-in-law.

If she hadn't married Eula's youngest brother, little Belle
would have been the one scrubbing and cooking for others, and
not the hired colored girl she liked to flaunt in front of Eula. Trying to balance the heavy platter of chicken, Eula struggled to slide
the big bowl of greens next to it without spilling everything. Now,
if she could just grab the pan of sweet potatoes, she could get out
of the kitchen in just one food trip. Eula was smiling to herself
as she started her careful way across the kitchen floor with her
burden when she heard the baby's cry.

"Momma, he just won't take it. Can't you speak to Papa?" Tillie's shrill voice verged on the hysterical.

Eula stopped and turned as she carefully reset all the serving dishes back onto Fedora's table. She walked toward the back bedroom where the commotion was getting even louder.

"Hush up, Tillie," Fedora hissed at her daughter. "If you can just keep yourself still and stop that dratted screeching, the baby will take the tit."

Even though the window was open to capture the windless air, Fedora's forehead was beaded with sweat. She stood alternately jostling Tillie's two-month-old son in her arms and pushing the infant's mouth at Tillie's exposed breast.

The baby, Little Ben, was as red as the strawberries due to come in next month. The little arms and legs flailed in all directions.

"Fedora. Tillie. Can I get you all somethin' to help out with Little Ben?" Eula stood in the doorway.

Being around babies still upset her, but the frantic scene in the room compelled her to offer whatever help she could. Both women turned their heads in her direction. Tears streamed down Tillie's cheeks. Tillie squirmed in the rocker her mother wouldn't let her leave, her hair hanging in loosening strings from its pompadour. Every time Fedora tried to push Little Ben's mouth onto her nipple, Tillie flapped her hands hopelessly in the air and rocked away from the baby.

"It ain't workin'," Tillie screamed at Eula. "Please, Auntie, talk to my father. I need Hettie."

"Hush yo' mouth before I smack you one." Fedora crooked the baby in her arm as she turned to the bedside table in the back room and dipped her finger into a half empty jar of honey.

Apparently uncaring of the sticky trail dripping across her carpet and her bedcovering, Fedora walked over to Tillie and smeared the honey on her daughter's nipple. The girl reacted as though her mother had caught her breast in a wood vise.

"Noooo." Tillie looked like she could swoon at any moment.

Eula hurried over and stood between mother and daughter, her heart racing. "My Lord, is there somethin' wrong with Little Ben?" She stared at the squalling infant, too frightened to reach out a hand to comfort her great-nephew.

"He's starvin' to death is all, Aunt Eula. Starvin' to death because of my father." Tillie shoved her breast back under the cloth of her bodice.

"He's doin' no such thing. You're the mother. You can feed him." Fedora held the baby in her arms as he frantically nuzzled at his grandmother's clothed chest.

"He does look hungry, Fedora." The last thing Eula wanted was to challenge her sister-in-law.

"He's hungry because Hettie's not here to feed him." Tillie rocked the chair hard. Eula feared she might just pitch forward and fall flat on her face.

"He drinks Hettie's milk best. 'Sides, mine is 'bout dried up. I can't wet-nurse no baby. Momma didn't wet-nurse me." Tillie shot an accusing eye at Fedora. "Grandma Thornton didn't wet-nurse you, Aunt Eula. Only colored did that. Why should I have to wet-nurse this baby?" Tillie folded her arms tight under her breasts, making them poke out all the more.

"Because it's an emergency. There's plenty of milk still in there if you just let this baby get started." Fedora took her free hand and pushed on Tillie's breast, setting up fresh howls from the young woman.

Eula knew better than to inquire on the whereabouts of Hettie.

"Emergency? Emergency?" Tillie's voice screamed out of her mouth. "You call having to cook for some family in Clarksville an emergency?"

"Your papa owed her to a friend. It's not for you nor me to question what Ben Roy says or does. He had to honor his word."

There was a catch in Fedora's throat. "Fact is, Hettie ain't here to-day, and she ain't settin' foot in this house no matter how much you scream and shout. And somebody's got to feed this baby."

"Did Hettie send any milk with him?" Eula ventured.

A colored woman could be milked like a cow and the liq-uid dripped into an empty Mason jar, Eula knew. Tillie aimed a trembling finger toward the carpetbag on the bed. Fedora stood unmoving, staring at it. Eula crossed the short distance to the bed and pulled out the Mason jar full of Hettie's milk. Without warning, Fedora thrust Little Ben into Eula's arms and started toward the door. Eula hadn't held a baby in more than twenty years. Doc Starter wouldn't let her hold her daughter after the girl had been born dead. He wouldn't even hand the body to Alex. Eula dropped to the bed, fighting to control her own mis-ery. The squealing child soothed enough to allow her to unscrew the lid to the jar. Unsure what to do next, she looked toward Til-lie who shrugged her shoulders at the doorway. Fedora turned around.

"Dip your finger in and see if he will suck it off'n them. I ain't touchin' it." Fedora answered Eula's unspoken question.

Eula stared at the jar of mother's milk, and her own eyes clouded with tears.

"What's goin' on in here?" The sound of Belle's voice snapped Eula's head up. "Oh, come on, let me do that. You all act like you ain't never fed a baby milk from a wet nurse befo'." Belle pulled Little Ben out of Eula's arms.

Dipping her fingers into the jar, Belle poked them into the baby's mouth.

The child sucked on Belle's fingers from tip to knuckle.

"This little one's sure hungry." Belle looked at the Mason jar. "I'm surprised Hettie's got enough milk to fill that thing up. Fe-dora, ain't she nursin' for two?" Belle pulled out a square of clean cloth from the carpetbag, dipped it into the Mason jar, and gave it to Little Ben.

Fedora remained silent.

"Colored women have lots of milk." A calming Tillie spoke up. "Her boy's four months. He eats after Little Ben's had his fill." Tillie buttoned her shirtwaist.

The baby's slurping could be heard throughout the room. Belle dipped the cloth into the milk while Little Ben fussed at its temporary absence.

"Fedora, don't that make three yella-skinned children Hettie's dropped?" Belle slipped the soaked cloth into the baby's mouth as Fedora turned in slow motion toward the door and moved her feet across the threshold.

Before she had gotten out of earshot, Eula's youngest sister-in-law turned on the next woman in the room.

"Eula, I do believe I saw that tenant of yours comin' out of the nigger church on Sunday." Belle soaked the cloth.

Every time Belle, who hadn't made it beyond the fourth grade, used that profane word, Eula winced. How could her baby brother have married a woman so unrefined?

"I'm not right sure what you believe, Belle. What tenant you talkin' about?" When Eula thought of the exchange in all the years to come, she would remember that Belle had led her into that trap like a fox treeing a rabbit.

"That nigg . . . , uh, colored woman on your mid-forty. What's her name?" Belle must have caught the frost in Eula's voice.

"You talkin' about Welles? That family tenant farmed our mid-forty last year?"

Glancing at Little Ben, Eula stood and started toward the door. Through the kitchen window, she could see Fedora standing outside, apart from the others.

"That ain't the way I hear it." The smirk in Belle's voice matched the one on her face.

"I heard her man's been gone for almost a year." Belle's voice sounded like it wanted to sing a church solo.

Standing in the doorway, Eula finally turned to her sister-in-law. What was the woman trying to say to her now?

"Nothin' to it. Alex hired a man to bring in the crop last fall, is all. Everthin' worked out just fine." She knew she should move her feet as fast as she could after the escaped Fedora. But, something in that curious look on Belle's face held her fast.

"I saw that Welles woman steppin' out of Bobby Lee's store with her belly 'bout as big as an August watermelon. And, the way she was dressed, I don't think I've ever seen such fancy on a nig-ger in all my life." Belle put Little Ben over her shoulder to burp.

Eula grabbed at her ear. She was certain that sudden roaring coming through the open window had distorted her hearing.

"What?" She could manage no other words.

"Your nigger tenant is 'bout to let loose another pickaninny on Thornton land. Tillie, come and get this baby."

Eula felt Tillie's groan. She could neither see nor hear anyone or anything else in the room.

"I wonder who the daddy is?" Nothing of a proper question lingered in Belle's voice.

By the grunts coming from Little Ben, Eula surmised that her sister-in-law had handed over the baby to Tillie.

"Aunt Belle, I swear you don't listen sometimes. Aunt Eula just told you 'bout the hired man. Of course he's the father. You know colored. They just rut around every chance they get." Tillie walked out of the room as Belle stood to smooth her crumpled dress.

"I don't believe that hired man was there long enough to give anybody a baby, do you, Eula Mae?" Belle swept past her.

Eula tried to make her feet move. There had to be some mistake. The woman…what was her name…couldn't be pregnant, not if her husband hadn't come home. Every imaginable thought poured into her head, but only one stuck to the inside of her brain like honey to a hive. She had to get home right now.

As she clicked the harness moving her horse faster, Eula's buckboard bounced on a rut in the lane. She could barely remember how she had gotten this far. She recalled stumbling out of Fedora's kitchen and mumbling something about forgetting her corn bread and she had to return home immediately to retrieve it. As she passed the stand of trees near her barn, she peered at the sky. The sun, a shade past its peak, told her it must be close to half past one. She had just missed the onslaught of men coming out of the fields and into the Thornton yard to begin the prayer dinner. She thought she spotted Reverend Hawkins as she made her hasty retreat, but she really couldn't be sure. She pulled the buckboard in front of the barn. Without unharnessing the animal, Eula led him to the horse trough filled with water, and ran into her own kitchen. Frantically, she reached for her journal.

Eula almost ripped the pages with her twitching fingers as they turned back to December, November, October, and finally September. All together the harvest had brought in over forty-five hundred dollars. Her books told her that after paying for food, supplies, and tenant needs for seven months, she and Alex should still have way over two thousand dollars. Grabbing one of her kitchen chairs and dragging it across her kitchen, parlor, and dining room floors to her bedroom, she stood it in front of the closet door. Gingerly stepping up onto its seat, she reached for the top shelf and began shifting boxes and bags until she felt the tin with her fingers. Dislodging a box of Confederate money left over from Alex's father that nearly spilled out over her head, she pulled down the tin. Eula wobbled off the chair, almost tipping it. She carried the box to the bed and dropped it down onto the feathered four-poster. Her hands worked to pry it open. The box was locked. Eula's mind rummaged over the whereabouts of the key. Remembering, she rushed to the closet and to Alex's funeral-and-wedding suit. There, in a breast pocket, she pulled out the key. Her hands shaking, she ran back to the bed and slipped the key into the lock. It turned easy as though it had been opened frequently in recent months.

Inside, Eula found, and tossed aside, the deeds for the house and land. She piled the sale papers for the animals on top of the bed. She scattered supply receipts across the floor. She dug her hands deep into the box until her fingers pulled out the envelope that should have been fat with cash. Her hands still trembling, Eula counted out one thousand four hundred fifty-five dollars and seventy-five cents. She shook her head. That couldn't be right. Her journal records told her they should have over two thousand dollars. She recounted. One thousand four hundred fifty-five dollars and seventy-five cents. Just like the records on her preserves in the smoke house, there had been no mistake. Over five hundred dollars was missing.

A wave of dizziness came up sudden from her stomach. She felt like she did as an eight-year-old when she slid off a slippery rock and fell into the slow-flowing creek on the far side of Lawnover. She clutched at her middle and reached for one of the posters on her bed. She laid her body against it, clinging to it like it was the rope Old Roy threw to pull her out of the murky waters. It could not be true.

Belle was as much a liar as she was white trash. Every man and woman in Lawnover, black and white, knew that Eula's brother Ben Roy was the father of Hettie's three children. But Alexander? The father of a colored woman's child? Never. She and Alexander hadn't conceived a baby in twenty years. Now he was nearly forty-four, and there had never even been a whispered hint that he had achieved fatherhood. If he had sired children, the news would have been all over Lawnover in less than two days. No, her Alex couldn't be the father, because he was incapable of making a baby.

Alex had never reproached her for her inability to bear him a second child the way any other husband would. Deep in her mind, she thought it might be because he knew he was partially to blame. Still, if Belle was to be believed, the Welles woman was pregnant. How could that be so? For all of her treacherous ways, Eula's youngest sister-in-law was right about one thing. The hand Alex hired last September couldn't be the father either. Even on those three mornings when she had awakened during harvest time to find Alex's side of the bed empty, she had gone down to the barn to see Isaiah Harris carry his slop jar to the outhouse. He had been in her barn every one of the fourteen nights of the September harvest. Yet, if it wasn't Isaiah Harris, who was the father of the Welles woman's baby?

The wooziness increased, and Eula felt the bile rise to her throat. The grandfather clock in her parlor bonged two. She had never laid down in the middle of the afternoon because of sickness in all of her married years, not even when she was racked with the fever. But maybe, just this once, getting off her feet might help her put that imagination of hers to rest. Her father had always told her that imagination in a woman was not only unnecessary but a dangerous thing. Eula eased herself on top of the coverlet, not caring that her shoes carried the dirt and dust of Ben Roy's backyard on them. The room felt warm though the window was opened wide to let in the mild, new-rose-scented May afternoon. She put her hands to the side of her head to push out the thoughts that no decent woman should carry. If she was really a good wife to her husband, she should be able to come up with the real reason for the short supplies, the missing money, and Alex's peculiar behavior over the planting.

With barely a word, her husband had put another hired man on the mid-forty to set the tobacco seedlings. That would have been of no particular concern to Eula. All the farmers knew that it was difficult keeping tenants, black or white, for more than two years at a stretch. But Eula had to learn from Jenny that the man, an out-of-towner, was married with three small-sized children. Worse, Jenny had added that none of the man's family was staying on the mid-forty. Yet, the Welles woman and her get remained.

Instead of evicting her as he should when a tenant stopped producing, Alex had allowed the woman and her children to stay, even though their man had been gone for almost a year. Why would Alex let a woman who could do him no earthly farming good live in his barn, while a hardworking man with a family had to travel two miles to and from town every day to tend the tobacco? Maybe if she closed her eyes for just a moment, these devil-placed thoughts might fade away and make room for the true answer. Somehow she knew that even Reverend Hawkins couldn't help cleanse her mind. She had to pray directly to the Lord for forgiveness for thinking the unbelievable.

CHAPTER NINETEEN

The two sixteen afternoon train from Nashville pulled into the Lawnover station right on time. The train, speeding to Chicago, stopped for only five minutes, and John, wearing his new cream-colored seersucker summer suit, scrambled to pull out his two valises from the overhead rack in the colored-only rail car. Kicking the box of gifts along in front of him, he moved toward the connecting carriage doors. John used his shoulder to open the heavy door and maneuver his belongings to the top of the stairs. The colored porter, standing on the platform at the bottom of the portable steps, stared up the station platform toward another white-coated porter two cars ahead. John's porter paid scant attention to his own departing passengers as they wrestled their boxes and string-tied bundles. John followed the man's stare, though he already knew what held the attention of his porter.

Two cars up the line from his own, steam hissed out of the undercarriage of the first of the whites-only train coaches. Colored porters there could expect tips, though they were seldom more than five or ten cents. Still, in times like these, every bit of change from four or five people at every stop could add up to substantial money. As John put one valise under an arm and juggled the second, he tried to lift up the gift box with his free hand.

"All aboard!" The disinterested porter called out, as a man dressed in an ill-fitting suit stood on the platform waiting for John to disembark so he could board.

For a fleeting moment, John wondered if the fellow was one of the fortunate ones heading for Chicago. The porter, finally turning back to his own disembarking passengers, reached out a hand to grab one of John's valises. On the ground, John lent the man one of his smiles as he fished in his pocket. It pleased him immensely to drop a fifty-cent piece in the porter's top pocket.

"Th-thank you, suh." The surprised train man could barely stutter out his appreciation.

Without a word, John winked and walked up the platform. With over a thousand dollars in his money belt, it felt better than good to show the world that John Welles was a man on the move. Judging by the time on the big round-faced clock on the platform, he figured he could rent a horse and buggy and be with Annalaura by three thirty. He nudged the gift box with his knee. The sturdy, rope-tied cardboard was stuffed full of presents for his family.

Every child had a complete outfit from underwear to shoes. Little Lottie even had bows for her hair. And, the doll, all made of cloth except for her head covered with real horsehair, would thrill his little girl. Henry had a fine wood-carved train. Cleveland would get a bone-handled knife. He knew Doug would take to the reading book he got for him. For Annalaura, he had gone wild.

Her pinafore was white with yellow trim over the ruffled parts that women liked. He had gotten her two dresses, one blue and one white to set it over. For the front of her pinafore, he bought a brooch that the man said was made of real shells from far-off California. And when he spread that money out on his bed, he could see her jumping in eagerness to let him scrub her all over with that sweet-smelling soap. He could already hear her moan her pleasure when he dabbed that rose water in all her secret places. Even Annalaura would grin and forgive him for being gone just a little longer than he wanted when she saw all that he was bringing home just for her.

John knew it was planting day even before the horse and buggy left Lawnover's wood-planked sidewalks. He could smell the new plowed earth, and the May air touched his face with just that right amount of warm and wet oozing out of it. The time was close to three thirty when he turned off the lane and up the path to the mid-forty barn. He reckoned Annalaura and the two older boys would be in the fields scattering seedlings right about now. He wondered if McNaughton had sense enough to put on some help for her.

He was surprised to see a tall, skinny boy of about ten standing just outside the smoke house door. The lad had apparently spotted the horse and buggy before John got a look at the child. There was something in the way the boy cocked his head to stare at the approaching buggy that told John the child's identity.

"Doug? That you, boy?" John jerked on the reins and the horse pulled up.

The child's eyes grew as big as a river lizard's. The smile coming from John was real.

"I swear, boy, I thought you was Cleveland, you is so big." John jumped down from the buggy, holding the reins in his hand.

"Papa? Papa is that really you?" His son's voice was still that of a child, and he was glad.

The troubles of a man would come on his boy soon enough. John wanted to make these last years of his Doug's childhood filled with some of the fun and ease the lad had missed.

"Well, what other man come ridin' up to yo' barn? 'Cose it's yo' papa." John swooped the boy into his arms, lifting his feet off the ground.

The child flung his arms around his father's neck.

"I knew you'd come back. I knew it mo' than anything." He squeezed his skinny arms all the tighter.

"Whoa, boy. You 'bout to choke me to death." John set the boy back on his feet and held him by his shoulders. "Whoee. You sho' have growed up. I hope all those new clothes I got fo' you will still fit." He jerked a head toward the box as he winked at his son.

Doug started toward the buggy, but with John's hands on his shoulders, his feet marked time in place. John's laugh boomed out in the afternoon sun.

"Papa, is you rich now?" Doug stopped his fruitless running and looked John up and down.

"Yo' papa's always been a rich man. I got you, yo' brothers, yo' little sister, Lottie, and yo' momma. It's just that now, I can show you all how rich I am."

The stunned look on Doug's face kept bringing on the pleasure. John couldn't stop the laughter, and it felt good. He hugged the boy again.

"Say, why ain't you in the fields? Ain't this the first day of plantin'?" He gave the boy a crooked half smile.

"How'd you know that? You must be a magic man and a rich man." The surprise on his son's face slowly gave way to a broadening smile.

John closed his eyes for an instant. All those Nashville months melted away in just this instant. He looked at his boy again.

"Is Cleveland in the fields with yo' momma?" Through all the joy he was feeling, the slim sound of silence broke through.

More curious than anything else, John stood up and walked around the buggy. With a hand over his eyes to block out the mid-afternoon sun, he scanned the fields near the path. Where were Annalaura and the other children? At least some of them should have been within seeing distance.

"Cleveland's plantin' tobacca with the new man and Momma's upstairs. She sent me down to bring up the pork chops."

For the first time, John saw the covered platter lying on the ground. Doug must have set it there when he first spotted the buggy.

"Pork chops? Where'd you all get pork chops in May?" That cracker McNaughton was being awful generous to the new hired man.

To get pork chops at the beginning of planting would have taken an advance so big that most tenants could never pay it back. Too excited to notice Doug's attempts at a stuttered answer, John grabbed the box from the buggy and headed into the barn.

Doug trotted along behind him. John barely noticed that there were now three cows in the stalls, and the oinking of the four sows in their pen just on the other side of the wall completely escaped his conscious mind in his haste to climb the ladder to the loft and Annalaura. He nearly stepped on one of the two dozen chickens in his way before he reached the bottom rung of the ladder.

"Papa's come home. Momma, Papa's back." Doug's high-pitched voice reached the landing before John could quietly slide the gift box on the floor.

He turned and tried to shush his son, just as the boy started his climb.

"Shh. Papa wants it to be a surprise." He was too late.

The oval-shaped face of a pigtailed girl of about six looked down at him.

First, the child scrunched her eyes in confusion then got down on one knee to peer at the face just coming into view. John put a finger to his lips to silence Lottie. But, like her brother, she was having none of it.

"Momma, Momma. It's Papa. I know it is. It's my papa." She jumped straight to her feet like a Jumpin' Jill.

John reached out a hand to stop his daughter from tumbling down the landing opening right on top of him. As he cleared the last rung, he picked her up as she wrapped both arms and both legs around him. The little girl covered his neck and face with kisses. He twirled Lottie around the room in a dance of triumph, bumping into a wall. He paid no notice as his eyes caught their first fleeting glimpse of Annalaura, but a full view of her was blocked by Henry hurtling at him faster than one of those Kentucky racehorses.

"Lottie, is he really my papa?" Little Henry pulled at the black high-topped shoe on his sister's foot.

The thought that the shoe was new and well fitted burst on his brain and fled when he saw Doug dive into the gift box.

"Papa brought us some presents," Doug announced as Lottie squirmed out of her father's arms and nearly ran over Henry getting to the box.

"Hold on, now. There's presents for everybody. Lottie, you and Henry, let Doug pass 'em out." He reached for his new breast pocket handkerchief when his eyes finally lit on the woman sitting at the table.

The kerosene lamp highlighted the little spray of sun coming from the window over Cleveland's alcove and played across her face. He was almost sure it was his Annalaura, but that look of surprise, mixed with a goodly amount of fright, confused him. He took a step toward her but stopped when he saw her face go pale underneath her brown skin.

"Annalaura, I knows I been gone awhile, but I can explain." Of all the faces he had pictured on his wife when she greeted his return, he hadn't seen this one.

He knew she'd be spitting mad, but this wasn't anger that he saw. He took another step toward her and thought she was going to fall right off that chair onto the floor. Chair? He remembered that when he left, the family only possessed two crates for sitting and no chairs. He waited for her to speak, and when her mouth looked like it was frozen into a face that had seen a lynching, John's heart picked up a pace. If it wasn't anger that he was seeing on Annalaura's face, then she must have passed anger and gone straight to don't care. He couldn't bear the thought. He unfastened the bottom button of his new suit and pulled out his shirt.

"Now, Annalaura, ain't no reason fo' you to take on so. I been workin' fo' us." John slipped a hand under the waistband of his pants and fumbled with his money belt. He undid the clasp and pulled out bills, piling them on the table. Fives, tens, and even twenties mounted. He kept his eyes on his wife who seemed to be barely breathing.

"Annalaura, darlin', I got us over a thousand dollars here." He swept his hand over the pile, knocking a few of the bills in her direction. "Sugar, we gonna get us our own place. Our own farm. Girl, stop yo' frownin' and let's get to dancin.'" He stepped around the table and pulled Annalaura from her chair.

His arm moved to encircle her waist.

"Mmm" strangled out of his voice box. "A... An..." His open hand lay inches from where her tight belly used to be. He stared at that big bulging thing that poked out in front of Annalaura.

The look of the living space rushed at him. He spotted the potbellied stove that hadn't been there when he left. He saw the tin of candied yams warming on the grate. The sweet scent of melting butter and sugar that should have filled his nostrils with pleasure brought only the taste of bile with it.

He tried to swallow but choked on a mouthful of nothingness. His arms moved without him willing them. He pushed Annalaura away.

"That." The word exploded out of him. He pointed at her stomach.

She stood stock-still.

"Annalaura?" The word squeaked out of him. Tears puddled in his wife's eyes. "Annalaura…you ain't…that…ba…you cain't…" He blinked his eyes to make the sight disappear. "What's in yo' belly, woman?" The words burst out of his dry throat.

He took in a deep breath, ready to hear that his wife had contracted some dreaded woman's disease. Something that men never learned about until their own women caught it. Something so terrible that it made the belly swell up like the woman had been poisoned. John grabbed the back of a second chair. His mind registered that the chair hadn't been there when he left. He swallowed, steeling himself, waiting for Annalaura to tell him that she was about to die of some awful thing that had no medicine cure.

"What's in there?"

She stood silent.

"What's inside you?" His voice clanged in his ears.

Annalaura's eyes turned in his direction.

"I want to know what's in yo' belly." He stepped toward her. "Tell me now, Annalaura. Damn it to hell, tell me now."

John didn't feel his arm move out from his shoulder, but he heard, rather than felt, the smacking sound the back of his hand made across Annalaura's cheek. He saw, rather than felt, her head snap back, and to the side as she stumbled against the wall that hadn't been there when he left. He sensed, rather than heard or felt, the commotion from his children behind him. He walked closer to his wife, the left side of her body punched into the wall, sliding down the whitewashed surface. Her hands hung limp in the folds of her dress. Her mouth stayed silent. Grabbing her shoulders, he roughly pulled her back to her feet.

"Annalaura, you ain't done this to me. Tell me in the name of God Almighty that you ain't done this to me." He didn't know how long he shook her, but the sound of her head banging against the wall finally entered his ears along with cries from either Lottie or Henry. He couldn't tell which. He spun his wife around and closer to the kerosene lamp on the table. His hand ran roughly over her stomach. The hardness greeting his touch caused him to throw her down on the table.

"Papa, no." He thought it was Lottie's scream this time, but it could just as well have been Doug. He pushed whoever it was away before he pulled Annalaura off the table and spun her around again. This time his arm flailed out at the other side of her face. The taste of someone else's blood felt strange flying onto his own lips.

"You ain't betrayed me, Annalaura. I know you ain't." He doubled his fist and smashed her in the right eye.

She began to slide down the wall again.

"You is the best woman in all this world." Pulling her to her feet again, his fist pounded at her left breast.

"You is the sweetest, smartest woman on all God's earth." There was moaning in his ears, but it wasn't coming from Annalaura. He had the strange impression that it was his own pain leaping out of some deep place.

"I would give this world fo' you. I done everythin' fo' you." This time his fist found her nose, then her chest, her ear, her eye.

Each time she slumped to the floor with her arms limp at her side. He pulled her to her feet. Still she said nothing.

"You gonna tell me, woman. You gonna tell me the bastard's name who give you this." He punched her in the stomach, the forehead, and with doubled fist, aimed back at her stomach.

Annalaura bent over and dropped to the floor, drawing her knees as close to her chest as she could.

"Kill me. Kill me, now. Just don't let yo' children see." She lay there with her eyes closed, ready.

"You damn right I'm gonna kill you, but I'm gonna kill that nigger first. I'm gonna kill him and make you watch." He reached down to drag her to her feet again when he felt something sharp jab him straight in the backside.

"Let her be. You ain't got no right to hit my momma. It was all 'cause of you." The voice crackled between boyhood and manhood.

John dropped Annalaura back to the floor and turned to look into the face of a wild-eyed twelve-year-old. The trembling boy held the pitchfork in his hands, and his eyes held the determined look of a man.

"Cleveland? Cleveland, is that you, boy?" He stared at his eldest, torn between joy and the most misery he had ever known. "Yo' momma, she..." Without taking his eyes off the boy, he gestured behind him to the fallen Annalaura.

"She did it fo' you. She did it fo' you." The boy's voice shook.

In his fear for his son, John searched out his other children. Over in the sleeping alcove, Doug held both Henry and Lottie close. Henry had his head buried under the bedcovers as he turned his back on the scene. Lottie and Doug sat frozen in terror. John knew it couldn't be helped. Someday he would explain their mother's betrayal, someday... Cleveland's words started to notch their way into his brain.

"Did it fo' me? What did she do fo' me, son?" He gained control over his voice.

"You ain't no good. You ain't no damn good." Cleveland jabbed the pitchfork in the air. "You left us all here to starve and freeze. You took all the money and all the food. What was she supposed to do?"

"Shut up, Cleveland. On your pa's life, shut up." Annalaura swayed despite her grip on the back of the chair.

John, startled, looked down at his now open palms. He lifted his head. Confusion roiled in his belly. The cupboards were full, his children wore new shoes and fresh clothes. He turned back to Annalaura.

"What did yo' momma do fo' me?" He glanced down at the floor where he stood. When he left, it had been full of knotholes. Now the boards were closely spaced, knot free, and good-sized rugs covered the sleeping places. How did Annalaura come by them? No Negro in Lawnover had money for such fancy this time of year, nor at any other time. No Negro…

"Cleveland, what did yo' momma do fo' me?" Fire and ice fought inside him.

"Cleveland." Annalaura croaked out the command.

John stared at the sleeping quarters. Where a thin sheet of cloth had been their only privacy, now stood a full wall and proper doorway.

"We was hungry," Cleveland called out. "We ain't had nothin' to eat but some dandelions in a whole pot of water. He gave her money and food and clothes fo' us. It was fo' us." The boy lowered the pitchfork, but John could see the firm grip his son still kept on the handle.

"No, son." Annalaura's knees buckled.

"If she hadn't let him stay, he was gonna throw us off the place." Cleveland's words came in jerks between sobs.

Out of the corner of his eye, John watched Lottie pull a porcelain-headed doll with light brown hair off Cleveland's bed and hug it to her little chest. Toys, food and plenty of it, new clothes. Even the dishes were new. He looked over at Annalaura who staggered to her feet. Her eyes stared frantic warnings at Cleveland.

"Boy…" John menaced.

"I'll tell you if you promise to never touch my momma again." Cleveland raised the pitchfork chest high. "If you don't, I'll kill you myself."

He turned to the woman he had always thought too good to be his wife. The swelling had almost closed both eyes shut. Blood ran from nose to mouth. A button was ripped off the bodice of her dress. A cut sliced across her forehead.

"You ain't had no right to go with no other man no matter what I done." The words croaked out.

Cleveland aimed the pitchfork directly at his back.

"I ain't meant to wrong you by leavin'. I did it fo' business, but if you think it was fo' somethin' else, then I reckon I'm sorry you didn't put mo' stock in me than that." Bile filled his throat. "But, ain't nothin' I could have done was so bad that you had to do this." Rage stoked his mind. "You ain't had no right to go with another man. You is my wife." He started toward her. The pitchfork scraped his side.

"She didn't go with another man." Cleveland's voice rose to the rafters. "Mr. Alex went with her."

"Say what?" John felt frozen in mid-step.

"She ain't had no say-so. Even I know that." Cleveland circled the pitchfork next to John's heart.

What difference did it make if his own son ran him through with a farm tool? His boy's words had already done that damage and more. "It's all right, boy. I ain't gonna touch…touch yo' momma if you is tellin' me that the owner of this here farm…Mc…he the one who…McN…bought all these things for you…Mm…and yo' momma. McNaughton." The name stuck in his throat.

"I am telling you that." Cleveland lowered the pitchfork.

Most of the air swept out of John's lungs. He turned to Annalaura and worked his mouth. Pictures flooded his head. Bad pictures. Awful pictures. His wife naked. White man...nak...

"I knows I wronged you, John." Annalaura stood behind the new kitchen chair, both hands on its back. "I knows I ain't never been the wife I should have been to you. I was just too 'shamed to tell you." The words came out of a mouth full of blood.

The roaring in John's ears made listening hard.

"Cleveland's tellin' you the truth. Mr. Alex did give us all this stuff, and he has been sniffin' around here a lot, and I knew what he wanted." She rubbed at her stomach. "You is right to beat me. He said he would bring food if I let him have breakfast here some mornings befo' I went to the fields."

"And you ain't known better than to trust a white man's word?" John nodded his head in disbelief.

"I know what you say is true. I was weak. I couldn't think how else to feed my children."

"And you let him climb into yo' bed...my bed...and give you a baby 'cause you was weak and couldn't think?" The rage roared back.

"No," Annalaura screamed as her figure swayed in front of his face. "What Cleveland saw was true. Mr. Alex was here in the mornings for breakfast, but this ain't his baby."

Out of the corner of his eye, John watched the surprise in Cleveland's face.

"This here ain't his baby." Pleading edged out of Annalaura's voice.

John inched closer. "A white man brings you food and gives you presents and you gonna tell me it ain't his baby? Who the hell baby is it then?"

His fists doubled up just as the pitchfork jabbed him in the small of the back.

"He was gonna throw us off the place if we didn't bring in the tobacco. You was gone fo' months. I thought you was never comin' back. Me, Cleveland, Doug, and Lottie worked so hard, but it wasn't enough. Even little Henry carried water to the fields. We just couldn't do it by ourselves, John." Her garbled voice rose to a shriek.

John nodded his no.

"Mr. Alex could see that. White men don't like to lose no money. He had to hire him an extra man just fo' the harvest." She ran out of air and had to stop to gulp in more.

"And?" Agitation rumbled in his chest. John turned to watch Cleveland.

The pitchfork lowered a fraction.

"I thought you was never comin' back. That I was too plain for a man like you." Her voice roamed over the loft. "That hired man make me feel like somethin' special. He talked real nice to me. Said sweet things to me." Annalaura struggled to grab in enough air to get out the rest of her words.

A pain thumped across John's chest.

"He wasn't good like you...you know...in the night." She gained control of her voice. "But I was lonely. He made me feel like a woman again." The tears started to fall.

Something wasn't right. Had his wife betrayed him with two men? Whose baby was this?

"The hired man? You laid with the hired man?" He advanced on her again. "If you is lying to me, Annalaura, I'll kill you." The pitchfork dug in deep enough to draw blood. John didn't care. "Where the hell is this Negro? What's his name? I'll beat the truth out of him, myself." He wanted to retrieve his valise from the buggy. His pistol lay inside.

The hard-to-understand words came out of Annalaura's mouth again.

"He ain't from around here. Kentucky. Gone back. Ask any-body." Her lips were now so swollen that he could barely hear her at all.

What was the truth? Had his wife slept, on purpose, with a colored hired man? Or, had she been forced into bed by a white man? She was lying, but about which one? He wanted to kill her and he wanted to take her in his arms all at the same time. He wanted to tell her how much he loved her. He turned to Cleve-land.

"Son, I ain't gonna hit yo' momma no mo'. But I ain't let-tin' her keep all this trash either. You can hold that pitch-fork on me all you like, but I'm throwing this junk out-ta here." John grabbed the kitchen chair from Annalaura's hands, walked to the landing, and tossed it down the ladder. "Doug, you and Lottie help me get rid of this mess while Cleve-land keeps hold of that pitchfork." As he swept up the new dish-es, he turned to his wife.

"I ain't sure who you laid with, but I do know it won't be me 'til I kill whoever he be. I ain't stayin' here tonight."

CHAPTER TWENTY

"Why did Papa throw my dolly away?" Lottie sat on the floor in front of Cleveland's alcove, her chin on Annalaura's shoulder.

Henry had his head in his mother's lap, his fingers rubbing at a spot of blood on her dress.

"Papa bought you a better doll, a prettier doll." It took all of Annalaura's fast-ebbing strength to calm her children's fears as she waited for John to thunder back into the house.

Her husband and Doug had wrestled almost everything Alex had given her down the ladder and out of the barn. The commotion had set the cows to mooing. John had even tried to dislodge the potbellied stove but, thankfully, even in his frantic state, he had realized that he couldn't put his hands on a red-hot stove. All of the clothes, pots, pans, toys, and especially the bed linens had been bundled up and dropped straight down the ladder opening. Annalaura reckoned that a better part of an hour had passed since John began sweeping the loft clean.

"But, why can't I keep both dolls?" Lottie, the tear tracks barely dry on her face, kicked at the doll John had pulled from his valise, knocking off one of the button eyes in the process.

Lottie had screamed in confusion and fright when her father snatched the other doll from her hands.

"Why is Papa mad at us, Momma?" Henry raised up from her lap and let his hand dab lightly at the swelling place on her cheek. "Did we do somethin' very, very bad?" Fright leapt out of the boy's eyes.

Annalaura laid her hand against his skinny wrist and let her youngest's open palm rest on her bruised cheek.

"Hush, now, both of you. Papa's not mad at any of you all." She slipped an arm around Lottie and pulled her tighter, though Annalaura's ribs pained her so much she could barely take in a breath.

"Papa's mad at Cleveland. I know he is 'cause Cleve's 'bout to stick him with that fork." Lottie started to whimper.

"No such thing. It's just that Papa's been gone so long, and he left me to take care of everthin' here and I didn't do a good 'nough job of it. It's me Papa's mad at, not you all." She hugged both children, but this time she couldn't stop the little cry of pain that made its way out of her mouth.

"But you took care of us good, Momma. Why ain't Papa happy?" Lottie ran her hand over Annalaura's torn dress.

"I done the best I could, but it's not what Papa wanted. He'll be mad fo' a little while, then he'll be back laughin' and playin' with you children befo' you know it." Annalaura didn't believe a word she had just uttered. Maybe these two young ones would take her story for truth, but Doug and Cleveland would be ten times harder to convince.

"He gone, Momma. Say he won't be back 'til he ki..." Doug, just clearing the last rung of the ladder, looked toward the little group sitting on the floor. "He say he won't be back 'til after he k-i-l-l the man."

Annalaura closed her eyes and wondered why she wanted to smile when Armageddon was falling all over her head. Thanks to Alex, her second son had finished a whole year of school, and the colored teacher told her that Doug could read, write, do his numbers, and spell better than most third graders.

"How you know he gone?" She let her sore face brush the top of Lottie's pigtails.

"He made me pile everthin' down by the lane and he took off in his buggy. He say he might k-i-l-l him two men." Doug dropped to the floor in front of Annalaura. He pushed the heads of Lottie and Henry deeper into their mother's body. "He took his pistol with him."

Annalaura had shown tears to John, but that was just to buy herself time to work out a plan that would keep her hotheaded husband alive. She tried to move the little ones away, but fell back against the alcove.

"What's the matter, Momma?" Henry jumped off her lap. "I won't hurt you. I won't hurt you, never." He threw his arms around her neck sending shoots of pain through half her body.

She kissed the tip of his ear. "Help me get to my feet. We got to go."

With Doug pulling and Lottie and Henry pushing, she struggled upright.

"Get yo' coats." Then, she remembered.

John had taken all their clothes, except what they had on their backs. "Never mind."

"Momma, where is we goin'?" Doug went down first and waited for Lottie, then Henry, to follow.

"Aunt Becky's." Annalaura started down. With each step jarring something loose in her belly.

The sun told her the time was about five o'clock, and the white farmers at the planting dinner should be heading to the Lawnover tavern for more celebrating. With the misery of her swelling eye shooting pain down the side of her face, Annalaura focused on the day of the week. Today was one of the times Alex had agreed to stay away from the barn, but he had made a poor job of honoring his promise to visit no more than one night a week. Most weeks, he came three, and sometimes four, evenings. Some nights, he just laid with her in his arms, whispering sweet things, and nothing more. Those were the times when she most had to remind herself just who Alex was.

Her feet weren't carrying her as fast as she needed. Now, everything on her hurt, and it had taken her almost five minutes to walk the little distance down the path to the lane. Standing over the pile of the family's former belongings, she spotted Cleveland, the pitchfork still in his hands. She saw little Lottie crane her neck toward the pile, her eyes searching for her lost doll. When Annalaura finally reached her eldest son, she slipped an arm around his shoulders and kissed his forehead.

"I knows you is too big to kiss, but I thanks you fo' what you done today." She whispered. "But I don't never want to see, nor hear tell, of you raisin' a hand against yo' father again. This fuss is between him and me. It ain't got nothin' to do with you." She let him go but kept a hand on his shoulder.

"I ain't never gonna let any man beat you like that ever again." Cleveland wagged his head at her.

"Cleveland, this ain't yo' worry, but I do have to ask a big favor of you." She squeezed the back of his shoulder. "I wants you to tell these words to Mr. Alex 'xactly like I tells them to you." The top of her boy's head still only came to the tip of her nose. To Annalaura, he was still her baby.

"Yes'm." His voice sounded deeper.

"Now, I'm thinkin' Mr. Alex shouldn't be botherin' us tonight, but if he do come, this is what I wants you to tell him."

Cleveland dug the pitchfork into the dirt next to the pile of clothes, chairs, toys, and even books. He kept both hands on the handle and leaned over it.

"Tell him that yo' papa, John Welles, is home. Tell him that John has a pistol with him." She stopped to make sure Cleveland understood the words.

"I can tell him that, Momma." Cleveland put a foot on the fork and pushed it deeper into the ground.

"Tell him the gun is fo' the hired hand, Isaiah Harris." Pain in her ribs rocked Annalaura. "Say to Mr. Alex, John is lookin' fo' the father. Isaiah." She waited for that glimpse of agreement in her son's eyes. "Tell it back to me, son."

"Papa's home, and he got a gun and he's goin' after Mr. Harris. I knows what to say, Momma." He looked down at the fork and the little piles of dirt it had scuffed up.

"That's good, son, but there is mo'. Make sure Mr. Alex knows that it ain't in yo' papa's head to do no harm to nobody else. He just wants to talk to Isaiah Harris. You understand that, Cleveland?"

"No, Momma. I don't understand. Papa said he might kill him two men. Ain't one of 'em Mr. Alex?" Cleveland stared straight at her.

She cupped her boy's face in her hands and pressed hard into his cheeks.

"Cleveland, you is twelve, and you is old enough to understand that no colored man can never, ever even think harm comin' to a white man. If the words come out of a black man's mouth, even if he don't really mean them, terrible, terrible things could happen. Things worse than cuttin' off the head of John the Baptist."

"Almost as bad as Jesus dyin' on the cross?" Cleveland's eyes grew large.

"Just 'bout as bad. What you think you heard yo' papa say ain't what he really means. No need to tell that to Mr. Alex, now is there?"

"No'm." Cleveland grimaced, and Annalaura loosened her grip.

"Make sure Mr. Alex knows that yo' papa only wants to speak to the hired man. Just the hired man. And, Cleveland, one mo' thing. Tell Mr. Alex it would be a kindness to me if he wouldn't tell nobody else that John is back with a pistol. Tell him I'd be pleased to have him visit us in the fields next week after my husband has come back to himself but not a day befo'." She tightened her grip on his cheeks again. "Cleveland, can you 'member all that? Mr. Alex ain't to come here fo' breakfast never no mo'."

Her son's hand reached for her wrist and broke her hold.

"Momma, I remembers every word."

CHAPTER TWENTY-ONE

The walk up the lane had taken the better part of an hour because of Annalaura. Her good sense told her that she had to get to Aunt Becky before John came back with the truth. She didn't need to lift her bruised face toward the sky to tell her that the sun was about to set on this day in no more than three hours. But the faster she walked on the wagon-rutted dirt road, the more air she had to take in, and with each breath, the more her ribs hurt. Doug had done a good job of keeping the young ones from overly fretting each time she stopped to steady herself at road edge. When they reached Thornton land, and Aunt Becky's cabin, Doug called out to the old woman, but all three children knocked and kicked at the door. Becky, with her all-seeing eyes, took one look at her niece and buried the scowl that crossed her brow.

"I knows it's too early fo' supper. Not but six o'clock, but I bets you chil'ren would like some peach preserves on some of Aunt Becky's biscuits, now wouldn't you?" Rebecca's voice did not match her face. "You all come set a spell."

Auntie slathered preserves on bread, grabbed two shawls to warm the children, and shoved all three outside. Annalaura eased herself onto the wrought-iron bed, grateful to Rebecca.

"Gal, let me take a look at them cuts." Becky rushed over to Annalaura, her arms full of jars and a tin box. She set them all down next to the pitcher of cool water. "What he hit you with?" Rebecca turned up the wick of the kerosene lamp set on a crate by the bed.

"Umm." Annalaura grimaced.

Becky stood over her niece. The woman's hands lifted Annalaura's chin. Rebecca took a quick look at the battered face, then ran her hands from neck to waist. "Don't look like mo' than his fists, but he done punched you in the belly."

"Aahh." Annalaura grimaced as another pain went through her middle.

With hands flying like they were thirty years younger, Becky opened jars and began mixing ointments, salves, and foul-smelling liquids on the upturned lid of one Mason jar. With her quick fingers, she dabbed Annalaura's cuts. Auntie opened another jar and poured a small amount of honey-thick unguent into the palm of one hand. She rubbed her hands together and patted the lotion all over Annalaura's bruised and battered places.

"Don't look like he touched the chil'ren, praise the Lawd. Bad business when a white man beat on you. If he gets mad 'nough, he takes it out on the whole family. Gal, did you tell him no when you shoulda said yes?" Becky's hands skimmed over Annalaura's lower body. "Ain't nothin' broke." Her inspection done, she sat on the bed beside her niece.

Whatever her aunt had doused over her started its work. Annalaura let her heavy eyelids close. Becky's fuzzy words swept in and out of her ears. Annalaura struggled to ease herself up in the bed. This was not the time to give in to sleep. She pushed away the damp cloth Becky tapped over her eyes.

"White man?" Her aunt's words registered in her head. "No. Alex ain't never hit me. John ..." She fell back onto Becky's feather pillow.

"Say what? If it wasn't McNaughton, who was...?"

"God help me, Aunt Becky. John, he's back." She could feel her tongue swell in her mouth.

"What you sayin'? John Welles is back, and he done found you like this?" Becky pressed open the tin box and took out a pinch of dried leaves. She dipped them in a fresh-poured cup of water and lifted the scruffy enameled container to Annalaura's lips. The elixir poured over Annalaura's chin, and down the front of her dress. She lifted a hand to right the cup.

"I ain't told him who it was." Annalaura managed a sip just as another pain gripped her midsection.

"John's back, Lawd Almighty. It's troubles. Troubles." Becky closed her eyes and began to rock on the bed.

In a voice so tiny it could barely be heard, the old Cherokee began to mutter words that Annalaura knew weren't English. Annalaura propped herself on the pillow and raised her voice as loud as she could muster.

"John. He don't know 'bout the father."

"Hard to keep a man from knowin' who the daddy. When a man think it ain't him, he gonna worry everybody 'til he finds out who. Old Ben Thornton, he knew 'bout Johnny." Becky's eyes refocused on Annalaura's face. She reached over again and wet the cloth in the tea mixture and laid it over her niece's eyes.

"The hired man. I told John it was the hired man." Annalaura felt Becky press gently down on the wet cloth, and its coolness soothed her.

"Hmm. Hired man, you say? That's good 'nough fo' a beatin' but not a killin'." Becky kept the cloth over Annalaura's face. "How long 'til yo' John find this hired man, and the truth?" She pulled the cloth away.

"I pray to God he don't never find out. I hear Isaiah gone home to Kentucky." Another pain wracked her, and she rolled to her side and drew up her knees.

"You'd better be hopin' that baby ain't comin'. That them pains is just from the blow he put on you." Becky handed the blue enameled cup to her niece as she moved toward the kitchen safe.

Annalaura heard her aunt rummaging through the drawers and shelves. Becky returned to stand over the bed.

"I'm goin' to Hettie's. Takin' the children with me," Becky announced.

"The children?" Annalaura's heart thumped through her sore ribs. "You can't take them to Hettie. Mr. Ben Roy will ask what they doin' there. You knows Mr. Ben Roy's a beatin' man. He'll make Hettie or the children tell him. If he finds out John's back with a pistol…" Annalaura grabbed the cloth and laid it tight over her forehead.

"Ben Roy?" Becky let a little smile creep across her face when Annalaura slid the cloth up her forehead to peek at her aunt. "Ain't no need to be 'fraid of Ben Roy. I still got the paper hid real good."

A new shot of fear filled Annalaura. "Aunt Becky. I can't have my children with Hettie if Mr. Ben Roy is at her cabin. It won't take nothin' but a minute fo' him to find out 'bout… 'bout…"

Rebecca's eyes began their backward shift to that other place where her mind sometimes dwelled.

"I done tole you, don't worry none 'bout Ben Roy Thornton. I gots the paper hid real good."

"What paper, Auntie?" Annalaura raised herself on the feather pillow, resting her back against its softness. She reached out a hand to pull Becky down to her. If she could lay her hands against skin, look the old woman straight in the eye, maybe she could bring her back before her auntie's lost mind put her children in harm's way.

"I'm takin' yo' chil'ren to Hettie's, then I'm gonna look fo' some of them herbs what will keep that baby from comin'. Baby ain't ripe yet." Becky jerked her arm away.

"It ain't the baby." Annalaura regretted the scream that forced itself through her broken lips. "I know when a baby's coming. I done had fo' of them. This don't feel nothin' like that. These pains will go away directly." A spasm rocked Annalaura. "Doug can watch the little ones while you go fo' the medicines. No need to bother with Hettie." Another pain jolted her body.

"Might be you can't stay here. Might be best fo' you to get gone." Becky's eyes were halfway to that other place. "Ben Roy's buggy. I'll speak to him." Becky turned toward the center of the room while Annalaura frantically reached out to grab her arm.

"No, Auntie. Don't go botherin' Mr. Ben Roy." The effort had lurched her to the edge of the bed, and a cramp in her stomach caught and held her breath.

"You don't know nothin' 'bout it, do you, girl?" Becky moved back to the safe and dropped to her knees. Bending down, she pulled out a lower drawer and swept an arm inside.

Fighting the spasm that didn't want to let her go, Annalaura heard Becky tapping on something for long seconds. She turned her head just enough to catch Rebecca's crooked grin as her aunt slammed the drawer shut and stood up. Her hands empty, Rebecca walked back to the bed.

"I ain't never tole you straight out, but I reckon it's time you finds out." Becky sat down beside her niece. "Ben Roy do what I say 'cause I got the paper." Becky looked toward the safe.

"The herbs, Aunt Becky. Go get 'em." Annalaura didn't know which hurt more, the pains in her body growing worse every five minutes, or her aunt, lost in that other world. "I got to get my head clear so I can keep John from this bad trouble I done made fo' him. Aunt Becky, I needs you to help me figure out what's best."

"I is helpin' you, girl. I'm takin' Ben Roy's buggy."

Annalaura snapped her hand around Becky's skinny arm. The shadows lurking in her mind of Alex shot dead and John Welles hanging from a tree, all because she hadn't tried hard enough to outmaneuver Alex, flooded into her head.

"Old Ben give 'most five hundred dollars for that horse." Becky's eyes stared at a far corner of the bed.

"Umm." With Rebecca sliding to that other place, Annalaura had to conserve what little strength she had to think of a way to keep John and Alex apart. "Aunt Becky, John gonna find out real soon 'bout the hired man." Why was the old woman rambling about events long past when fresh disaster faced them all in a day's time?

"Five hundred dollars, he did." Becky rocked on the bed.

"I need help. I got to find me a way to get that gun away from John befo' he…befo' he kills Al…I can't allow that." Annalaura pinched down hard on her aunt's arm. "But I can't do nothin' 'til these hurts leave me. Please get me some of yo' herbs?"

"Help you?" Becky patted Annalaura's arm. "That's what I'm tellin' you, gal. Ben Roy gonna give us the buggy. I'm gonna find someplace to put you 'til the baby come. Someplace where yo' John can't find you. Alexander McNaughton neither." Becky stood and walked to the door, where Lottie, Henry, and Doug snuggled under her warm wraps.

Annalaura eased up in bed and struggled to dangle her feet over the edge of the mattress. She couldn't let Becky take her children.

"Not Mr. Ben Roy. Please don't go to Hettie. Mr. Ben Roy could be there." The pain in her ribs wrenched the breath out of her.

Almost at the door, Rebecca turned back toward her.

"Ain't you heard nothin' I said? Ben Roy ain't gonna tell nobody a word, and he ain't gonna start no white man's ruckus either 'cause he knows what I know." With quick steps Becky crossed the floor and sat down on the bed beside her niece. She slipped an arm around Annalaura's shoulders and leaned her niece's head against her chest. Her aunt's comforting arms helped ease some of the pain.

"I'm takin' yo' chil'ren to Hettie. I'm gonna take Ben Roy's buggy to find somebody to take you in fo' one or two weeks 'til yo' baby come. Where can't neither John nor Mr. Alexander get to you. Baby stay with them awhile. If the baby's color come in dark, maybe John might let you bring it back. Now, I'm gonna pick you some herbs to keep that baby in you 'til its time. Ben Roy ain't gonna bother none of yo' chil'ren, 'cause he know I got the paper."

CHAPTER TWENTY-TWO

The sun readied to shut down for the day, though Alex had tried by hours to beat its demise, and get back to the mid-forty. After dropping the new hired man off there right before sunup, he had spent the time before the planting and prayer dinner setting up the rest of his acres. He hadn't even gotten to the Thornton place until close to three o'clock. With Reverend Hawkins droning his prayer a good thirty minutes, the dinner hadn't been over 'til way past six. After asking Tillie and Wiley George to check on Eula, who had strangely gone home before he arrived, Alex finally made his excuses and left to pick up the hired man and bring him back to the main barn. Since Eula had taken the buckboard, he borrowed Ben Roy's high-seated wagon and Fedora's slow-stepping mare.

Alex watched the day's shadows grow longer as he whipped at the horse. If he could get to the mid-forty twenty minutes before nightfall, he might find Laura before the hired man came in from sowing seed. He knew this was not one of those nights she had agreed to his staying, but a quick kiss and a touch could do no harm to the baby. He gave the reins two rapid flicks, but Fedora's horse, unaccustomed to a quick pace, decided to slow down even more. Wishing for the gray, Alex finally marshaled the old animal down the lane. He trained his eyes on every foot of the familiar road knowing that when he cleared the stand of sycamores a hundred yards distant, the path to the mid-forty would be no more than a minute's ride away. He looked up at a sky filled with deepening reds, oranges, and yellows. Alex reckoned he still had fifteen minutes of daylight before cooling evening arrived. He hoped the hired man was as good a worker as he pretended, and wouldn't leave the new-plowed fields until after the sun had settled in for the night.

In answer to Alex's constant snap at her flank, the horse finally got the message and quickened her pace. With the sycamores behind him, he spotted the path and the figure of a standing child, dwarfed by a large pile of what looked like household furnishings. Sticking out of the heap were the four wooden legs of a chair turned bottom-side up. As Alex neared the path, he pulled on the reins so hard the horse nearly reared up on her hind legs. Young Cleveland took a half step forward to greet him.

"What's this?" Puzzled, Alex pointed to the pots, shoes, coats, skillets, quilts, dresses, cotton sheets, dolls, and dishes.

Half buried beneath the blanket that just two days ago had served as the cover separating the open alcove doorway from the rest of the living quarters was Laura's blue serge coat. The new hired man, sitting on the ground at the edge of the pile, stood up, removed his sweat-stained straw hat, and walked a few steps back into the fields. He could feel the man's eyes sidle in his direction. Alex grunted his dissatisfaction at the tenant's too-early quitting time. Cleveland looked at the family's belongings and then turned back, his eyes staring down at the wheels on the buckboard. The boy shrugged his shoulders as Alex followed the tilt of the lad's head.

"Momma says to tell you that my papa done come home."

Alex shook his head trying to clear his ears. The boy stood somewhere between pleased, confused, and frightened.

"Your papa? John Welles is home?" The man had been gone almost a year without a word to anyone. What the hell was the nigger doing back in Lawnover? Alex pulled out his big square handkerchief and swiped it across his forehead.

Cleveland nodded his head. Welles back in town, and for what? Alex looked at the tumble of clothes and furniture. Whatever brought the nigger back to town couldn't hold a man like him for long. Unless... Alex glanced over at the hired man who stood flat-footed, slowly twisting his hat in his hands. Welles was no ordinary hired hand. He would never stand there holding a cap with his neck bowed like he meant it. John Welles would always tip that head just short of respectful or let those eyes roll up a little bit too high. An uppity nigger like John Welles was nothing but trouble. Alex took another look at Cleveland and sat up in the buckboard. The boy dragged the toe of his shoe back and forth in the dirt.

"Welles is home?" The question wrenched Alex's body just as much as the first time he asked.

"Yes, suh, he done come home. Momma say to tell you that he lookin' for Mr. Harris."

"Harris? You talkin' 'bout the hired man that helped bring in last fall's harvest?" The very man Laura had claimed as father of their baby?

Alex peered at Cleveland. Laura must have told John Welles the same story she tried to peddle to him about who'd fathered her baby. He jumped down from the buckboard and walked over to Cleveland, laying a hand on the boy's shoulder. Out of the corner of his eye, he spotted the half-surprised, half-scared look on the face of the hired man.

"What else did your momma tell you to say, and why ain't she here tellin' me all this herself?"

Cleveland raised his eyes to Alex's shoulder. "She say that I is to tell you that papa have a gun, but it's just to take with him when he go to talk to Mr. Harris." The boy recited the words his mother most likely put in his mouth.

Alex kept his hand on the boy.

"Momma say the gun ain't fo' hurtin' nobody. Not even Mr. Harris. She say Papa just a little upset with that hired hand."

"Gun? You say yo' papa's runnin' the countryside with a pistol?" Alex lifted his eyes to the barn window. "Is your momma in the barn?" He took a step up the path while the hired man walked even deeper into the darkening rows of new-sown seed.

"No, suh. She ain't in the barn." Cleveland's voice sounded alarm. "She took Doug and the little ones over to Aunt Becky's."

"Where's your papa? Did he go with Laura?" Alex dismissed his misspeak. Calling Annalaura by the special name he'd given her could make no difference to any of them if John Welles really was back, and with a pistol.

Cleveland stood silent. Alex walked toward the barn, rushing thoughts flooding his head. Welles was going after the man Laura claimed to be the father of her baby. A nigger, a pistol, a wife big with another man's baby were a dangerous combination. Alex stopped and stared at the window in the loft—that very same window where the moon had played its silvery light across Laura's naked body when the two made love. A dozen horrors ran through his mind. What had Welles done to Laura?

He struggled to keep his face and body still as he turned back to Cleveland. One thing was certain. John Welles could not stay long in Lawnover.

"Is your papa with your mother?" He whirled around to Cleveland.

"No suh, he ain't." The boy finally answered. "Don't rightly know where he is. Momma say Mr. Harris might be in Kentucky."

If the boy was telling the truth, Alex thanked God. Laura was safe for now. He gestured to the hired man to climb into the wagon. The beginnings of a plan laid itself out in his mind. John Welles couldn't be allowed to stay in Lawnover. He couldn't be allowed to lay claim to Laura.

"Momma say I was to ask you one mo' thing." The boy's voice was a whisper as the hired man sat in the back of the buckboard, his knees hunched up to his chin, his face turned toward the chirp of a night bird.

"Yeah?"

"She say it would please her most kindly, suh, if you come visit us in the fields next week, but not a day befo'. She say, it might be good if you don't visit fo' breakfast no time soon, neither." Cleveland sucked in a lip. "One last thing, Mr. Alex, suh. Momma say please kindly take these things away."

The Lawnover store hadn't changed much in the thirty years Alex had gone in and out of its doors, other than that Bobby E. Lee Thompson ran it now since his daddy, Andrew Jackson Thompson, died some ten years back. The building still had that big main room that sold everything from galvanized nails to barrels of brined pigs' feet to baling wire to calico cloth for the women. The two windows on opposite sides of its walls, along with the kerosene lamp that burned even in the daytime, gave the place enough light so a woman could tell blue thread from black. Bobby Lee and his wife worked the store pretty much through all the daylight hours six days a week, twelve months a year. During the busy times, like right after the money came in for harvest and when supplies were needed to set up the hired hands for planting, Bobby Lee would take on extra help from some of the poor whites down by the tracks.

Bobby Lee only allowed colored to come in two at a time and that was only a man and a woman, or two women together, but never two colored men at once. No matter how many niggers were lined up outside, and sometimes there might be a dozen or more, or how many were inside, Alex knew they had to step aside when he walked up to the counter. Even if the colored woman had her calico yard goods already cut for her and her coins on the countertop ready to push to Bobby Lee's wife, careful not to let black hands touch white, she would have to stand aside 'til he got his business done.

Between his and the Thornton farms, the Lawnover store was the only buying place for five miles around, for either colored or white. Every farmer in the area had to stop by Bobby Lee's at least once a month for supplies. It hadn't been two weeks since he brought Eula by to pick up some lard and some sugar while he went to the blacksmith shop to repair the rein for the gray.

Tonight, it was after dark and the main business at the Lawnover store was over. The front door was closed and latched. Once he dropped off the hired man at the McNaughton barn, Alex switched over to Eula's horse and rig. Coaxing the buckboard and the wheezing horse around back of Bobby Lee's, he led the animal to the water trough. Inside the store he heard the guffaws.

On just about every Friday and Saturday night when it wasn't harvest or planting time, Bobby Lee opened up his back room for poker games. Most game nights, five or six of the farmers would gather. But the first day of planting was special. After all that planting and praying, the men needed to end the evening with a little fun. Bobby Lee might have twelve or fifteen farmers in the store tonight. If he did, he would put the overflow into the store's main room. Only the regulars like Ben Roy got the use of the back room.

While Eula's horse was taking in water, Alex walked across the way from the hitching post to the log-hewn building. The light from the lamps shone through all three windows, even though curtains covered only the one in the back gaming room.

It took Alex a few seconds after he opened the back door to spot Ben Roy through the brown cloud of cigar, cigarette, and pipe smoke. The kerosene lamp sitting on a highboy right over Ben Roy's left shoulder shone directly at the back door and at any newcomer. Those already in the room knew who had entered long before the late arrival could make out the outlines of the pork and pickle barrels lining the walls.

"Alex, 'bout time you got yo' ass over here. Come on and set a spell." Ben Roy had left the planting party at his own home no more than thirty minutes before Alex, yet he was already halfway into a tall Mason jar of Tennessee whiskey. His eyes finally adjusting to the glare, Alex made out the uncovered planked wood table set in the center of the room surrounded by boxes and barrels piled shoulder-high to the timbered ceiling. He made his way around a big barrel of sweet-smelling sorghum molasses and another of pickling hog heads. Ben Roy, Wiley George, two other Thornton kin, a farmer from down county, and Bobby Lee were already sitting around the table, with Ben Roy fumbling with a deck of cards. Bobby Lee grabbed a Mason jar of whiskey as he scuffed his chair backward to stand. Clapping Alex on the back, he almost pushed him into the vacated chair.

"Here's hopin' your new hired nigger sticks it out this time." Bobby Lee reached for the first in a line of empty Mason jars standing next to the kerosene lamp behind Ben Roy's head. Bobby Lee handed the container to Alex. "If that nigger don't work out, I got another one been 'round here beggin' fo' a place to farm." Bobby Lee took a swig of his own homegrown mash liquor and walked through the door into the front of the store where, judging from the cursing, spitting, and laughing, the second poker game was heating up.

"We're playin' five-card stud, no deuces wild." Ben Roy tapped the table. A mound of greenbacks lay in the center.

Alex frowned. Big money like that usually was gambled only after harvest. Planting time most often meant quarters and half dollars, but any game with Ben Roy usually called for betting more than most farmers wanted. Winning or losing at gambling was not what had brought Alex to Lawnover this night, but he had to bide his time. He pulled out a crumpled dollar bill from his overalls pocket and tossed it on top of the money pile.

"Hey, Bobby Lee. Send Hettie in here." Ben Roy shuffled the cards as his shout went through the closed door into the main room.

"I sho' hope to hell you give me some better cards than you did last time." Wiley George looked like he was enjoying the aftermath of his second Thornton family planting party just a little too much.

Alex saw the other Thornton kin shoot the boy a warning look.

"It ain't the cards, you dumb bastard. You hold your liquor worse than a ho in a white trash bawdy house." Ben Roy chomped down on his cigar as he deliberately blew a large puff of smoke into his son-in-law's face.

Wiley George turned his head and took another gulp from his Mason jar. Ben Roy slapped a card face down in front of Alex.

"Lay offen him, Ben Roy. You know Tillie and that new baby got him goin'." The Thornton middle son, who thought he was the better man with his fists, challenged Ben Roy.

Another card slipped down in front of Alex, its blue-patterned back staring up at him. He let his eyes travel around the table checking on how much liquor had been consumed. This was not the night he wanted the Thornton boys engaged in one of their usual brawls. He needed them at least part of the way sober to hear what he had to say.

"I reckon I know what's got Wiley George goin' as good as you do." Ben Roy grunted at his younger brother just as Hettie opened the door carrying a big jug in one hand and a platter of leftover fried chicken in the other.

"Set that chicken plate down and pour us some more whiskey, gal." Ben Roy barely looked at his woman as he laid a third card in front of Alex.

Hettie bobbed her head as she circled the table behind the men, refilling each glass jar. As she poured Bobby Lee's home brew, Alex sneaked quick glances at the woman every man at that table knew Ben Roy had bedded for six years. Her brown skin may have been a shade fairer than Laura's, and her hair might have been a degree less crinkly. It was hard to tell about the shape of her body since she still carried much of the weight of her last pregnancy. But, remembering her from before, Alex could tell Hettie's body had never been a match for his Laura's curves and firmness.

He admitted that Ben Roy's Hettie once had a bit of prettiness about her, but that had faded over the years. He looked up toward her eyes. Sensing his glance, she looked back at him, paled, became flustered, remembered her place, and hurriedly backed away. Ben Roy hadn't noticed any of his woman's antics as he laid the fourth card before Alex.

"Wiley George, you think you gonna need some help readin' them cards?" Ben Roy snickered at his son-in-law as he placed the fifth and last card in front of Alex.

"Don't need no help readin' aces and kings." Wiley George clipped off the answering challenge.

Everybody knew that Ben Roy hadn't exactly approved of Tillie's marriage to the Jamison boy, just as he'd never fully accepted Alex into the Thornton ranks. Both the Jamisons and the McNaughtons farmed acres too few and too poor to be in league with the Thorntons. Alex recognized the taunts Ben Roy tossed at Wiley as the same ones he'd fielded himself more times than he cared to remember. Alex picked up his poker cards. Besides a pair of nines, he held only an ace, queen, and jack, all of mixed suits. Gambling had never meant anything to him other than throwing away good money. Sometimes, he thought that was the reason Ben Roy insisted that he sit in on the poker games with him. It was just another opportunity to flaunt the Thornton money in front of a struggling in-law.

"If you readin' aces and kings, Wiley George, sweeten the pot." The Thornton cousin sat with his lids half closed.

"Big talk is the onliest thing Wiley George got of any size on him. Everything else is puny." Ben Roy guffawed at his own slight of his daughter's husband. He pulled out another dollar bill from his work shirt pocket and pitched it onto the pile of money in the center of the table.

Hettie, the jug now almost empty, turned to leave. Without looking in her direction, Ben Roy jerked hard on a handful of skirt. As she stumbled toward him, he lifted the back of the garment and ran his hand up the inside of her legs and jammed it hard into her crotch. Hettie flinched. A little grunt escape her mouth as Ben Roy rubbed his hand back and forth between her thighs. He let the skirt fall back in place as he delivered a smack across her butt hard enough to push the unhappy woman against the edge of the round table.

"Now, git," he commanded as he looked around the table for player hits.

The younger Thornton brother signaled for two card replacements while Alex stared at his own. Despite his poor poker-playing skills, he had to play it smart tonight. When Ben Roy trained his eyes on him, Alex discarded the three face cards and kept his pair of nines.

"You either got a hell of a hand or you need help readin' them cards like Wiley George." Ben Roy stubbed out his cigar and tossed it in the spittoon.

Alex picked up a jack, a seven, and a third nine. All Thornton eyes were trained on him. With his trio of nines he doubted he could beat a Thornton hand, but they were waiting for him to add to the pot. He reached back into his overalls pocket and pulled out a silver dollar. The thud it made as it crashed into the mound of bills was the only sound coming from him. If he'd learned one thing in twenty years of poker playing against Ben Roy, it was to keep a straight face and do almost no talking, no matter how hard his brother-in-law pushed.

"Bobby Lee ain't skimpy with his liquor. Take yo'self a drink, Alex." Ben Roy dealt himself one card before his eyes scanned the table for new hits.

Funny, Alex reminded himself, how Ben Roy's flat, brown eyes looked just like Eula's. Looking into them was like looking into the bottom of a dirty coal pail.

As if by invitation, the belly-bulging down county farmer picked up his Mason jar and drained it empty. All in a pile, the farmer spread out his cards—two pairs—one of eights, the other of fours. The man clamped both hands around the empty Mason jar. Wiley George threw his cards on the table in disgust. A little grin started to play across the farmer's face as he eased up on his grip of the Mason jar and leaned toward the mound of bills.

"Well…" The broad-shouldered Thornton cousin drew out the word as though it had four syllables as he laid his cards on the table. Three sevens showed their faces.

A grimace flickered across Ben Roy's lips but disappeared. He turned down his cards. The younger Thornton brother reached for his own Mason jar. The down county farmer looked as though his prized sow had just been shot. Once again, all eyes at the table waited for Alex. He checked his cards again—a seven, a jack, and three nines still remained in his hand. Slowly, he spread them on the table.

"I'll be damned," Ben Roy exploded, "if brother-in-law ain't won a round." He pushed the pile of money toward Alex while the older cousin scowled. "Hettie, gal, get yo' ass in here." Ben Roy pulled at the string dangling from his pocket and lifted out the packet of chewing tobacco. He pinched off a wad and popped it into his mouth.

With as much casualness as he could muster, Alex slid the entire pile of money back to the center of the table. He needed far more than money this night. "Let it ride. Deal, Ben Roy."

As the playing cards circulated to the left, Alex studied each man trying to judge the best time to bring up the subject. Liquor was having its way, with Wiley George leading the pack. After losing the last hand, the down county farmer looked even more glum and desperate as he tapped at his empty glass. The Thornton kin still held sober enough heads. Ben Roy was the key to getting rid of Welles. The fifth card landed just beside Alex's hand. He picked up all five. An ace, two queens, and two tens greeted him. He knew he already held a better than decent hand as he picked up his untouched Mason jar and brought it to his lips. He saw Ben Roy give him just the slightest nod of approval as the dealer scanned the table for hits.

"Damn it to hell, Ben Roy. Can every goddam card you deal me be this bad?" Wiley George threw down four of his five cards.

"Watch yo' mouth." Ben Roy's younger brother looked out from under his sandy brows to warn his niece's husband.

"He don't mean nothin' by it. Wiley George is just havin' a bad run of the cards. Can happen to anybody." While the wide-shouldered cousin tried his hand at peacemaking, Alex went over his words again in his head.

"Better not have meant nothin' by it. Wiley George, just what are you good for? You can't play cards, you can't hold your liquor, and you can't take decent care of my daughter. Just what the hell can you do?" The sound of Ben Roy's rising voice brought Bobby Lee through the door and into the back room.

"You boys need somethin' else in here?" Bobby Lee walked over to the platter of chicken sitting on top of a barrel of crackers.

Now was Alex's chance.

"Bobby Lee, you say you got another nigger lookin' for hired-out work?" Alex glanced up at the proprietor but kept focus on Ben Roy. Alex swept the table with his cards once.

Ben Roy laid another card face down in front of his brother-in-law.

"I thought you was gonna be all right with the nigger you just got." Bobby Lee came over with the chicken. The down county man took himself a thigh but the three Thorntons waved the proprietor off.

"That's just it. I don't need no more hired men. Got too many as it is. That no good nigger John Welles come back today." He said the name slow, but he held his voice steady like it didn't really mean everything to him.

Alex let his eyes slide to his left to catch a secret glimpse of Ben Roy who sat staring at his cards. Had his brother-in-law heard? "Place don't need two hired men. 'Sides, that Welles is a no good nigger." Alex picked up his fifth card and slipped the third queen in next to the other two. He had a full house. He knew not to make a move, not to make a big show of adding more money, nor to let a muscle twitch in his face. In this game of poker, when a man held a winning hand, he was the only one in the room who needed to know until the very last second. But the hand Alex most wanted to win wasn't in any poker game. Nothing but besting John Welles would do, and Laura was the pot.

"What's no good 'bout this nigger?" The down county man asked as he scowled at his own cards. He swept the table twice, and Ben Roy delivered him two fresh replacements.

"Left me right after plantin' last year and ain't showed his black ass back in these parts 'til today." Alex slowly reached back into his overalls pocket and pulled out a second silver dollar. He slid it casually toward the pile of cash.

Ben Roy caught the action.

"How'd you come to know he was back in Lawnover?" Ben Roy let the words slip out of his mouth.

Alex watched him discard a card, take a replacement, and pull out two greenbacks from his shirt pocket. Slowly, he shifted his eyes to Alex as he waved Bobby Lee and his chicken platter away. Bobby carried it into the main room. Alex's mind was a whirlwind of concoctions.

"Picked up my new hired man on the mid-forty tonight. Welles's boy said his pa had been back around the place." Alex held on to his cards, careful to avoid Ben Roy's eyes.

"The nigger's back on the mid-forty? I thought for sure he was gone." Wiley George spread all five of his cards face down on the table as he finished off the contents of his Mason jar.

Alex didn't answer.

"You seein'?" Ben Roy jabbed a finger in the direction of his cousin, who laid out three tens. The self-appointed Thornton patriarch turned to his younger brother, who laid his own cards face down on the table. Ben Roy lifted his fisted cards to his chest and turned back to Alex.

"That Welles nigger come back to look in on his wife and kids is all. He's got a mad on 'cause his wife's got a full belly." Ben

Roy shrugged his shoulders. He paid more attention to the down county farmer when the man laid his cards face down on the table than he did to Alex.

Though the May evening was mild, Alex watched the sweat pop out across the hapless farmer's forehead. Other than making for a tight summer, what did the man have to fret over? It was nothing compared with the danger to Laura.

"Once he smacks her around a time or two, gets it out of his system, he'll haul his ass out of Lawnover." Ben Roy inclined his head toward Alex. "Take Bobby Lee's new man to help you out." Ben Roy made no move to show his cards.

The thought of Welles laying a hand on Laura brought up the bile in Alex's throat. "That ain't likely. Not on his own. John Welles is an uppity nigger. His boy says he carryin' 'round a pistol." Alex let the words ease out of his mouth.

Hettie reentered the room carrying the jug. Judging by how tightly she gripped it, Alex guessed it to be full. Ben Roy's eyes were still on his own cards.

"Pistol? A nigger don't need to be carryin' 'round no pistol." Wiley George held out his Mason jar to Hettie for a refill.

"Hettie." Ben Roy's voice bounced off the bundles, barrels, and crates in the small back room as the woman stiffened her body. "Don't pour that fool another drop. I ain't carryin' no drunk home to my daughter." He turned back to Alex. "Niggers carry pistols even when they go to church. Long as he ain't carryin' it 'gainst no white man, who the hell cares?"

"The boy says Welles is after the father of his woman's baby." Alex locked eyes with Ben Roy, who had taken a quick glance away from the cards in his hand. "A nigger takin' a gun to church is one thing, but a crazy nigger with a loaded gun runnin' 'round the countryside after dark is another. It just might go off against anybody." Alex held Ben Roy's gaze.

"Maybe Welles slipped back in town last fall for a night with his woman. Who's to say who the baby's daddy is." Ben Roy still held his cards clamped to his chest.

"That nigger needs that gun taken away." The down county farmer held up his glass for a refill.

Ben Roy rolled his eyes, and the farmer set his Mason jar on the table only a quarter filled.

"You gonna be the one to take a loaded gun from a crazy nigger?" Ben Roy turned to spit out the wad of tobacco he'd been chewing, spewing brown specks across the table. "Alex, let's see yo' cards."

Alex's throat had gone dry. He couldn't speak even if he had thought it a good idea. Instead, he laid out his three queens and two tens. He heard Ben Roy's big intake of breath just as Hettie approached him with the jug in her hand. Alex glanced down at his own almost full Mason jar and nodded her off. Ben Roy threw his cards to the table and pushed the pot toward Alex.

"You been a lucky bastard tonight." Ben Roy leveled his eyes at him. "Every man here wants to have that kind of luck this plantin' season. Put the seed in the ground, hope the rains come and go when they 'sposed to, fight the bugs so they don't eat yo' leaves down to nothin', and pray that the niggers will stay in the fields. That's the kind of luck every white man wants this time of year. Unless it's somethin' powerful bad, ain't no need to rile 'niggers up with trouble right at the start of the season. A nigger will sit down quicker than he'll work. Don't give 'em no excuses."

"A nigger runnin' around the county with a loaded pistol, crazy enough to shoot anything and anybody, white or black, coming across his path...that's bad business." Alex looked at the men at the table.

Hettie, on her way to Ben Roy, slipped on some of the tobacco spittle that had escaped the spittoon. Catching herself, she splashed the liquor mash from the jug across the poker table and onto the deck of cards Ben Roy was shuffling. Almost before Alex could blink, Ben Roy's arm shot out and backhanded Hettie hard across her new-mother's nursing breasts. Still clutching the spilling jug, the woman doubled over in pain, one hand at the bodice of her dress.

"Leave the damn jug and get the hell out of here." Ben Roy wiped the cards clean on his shirt as Hettie scurried into the main room.

"I reckon that's it for me for tonight." The down county farmer scraped back in his chair. He turned to Alex and almost whispered to him. "If you need me to help out with that uppity nigger after harvest, you come on back to me."

"Me, too." The Thornton cousin gulped down the contents of his Mason jar. "That nigger's just gonna run around a lot tonight. Get liquored up and find him some other nigger to shoot in the ass. He'll light out of here by mornin'."

"Two or three men tonight to catch this nigger and run him out of Lawnover is all I need. He ain't nothin' but trouble for all of us." Alex swept his eyes between the Thornton kin and Ben Roy.

Pushing the deck of cards aside, his brother-in-law leaned toward Alex, his elbow on the table, his hand half shielding his mouth.

"Hettie's got a tan-skinned cousin come to visit. Not but thirteen, but I reckon she's trainable. You can help yo'self to her." Ben Roy may as well have been speaking Geechee to Alex's ears.

Why in hell would his brother-in-law think he wanted a thirteen-year-old child? All Alex could do was nod his head in confusion.

"I don't mean nothin' serious like a lynch..." Alex realized his error almost before he spotted Ben Roy's eyes narrow to half the size of a lead point. He shook his head and hurried off the memory. "Just need a few of us to make sure Welles knows he ain't welcome back here in Lawnover after what he done." Alex watched Ben Roy shift a new wad of chewin' tobacco from one cheek to the other. He said nothing, as Wiley George, his head bowed down toward the bare table, glared at his father-in-law under his brows.

"You talkin' 'bout bad business." Wiley studied the tabletop like he was counting each and every stain ever put on it by a poker player. "Seems like to me, it's bad business if a nigger don't stay put when it's plantin' and growin' season. Ain't right for niggers to shuffle off whenever they take a notion. Only a white man gets to say when a nigger goes or stays." He finally lifted his eyes to his father-in-law. "If you was to ask me, I'd say that nigger needs to learn him a good lesson that'll stick with the rest of 'em too." Before Wiley George finished, the down county farmer pushed back from the table and rose to his feet.

"I just put me in eighty acres with one pretty good hired hand. But he got six children, five of 'em boys and all of 'em of good size." The farmer patted at his now flat pockets as he turned toward Alex. "With all them children, I don't reckon my nigger gonna run off, lessen there's trouble. I can't afford to have me no trouble." He held out a hand to shake Alex's. "If that nigger of your'n still needs a good learnin', call on me after harvest."

"Alex, you ain't got nothin' to worry about. My money's on that nigger gettin' out of town once he's done a little drinkin', some fightin', and a little harmless shootin' with that pistol. He ain't gonna turn that thing on nobody." The cousin flexed his shoulders as he stood, stretched, and reached for his empty Mason jar. His own jar refilled, the man slipped into the front room. Ben Roy turned toward his younger brother.

"Take this fool on home to Tillie." He jerked his head toward Wiley George. "God gave a goose a double more portion of good sense than he gave you. You don't stir niggers up when you need 'em. Fifteen farmers in this part of Montgomery County depend on them hired hands to bring in the crop, and you tell me that now is the time to teach them a lesson?" He turned full on his son-in-law. "When you rile up niggers, it better be over some- thin' good and worth the trouble 'cause there could be hell to pay for more years than you wanna count." Ben Roy slumped back into his chair.

The younger Thornton grabbed Wiley by his collar and pulled him to his feet. The new father wobbled. Little brother Thorn- ton put an arm around Wiley's waist and half dragged his niece's husband out of the room. Ben Roy reached for the last of his whis- key. He drained the jar, started to call out Hettie's name, changed his mind, and turned to Alex in the now quiet room.

"Funny 'bout the Welles woman and her baby. Been a lot of years between babies." Ben Roy leaned his elbows on the table. "You sure 'bout that baby? Could some other nigger have come in there?" Ben Roy kept his voice low.

"I'm damn sure 'bout the baby." Alex's voice boomed.

"If you're sure 'bout the daddy…high-yella babies born in these parts stay put for a lot of years." Ben Roy let loose with a stream of tobacco juice. "Anybody can take a look at the child from time to time. 'Course, could be troublesome if the momma moves on to some other man's acres." Eula's brother nodded his head toward the door leading to Bobby Lee's main room. "If a man took a mind, he could always come here to town and take himself a good look. The momma's bound to bring the child by at least once a month." Ben Roy squeezed the deck of cards tight between his hands. "Baby or no, if that nigger goes back to his woman, works like he ought, and don't cause no trouble, ain't no- body in Lawnover gonna drive him out of town. That's the way of it."

The building went silent in Alex's ears. The clink of jars and the cussing from the front room stopped. The smell of sorghum turned sickly sweet. The brined pickled feet let off the stench of ten-day-old pig slop. Alex worked his mouth to speak. Ben Roy raised a hand that the kerosene lamp silhouetted against the table into long snakelike shadows.

"You think about Hettie's tan-skinned cousin." Ben Roy laid a hand on Alex's arm. "We can't have no trouble right now. Troubles don't go 'way quick. They have a way of lingerin' long and makin' you wish things was different...wishin' you hadn't done what you..." Ben Roy's eyes drifted off an instant. "Get on back to my sister, and do what you ought, 'cause that other one, that Annalaura, she ain't available no more. Her husband's done come home. As long as he's around, she's John Welles's woman. Ain't nobody 'round here gonna run him outta town over a baby that belongs to another man. You got to let her go, Alex. It's over."

CHAPTER TWENTY-THREE

The clock struck eleven. Eula felt each strike bounce around her skull like apples jostling in a bushel barrel after the fall pick. Funny the things that went through her head since she'd taken to the bed nine hours ago. Not that she slept even one minute in all that time. Silly little things played in her head as she lay there staring at her white-painted ceiling and daisy-printed wallpaper, like the first time the grandfather clock had appeared in her parlor. It hadn't been new, of course. She and Alex couldn't afford new, especially in those days. Alex had bought it at a Clarksville auction just two weeks after her thirtieth birthday. She always liked to make believe it was a present from her loving husband, though Alex never said one way or the other.

The clock's time had always been right on the strike. Eleven o'clock, and she hadn't spoken more than a dozen words to her husband in days. As good as she'd been at keeping the pain away these long hours, sometimes those other thoughts crept into her head. Sister-in-law Belle, missing preserves, the money box lighter by five hundred dollars, all insisted on tumbling around in her brain, forcing her to find another way to push them back into that wonderful place of forgetfulness.

Eula rolled to her side and remembered something about her feet. She had managed to unbutton her shoes and drop them to the floor when the clock had struck six. But she still hadn't found a way to remove any of her other clothing. The house was dark with the moon only a quarter full. Since it was just mid-May, Eula guessed it was probably still chilly enough this close to midnight to warrant slipping under the bedcovers. She would have done just that if her body and head could tell the difference between hot and cold, comfort and misery. Everything about her had gone numb. Other than the hourly sounding of the grandfather clock, her ears had mercifully screened out the sound of Belle Thornton's hateful voice.

Lying on her right side, Eula could see her half-shut bedroom door. She wanted no part of staring at a closed door, counting the hours until it would open. She rolled over to her left and lay her forearm across her eyes. Now she would neither hear, nor see, nor feel Alex, but the smell of him lingered on the feather pillow next to her head. She lowered her hand to cover her nose and mouth and went into herself so deep that the sound of the back porch and kitchen doors opening and boot steps striding across her pinewood floors made no more sense to her than the little breeze tickling her windowpane.

She finally caught snatches of sound that might have come from a human voice, but she had the feeling that the noises had been repeated over and over before they woke up her ears. It was the unsure touch on her shoulder, rather than the harsh light from the kerosene lamp, that finally forced her mind to come partway back from that quiet, safe place.

"Eula?" The voice was uncertain, concerned, and befuddled.

She kept her eyes shut. She had no desire to answer that strained voice.

"Eula Mae, you sick or somethin'?" The voice sounded tired and downcast.

The hand on her shoulder became more certain, more familiar. Though she didn't want it to happen, her ears slowly returned to their job. Outside, somewhere, that little breeze kicked up and rustled the new leaves on the trees. A weight dipping down the small slice of mattress behind her back told her that the owner of the voice had leaned on the bed.

"Can I get you somethin'?" The sound of the voice shot through her.

Eula rolled on her back as though a good gust of wind had pushed her over. Her eyes flickered open.

"What?" She stared at her husband.

Alex stepped back from the bed and lowered the lamp to her face. He scanned the light down to her feet. The glare blinded her and kept her from reading his eyes to see what could have possibly prompted him to offer help for the first time since their baby di ... She pushed that thought back into its rightful hiding place.

"How long you been layin' here? It's 'bout midnight, and you still got your clothes on." The sound of concern in her husband's voice woke up her worry over him, and she hated the bother.

Eula raised herself against the headboard, a pillow at her back. She reached to move the light aside. As Alex set the lamp on the bureau next to their bed, she caught a glimpse of his face. His mouth drawn down in weariness, his cheeks sunken in, he looked as though he had lost the battle with a swarm of tobacco locust.

"I'm a little tired, is all. But, you...uh...didn't the plantin' go well?"

She readied herself for his quick burst of annoyance and then his silence. It was not as if anything she ever did could warrant true anger, or any other real feelings from the man. Whatever outbursts he had were over in less than a minute.

"Plantin' went just fine. Could do as well as last year. You sure you all right?" He walked around to his side of the bed, unbuttoning the straps of his overalls as he moved.

Eula mustered a shake of her head. Thoughts of missing money and missing nights rammed back into her mind. She watched Alex as he sat on the edge of the bed and removed his boots. The light from the kerosene lamp cast his face in half shadows. She hadn't noticed before that his eyes looked quite so haggard.

"You feelin' a little warm?" Alex placed the back of his hand against her forehead.

"I'm mmm." If she dared, her hand would have been the one to reach up and check Alex for fever. Her husband was not in the habit of checking on her health.

"Let's get you under the covers." Dropping his overalls, he scooted onto the bed.

Alex reached behind her neck to unbutton the apron she had put on fresh this morning. Before she could reach out a hand to stop him, he pulled the garment away, the untied strings dangling, as he dropped the muslin to the floor. What was he doing? Alex tugged her shirtwaist free from her skirt. When his hands reached for the buttons, Eula slapped her hand over his before she could get her mind clear.

"No. I mean...I'm not sick. I'm just tired. I can do it myself." Her hands fumbled with the buttons before she remembered that she had never taken off her clothes with him looking straight at her.

If he did happen to walk in when she was changing, she just stepped behind the chifforobe door, turned her back, stepped out of her petticoat, and pulled her nightdress over her head, all before he could notice. Eula's shaking hand stalled at the button over the center of her chest. Alex finished the job. She held her breath as he pushed the shirtwaist back from her shoulders. In her confusion, she moved to stop him before she remembered. She only wore an everyday chemise. Was Alex checking to see if she was properly dressed?

"My corset, too tight. I need…"

"I reckon I haven't always given you what you need. If you need a new corset, I'll make a way…" He slipped her skirt over her feet as he looked at her face.

What she needed? Make a way? Did Alex have some money worry that a good wife should have seen and sorted out?

"You already give me everything I need." She stumbled out the words as the dwindling numbers in her journal and the missing supplies in her storeroom flashed into her head. Did the missing food and five hundred dollars go to pay some debt he hadn't bothered her with? Had Ben Roy gambled her husband out of some money?

Alex slipped his hands to the bottom of her chemise and began sliding it up her chest.

Eula laid a hand at her bodice and scrunched up the loose fabric, her fingers squeezed so tight, they hurt. Alex hadn't seen her naked in full kerosene light in years. He pulled her back when she reached out an arm to turn down the wick. Had she paid more mind than she ought to her mean-spirited sister-in-law? Was the real answer gambling?

"No, I ain't given you everythin' you need. I ain't never told you how much it means to me how well you run this place."

The quick intake of her own breath sent a charge straight to Eula's chest. She let her tight grip on the chemise loosen. Her eyes closed as Alex slipped the garment over her head. Her hands dropped to her side, not bothering to cover the breasts she always tried to hide from him because they hung flat like empty socks laid over darning balls. How could she have let herself pay mind to the silly prattlings of her brother's wife? The real problem lay with Ben Roy all along.

Alex ran his hands the short distance from her belly to her breasts. A breath came in and she held it as his hands worked her drooping bosom up her chest to where it used to blossom.

The heat coming from his body as he leaned in and parted her lips with his mouth set up a sweat all over her own body. Something foreign found its way into her mouth. Was it his tongue? She wasn't sure if he was searching for hers or not, but she let him find it. He pressed her bunched up breasts against his rough cotton work shirt as his tongue encircled hers. Before she could will it back, her tongue pressed into his.

She let her arms slowly reach around his back. Alex kissed and released her lips. She flickered open her eyes just as his flushed face drifted to the windowpane.

"I'm glad it was you." Alex's voice carried the husky sound of a man struggling for breath. "You and not Bessie." He moved to take off his shirt and summer drawers.

Eula chanced a look at his manhood. It had made a full rise.

"What?" She managed to get out the word. She saw her reflection in Alex's eyes. Did he really want her like a man hankers after a woman? The calendar on the pantry door conjured up in her head. Tonight was Tuesday.

"I could of been like Wiley George. Worse." Alex leaned toward her again and kissed her on the cheek.

"You're the best wife I could of found. I'm not a man born with good luck. Without you, I reckon I would of lost this farm." Alex's hand squeezed her breast.

She sucked in her upper lip. Alex was saying things to her that he'd never said before. Though she'd never known her husband to be a drinking man, did his words come from the liquor served at Bobby Lee's? Was that how Ben Roy did it...got her husband drunk?

"No such thing. I just always want to be a help to you because I…"

Eula had loved Alex for sure since right after the baby, but she had never said the words. And Alex had never said them to her. Was he trying to say them now? His eyes caught hers again.

"It was a blessin' that Bessie was taken when I finally came callin'. She was pretty, but pretty goes away and a man's left with nothin'." He slid his hands around her hips to the place where her thick thighs came together.

Alex let his fingers stroke midway between knee and her triangle. Eula grabbed another gulp of air. With the pleasure feeling spreading between her legs, she looked at Alex as his eyes fixed on the windowpane.

"Every man in Lawnover was wantin' Bessie. I don't fault you for that." She let out a sigh as her legs spread open just enough to still remain a lady. How silly she'd been.

Alex's hands moved between her thighs. "It wasn't much I done to get you, but I'm thankful you're my wife." His fingers played in her triangle.

Eula bent her knees. The muscles in her thighs jerked. She fought to press her hips into the mattress to stop her legs from throwing themselves wide open. She battled the urge to lift her arms to his shoulders and pull him down on top of her. Scattered bits of pictures jumped into her mind, and right out, again. Liquor, money troubles, swollen-bellied colored women, the lying lips of sister-in-law Belle, Alex's love for her finally finding words, spun around in her head.

Eula arched her body into Alex, allowing her legs to gap a little more than was proper for a lady. She sniffed to catch the smell of Bobby Lee's home brew. She wanted to swim in Alex's embrace, answer his exploring fingers, sweep his ears with words of her love, but if he was a little bit drunk, he would hate her in the morning for behaving like a roadhouse tart.

"Alex, I try to be the wife you deserve because I know I haven't served you as well as I ought." She grunted as Alex's finger slid all the way inside her triangle. He had never touched her like that in all their years together.

"Mmm" was all she heard from him.

"A good wife…ooh…a good woman…my Lord…would give you babies…oh, my Jesus…I…"

"No. No talk 'bout babies tonight. No talk 'bout babies, ever." His voice sounded gruff as he pushed his manhood inside her.

Eula lay in what felt like a field of magnolia blossoms that tingled shivers up and down her body when Alex exploded inside her. He grunted out a sound, and her mind drifted to her eighth grade schoolteacher who taught her about the emperors of Rome back in the old days. They crowned their heroes with the leaves of a victory tree. The ancient Romans plucked the fragrant leaves right off the branches of the laurel and wove them into a thornless crown that they set on top of the head of their most glorious heroes. Had Alex just crowned her his empress? She nuzzled his cheek when he didn't roll off her and turn his back like he always did. She let out a satisfied breath, and Belle Thornton disappeared into the daisy-printed wallpaper.

Though her husband hadn't quite finished the sixth grade, he must have heard parts of that lesson on the laurel wreath because the slightly garbled word bursting from his mouth was loud, drawn out, and laid sweet upon Eula's ears.

"L-a-u-r-a."

CHAPTER TWENTY-FOUR

Something was wrong. Something was very wrong. Annalaura had long since let go of the idea that the pains twisting her body came from the blow John had struck at her belly. Though none of her other four children had given her this much trouble getting born—nor had they come early—they had all belonged to John Welles. How could the father of a baby make that much difference? The latest big cramp eased up, and she let herself take a breath. She grabbed at one of the three cotton blankets Aunt Becky kept tucked across the bed, summer and winter. All three were drenched in her sweat, her broken bag of waters, and the plug of blood from her womb. This baby was definitely on its way, and Aunt Becky hadn't come back to the cabin.

Hours had passed since Rebecca took the three youngest over to Hettie's. The ever-closer pains faded most of Annalaura's sense of time, but the low-burning embers in the fireplace told her daybreak couldn't be more than four hours away. Even the kerosene in the lamp burned low.

Right after Becky had gone with the children, her water broke and it was all she could manage to struggle out of her shirtwaist and skirt. Annalaura had tried to raise herself to refill the lamp and stoke the fire only to be wracked by a pain so strong that even setting one foot on the floor caused her more misery. Was she suffering God's punishment for her sin against her husband?

Another cramp wrapped her in its grip. Where was Becky, or even Cleveland? She had stationed her boy at the gate to warn Alex away. After that, Cleveland had probably gone back to the loft to await her return, not knowing how much his mother needed him. She prayed that her boy would worry over her and come to Becky's cabin. As she held her breath against what felt like a thousand tobacco spearing sticks jabbing at her insides all at once, she remembered that her twelve-year-old would never venture out after dark. John had trained him too well. Colored weren't safe wandering the lanes after nightfall.

The spearing sticks did their worst and started to ease up. If she had a timepiece, she would know for sure that the pains knotting her insides into a hot ball of fire were coming every five minutes and holding tight for well over a minute. She frowned, drew in a long breath, and knew her body was tiring much too soon.

It wasn't that dying would be so bad. Being dead had to be better than the double portion of misery dragging her with it right now. But who would see after her children? John would take Cleveland and Doug—they were of some size to be of help. But Lottie was a girl, and Henry, little more than a baby.

Before she could worry after her two youngest, a poker, hot from a roaring fire with butchering knives stuck all around it, let itself loose in her belly. Annalaura rocked on the bed in time to her own yells in a fight with the red-hot poker. In what felt like an hour, she sensed the poker start its cooldown. Her forehead beaded in sweat, her breath came in short bursts. She lay gasping on her aunt's bed, the covers tumbled tight around her. A hard tap at the door brought the first burst of hope.

"Push it open, Cleveland. Hurry." She fell back against the flat feather pillow. "Yo' momma needs you bad."

The door slammed against the cabin wall, but her head felt too heavy to lift.

"My God, Laura, is it the baby?" The sound of Alex's boots bounded across the room. Her world suddenly turned to a blur of dying fireplaces, dying lamplight, and dying men.

"No. Gawd. Ughh. Mmm. You can't be here. You got to leave. Cleveland…"

"It's the baby." Alex's hands tumbled over themselves in his hurry to untangle the blankets that wrapped her body.

He bent closer, looked into her face, and frowned. Annalaura took in short, quick breaths. She had to warn him out of the cabin. He stopped fumbling with the covers and moved to retrieve the low-burning lamp.

"Shit. Where's the kerosene for this damn thing? It's dark in here." He swung the lamp over her face.

The little flicker of light was weak, but allowed her to catch just a quick glimpse of his face. Another pain moved up, and she held her breath. The lamp thudded to the bedside stand. The old bed dipped down as Alex knelt beside her.

"You got to breathe, Laura."

Her eyes cranked open under Alex's rough hands as he grabbed her shoulder and pulled her up in the bed. His hands beat back the offending blankets and suddenly stopped. She watched him bring his hands to his face. Alex played his fingers under the light from the kerosene lamp. Both hands were smeared with her blood.

The floodwaters signaled their retreat, and Annalaura watched Alex stare at one hand and then the other before he grabbed at the lamp and swung it back to her face. Her neck and shoulders pressed against the bed headboard. She let the air make its way back into her. She had just enough strength to lay an arm against Alex's chest as he knelt over her.

"Go. You gotta leave. John...my husband...he back...pistol. Please go."

"Your face? What the hell happened to your face?" Alex leaped from the bed.

Didn't he hear her? Annalaura bit down on her bloody lip as she tried to make her ribs move to take in more air. She had to get Alex out of the cabin.

He scrambled around the room, filling the lamp. She heard Alex's boots stomp back across the floor to her.

"Now." She moaned. "You gotta go now."

The mattress sagged under Alex's weight as the bright light from the refilled lamp swung across her face. She closed her eyes all the tighter until the lamp moved away.

"That bastard hit you, didn't he?" The sound of Alex's voice frightened her all the more.

A cloth dampened in cool water dabbed at her eyes, lips, and all her cut and sore places. She sensed his hot breath of anger fan her face. She couldn't have Alex mad at John and John mad at Alex. If only God would take these awful pains away so she could sort out this mess.

The first shock wave of cannon thunder rolled into position in her belly. She heard Alex lift the pitcher on the nightstand and pour fresh water over the cloth.

"Where's yo' aunt? Where's Rebecca Thornton?" He turned back to her and laid the coolness against her cheek.

The cloth's comfort was no match against the cannonballs ripping her insides to shreds. The battle caught her breath and held it as she grabbed for life wherever she could touch. She dug her fingers into her lifeline as the battle raged.

"Take a breath, Laura. My God, take a breath."

Hands grabbed her shoulder and pulled her body out of a deep hole just as the cannons ran out of powder. Her eyes opened as air poured back into her body. She stared directly at Alex. Annalaura remembered that his eyes were a milky blue, but she had never seen such worry in them. He sat next to her on the bed, cradling her head against his chest.

"Mmm." Her voice wouldn't work.

She pointed to Becky's food safe. She clutched at Alex's arm, and her fingernails dug in hard, drawing his blood.

"Where's the doctor?" Alex's arms wrapped tighter around her.

His mind must be unraveling. He knew as well as she that no colored in Lawnover could afford a doctor. With one hand, he grabbed Becky's feather pillow and plopped it under her back. He swept the other down to the blood-speckled cover, gave her a puzzled look, and jumped off the bed.

"I'm goin' for help." He started for the door.

"Nooo." Her scream rushed out as a new rumbling started in her belly. "No time. Baby comin'." If she could, she would have swallowed back her words. She couldn't bring this baby into the world by herself. She needed help, and right now. But if Alex stayed...and John...

"Oh, my Lord...uhhh...Go. Go, now."

Almost at the door, Alex stopped, turned, and stared at her. "Becky. I'm goin' for your aunt Becky." Panic spurted out of his mouth. His hand reached for the door latch. "Where's your aunt?"

"No good...took...Doug...Lot...Hettie..." The scream jumped out of her mouth before she could corral it.

He ran to her side just as the pain took all of her air. "Hettie? You sayin' Rebecca's gone to Hettie's?" Alex shook his head. "No good. She's with Ben Roy. Don't know if he's done with her yet."

As her insides fought to burst through her body, Annalaura tried to lift an arm to reach out to him.

"Safe. Becky's safe. Knife. Then go." The pain eased up just enough to get the words out.

Alex didn't move.

"Knife to cut the pain. Put it under the bed." She nodded to-ward Becky's safe before she sank back into the pillow.

Alex started to pace the floor, ignoring her. He threw more kindling into the fireplace and poked the embers into flame as he stared at her.

"Birthin' a calf." The frown lightened as he muttered.

A moan pushed out of Annalaura's bruised lips. Becky was beyond her reach and could offer no help. And now Alex was talk-ing out of his head. She watched him drop the poker to the brick hearth. He rushed to the other side of the cabin. Alex fetched a bucket of water, Becky's dish-drying towels, and a knife. Annal-aura turned her head to see him set the pail in the flames of the fireplace and splash the knife into the water before he returned to her side. She inched a hand out to him again.

"My grandma said…knife under bed…cut pain." She let her hand fall against the bedcovers as she felt the winds of a tornado begin their slow wind-up in her stomach.

She said her last prayers. Lord, take pity on my motherless children. Let Alex get out of this cabin before John gets here. She closed her eyes, the better to see death coming.

"If it's like birthin' a calf, the hot knife will cut the cord clean." Alex climbed on the bed, knelt behind her, and shifted her weight from the pillow to his chest.

Calves. Cows. What was the man talking? The winds of the tornado picked up.

"Ahm…my God. It's stuck. Can't get it out." The iron bar moved to her belly and held her fast. If only dying didn't hurt this much.

"It'll come." Alex, his voice carrying a sudden strength, took her hand, and with his, slid it down her belly.

"When a mother cow gets stuck like this, I rub on her belly to get her to moo it out. Each time we rub yo' belly, you grunt it out." Alex shifted her body higher up against his chest.

Annalaura let her head rest under his chin, her knees bent. Alex was right. This was a less hurting way to die. She felt the strength of Alex's grip on her hand as he rubbed down her belly.

"It's comin'." The scream burst out of her as the old cabin splintered into a hundred logs all rushing to get out of her at once. "Alex, help me. It's comin'." Her eyes clamped shut, she felt him shift her weight from his chest back onto Becky's wadded-up pillow and bedcovers.

Alex moved down to her spread legs. She opened her eyes enough to see the top of his head. Dozens of logs jammed inside her as each one turned and twisted to find the opening.

"Help *meeee*."

With death tightening the baling wire, somewhere Annalaura felt the hand of Joshua reach in to free the jam just like he fought the battle of Jericho in the Good Book.

"Laurie, another grunt. One more good grunt." It was a saint's hand she felt, but Alex's voice she heard.

"Can't Alex. I got no mo'." Though the sainted hand wrestled with the devil, the logjam started its move back up into her belly. Even the saints couldn't save her.

"I can touch the head. Laurie, you got to grunt one mo' time." Alex laid one hand on her belly and pushed down. "Give me yo' hand."

Did he want to hold her hand when he bid her good-bye? She hadn't asked for another man in her bed, or in her life, but if one had to come, she would thank the Good Lord when they soon met, that he had sent Alex. She stretched her hand toward him. The tips of her fingers brushed his. At first touch, Alex grabbed her fingers and squeezed hard. A new pain shot sharp jabs up her arm, and her yelp exploded into the room. The logs, stuck together in her womb, splintered apart and began to slide out of her belly, one by one. Annalaura dropped her head back onto the pillow, her hands limp in the muddled bedcoverings.

"Um." The broken bits of timber eased out, and air oozed back into her chest.

"I've got it," Alex shouted.

Annalaura lolled her head to the side in time to see a little smile cross Alex's lips.

"I've got…Laurie, I think it's a girl." He lifted his surprised eyes to her face.

She felt the muscles in her cheeks work themselves into a weak half smile. Alex's eyes flitted from her back to the baby. She saw the light in them move from bright surprise to fear. He moved a bloody bundle into Annalaura's line of sight. She turned away.

"Ain't she supposed to cry?" He whispered the question like he knew he was sitting in a death room.

"Hold her up by the feet. Smack her bottom." Annalaura's eyes closed when she heard the light tap on the baby's backside. Sensible thoughts started to make their way back into her head. Maybe the Lord wasn't going to take her tonight after all.

"Harder." She felt her voice growing stronger.

As she let her chest take in more welcome air, she smiled at Alex. Even if he didn't know how to do this part, she wished she had the strength to tell him her thank-yous for all the rest. The second, louder slap brought a familiar wail that filled the cabin.

"She's just fine," Annalaura announced. She hadn't wanted this baby. She knew that nothing but a lifetime of trouble awaited them both. Still, she needed to know if the child had all her fingers and toes. Annalaura would do what she had to soon enough. But for now, it was best if she didn't set eyes on Alex's baby.

Alex stared at the infant as though he'd never seen a newborn human before. Then Annalaura remembered. Hadn't his own firstborn come out dead? If Tennessee allowed, she would take

Alex in her arms. Another gulp of air, and Annalaura pushed that thought away faster than any of the others about the man who had just saved her life.

"Let her down and clean her up." Those were the only safe words to say to him.

Alex's face showed confusion as he looked for a place to lay the baby. He reached toward her stomach.

"No. Lay it on the bed. I don't need to see it." The words came out too late. As he wiped a damp rag over the baby's chest, Annalaura caught a glimpse. A new fright washed over her.

"Alex, what do she look like?" Please, Lord, let the herbs have done their job.

"She's good. She's better'n good. She's perfect." The sound of wonder seeped into Alex's voice.

"But what do she look like?" Annalaura pressed.

Alex lifted the baby toward her, and she wrenched her head toward the far cabin wall. She knew she had to care for this child, but if she could put off looking at it just a bit longer…

"No. I don't need to see it. Just tell me." She caught his confusion in that little shrug of his shoulders.

"I reckon all her parts are here, but is she supposed to be this little?" That edge of fright hadn't left his voice.

"What color?" Annalaura knew what Alex didn't.

Colored babies often came out with pale, alabaster-looking skin, only to darken nicely in the first few months. But that first quick glance she'd had of Alexander's child told her that this baby's color was all wrong. The infant's skin showed a creamy pink, not a golden, fried-potato brown. Maybe there was still hope. Aunt Becky told her that a colored child's true color stayed hidden behind the ear. Many a light-skinned newborn child was lucky enough to turn a beautiful chocolate brown within three months. And, if Aunt Becky was right, the truth lay there all the time, just behind the ear.

"They're blue." Alex shouted the word in the room.

"Blue?"

"Yeah, her eyes are blue...like...like mine." His voice dripped pride.

He cradled the baby in his arms, stroking a finger over the child's foot. He caught Annalaura's eyes staring at him and returned a funny little half smile like he couldn't quite trust the good fortune his own eyes were telling him.

Her heart spiraled down into her chest. Only fair-skinned colored children started out with blue eyes. The darkest they ever showed was a greenish-brown.

"Behind her ear. Look behind her ear." Annalaura tried to keep the fright out of her voice, but the worry crept in.

She held her breath while Alex shot a puzzled look at her.

"What's behind her ear?" She shielded her eyes as he turned the baby, but not in time to escape a glance of the top of the child's head.

"She don't look no different there than anywhere else." Alex shot her a puzzled look.

Of all the pains that had ravaged her body in the last hours, this one hurt her heart the most. Alex reached around for one of the unused cloths and wrapped it around the squirming, squalling infant.

"This ain't warm enough." He looked for another clean drying rag, found none, and grabbed an unsoiled corner of the bedcover.

The baby's cries settled into soft little mews. Carefully, Alex stood, holding the infant in his arms, trailing the end of the cover behind him. He walked to the safe and returned with a Mason jar. He handed it to Annalaura.

"Take a sip of this." He sat down beside her with the baby still in his arms.

Annalaura turned her head as she brought the cup to her lips. She sipped Aunt Becky's best medicinal whiskey. Its smooth warmth soothed her all the way down to her ravaged insides.

With one hand Alex took another cloth and finished wiping away the blood between Annalaura's legs. As he held the baby in the crook of one arm, the color of the infant's still damp hair registered in Annalaura's mind. Tufts of burnished gold covered the child's head, and Annalaura fought against a fresh wave of misery.

"She don't look real. She looks just like a doll." Tossing the rag on the pile of tousled covers, Alex turned the baby toward her.

Before she could shout her no, it was too late. Annalaura got a full look at the child she had just delivered.

"What're we gonna call her?" Alex looked down at the drowsy infant girl.

Even with her head still clouded over worse than a winter's day, Annalaura already knew that she had asked too much of Alex. If he'd been in Becky's cabin, even little Henry would have seen that the mind tottering on the edge of some unreal place was not Aunt Becky's. It was Alex's. What are we going to call her? There could be no "we" when it came to this baby. Not in all of Tennessee had there ever been a "we" for a colored woman's baby with a white man. Annalaura looked at Alex as he held the child like she was that newborn calf he talked about. He touched her soft and gentle like she was the pure gold the wise men brought to the Baby Jesus. Didn't he know, didn't he understand that he could have no parts of this baby? No white man could claim a colored child as his own. What little bit of a mind she had coming back to her, Annalaura had to spend on easing Alex out of the cabin and away from all thoughts of a "we."

"Becky say it might be best to let the child stay down county fo' a bit." She said it gently.

"Down county? Why would I want her there? No, my daughter ain't leavin' Lawnover." He snapped his head toward her, his voice carrying a sting in it.

Annalaura squinted over Alex's shoulder. How much time 'til daybreak? How much time until John found her and the child? How many more hours until he found Alex and pulled out that pistol? She shut her eyes tight as turmoil roiled up in her chest again. She had to find the strength to bring Alex back to his senses and wash his mind clean of any thought of a "daughter."

"Baby's mine, Alex." She let the words flow as soft as she could. "It can't be none of yours."

His eyes stayed on her face, and a slow smile started at the corners of his mouth. All the words went out of her head when Alex leaned forward to brush his lips over her cut and bruised mouth.

"I know she's mine, Laurie." The words were low and sure. "I know it more sure than anything. I can feel it all the way here." He tapped the pocket of his gray shirt. "She's the most beautiful thing I've ever seen, and she belongs to me."

Annalaura sat stiff on the bed, afraid to move, wondering if he was going to kiss her again.

"Dolly, I want to call her Dolly."

Alex reached to stroke the side of Annalaura's cheek. She closed her eyes and for a moment breathed in the healing touch of his hand. The soreness melted away quicker than any Cherokee salve Rebecca ever rubbed on her. Annalaura forced her eyes open to stare at the glare from the lamp. She needed its hot, yellow light to remind her that the devil had lost one battle to take her away with him this night. If she couldn't set her mind on the right road and put away those other thoughts, that red-coated fella was there to remind her that he wasn't through with her yet. Why else did things that could never be keep planting themselves in her head?

She looked toward the curtained window. There was no time for foolishness. Every second in this too-short night had to be spent making a plan to put a considerable distance between Alex and John, between herself and the devil.

"It might be best for the baby if John don't see it right off. Down coun..." She started off as slow as she could.

Alex laid the sleeping baby on the bed. He took Annalaura's hand in his.

"If John Welles lays one hand on her or you, it won't take me no time to kill him." Alex's voice came out strong and certain.

A chill ran from her shoulder blade to her tailbone. Alex released her hand and reached over to pick up the child.

"I'm takin' her to my place."

A horde of white-robed night riders rode into Annalaura's head. Carrying the baby, Alex moved toward Becky's safe.

"Yo' place?" The words rushed out on a shriek. "You can't take her to yo' house. She just born. You'll kill her if you take her out in the night air." Another wave of fear welled up in her stomach.

Alex pulled an old shawl, brown from age, from a drawer and wrapped it around the baby.

"Give her to me. She needs to be fed." Annalaura pushed herself up farther in the bed.

Alex stood by the safe, patting the shawl-wrapped baby. Annalaura leaned forward in the bed, her arms stretched out as far as they would go, willing Alex to come to her. With his face set hard like she'd never seen before, he started slow steps back to the bed. As though she knew the trouble she was in, the baby started wailing. If John came to Becky's cabin and heard the cries of a newborn... When Alex stepped close enough, Annalaura tugged at his pant leg.

"Alex, please. I needs to feed her."

He stood looking down at Annalaura, his jaw muscles locked tight, the baby's wails coming louder.

"When can she leave?" Alex looked at the child, then back at Annalaura. "When can the two of you leave?"

Annalaura tried to walk her hands up his leg to the shawl-wrapped baby. Alex took a step backward. Behind him, she watched the darkness that had covered Becky's window curtain all these hours show signs of letting go. Daybreak was about to cut through the night. Annalaura let her hand drop from the edge of the shawl to Alex's leg. She laid on gentle strokes just above his knee.

"We both got to get a little stronger, but that ain't gonna happen if you don't let me feed her." She succeeded in keeping her voice steady.

Alex turned away and walked to Becky's wood-block table, where the light from the kerosene lamp couldn't reach him.

"If you say you and Dolly can't leave now, I'll just wait here 'til you can." He kicked Becky's shored-up chair from the table, but he didn't sit in it. "Where's the old woman's shotgun?"

Annalaura fell back on the bed, her tired arms dropping on the mussed covers. The baby thrashed in Alex's arms as he scanned the walls. She watched him step around the broken chair and walk to the fireplace wall, where Annalaura remembered Becky kept the shotgun. Thank the Lord, that rusty old blunderbuss was gone. Alex peered at the empty hook, turned, and stomped at every floorboard in the cabin that looked loose. The newborn filled the room with her cries, and her mother's heart with fear.

"Listen to me, Alex." She had no more time. "Give me Dolly, now." She pushed herself upright in the bed, struggled her feet out of the covers, and stretched them to the cold floor. She felt the old floorboards skidding out from under her as she started to slip off the bed.

Alex blocked her slide with his free arm and chest. He laid the baby on the bed and took her in his arms.

"I ain't gonna leave you here for that nig...for that bastard to come after you again." His lips brushed her ear with a softness, but his voice sounded hard.

Alex shifted her back in bed to the squalls of little Dolly. Annalaura reached a hand toward the shawl-covered bundle, her eyes away from him. She gathered the baby in her arms, unbuttoned her chemise and set the little mouth to her breast while Alex smoothed the blankets around her. Dolly lost the nipple, screamed, and Annalaura put her breast back into the infant's mouth.

"I want the two of you to come to the farm." Alex settled in on the bed next to her. His voice carried the sound of wonder.

As the baby suckled, Annalaura let his hands lean her body against his chest. Alex stroked a finger from her breast to the baby's puffing cheeks.

"He ain't comin' after me again, Alex. He already took out his mad on me." She was too tired to move her body, and there was no time to push back how good she felt. "He won't hurt the baby either. When he takes one look at her, he ain't never gonna want to see me or her again." Maybe telling Alex the truth would get him out of the cabin.

If John Welles wanted her dead, he would have done the job when he first saw her fat belly in their barn. Cleveland, and his pitchfork, would never have stopped John if he'd really meant business.

"How long before he gets outta Lawnover?" Alex's hand played between the baby and her breast. His voice carried more calm, but Annalaura heard the purpose in it.

"If he don't meet up with you, no more'n a week." She tried to make her own voice sound casual as though his life and John's life weren't hanging on a thread thinner than any ever sold by Mr. Bobby Lee to colored.

"Can't wait no week." Alex raised up on the bed and fumbled through the blankets until he uncovered her shirtwaist and skirt. Shaking them free, he pushed them toward her. "Soon as you feed the baby, put these on. Night air or not, I'm gonna take you both to my place."

"We can't ride out nowhere, tonight." Annalaura shuddered, and the baby's tiny mouth fell away from her breast. "In a week, maybe..."

Alex bounced off the bed. Scouring the floor, he reached down to retrieve her boots.

"Let's get some clothes on you." He grabbed at her foot and tried to jam on the shoe. She pulled her leg back.

"Can't do it, Alex."

"I know it's soon. You can rest when I get you home."

"That ain't it." She swallowed trying to bring up more strength. He stopped buttoning the boot to look up at her face.

"Me bein' there might not set too well with yo' wi... with... Miz McNaughton."

Clutching the sleeping baby, Annalaura watched Alex's brow furrow into a scowl. He looked like he'd just heard her say that roses bloomed straight out of snow for all the sense her words made.

"What in the name of the Good Lord has Eula got to do with this?" He stared at her. "I left her asleep." Alex slipped another button through its loop, looked up at her, his eyes bright. "Matter of fact, once you finish yo' layin' in, you can help her with the cookin' and cleanin' and such. She'll thank me for bringin' in help." He went back to the shoe.

"Thank you?" Annalaura fought back a tremble that shook her shoulders. "Alex, it's just that I fear that the surprise of me and little Dolly livin' there without much notice might... well... it could be a might sudden."

He fastened the last button.

"Besides, I got fo' other children." She kept her voice as gentle as she could.

He slipped on the second shoe.

"I don't reckon yo' missus wants fo' children and a baby clut-
terin' up her house."

His hand on the bottom shoe button, Alex looked up at her
at last. Annalaura took in a breath as she watched the slow nod of
his head. He had heard her after all.

"Well, a house full of youngsters might take her a spell of gettin'
used to." Alex tapped at the shawl-wrapped baby as his eyes settled
on the far wall of the cabin. "I reckon Cleveland and them can stay
here with yo' aunt."

"This cabin sets on Thornton land, Alex. Mr. Ben Roy might
not take too kindly to..." Annalaura bent her head toward the
baby, but she let her eyes search out Alex's face.

"Could be so...if Ben Roy...Thornton land..." When he
raised his eyes to her, they blazed. "Then I...we...me, you...the
baby...we can all go off to Chicago." His hands dropped from the
button as he moved back to the bed. "I've got enough money to
get us a start up north. Eula can have the farm. I can find a place
for Cleveland. Maybe for Doug, too, if I pay a farmer for his keep."

Annalaura couldn't tell if the pile of words spilling out of his
mouth were for himself or for her. Either way, his second plan was
worse than the first.

"I reckon the colored preacher will take Lottie and Henry if I
give him some money."

A second tremor shook Annalaura. Did he really believe
what he was saying? Chicago. She'd never seen any colored person
who'd ever come back from that northern paradise once they'd
left Lawnover, but she'd heard all the glory talk from their jealous
kinfolk back home. But even if Chicago did sound close to God's
heaven, Annalaura knew that not even in that place could a white
man live in the open with a black woman.

Annalaura looked down at the sleeping baby. This little one
would need more than Aunt Becky's Cherokee medicine to spare

her all the misery that life was going to throw at her. How could her little girl survive when she had a mother so overcome with worry that her milk was bound to taste worse than rancid butter. And her father? Didn't Alex understand that white men who got too close to colored also got killed? There could be no running off to Chicago with a colored woman and a half-colored baby. The trees in Montgomery County had limbs on them marked for white as well as black. Dolly could be an orphan before the next sunset. Annalaura had to try again.

"Their father...John...he's gonna want the big boys. Ain't no need to pay for their keep." If she started to agree with him, he would soon see that his plan was impossible.

"I don't want Welles nowhere near any of the children." Alex shook the bed with his shout. "Not Cleveland, not Doug, not you, not Dolly. I want his as...butt out of Lawnover." He laid his arms around her shoulders, pulling her closer to him. "Once spring plantin' is over...Let's just say Welles will be happier if he gets out of Lawnover sooner better than later."

Annalaura clenched her grip on Dolly. Her whole body started to shake. What could she do to make Alex understand that if he stirred up the white farmers over her—a colored woman, any colored woman—both he and John would be dead? John would be found hanging from the branch of an oak, and Alex would meet up with a runaway wagon.

"I don't want no trouble, Alex. Not fo' John, not fo' Miz McNaughton, not fo' you." She had tried almost everything.

Her body and mind had little more to give. Careful of little Dolly, she twisted around and slipped her free arm around his shoulders. She leaned into him and pushed her tender breast into his chest. She readied herself against the pain and kissed him hard on the lips.

"Alex, you gotta help me make this work." She released his lips and looked into his eyes. "You gotta let me handle John. He ain't gonna hurt me nor this baby. Without you doin' a thing, John gonna light out of Lawnover before the week's out." She nuzzled her nose against his ear, raised her hand to his neck and stroked the side of his face. She watched his eyes. She had him captured in her gaze. "Let me have two days, just two days, and I promises you that I will bring Dolly to yo' house. I'll stay low 'til yo' missus get used to us bein' there. Just, please, darlin', let me bring Henry and Lottie 'til I can find somebody good to take 'em in." She kissed him again.

Little Dolly, squeezed between the two, started to whimper.

Alex leaned away from her and laid a hand on his daughter.

"You'll move in with me in two days and bring the baby?"

Her time had run out. If this was the price she had to pay to keep alive the two men who had captured every feeling her heart ever held, then she would make the bargain.

"I'll do whatever you say and be glad for it. Just, no more talk 'bout John. He don't want my face to give him reminders. He'll be outta Lawnover in two days' time." She let her head fall back on his chest. She could fight no more.

Alex kissed her forehead as he eased her back onto the pillow. He smoothed one of the rumpled blankets over her, bent down to kiss the top of Dolly's head, and headed for the door. As he opened it to let in the first pale gray streaks of the new day, he turned and looked back at Annalaura.

"I love you, Laurie. Thank you for the baby." He was gone.

CHAPTER TWENTY-FIVE

The pink of the sky settled in and brushed away the last of the night. If the day was going to be hot, cool, or middling warm made no difference to John. If the newly turned earth scented the fields with wild primrose or mule dung was of little notice to him. Every thought in his head, every picture before his eyes, every sound in his ears, and every touch upon his skin was fixed upon the barn and the mid-forty. Last night had been no different.

He had passed most of it sitting upright in the little lean-to right behind the colored Baptist church in Lawnover, hearing their voices and seeing their intertwined bodies as he waited for daylight to banish the night. His only company in that long space between sundown and sunup had been the hired man's words that kept playing in his head, and his own black-handled pistol. He had run his hands over the weapon so much that it was a wonder he hadn't rubbed off all the black.

As soon as that first gray light of dawn brushed half the sky clean of the dark, he had made his way over to the blacksmith's shop, awakened the drowsing man, and rented a horse. Now, it took all he had not to whip the animal into a frenzied pace to reach the barn and Annalaura, and whoever else she might have in there. So far, he had won the fight to keep the bile down in his stomach. The pictures plaguing his mind left him no room to plan anything beyond what he knew had to be done on the McNaughton acres.

As the horse trotted down the lane, John struggled to keep enough of his wits about him until he could get the job done. Then he would welcome mindlessness. Riding as sedate as a preacher's wife was the first thing he had to get right. A colored man riding a horse at breakneck pace down a country lane would stir up the suspicions of any early rising cracker farmer. By the time he turned off the lane and onto the path leading to the mid-forty barn, the hired man's words were beating a tattoo in his head.

He'd had no real trouble finding the man, despite Annalaura's claim that her so-called lover had hied himself off to Kentucky. A few well-asked questions at the colored juke joint down near the river bottom let him know that Isaiah Harris, along with his new wife, was staying the night in the colored principal's back room. The two planned to catch a ride the next morning for a tenant farm ten miles south of Lawnover. As John's horse made its slow way to the hitching post, his head swirled with bigger-than-life pictures of the hired hand, Annalaura, and her lie. When he first set eyes upon the rather flabby-looking man, John knew something wasn't right.

Harris couldn't look him in the eye, only at some place between his eyebrows and the middle of his forehead like John bore the mark of Satan. As soon as he spotted that look on Isaiah's face, he knew the truth. John knew that look. It was the same one black men all over the South gave one another when a man's woman had just been made some white man's whore. Even before the first real words passed between the two, John read all the answers in that look of Isaiah Harris. No black man had fathered Annalaura's baby.

John's heart beat faster as he climbed down and tied up the rented animal. Walking through the barn, he neither heard the cows grazing at their hay, nor smelled the pigs, happy in their swill. He put one hand on the side of the ladder and stopped. He had clamped down so hard on his lip that the taste of his own blood stained his teeth and flowed into his mouth.

John began the slow climb up the ladder. A trembling Cleveland greeted him. The boy still held the pitchfork.

"You promised you ain't gonna hurt her no mo'." The boy raised his voice.

"I ain't come here to hurt yo' momma. I come to talk." Halfway up the ladder, John tried to peer around his son.

Cleveland shoved the sharp tines two feet from his father's chest. John's ears finally cleared of the hired man's voice, only to have it replaced by a strange silence in the loft. Where were the sounds of a crying Henry and a pouting Lottie?

"Where's yo' momma?" John moved to climb up one more rung, but neither Cleveland nor the pitchfork budged.

"She don't wanna see you."

The fork brushed his shirt.

"I wanna see her." John grabbed a corner of the metal tines and jabbed the wooden handle into Cleveland's little chest, knocking the child onto his bottom.

Before the boy could regain his feet, and control of the pitchfork, John bounded up the last few rungs of the ladder. Throwing the fork to the opposite side of the room, he reached down with one arm and scooped up Cleveland.

"You a good boy to look after yo' momma. It's just what I wanted you to do when I had to be away." John watched his son's face dissolve into tears.

He wrapped his arms around the child as the wetness dampened his shirt. John kept his hand firmly around Cleveland's head, grateful that the boy could not see his own throat swallow back the beginnings of unmanly tears. What had he done? Had he left a child to do a man's job?

"Stop yo' blubberin' now." He meant his voice to sound gruff.

"Papa. It ain't her fault, it ain't..." Cleveland spoke on great gulps of air.

John released his boy and looked around the empty loft.

"I ain't meant to hurt yo' momma. Just lost my head fo' a minute. Won't do it again." He laid both hands on the boy's shoulders. "Cleveland, you done the job of a man whilst I was away, and I'm feelin' good 'bout that." He heard the sobs simmer down in his son's throat. "But, I'm back home now, and it's the business of a full-growed man to look after you all. Where's yo' momma and the others?"

Cleveland rubbed his eyes with his shirtsleeve. "I reckon I can't tell you that."

"I can understand that, son." John sorted it out. Rebecca Thornton. "When you next see yo' momma, tell her to find me in Lawnover when she get ready. I'll wait fo' her there." He patted Cleveland on the shoulder and walked down the ladder.

The pile of white man's junk lay at the end of the path as John galloped the horse toward the lane. The bile lurched up from his gut, and he yanked on the horse's reins. He stared down at the debris. The feel of two red-hot pokers burning deep into his eyes would have soothed him more than looking at what was on that stack of goods. John couldn't recall how he got off the horse, nor how long he'd stood shredding, stomping, tearing, and kicking at the pile when he remembered the matches he carried in his pocket. He struck one and threw it at the mass. When the flames licked too slow at a new patchwork quilt, he tossed in another match. He remounted the horse. The low-burning fire made slow work of the stack. To his satisfaction, the little flames lapped at a woman's blue serge coat.

Dawn came into full bloom. He kicked at the horse's sides to quicken the pace and get away from the nightmare misery of knowing what had happened to his wife in his very own bed. The sour taste of bile rested just at the back of his tongue.

How could she let this happen? He dug his heels into the horse's side and snapped the reins. Why didn't she just kill that cracker herself when he came near her?

His throat felt sore, raw, from the cries flying out of his mouth. The labored snorts from the horse made their way from his ears into his brain. He eased up on the animal when it nearly stumbled at the fast pace John had urged upon it. His head throbbed with the furnace-red heat of his anger. Something gnawed at him.

When Alexander McNaughton set his sights on his Annalaura, there was no way for her to win. If she killed him, it wouldn't be no time before her neck was stretched to a tree. And, if she didn't, if she let him have his way, well, she was still lost to John.

As Becky's cabin loomed into view, the gall puffed out his cheeks until he won the battle to push it back down into his chest. Turning onto Becky's path, he laid his hand on the pistol tucked under his shirt and in the waistband of his pants. It was the only thing that could keep him calm enough to talk to Annalaura.

"Becky, open up this damn do'. I know she in there." John pounded on the old door until he felt it on the verge of splintering.

"Get yo'self gone from here, John Welles. You ain't nowise welcome." The old voice sounded like it came out of a deep well behind the closed door of the cabin.

"Becky, it won't take me no time to kick this damn thing in." John delivered the first blow with his foot and the old wood showed the beginnings of a faint, jagged crack. He readied his boot for the second assault when the door creaked open no more than two inches. He couldn't make out Becky's face in the gloomy slit of an opening.

"I'm tellin' you fo' yo' own good. Get gone from this place."

A bandanna still wrapped around Becky's head made John believe that she had just come in from the outside. He had no time to deal with a crazy old woman. He leaned his shoulder into the door and shoved it open. Once inside, he stopped an instant to adjust his eyes to the dimness, only to feel cold, hard metal pointed between his shoulder blades. Slowly, the specter of Becky coiled around in front of him, holding a blunderbuss of a gun older than John himself. As she moved, she pressed the weapon into his skin, ending up with it dug deep into his chest, right over the heart.

"I ain't of a mind to tell you again. You ain't layin' another hand on my niece."

"It ain't Annalaura who needs a hand laid to her." He didn't know if Becky's old gun could still shoot or not, but he couldn't afford to have it go off at him before he had a chance to do what he must. His eyes began adjusting to the duskiness.

The old woman's mouth was set in a thin line, and those Cherokee eyes stared up at him like she was trying to put out a hex.

"Ain't gonna be no layin' on of hands. You gonna leave." Becky had stationed herself between John and the sleeping area of the cabin. With his eyes rapidly taking in the dark, John had no trouble looking over the old woman's shoulder.

There, in the bed, lay a tousle of blankets and pillows. Under it had to be Annalaura. He tried to take a step toward the worked-iron bed, but Becky's old arms held the strength of a mule team driver as she blocked the way with her gun.

"I means no harm to Annalaura. I just needs to talk to her." He reached into his waistband.

Before he could pull out the pistol, he heard the squeeze of Becky's finger on the trigger. He lifted both hands in the air.

"Hold on there, Rebecca. I'm gonna let you hold my pistol to show you that I mean no wrong to Annalaura."

"I got this gun offen Old Ben Thornton, and I knows how to use it, too. And I ain't too old to push yo' worthless body outside once I done killed you." The steely eyes were still on his face when the cry went out into the room from the mound of covers on the bed. The sound was quickly stifled by the now moving jumble of blankets.

"What the hell's that?" John asked in the direction of the sound. "Annalaura?" He started toward the bed, saw Becky's mouth move but caught only a bit of the sense of her words.

"Pistol...my hand...real slow..." The blunderbuss lowered and circled his waist.

He felt the old gun lift the pistol out of his waistband and knock it to the floor.

"Knives. You got knives?"

"Knife? Ain't got no knife. Annalaura? What is that?" He brushed past Becky and reached the bedside in no more than three strides.

"Mind my words. Touch her and I'll kill you." Becky was right behind him, though his eyes were fixed on the bundle in the bed.

Something that sounded strangely like the wail of a tiny infant started again as Annalaura pushed herself up onto the pillow. The sight of her battered face sent waves of surprise through his body.

"Annalaura, I ain't meant to…my mind…seein' you…" He reached out a hand toward her swollen cheek, but she turned her head away. He followed her eyes down to the sound of the cries.

They came from something wrapped in one of Becky's old shawls. He pointed to the bundle. The rancor threatened to reappear in his mouth at any moment.

"What's that you holdin'?" Could it be a cat?

Annalaura turned her face back to him.

"John. There's a way we can make this right."

How could her voice come out so quiet, so settled, so steady, when the whole world had just spun itself down to hell?

"Right? Make it right?" His whole body shook as he pointed a finger at the bundle. "That's a baby. You done birthed another man's bastard chile, that's what you done." His shouts shook his own body.

Waves of heat swarmed over him. Annalaura dropped her head and clutched the bundle all the tighter.

"We can try to make it right." Her words were low like she didn't believe them herself.

"Right don't come easy to yo' mind, do it?" His words burned his own mouth as he spit them out. "You layin' there talkin' to me 'bout makin' it right? Was it 'right' fo' you to lie to me?" He wasn't sure she could hear his scorched words. "Was it 'right' to tell me it was Isaiah Harris who done give you a baby last fall?" Without warning, even to himself, he jabbed a hand at the shawl only to feel the quick stab of cold metal under his armpit, jamming his arm upward and away from the bundle.

Annalaura's body shook even under the blankets. He saw her eyes puddle with tears.

"John, ain't nothin' I can say to make it like it used to be. I can't take back what I done. But fo' the children, we got to try to make it better, not worse." She sucked in her lower lip as she brought the still-covered bundle to her chest.

He could hear the squalls of a newborn.

"Worse? Hell, woman, how could it get mo' worse? You laid with a man who wasn't yo' husband like a common whore. And, now, you done give him a baby." He tried to clear his throat of the snake's venom that threatened his voice, but it was no use. "And it weren't no hired man you laid with, either." He jerked his head toward the covered bundle. "Let me see that."

The blunderbuss raked across his back. Annalaura swallowed hard as she tried to quiet the wailing bundle.

"She ain't to blame. It's all on me. I done it." The tears finally began their trail down his wife's cheeks as she glanced down at the shawl.

"She? You done give that damn white man a girl?" He wanted to double over right then and there, and let the bile finally make its way out of his mouth.

"I knows I'm no mo' good to you. I ain't askin' fo' me or fo' this chile, I'm askin' fo' Cleveland and Doug." She kept her eyes on him like she was willing him to look her in the eye like she was a decent woman again. "I'm askin' that you pay mind to them. You got money now. You take all of it and go back to wherever you was this last year and make a place fo' the boys." She stopped and swallowed.

Annalaura tried more than once to clear her throat. When she finally had sound, John heard the hoarseness in her voice.

"I'll send Cleveland and Doug to you as soon as it gets quiet 'round here." She looked at him like he was supposed to understand her words.

"You damn right I got money now. I earned it all for us, for you and Cleveland and little Henry…" All those long, big city months at Miz Zeola's came flooding back to him. "Right now, I wouldn't give a bent penny to a tart like you."

He had lain with Sally and the colored schoolmarm, but neither of them had meant a thing to him. God knew he had done
the deed for Annalaura, and not against her, so why was the Lord
visiting this awful punishment upon him? If he'd been wrong to
do it, still, wasn't no need for God and Annalaura to get back at
him this way. Not this way.

"You damn right I'm gonna take Cleveland and Doug with
me, but not befo' my business here is finished."

Annalaura's head started a frantic shake.

"Them boys need you. They needs their daddy." Her voice
rose as she pulled the blanket half across her chest.

Though he couldn't see, he knew she was suckling that new
thing in the bundle. A white man's bastard with its mouth on his
wife's tit. The bile strangled his tongue.

"Take them with you now if you feel like you have to." Her
voice trailed away.

She looked up at him. Did he see a plea for mercy in those
beautiful eyes?

"Cleveland's of some size and can help. So is Doug, but he still
young. I'd like to come visit my boys sometimes if that be all right
with you?" Trembling joined the pleading in her voice.

"Come visit? You wanna look in on Doug and Cleveland?
Why in hell would I let my boys see a mother who ain't nothin'
but a worthless everyday slut? I bet this wasn't the first white man
you done slept with either, now was he?"

The blunderbuss almost poked a hole right through his back.
Annalaura's lip crumpled, and she looked as though he had slung
the rope around her neck himself. He couldn't help it. Somebody caused this mess. And if it wasn't Annalaura—as much
as he wanted to believe otherwise, something told him it wasn't
all McNaughton—then who was it? John's head felt ready to
explode.

"What you think you know 'bout it?" Becky's voice dripped with menace and the blunderbuss held steady.

"Rebecca, I ain't gonna lay a finger on Annalaura, but I can't say as much fo' you." He drew back a hand.

Becky's mouth set as hard as blacksmith iron. The sound shot out of the tousle of covers.

"John. It ain't Becky. It ain't the baby. It's me who done wronged you. You don't never have to look on my face again after this night." She swallowed hard. "Doug's at Hettie's. Becky will fetch him here, and the three of you can leave Lawnover this mornin'."

"Well, I reckon you got it all worked out. And yo' white man will take care of Lottie and Henry as soon as you let him back in yo' bed? He'll buy Lottie some mo' pretty-haired dolls? Maybe a drum for Henry?" He whipped around toward her, crashing his fist down so hard on the table stand that the water pitcher skittered to the floor and shattered into a dozen pieces.

The surprise of his action startled Becky and she almost dropped the old gun.

"I ain't havin' it, woman. That cracker ain't gonna have a chance to get his hands on my children. Not none of 'em." He let his eyes narrow to slits. "I will have all of 'em with me." Cleveland, Doug, Lottie, and Henry. I'll have 'em all."

Annalaura looked worse than when he'd punched her.

"But Lottie and Henry is too young to leave me." Her eyes tried and failed to blink back more tears.

"Ain't no chile too young to leave a ten-cent whore." His words banged around the cabin. He saw Annalaura fall back onto the pillow.

She looked like she was dying. He knew his words slammed hard, crushing every hope, every prayer, and every plea for mercy in its path. He could see the light go out of his wife's eyes, but what she couldn't see was what that sledgehammer was doing to his own heart. Every mean word, every cruel name he let spark out of his mouth and aimed straight at her, did not belong on those brave shoulders. Even a fool, crazy mad like he was, could see that it wasn't Annalaura who deserved the stoning. But he couldn't fix his heart, nor his mouth, to tell her that. None of this was the blame of Annalaura. Even with all of his hurt, he knew that none of the fault lay at her feet. That damn cracker.

"He's right, Aunt Becky," Annalaura's reed-thin voice pronounced. "I'll send all yo' chil'ren with you as soon as you is ready for them."

"I'll be ready as soon as I kill that cracker."

"You ain't killin' nobody." Becky stroked his earlobe with the gun. "You gettin' yo' ass out of Montgomery County as fast as yo' legs can carry you."

He turned around to face her. "You think I'm gonna run? You think I'm gonna let some cracker ruin my wife?"

This was not the time to let the women know that Annalaura was everything to him. She always had been ever since he picked her out from the edges of that crowd of silly women always around him.

"Night riders will kill you dead." Becky's voice was low, soft, and certain.

"Old woman, do you think I is afraid to die?" He couldn't tell Rebecca Thornton that he was already dead. That he'd died yesterday afternoon when he first saw Annalaura's swollen belly.

"Ain't no white man gonna put his thing in my woman and get away with it even if she ain't nothin' but a worthless slut." He couldn't bear the pain.

What he really wanted more than anything was to wrap his arms around that wounded body, that shattered mind, and tell her that all of her misery, all of her shame, all of her pain belonged on his soul, not hers. He longed to tell her that he loved her far more than anything else in this world. But he couldn't say the words. When he spoke, all that came out were devil thoughts and low-down names that he could never mean against her in a thousand years. John knew the real whore, and it wasn't Annalaura.

"You is a bigger fool than I took you fo'." Becky waved the gun around. "First, you run yo' ass off to God-knows-where for most parts of a year. Then you hauls yo' sorry self back home and bad-mouths Annalaura when she ain't had no mo' say in what happened than little Henry. Next, you talk 'bout killin' a white man." The gun steadied again and its aim was dead at his heart. "You think you can kill a white man and that's gonna be that? He dead and you dead and you got no mo' worries?"

Although he hadn't seen the telltale wad in her cheek, the old woman spit out a stream of weak tobacco juice.

"Ain't you got sense 'nough to know that it ain't just you who gonna die?"

"Crazy old woman." He muttered in Becky's face. Why didn't she shut up? His heart couldn't take the truth right now.

"They'll string up my Annalaura as sure as you standin' there. They'll say she stole all that stuff offen that white man." Becky waved the gun in the air.

"Woman, you is crazy as a bedbug. Why would they put a hand to Annalaura? She ain't the one gonna kill that cracker. Lawd knows, she sho' should have." He turned a glare on his wife that he did not feel or believe.

"You know as well as me that every white farmer in these parts know that Alexander McNaughton been layin' with my girl. If you kills him, they gonna kill you and her, too, so she won't be 'round to tell the truth of the tale." Becky's words only chunked away a part of the fuzz in his head.

That he had to die was all right with him as long as Alexander McNaughton got dead first. But Annalaura couldn't be part of the killing.

"Hettie ain't dead, and she's laid up with Ben Roy fo' most six years."

"If a black man kill Ben Roy, white men will kill Hettie, all them children, and the nigger who done the first killin', all in one night." Rebecca confused him with her Cherokee reasoning.

"And it won't jest be you and Annalaura. It'll be Cleveland. They'll call him a 'complice. He's twelve, big enough for white mens to hang. My Johnny wasn't but seventeen when they hung him high."

The barrel of the gun suddenly pointed to the floor, and the old woman's arm dropped to her side like soft butter. So this was why Becky was talking crazy. It was all about her Johnny. A wave of relief swept over John.

"Aunt Becky." Annalaura jerked up in the bed, her voice full of alarm. As she sat up, the covering blanket fell away from her breast and the suckling baby.

John turned to look at that face, the color of cream from a fresh-milked cow. A blue eye flitted open and then closed. Ignoring Becky and her dragging shotgun, John walked over to the chair and plopped down in it. His legs turned weaker than water corn bread. It was true. Alexander McNaughton had fathered Annalaura's baby. To see the living proof with his own eyes left him searching for the cabin window to let in more air. He turned to the old woman.

"Rebecca," he kept his voice steady. "I ain't seventeen, and I ain't yo' Johnny."

She turned a rheumy eye toward him. "Seventeen. Weren't but seventeen." She stared at John as though she thought he should have been there on that long-ago night. That he should have been the one to pull Johnny out of harm's way all by himself.

"They killed yo' boy over nothin'. They'll kill me over somethin'." John kept his eyes on the Cherokee.

"Old Ben Thornton said he could have that hoss." Rebecca lifted her head toward Annalaura. "Old Ben was my Johnny's daddy, you know."

"Becky, I've known that story since before I married Annalaura... yo' niece."

"Like that one." Rebecca ignored him as she pointed to the baby in his wife's arms. "My boy had the light skin like that one, and that ain't never set well with Ben Roy."

"Aunt Becky, fetch me a quilt, I'm cold." Fear leaped out of Annalaura's voice.

"Old Ben said he wanted our Johnny to have that hoss." Rebecca looked at an empty space between herself and the front door. "Was the only decent thing he ever did fo' me. I think he done it to spite Charity. He had her first, you know. He took my momma, and when he got tired of her, he lay on top of me even when he knew I was his own flesh and blood. That's a God's sin, you know." Becky nodded to the vacant space.

"Auntie," Annalaura called out.

"It was a big roan and the best thing on this here farm." The woman ignored the girl she had raised. "I was there when Old Ben said Johnny could have it, but his oldest boy, Ben Roy, took a jealous streak."

John struggled to his feet. Becky, lost in her world, ignored him.

"Ben Roy always hated Johnny 'cause Old Ben took a shine to the boy. To vex Ben Roy, he would give Johnny little things like a toy that Ben Roy wanted first. A pair of shiny high-button boots fo' Johnny, even if they wasn't new, whilst Ben Roy got new, but they was only work shoes. Then, he sold my boy the best, that big, pretty roan—worth 'most five hundred dollars. He give it to him fo' one silver dollar. And he give him the God's truth legal sale papers." There was pride in Rebecca's voice. She took a step toward John, the barrel of the blunderbuss bumping along as she crossed the cabin floor.

"Aunt Becky, my quilt, please. The baby's gettin' cold," Annalaura pleaded.

"When Old Ben took sick and died, Ben Roy told everybody that Johnny had come by the hoss illegal. Ben Roy riled up them night riders, and they came fo' my boy. Johnny tried to tell 'em he had the papers, but Ben Roy tole them riders not to listen, that my Johnny was a liar." The old neck swiveled from the empty space to her kitchen safe, slow like a gate on a rusty hinge. She looked at the floor beneath the bottom drawer.

"I had them papers hid all along. Right there in the false bottom of that drawer." The eyes blinked. "But I ain't had no time to get them papers to the night riders. They killed my boy befo' they had a chance to see that everthin' was all legal. It was Ben Roy, Johnny's own half brother, who threw that rope over the tree, and he knew all the time that his daddy done give Johnny them papers." The gun thudded to the floor.

John rushed to her side and guided Becky to the rickety chair.

He tried to give her a sip of her medicinal whiskey when he heard Annalaura shudder. He couldn't bear to look upon his wife's face as he walked across the floor, stooped, retrieved his pistol, and headed for the door.

"Have my children ready to go as soon as I tell you." At the doorway, his back to her, he paused and called over his shoulder. "I may not kill that cracker tonight. Maybe not even tomorrow, but I'm gonna get black man's justice offen Alexander

McNaughton. You just worry on it." He let the door slam behind him.

Mounting his horse, he nudged the animal in the side and let him have his head. He knew what he had to do, but he hadn't yet sorted out the when and the how of it. The sun was well placed in the sky, and it was halfway to noon already. When the horse reached the lane, the animal slowed its pace, waiting for the tug on the reins. Right would take him across Ben Roy's acres and onto the roundabout back road to Lawnover. Left would take him back to the mid-forty and right past Alexander McNaughton's house to the direct road to Lawnover. Whichever way he went, some farmer would see him. And no colored man not working on some white farmer's land had any business astride a horse riding up and down country lanes during prime work hours. He jerked the reins to the left and let the animal find his own pace.

As the horse clopped closer to the McNaughton place, the nightmare vision that hung in his head of another man touching Annalaura churned at his stomach. When he blinked his eyes to make the spectacle go away, he could see the leaves on the trees move slightly. He supposed the day had brought a slight breeze with it, but his outside body had gone numb. There was no feel of the warming sun on his arms, or the touch of the light breeze brushing his cheek.

John neared the McNaughton back-forty, where a little stand of cherry trees stood twenty yards distant. The buds on the limbs were full, but they hadn't yet blossomed. Normally, he could taste their promise, even this early in the season, but now, all that was on his mind, all that he could see, was Alexander McNaughton putting the sweet honeyed lips of his Annalaura into his own white mouth. And worse.

He couldn't recall how he got to the ground, nor when the horse stopped near the little stand of cherry trees. He only knew that his knees barely made it to the grass when all the bile stored up over the past twenty-four hours spilled out over the fresh green carpet. He couldn't stop. His woman had been dirtied, defiled, and his world told him he had to take it like it never happened. To hear Becky tell it, half the colored population of Lawnover would be murdered before tomorrow sunrise if he touched one hair on McNaughton's pale head.

Cleveland, and even ten-year-old Doug, might swing from a tree. Little Henry would wind up in some workhouse, while Lottie would become another white man's plaything before her seventh birthday, all because he dared do what any husband on this earth had a right to do.

Becky and Annalaura would have him believe there was justice in running away. Justice and honor in swallowing his words and tipping his cap to every white skin, if that's what it took to keep his children safe. Didn't those women know there were worse things than not being safe? The bile grabbed him, and he retched to get it out. All of it had to be gone to cleanse his own soul before he died of the pain.

Ten minutes, maybe twenty, passed before he had the strength to try to stand. He reached for a branch to help pull himself to his feet, but its suppleness reminded him of Annalaura. In time, the cherry buds would deliver rich, ripe, dark fruit. But time would never deliver Annalaura to him the way she was. How could he ever mount her again when all he would ever see and smell when he came near her from this day on would be Alexander McNaughton? He rolled to his side, pulled his knees to his chest and squeezed his eyes so tight that the pain came to his head.

"Forgive me, Lord Jesus. I can't let this go, though I knows a good man should. It's best fo' me to keep on livin' so I can take care of my children. I knows it's best to stay breathin' so I can look after Annalaura though she can't never know it." At the sound of his voice, the horse quieted. "But, Lord, I is weak. A better man than me would say nothin', do nothin' that would bring harm to his family. But I ain't got that kind of strength in me, Lord. I can't stand by and let another man soil my wife." His throat felt raw, scratchy, from the retching and the shouting to the sky. "I know that because I can't turn it loose, more'n me will die. Lord, I prays you will show me a way to make it all go quick for them." The tears broke through like a spring river flowing over an earthen dam. "I don't care nothin' 'bout myself. Ain't no torture night riders can put on me worse than this hell I'm already in. To spare them the fright, if it be Yo' will, Lord, I will shoot Annalaura and all of my children in the head befo' the night riders get to them to spare them the fright. I just prays fo' you to show me the way."

John didn't know how long he lay there, but when he finally came to himself, he saw the sun filtering through the tree branches. It was directly overhead. As slow as though he carried the chains of his slave ancestors, he moved to his feet. He knew what he had to do and when. He was finally ready.

CHAPTER TWENTY-SIX

Alex dug his heels into the gray. Only when the horse failed to quicken his pace did he come back from his daydream. Out of habit, he looked at the sky. The sun told him he had one more hour of daylight. No wonder the animal could not give him what he'd asked. Since dawn's light, when he left Rebecca's cabin, and Laura, he'd ridden the animal hard. Alex eased up on the reins. He patted the horse's neck. There was no rush to hurry home. Nothing there but Eula Mae. And the cradle, of course. That rush of pleasure that thundered up from his gut when he least expected it washed over him again. Ever since she, his Laura, had agreed to move in with him, Alex had struggled not to let his excitement show in front of the other farmers. That's why he'd ridden the gray all the way to Clarksville. To Clarksville, where he could buy clothes and toys for his baby, and even pretties for his Laura. All without too many prying eyes. His smile broadened. It felt good to his soul to realize that he had just become a father. And, better yet, his baby and her mother would soon be under his roof. Now, away from peeping eyes, it was all right to grin all the way home. He felt like he had just brought in the biggest cash crop in the whole of Tennessee.

John mounted his rented horse, his stomach still cramping from all the retching he'd done. He aimed the animal up the road. As he settled himself on the broke-down horse he'd paid a pretty penny just to rent, he shook his head. What foolishness was he thinking? What did money mean to him or to any of them now? He had to do what must be done. He slid his hand into his overalls pocket— his old work clothes. He'd dug them out special this morning. It wouldn't do for a Lawnover colored man to be seen wearing city slicker clothes. Not this day. John reached a hand inside the pocket and pulled out the pistol. He held it by the hard metal butt. He'd wanted a fancier revolver, of course, but at the time he bought it, there had been no money for such frippery. Back then, in his early days in Nashville, he'd scraped together every penny just to get by. Twenty acres. That's what he'd wanted. Twenty acres to make a stab at earning a decent living for his children and...Annalaura. The gall clambered to his throat again, and he pulled up on the horse. He looked at the sun as he dismounted. There was still time. He just had to sort out the order. With planting season just starting, McNaughton wouldn't be getting home 'til dusk. And here it was, a good hour left of daylight.

The gray bobbed his head like he was saying his thanks to Alex for slowing the pace. Alex rubbed the horse's flank. No harm in letting the animal take a break. He spotted the old oak that told him home was just two miles away. He led the animal off the road. There was a tiny spring just a quarter mile distant. Let the horse have a drink. Besides, he supposed he could use the time to figure out the sleeping accommodations once he got Laura to his house. There was that spare room, upstairs next to where he and Eula slept. His wife used that one as her sewing place. No problem there. He'd just find another spot for Eula's sewing stuff. Maybe outside in the store-house. Alex trotted by the oak tree and turned the animal's head to the left. His mind drifted back to the sleeping arrangements. Having two women with beds on the same floor just might not work. He sensed that Laura's passion for him was growing. It wouldn't be too much longer before she screamed out her nighttime feelings for him. Suppose her moans woke Eula Mae? No, he'd have to come up with something different. He spotted the little stream, dismounted, and led the horse to water's edge. As the stallion drank his fill, Alex reached into the saddlebag. He fumbled underneath the wrapped doll he'd just bought for his new daughter and pulled out the pistol he always carried to Clarksville. Laura had asked him to let her handle things. Two days, she said. Two days and she'd make sure the husband wouldn't bother them anymore. One week and he'd be out of Lawnover for good. Alex snapped open the bullet chamber. One. Two. Three, four, five, six. Fully loaded. "Just in case." He spoke out loud with only a horse to hear him.

John leaned against the tree trunk, mindful of the time. The sun said about forty-five minutes 'til setting. His pocket watch told him it was half past six. There was enough time to sort it all out, but when he started to put his mind to it, his belly told him no. He rechecked the bullets in his pistol. Yep. Six of them. One for McNaughton, that was for damn sure. One for Annala...His head started its throbbing again, and his eyes their watering. He knew what had to be done. The Good Lord knew what was right. No man could be expected to have his wife dirtied the way McNaughton had ruined his Annalaura. It would pleasure John no end to put a bullet straight between McNaughton's eyes. Yes, he wanted the man to look him full in the face when he pulled the trigger—so the farmer could see just who was delivering what he had coming. But when it came to the part about who he had to shoot next, John couldn't order it out in his head. Another mile and he'd be at the turnoff to the barn where his family lived. Cleveland would still be there. His boy was only twelve. He'd acted like a man, and for that John was proud, but in God's truth, the boy was not yet full grown. Should he shoot Cleveland after McNaughton? Or before? The cramp rolled up so fast from his belly that it forced John to his knees, and four minutes of dry heaving. When the knives in his gut finally quit their chopping, he took out his handkerchief and wiped his face. "Let me just lean here for a minute." He guessed he was asking permission of the Lord. The Lord's answer must have been yes, because he still had thirty minutes before he had to lay in wait in the shadows of McNaughton's barn.

The gray whinnied his satisfaction, but Alex was in no hurry to remount. He was still mulling over who was going to sleep where. Eula's pantry might make a tidy little room for Laura and his baby. "My baby. My very own little girl." Alex rummaged the saddlebag again and pulled out the parcel the shopkeeper had wrapped. He lowered himself under the tree and undid the string. He looked at the porcelain-faced doll he'd bought for his daughter. Daughter. Every time the word entered his head, he felt like pinching himself. Yes, he was going to have his child and Laura with him tomorrow. He closed his eyes and let his mind drift into that place of happiness that only came when he thought of her—Laura. "One more week and it's all over." The words whispered out of his mouth so soft, even the horse couldn't have heard. "One more…" The caw of a hawk jolted him out of his dreaminess. One more week was a hell of a long time to wait for John Welles to get his ass out of town. Alex felt around the ground for the pistol he'd laid under the tree. Laura had pleaded so. Yes, she was certain she could get John Welles gone from Lawnover. Alex picked up his pistol and stroked the barrel. "That would surely be best." His words were loud enough for horse or man to hear if they cared to listen. "That would keep Ben Roy, and all those other afraid-to-spit farmers, quiet." He tucked the gun into the back of his britches' waistband. "But if that nigger lays another hand to Laura, he's dead, planting season or no." Alex placed the doll back into her wrapping paper. It had been a hard night and a long day. "Twenty minutes 'til dark. No need to face Eula tonight. Tomorrow will do. I'll just take myself a little nap."

The rented horse was not the swiftest thing on four legs, John declared. No matter, there was McNaughton's barn just up ahead. There were still ten more minutes 'til nightfall. John slowed the horse, raised a hand to his eyes and scanned the fields on either side of the road. No sign of McNaughton. Good. He reined in the horse to a slow trot as the side path off the main road came into view. Nobody else on the road. McNaughton wouldn't be home before dark. John's only worry was Miz McNaughton. At dusk, she would be heading to bed. It wasn't like she was a colored woman who had to tend the fields from sunup to sundown, then fetch and carry for her own family 'til the moon was good and set in the sky. McNaughton's wife was a white woman, and every white, churchgoing farmer's wife took their night's rest right after sunset. The last red-orange glow of the sun had just sunk below the horizon. There it was. The path to the McNaughton house. John slipped off the horse and tied the animal to the sycamore tree. If Miz McNaughton happened to be about, it would not do for her to see a colored man riding to her back door on a horse. John walked slowly up the path toward the red barn, his head down the way a respectful colored man should hold it. He sidled his eyes toward the main house. A lone lamp shone from one bottom floor window. Upstairs, another lamp lit a window. Good. Miz McNaughton was readying herself for bed. The downstairs light meant McNaughton hadn't made it back yet. John moved to the far side of the barn. It was a risk. The pistol shot was sure to wake the wife. She'd most likely look out the window, but darkness would cover him. He would have to scoot around the back of the barn and get out of the woman's sight if she took a notion to come outside for a look around. If he made a clean shot, McNaughton ought to drop without a sound. That way, maybe the missus would let everything be 'til morning. In the twilight, he spotted Miz McNaughton's buckboard at the far side of the barn. He eased toward it and squatted behind one of the big-rimmed wheels. He was good and out of sight now to anybody coming up the night-dark path toward him. John pulled out his pistol, scooped up a handful of dirt and rubbed it across the barrel just in case the moonlight reflected off the gun barrel. He was giving McNaughton no warning.

Something furry scurried across Alex's foot. A squirrel? A chipmunk? Whatever it was took him out of his dream about Laura. He ran a hand over his eyes and looked around for the horse. Night had fallen hard, but he spotted the animal where he'd left him, loosely tethered to a branch near the stream. Alex gathered his belongings and returned them to the saddlebag. He reached behind him. The gun was still there. Nice and snug. Not that he expected any trouble. But it was getting harder to keep his promise to Laura. He mounted the horse. Hell. He had only one more day, and she'd be there in his kitchen. In the pantry he'd fix up for her. He'd have to get a good-size bed, of course. No need for the two of them to be cramped like back at the barn. He felt a warming in his pants as he headed the gray back onto the path to home. The gentle rocking of the animal as it trotted up the road to his house jostled the gun into his back with each step. He laid a hand on the handle and readjusted the revolver. "Just in case," he muttered.

Full dark had fallen and tonight's moon was not quite a quarter in the sky. The upstairs light had gone out. John's leg cramped from staying too long in his crouch. He sat long-legged to give his muscles a rest. He kept his eyes on the road.

The clop-clop of the horse did little to help Alex keep awake. That nap had not really done the job. But no matter. There was his house. He couldn't make out the color in this sliver of a moon, but he knew every inch of the silhouette. Clop-clop, the gray approached the path leading to his property. "Damn, if this horse don't know the way home better than I do." Clop-clop. One more day and he'd have his Laurie in his arms.

The cramp eased in John's leg. He shifted to his knees and crouched behind the back wheel of the buggy. As he settled himself, his shoulder brushed the spoke and sent up a little creak. "Damn thing needs oiling. Can't McNaughton do nothing right?" John mumbled. He peered up the lane for what seemed the one hundredth time. Nothing except the occasional rabbit. He clicked open the gun. Six bullets. The first for McNaughton. The second for...for... No. It couldn't be Cleveland. Maybe, he'd go after Annalaura next. Bullet number two for her. But what about the baby? Sure, it looked as white as snow, but could he really put a bullet into a baby? The gall swarmed up again. Aunt Becky had told him to swallow seven times quick when that happened. It hadn't worked at all today, but now was not the time to start retching again. He swallowed four times before he let loose with one dry heave. He snapped the gun closed. Snap.

Clop. Clop. The gray made the turn with very little direction from Alex. "Where the hell am I going to sleep tonight?" Alex asked out loud. Not with Eula, for sure. He'd make himself a pallet in the pantry. He smiled. Tonight was as good a time as any to get used to sleeping in the little room. Clop. Clop.

The sound came at him like a heavy hailstorm. Clop. Clop. A horse. McNaughton's horse. John leaned into the buckboard wheel. Creak. In the darkness, he could see no figure, but sure as hell, that was McNaughton. As his eyes strained at the pathway to the house, his brain told him to sort out the order. Quick. First, McNaughton. Second, Annalaura. Third. Who? Which of his children would he have to kill next? Not Cleveland. Not that soon. Doug? Oh Lord, no. That was his smartest child. He'd make something of himself one day. Then it had to be Lottie. Lottie? His only girl? Sweat poured off John. His hand felt slippery against the butt of the gun. Clop. Clop. Good God. There he was. A horse and rider. Decide. Decide now. John leaned into the buckboard wheel. Creak.

What was that? Alex pulled up on the red reins. Sounded just like that creaky wheel on Eula's buggy. What was she doing out here at this time of night? Clop. He slowed the horse 'til the gray barely moved. Alex pulled out his gun.

Sweat swarmed down John's forehead and into his eyes. He had McNaughton in his sights. His finger stroked the trigger. One little squeeze. That's all there was to it. One little squeeze, and goodbye to a no-good, rapin' white man. She rose up out of nowhere, or from that place Becky called "beyond the pale." Annalaura's face with a body that looked made of rippling water popped into his head and would not move away. Worse. The figure blocked his view of McNaughton. John's gun hand shook as he stared at the thing Becky called a 'Parition. Some Cherokee women possessed it—a force as strong as fury that took hold of them and pushed their will into another person's head. Once it was in there, no power on God's earth could make it leave until the thing got good and ready. Even so, John jerked his head hard. Anything to make the Annalaura 'Parition go away. The vision that chilled to the soul wouldn't budge. John took his gun hand and swiped at the image clouding his eyes. No good. He leaned into the wheel to look around the thing. Creak. There was just no getting away from Annalaura.

Creak. Alex pulled up on the horse. He leaned forward and rested the side of his face against the gray's neck. Something was out there. Could be a coon. Could be a possum. Best not to take any chances. He let up on the reins, and the horse ambled toward the barn.

Annalaura's mouth moved, but she still shrouded John's target. Then, like a hammer dropping down on a nail, the 'Parition called out the names of their children. Cleveland. Doug. Lottie. Henry. Oh, Lord. He'd forgotten all about little Henry. He'd have to kill him too. The 'Parition moved closer, and with a force stronger than he'd ever known the flesh-and-blood Annalaura to show, the thing that looked like the woman he loved pushed him back from the wheel. Whatever it was dropped to the ground and got hold of his feet. It pushed them backward and away from the wagon wheel. To keep from falling, John reached out a hand to steady himself against the side of the barn. Two more steps and he'd be behind it, out of sight of anyone coming to inspect the buckboard. He dug in his heels, flailing out. The 'Parition grabbed his gun hand and jammed it against his chest. A force stronger than a mule pushed him behind the barn, and out of sight of curious eyes.

The gray halted at the barn door. Alex slid off. He peered over at the buckboard as he flattened himself against the barn wall. He sidestepped toward Eula's buggy. The black silhouette, with its high seat, stood undisturbed. Alex stared inside the open contraption. Empty. He let his eyes travel to the undercarriage. Nothing. With the gun cocked and pointed, he checked the front wheels.

No change. He slipped along the side of the buckboard toward the back wheels. Snap. His shoulders tensed and his breath stuck in his chest. Gurgling for air, he raised his gun arm, sighted as best he could, and aimed his pistol into the darkness. A raccoon ran from the back of the barn and straight into the wheel of Eula's buggy. Creak. The stunned animal staggered away. Alex sucked in a mouthful of air. "Hell, ain't nothin' but a coon." He laughed out on a burst of air as he lowered his gun arm. Alex shrugged that burst of fear off his shoulders as he moved to the front of the barn. "All right, horse. Let's get you settled in for the night."

John's breath came in spurts. McNaughton ought to be dead. But the way Annalaura had lied to protect the man…All that new stuff McNaughton had given her? White men didn't give black women fancy presents unless they were sweet on them. More gall coated his throat. He did Rebecca's seven-swallow routine in quick succession. Was that the truth of it? That fool white man had real feelings for Annalaura? He leaned against the back of the barn, both hands clutching his stomach. John's chest burned, and his head felt like it was going to cave in on itself. Annalaura, Henry, Lottie. Cleveland. Doug. Even McNaughton. They all did a whirly-twirly dance before his eyes, each one reaching out a hand to squeeze his heart. That farmer ought to be for sure dead, but McNaughton was nowhere near good enough to take the lives of John's four children to the grave with him. His breathing slowed, and his head quit throbbing. The Annalaura 'Parition began a slow fade into the blackness of the night. If white men found out McNaughton had honest-to-God feelings for a colored woman and was careless enough to let them show, they'd kill him themselves. One thing to use her, another thing to love her. The sweat began to dry on John's forehead. His lips forced themselves into a crooked smile. "This white man ain't worth it. Not if the price is my four babies. Not even An..." Leave his killing to those of his own kind.

With the gray settled for the night, Alex walked through the porch door, a half smile twitching across his lips. He'd pull out that old cradle and get it set up for his new baby. His own Dolly. Tomorrow he'd have both mother and child with him. The porch door snapped closed behind him.

John waited fifteen minutes by his pocket watch. He never did see a lamp relit upstairs. But at least two more lamps blazed on the first floor. Whatever that white man was up to would do him no good come morning. McNaughton could live. For now. But he'd never have Annalaura. John bent double and made his way back to the main road and the rental horse.

CHAPTER TWENTY-SEVEN

That first pale light of dawn filtered under Eula's eyelids and gently brought her out of sleep. But before she let the day come into focus, she stretched out an arm to search for that unfamiliar tingling "down there." It had been with her through all of yesterday with its heart-pumping exhilaration. She wanted to revel in that strange pleasure as long as she could. Disappointed that it was fading, she re-created the memory of that amazing night in her mind. Even though Alex hadn't been beside her in the morning when she rolled over to greet the new day, she had been filled with such pleasure and awe that she paid little mind that he hadn't shown up back at the house 'til close to suppertime.

He had gone to Clarksville, he announced upon his return, and brought back a package wrapped in brown butcher paper. She didn't believe she'd shown him impatience when he said she'd have to wait until tomorrow for its opening, but everything she thought she knew about her husband had turned inside out. The man who had been as predictable as the planting and prayer dinner had become a man of surprises.

Eula let her eyes drift to the first light at the window as she remembered her excited anticipation of last night. That she had to wait until morning to open a package was of small matter. Her husband had gotten her a gift, and it wasn't even her birthday. But it wasn't a butcher-paper-wrapped surprise that she'd wanted from Alex when she climbed into bed beside him last night.

First, she had debated if she should take off her own clothes or let him do it. When she saw him with his eyes closed and the kerosene lamp dampened, she shakily stood beside the shut chifforobe and, in full view in the dimly lit room, shed her corset and donned her summer gown. Alex never opened his eyes that she could tell, and by the time she crawled next to him, she was certain he was asleep. Perplexed, she finally eased off to dream, wondering what he would expect when he came after her in the morning. Whatever it was, she was determined to give it to him.

When she finally let this morning float into her mind, she quietly turned her head to the pillow beside her. Like yesterday, Alex's side of the bed was empty. A quick frown furrowed her brow, but she banished it just as fast as it came. She climbed out of bed and hurried to dress. She had to ready breakfast for her husband, and she had to be ready for whatever else Alex might want this morning. Eula giggled. Not since their first year together had he ever wanted her in the morning. She said a quick prayer for forgiveness at the sinful thought as she hurried to the kitchen.

Her mind lingered on the faded warmth of two nights past as she swung into her kitchen to find Alex sitting in a chair, a dusting rag in his hand, his head bent down over something sitting on the floor. Her gasp brought Alex's head up sharply from the object he was polishing. It was the smile on his face and the pure delight shining from his eyes that first made her feel like she'd fallen through February ice. She didn't know how long she stood there staring at her husband and the baby rocker. But she supposed it was long enough for him to speak first.

"Look what else I've got." He pointed to the butcher-wrapped package he'd brought in yesterday, completely ignoring the pain that spilled out all over her at the sight of the twenty-year-old cradle.

Alex had cut down the trees and sawn and hammered the cedar and elm pieces into place with his own hands. It had taken him over three months to ready it for their child. With their own precious baby so long gone, how could he bear to touch that wood again? Before she could nod her head nay or yea, Alex tore into the paper wrappings. Inside, the painted porcelain face of a child's doll emerged, its blonde hair made of bleached horsetail. As the paper came off, arms, legs, and a body stuffed of excelsior stared up at her.

"Alex, it's a baby doll?" Her question matched the look on her face. One heavy arm pointed to the toy and then swung to the cradle Alex stroked with such tenderness. What had brought his thoughts to their dead daughter after all these years? "What am I to do with a baby doll?"

"I'm gonna set you down, Eula Mae." Alex walked over to her and slipped both hands to her shoulders.

When he looked at her, Eula could have sworn that she saw real caring in those blue eyes. Was this the way of men after twenty-one years of marriage? Did they blow hot one minute and then act like you mattered no more than a gnat the next? Before she could blink again, he pulled her close, hugged her to his chest, and propelled her toward the kitchen chair he always took.

"I couldn't have done no better." He brushed her forehead with his lips.

"I got to get your breakfast on." It was the only thing that came to mind.

"That's just it, Eula. You been cookin' and cleanin' this place since the day I brought you here. Brought you to a po' piece of land." He took her big work-reddened hands in his.

Of all the things that she hated about her large, awkward body, her hands came high on the list. She felt Alex's strong fingers stroke them like they were made of the most delicate Nashville silk. He brought them to his chest.

"You're a Thornton girl, you deserve better."

"I been a McNaughton woman for twenty-one years." What was he saying to her?

"You're the best wife I could have picked. You keep this place spotless and your cookin' is more than tolerable." He lowered her hands to his knees. "I ain't never heard a mean, nor a nay-sayin', word out of you."

"Work ain't nothin' to me, Alex. I'm the oldest girl with four brothers." She stumbled out the words. "Of course, I can work."

"You're a Thornton woman. Fedora has lots of help. Even Wiley George got Hettie for Tillie. It ain't right that you don't have help after all these years." He bobbed his head.

"Fedora needs all the help she can get, and Hettie's wet-nursin' Tillie's baby until my niece can get the hang of it." In her confusion, she put a half smile on her face. "Wiley George can't afford to keep a real hired girl."

"I wouldn't be much of a man if I couldn't give you what you should have, now would I?"

"That's not the way of it," Eula managed.

"I'm gonna set you down."

"Alex, I'm not near 'bout worn out yet." Was that what he thought of her after their astonishing night? That she was too old and too broken down to do what a good wife ought? That she needed help?

"I ain't gonna let you get worn out, Eula. I'm gonna get you a hired girl." Alex couldn't have sounded more jubilant.

"A hired girl?" She couldn't remember who let go first, but her rough hands were suddenly free. "I don't need no hired girl."

Alex moved back to the rocker. "Of course you do. She'll do a lot of the heavy work around here. She's a strong woman." He laid a hand on the cradle and set it into gentle motion.

"Nooo." Eula felt her stomach sway in time to the old baby crib. He knew how she hated to look upon it.

"Best part about the hired woman is that she's comin' with company." He ignored her cry as he gave the cradle another gentle push. He laid the baby doll in it. "I know it's been hard on you all these years since you lost the baby."

"Please, Alex, put it back," she whispered as she turned her eyes away.

"It took me hard, too...the loss...God's will, I said. Best not to dwell on it." He left the cradle and walked back to her. "But that ain't helped much. I still felt mostly like I was missin' something. A baby will put life back into the both of us." He stood there looking down on her as though every word he said didn't feel like he was slicing the skin right off her bones.

"I can't talk about no baby." The tears were on the verge of falling, but Eula knew her husband would never tolerate them. She blinked them back.

"The hired woman will be here in a few days and she's bringin' a baby with her." He grinned at her.

Eula swallowed her spit so many times she was sure it would dry up in her throat before she could get the words out.

"Baby? What baby?" Missing preserves, disappeared hams, lost nights, her silver-trimmed wedding bowl, all popped out of their hiding places and marched before her eyes. She knew the answer.

"Looks like I've got to let out the mid-forty to some new tenants." His eyes didn't meet hers.

"The mid-forty?" Her voice croaked.

"Yeah. The new hired man's family is movin' in. The other one...the woman on the mid-forty...she'll make a very good hired girl for this place." His eyes slid back to the cradle.

"The...the woman on the mid-forty..." The words coming out of her mouth belonged to another voice. "Her name. What is the name?" If Alex could speak the syllables, could she bear to hear the sound? She glanced out the kitchen window.

The sun, the new leaves on the trees, the blue on the jaybirds, all looked painted, unreal, frozen into their places like on a play-acting stage. Only her breath, trying to fight its way out of her tight chest, made any noise in the room. Hours passed as Eula watched Alex's mouth set itself to form the words.

"It's Laurie…ah…Annalaura. I mean Welles…Annalaura Welles." Alex's face showed that he had no idea that the stops and starts of his voice made her ears hurt.

"Laurie…" She let her mouth form the noises into order and push them back out into the dull, dead world that was now hers.

She heard the pantry clock tick five times. Each click felt like a knife cutting the inside of her throat. Her one night of perfect, exquisite pleasure banged against those sounds coming out of her husband's mouth. The only laurel wreath Alex had called out in ecstasy that night belonged to Annalaura…Laura Welles.

"The ba…baby?" She coughed each syllable through the heavy grit of sandpaper.

Alex finally turned his eyes back to her. "Dolly. Her name is Dolly." He said it like he was praying soft in church. He said it like it was the most precious name ever to fall off the tongue of humankind in the history of the world.

Only the sudden knock on the porch door at ten o'clock in the morning stopped her body from sliding from the kitchen chair to the floor.

"Mornin'." Ben Roy stepped through the back door. Eula barely noticed her brother.

"Mmm." Alex's curt response glanced off her ears without leaving a dent.

She paid no mind when Ben Roy walked right past her husband and stared at the black cast-iron skillet she had set out last night. Only the rustle of a go-to-town skirt hovering near her told her that Fedora must have followed Ben Roy through the open door. Why these two were paying the McNaughtons a morning visit took second place to Eula trying to stop her kitchen from spinning. She put a hand to her head and leaned heavily on the table. She felt Fedora lay a hand on her shoulder. She had no strength left to even wonder at the why of it from a sister-in-law who had never expressed any fondness for her.

"Took Fedora over to Bobby Lee's this mornin'." Ben Roy kept staring at her skillet.

She thought she had cleaned it good last night, but for the first time in her life, she didn't care. Fedora's hand dug into her shoulder. Even though she sensed anger coming out of Alex, she didn't have the will to look at him.

"Uh huh." There was an unmistakable eagerness in Alex's voice to get his brother-in-law out of the house.

Ben Roy still stared at her skillet like it might throw itself off the stove if he didn't keep a close eye on it.

"Talked to Bobby Lee this mornin'." Ben Roy kept his eyes gripped on the skillet.

"What can I help you with, Ben Roy?" Alex sounded impatient.

Ben Roy turned halfway around to face her husband.

"Bobby Lee knows of some niggers that can help you out."

Fedora's fingers dug deep into Eula's arm. She lifted her head toward the two men standing on her kitchen floor.

"I already got enough hired hands to work my acres." Now Alex sounded annoyed as well as impatient.

"You gonna need mo' help on the mid-forty." Ben Roy puffed out his cheeks.

"Don't you worry none, the mid-forty will be all right." Alex stared down Ben Roy.

Fedora's fingers dug in so hard that Eula squirmed away from the pain.

"Bobby Lee was up in Clarksville way early this mornin'. He saw that nigger, John Welles, pull out on the eight ten train." Ben Roy slipped a hand into a pant pocket.

"What?" Alex drew the word out long, but at its end, Eula was sure she heard pleasure and relief.

Ben Roy gave a fast and strong shake of his head after shooting a quick glance toward Eula.

"Welles is gone? He left town?" A smile started across her husband's face.

"Took the whole damn family with him."

"What?" Alex shook his head, his eyes blazing. "What you say?"

"Even his wife." Fedora aimed each word at Alex.

"Took every damn one of 'em." Ben Roy spat out an imaginary stream of tobacco juice on her kitchen floor. "Took his fo' kids and even that old woman—Rebecca."

Eula's eyes moved to Alex. Nothing on her husband moved. Even his eyes had gone numb.

"Nigger must have stole him some money 'cause he bought one-way tickets fo' all eight of 'em," Ben Roy added.

"Eight of them," Fedora repeated.

"Welles, his fo' kids, Becky, the woman, and…" Ben Roy stopped.

"Bobby Lee's wife said the woman just had a baby two days ago. Colored," Fedora clucked. "Don't even allow their women proper lyin' in time, but then, I don't reckon a colored woman needs much of that anyway. Birthin' comes easy to them."

Ben Roy turned toward Eula. "I reckon Welles wanted to get his woman and the new baby away from that man who was botherin' her…that hired hand from last harvest. What was his name, Fedora?" Ben Roy kept his eyes on Alex.

"Harris somethin' or other." Fedora's hand stroked Eula's shoulder.

Eula stared at the floor and wondered why it was fast rising to meet her face. Ben Roy's arms wrapped around her. Her brother sat her back on the chair. Fedora laid a wet cloth across her forehead.

"It's a damn lie." Alex exploded across the kitchen.

Eula's closed eyes flew open as the tornado that was her husband brushed roughly past Ben Roy and stormed onto the porch. Through the open door, she heard kettles, supply barrels, water pails, metal-tipped leather straps, and nails, all crashing and clanging together. Alex thundered back into the kitchen, the shotgun in his hands.

"You comin' or not?" He looked like a man possessed as he shouted at Ben Roy.

"Comin'? Where the hell you think we goin'?" Pushing Fedora almost onto Eula's lap, Ben Roy rushed up to Alex.

"For God's sake. To catch that damn train, of course." Alex turned toward the back door, but Ben Roy wrapped an arm around his shoulder.

"You ain't doin' no such a thing. Hell, man, that train done left Clarksville two hours ago. It's clean to Kentucky by now. You can't catch no train." Ben Roy took a quick look at the women, jerked his head toward Fedora, and slammed the porch door.

"Let's get you to the parlor and onto yo' settee," Fedora soothed. "You can rest better there. You been workin' too hard, Eula Mae." Fedora kept her eyes on the shut door.

"If you ain't goin', then get out of my damn way," Alex's voice shouted through the closed door. "I'm after me a train."

"And what the hell you gonna do if you catch that train?" Ben Roy yelled at Alex.

"The same damn thing you and Wiley George should have helped me with two nights ago," Alex roared. "Run that nigger out of town."

"He is outta town, damn it. He left this mornin'. Ain't that what you wanted? Bobby Lee says the tickets was one way fo' Chicago. They ain't comin' back. Not none of 'em." Ben Roy's barked words were lost in the moan of pain Eula heard erupt from Alex's throat.

She felt Fedora try to pick her up bodily from the chair. Eula clung to the edge of the table.

"That's a damn lie. He's takin' her against her will. I'm gettin' her off that train. She promised me…" Alex's shouts could be heard straight to Lawnover, Eula was certain.

"She's the man's wife. She can't make you no damn promises," Ben Roy shouted right back at her husband. "Alex, it's over."

"I can't. I can't do it. Don't you know that I can't let her go? I love h…" The sound of fist against flesh and bone rocketed through the porch door.

Eula felt Fedora lurch at the commotion.

"Are you fo' sure crazy? You can love her all you want, you just can't say it out loud, and you sure as hell can't keep her." The sounds of a scuffle bumped out of the porch as Ben Roy shouted.

"I'm gonna bring her back. Her and my baby. It's me she wants, not that n…" Bone against muscle shook the room.

From the crashes on her porch, Eula was certain that not even one wall would be left standing.

"You ain't doin' no such a thing, and you ain't sayin' them words to another livin' soul. Talk like that will get us all killed," Ben Roy panted.

"I don't give a damn." The sounds of wrestling on the floor blasted into the kitchen.

"You'd better give a lot of damns, 'cause ain't no power on earth gonna let you love a colored woman and live it out loud. Not here in Tennessee." Ben Roy struggled for breath as the most soul-rattling sound Eula ever heard emerged in a keen, low moan from her husband.

Eula lurched in a haze. Fedora shouted words at her that she couldn't understand. Her sister-in-law may as well have been speaking Geechee.

"What you gonna do with that?" Fedora's face went white. Eula followed the short woman's horrified gaze to her own hand, where she held her just-sharpened chicken-butchering knife. Fedora pushed on Eula's hand with all her might, but it felt like a ladybug crawling up her arm.

"I'm goin' to kill Alex." She said it just like she asked her husband if he wanted a third cup of breakfast coffee.

Eula started toward the door, each foot feeling like a dozen horseshoes were nailed to it. Almost at the porch, she didn't see it coming. The chair crashed across her back and she stumbled. The knife skittered from her hand. Fedora kicked it to the other side of the kitchen.

"Get on into this parlor, now." Fedora put her full weight behind her sister-in-law and shoved her into the front parlor.

Eula's feet stumbled out from under her but not before Fedora gave her a final push in the direction of the settee. Eula fell more on than off of the horsehair-stuffed sofa. Fedora grabbed both of Eula's feet and draped them over one arm. She pushed a pillow under her head and started for the sideboard after she first slammed the door to the kitchen.

"Where the hell does Alex keep the key to the whiskey?" Fedora began pulling out drawers and opening doors.

The sounds coming from the back porch were now too muffled for Eula to hear.

"Bottom drawer. In the matchbox." Eula watched her sister-in-law fill two glasses almost to the top. Did Fedora actually think strong drink was going to help?

Walking to the settee, Fedora pushed a glass in Eula's hand as she pulled up a straight-backed chair.

"Where's yo' rose water? You got fresh lavender soap?" Fedora's words grated on Eula's ears. "Day after tomorrow, me and Ben Roy will take you over to Clarksville. I know a place where all the wives go. Yo' momma told me 'bout it."

Eula pushed herself up on the settee, looked at the amber liquid in the glass, and brought it to her nose. It smelled like tar paper.

"You can get black bloomers there." Fedora kept up her chatter. "They just cover the crotch and got pretty lace 'round the edges." Fedora stopped and took a deep swig from her glass. She coughed once and leaned in closer. "Eula, you payin' me any mind?"

"Alex don't think a lady should take a drink unless she's close to dyin'." Eula looked at the full glass in her hand and sloshed it around, not caring that some of the liquid dripped onto her tapestried settee. She raised the glass, nodded her head toward Fedora, and took in one large gulp of whiskey. Eula held it in her puffed-out cheeks until it burned, and then let it flow down the back of her throat.

"You listen to me," Fedora commanded, but her words held about as much force as Tillie's new baby, Little Ben. "It's a woman's job to keep her husband happy, especially if he's off with a colored woman. Now, this place has got short corsets that are made to push 'em up and out just like when you was twenty."

How many of these whore clothes did her sister-in-law own? Eula wondered.

"Fedora, to keep my husband in my bed, you want me to dress and act like a Clarksville trollop." She took another deep swallow of the whiskey. "I'd rather kill myself." She spit the word out at her sister-in-law.

The slap across her face came sudden and hard. In fact, if she hadn't seen Fedora standing there with her open palm, Eula would have sworn that the woman struck her with a closed fist loaded with buckshot. The whiskey spilled all over the settee.

"Who do you think you are, Eula Mae McNaughton?" Fedora was a head shorter, but right now, she towered over Eula. "Who told you that you could kill yo'self?" Fedora tossed her head back and started to laugh.

"Fedora?" Had her sister-in-law gone as mad as Alex? "Take yo'self another drink." Eula sat up straight as she tugged at Fedora to sit beside her.

Fedora could not be moved. "You sit there like you are the queen of all the Thorntons. Always did think you was the best of us. The best cook, the best canner, the best at managin' the farm. Yo' husband never had to say a harsh word to you, nor lay a hand to yo' head 'cause you never did nothin' wrong. Everthin' you touched was right." Fedora screamed every word at her.

"Fedora...no...I never thought I was better. I..."

"You're a damn liar, Eula Mae. And now you think you're too good to have yo' man climb into bed with a nigger woman. You think your stuff is so special, so pure, that you should be the only white woman in Lawnover, hell, in all of Montgomery County, whose man ain't never laid with a black woman." Fedora finished off the whiskey and threw the glass to the floor.

Eula watched it roll, unbroken, on her carpet. "Alex wouldn't...he couldn't."

"Why is that? Because he loves you so much? 'Cause he can't live without you?" The steam suddenly shot out of Fedora, and she flopped, deflated, on the settee beside Eula. "Don't you know it ain't got nothin' to do with how well you cook, or how many preserves you put up for the winter, or how clean your kitchen, or how many times you write in that damn journal of yours?"

"What…what was it then?" She welcomed Fedora's arms around her shoulders.

"Eula, you ain't the first in this family whose man took up with a colored woman." Fedora swallowed hard. "You know as well as me that Ben Roy got three yella bastards by Hettie. And, yo' own daddy, Old Ben, had that yella Johnny by that old woman all you Thorntons is scared of—Rebecca."

"That can't be right. My pa never…"

"And, if you're thinkin' Rebecca was the only woman yo' pa put it to, you're wrong. I hear tell there were at least a dozen others." Fedora sounded so sure.

"I don't believe you." Eula stared at her sister-in-law.

"Everybody in Lawnover knows the truth of it 'cept you. Kept it from you because you're his daughter." Fedora took her arms from around Eula's shoulders and folded them in her lap. She stared down at her hands.

"Does Tillie know about Hettie?" Eula managed.

"Not yet, praise the Lord." Fedora looked at Eula with hollow eyes. "Wiley George don't have a colored woman yet, far as I know, but he will. It's the way of a Southern man. It ain't nothin' you done or didn't do, Eula. You just been lucky that it took Alex twenty years to find him a black woman. All men do it, and it's just somethin' we wives have to get used to." Fedora let the words come out of her mouth like there was no other way to it in all this world.

"Well, I'll be damned if I'll ever get used to it. I'm leavin' Alex. I'll go to Kentucky with Bessie." She shrieked her agony when Fedora's second blow landed across her mouth.

"Ain't gonna be none of that. You ain't disgracin' this family. There'll be no Kentucky. Ben Roy won't have it no other way." Fedora was on her feet, towering over her again.

"No." The sobs finally came. "I'll never stay with Al…that bastard."

"Oh, yes, you will. You'll bear it the way the rest of us have. You ain't never gonna mention none of this to Alex. Is that clear?"

"The hell I won't. I'm gonna kill Alex if I don't leave him first. I'm..." Her sobs drowned the words in her throat.

"No, you ain't. Now, this woman's gone, but if he takes up with another, you're gonna pretend that you don't know nothin' 'bout it. Like you barely know her name. You ain't never gonna say a cross word to Alex, because if you do, it's only you who bears the hurt, not him." Fedora stooped and picked up the empty glass from the carpeted floor. She marched to the sideboard and refilled it. Wiping the rim, she handed it to Eula.

"I don't think I can do that..."

"Oh, you'll learn how quick enough."

"And if I can't? If I complain out loud to everybody who will listen about what...what Alex done to me?"

"They'll take you for a fool and a disgrace." Fedora reached for the whiskey bottle. "Not a disgrace to your husband, but a disgrace to every married white woman who ever lived in Lawnover. If you complain that yo' husband is cheatin' on you with a nigger, then you're telling everybody in all of Montgomery County that a colored woman is the same as you. That she's as good as you. That she's even better, because she's got yo' man. Eula, you can't do that." Fedora took a deep swig from the bottle.

"He said he lo...loves...her. He said he loves a...nig..." The word ripped out of her gut.

Fedora lowered herself slowly to the settee. "That's why you can't never complain. Not to nobody. Different if it was another white woman he said he loved. Then you been wronged fair and square, and you can cry and scream all you want. Everybody will come to yo' side. But when it's a colored woman, it just can't be the same. White men ain't supposed to love black women over us.

My Lord, if we acted like that was true, there wouldn't be no sense to this world." Fedora patted her shoulder. "Never you mind, Ben Roy will make sure you never have to hear those words out of Alex's mouth again." She slipped an arm back around her shoulders. Her voice was full of sorrow.

Eula saw the floor coming up to greet her again. Fedora grabbed her hand and squeezed her wedding ring.

"You feel that?" She dug the too-tight ring into Eula's skin.

"Umm."

"You feel that ring on yo' finger, Eula Mae? You'll always be the wife. Let that be yo' comfort. He may be in her bed every night. He may even tell her that he loves her and mean it with all his heart. But that black woman will never have what you have. God and the law will always see to it that you come first."

"What do I care 'bout bein' first with the damn law. What do I care 'bout bein' first with God? What about his heart? I need to be first in his heart." The tears ran down her cheeks and onto her shirtwaist. "I want Alex to say those words to me…that he loves me. Only me." Eula pulled at the bodice of her dress so hard that one button clung to the garment only by a single thread.

Fedora slipped both arms around her, pulled her close, rocked her in her arms.

"Men think different than we do. They have their colored women for their own silly fun, but they have us fo' wives." She smoothed Eula's hair. "Alex is just talkin' crazy right now. He don't really want to trade." She sounded so certain.

"If he could, he would." The words rode out of Eula on a great wave of sobs.

All the years with Alex slipped in front of her eyes. Everything about her husband played over and over in her mind. She knew when he was happy, when the planting had gone wrong, when the harvest had gone right, when he was pleased, what he disliked, what and when he wanted more, when he wanted quiet, when he wanted laughter. Even the passion he'd shown two nights ago fit into the picture puzzle that was her husband. It had been there, simmering deep down in the center of him always. Now, somewhere, at her own core, she knew she'd never been, and would never be, the one to unlock that power. The woman...Laura...held the only key.

"If he could, he would." Eula repeated the sounds that squeezed out of her mouth in a soft moan.

Fedora squeezed the ring again. "You will get through this, Eula. Every other white wife in Lawnover married more than five years has lived through the exact same thing you're goin' through right now."

"Belle? Cora Lee? Jenny?" Their pain couldn't be as great as hers. She loved Alex. Did Fedora love Ben Roy like that?

"All of us. Don't worry none. Alex won't never talk about this day again. You ain't seen Ben Roy bring Hettie anywhere near my house, now have you? Why do you think I wouldn't allow Ben Roy's woman to come serve the plantin' dinner and prayer when Tillie carried on so? Your brother knows better than to parade his colored whore in front of me. All the men do." Fedora put her hand on Eula's whiskey glass and tipped it to her sister-in-law's lips.

As she drank, Eula knew the woman, Alex's woman, was no whore. He couldn't love her if she was.

The parlor door slammed open, and Ben Roy walked through, Alex's shotgun crooked in one arm.

"Let's get outta here, Fedora." Ben Roy spoke through blood-oozing lips. One eye was swollen almost shut, and a large lump had made an appearance on his forehead. He turned to his sister. "Eula Mae, get on in to yo' husband. He's in the kitchen." Ben Roy crossed the floor of the front parlor in two strides, grabbed Fedora by the wrist, turned, and stalked out of the house.

Eula eased up from the settee as though she'd been the one in the fistfight. Her feet wanted to take her into her bedroom, away from Alex, away from Fedora telling her to be brave, away from Ben Roy ordering her to comfort her scoundrel of a husband, away from all thoughts of... She wanted to climb into her bed and pull the coverlet over her head, go so deep into sleep that she would dream only of darkness. She turned her head toward the parlor door leading to the kitchen. Alex was in there. What could she say to him? Nothing, as Fedora suggested? Everything, like she wanted? Cajoling like Ben Roy ordered?

First one foot, then a second, led her toward the bedroom. She stopped in her tracks. Through the partially cracked door, she spotted the neatly made bed. The bed where Alex had lain with her two nights ago. Lain on top of her, and lied with his body. Her stomach churned as she moved like a stiff scarecrow into the kitchen.

Alex's usual chair was empty. Whether Ben Roy put him in there or he just didn't care, her husband sat at her regular place at the table. Alex must have heard her walk into the room, for he turned a cheek reddened with an upcoming bruise toward her. His moist eyes looked right through her. He turned his head back to the crib and rocked it slowly. Moving like a rusted plow badly in need of oiling, he picked up the porcelain-headed doll and brought it to his lips. He rubbed his face against the horsetail hair.

On the kitchen table within easy reach was the knife. Ben Roy must have picked it up from the floor. Slow like she was treeing a possum, Eula inched her hand toward it. Alex paid her no mind. Grabbing the handle, she slid the knife as quiet as she could toward her. Even though it was twenty-one years old, the rocker was so well made that only the whisper of a sound came from its runners as Alex let his hand keep it in motion.

Eula brought the knife before her eyes, both of her hands clasped tight on the handle. She twisted it in the almost-noonday sun. A ray caught on Alex's yellow hair. She wondered what it would look like drenched in the red of his blood. She switched the knife to her right hand and took a step toward him. Her feet moved like great lead weights had been sewn into her cotton stockings. Standing right behind him and breathing hard, she wondered that he hadn't noticed her. She brought the knife handle to her right shoulder, the blade pointed straight at the middle of Alex's back. She closed her eyes and willed her arm to move with the strength of David in his battle with Goliath. The heavy image brought up a laugh from her gut that she failed to keep down.

Alexander McNaughton was no giant, and she wasn't a weak but brave child. She was poised to plunge a knife into the back of a cheating, lying husband, and he hadn't even noticed. That was just it, Alexander McNaughton had never noticed her—not to hurt her, not to hate her, not to love her. And if she did plunge the knife into his back, straight through to his front, and he turned his dying eyes toward her, he would only wonder at her actions. In his mind, he had done nothing to cause her harm, nothing to inflict pain. He had done nothing wrong. He would go to his Maker with innocence in his mind, pondering what had driven his wife to such an uncalled-for act. The laugh came out of her mouth garbled. It sounded more like she was wishing him a cheery good morning.

"Sorry 'bout breakfast. I'll get yo' pork chops on fo' dinner." She lowered the knife and laid it on the table as she moved her lead feet to the stove. Behind her, she heard Alex pick up the cradle and carry it back to her pantry.

As he walked past her like a dead man, she caught a glimpse of the porcelain-faced doll inside. For long seconds, she stood at the stove, a lit match in her hands, wondering what to do. Should she follow him into the pantry? Should she tell him something about loving him so much that she could die of it right now? That she could forgive him? The match singed her fingers, and she blew it out. She took a step toward the pantry. Trying to find a way to put her feelings into words, she moved almost to the door. Alex turned those vacant eyes on her. She reached out a hand to him just as the pantry door closed. She felt for the knob. She heard the pin drop into the latch. He had locked her out.

No thoughts came into her head. All the pain had left her heart. All the agony had fled her soul. She felt nothing as she walked to her safe. She didn't need her calendar to tell her that it was time to check her journal records. She reached up on the shelf and pulled out her account book. She laid it open on her table, reached for her pencil, and sat down. Thumbing through the book until she reached the Planting page, she began to write in her careful hand. Under Vegetables she wrote String Beans: 10 rows. Corn: 20 rows. Lima Beans: 5 rows. She had always been proud of her nicely squared-off handwriting, and though she couldn't feel the pencil in her hand this day, she saw that her writing was still meticulous. She turned to a fresh page to continue her accounts, but without her hand or her head willing it, the pencil lead began to write.

May 21, 1914
Township of Lawnover
State of Tennessee

I, Eula Mae Thornton McNaughton, testify that this day I have become, at last, the perfect Southern wife. I now know to the core of my being the lessons my mother, and her mother before her, tried to teach me. On the eve of my wedding, when my mother told me that my husband would give me pain beyond all imaginings, I foolishly thought she spoke of his breaking of my flowering. Now, I know that it was my soul that would be shattered. It is because I am condemned to never be a whole woman that I make this testimony.

This day I resolve to do what I must. If, and when, my husband ever returns to my bed, I will hold him harmless for any pain he has ever put on me. I vow to never bring shame to him, or his name, by letting the world know that my entire life, and my love for him, have been betrayed in the most foul way. None will hear the cries that I dare not release from my chest even though each one strangles the breath out of me. If my husband ever again puts an arm around me, or even his lips to my forehead, I will never allow him to see the sorrow that drowns my heart. Beyond all doubt, I know that he wishes with all his being that the shoulder he touches, the lips he brushes, the breast he caresses, belonged to the body of another.

When he looks through me, I will always pretend that I don't know that it is the love of another he prays to possess. To my God, this day, I resolve to be the best white wife who has ever lived in Tennessee.

Eula McNaughton

In letters no more than tiny pricks of the pencil to the middle-aged eye, the words printed on the right-hand edge of the paper running up and down read *Alexander McNaughton loves Annalaura Welles.*

She punched the pencil deep into the book, but she could not bring herself to scratch out the words. Carefully closing the journal, Eula pulled her usual kitchen chair to the safe, climbed on it, and reached to the top shelf to move her silver-tipped wedding tureen. She tucked her journal behind it knowing she would never touch it again.

Not bothering to look where she landed, Eula stepped off the chair, grabbed a pitcher, and walked into the shambles that had been her porch. She pushed aside her now dented tin bath-tub to reach the pump handle. Filling the pitcher with water, she returned through her kitchen, picked up the butcher knife, and retreated to her bedroom. She barely glanced at the bed as she poured water into the blue-flowered basin she had bought for herself as a remembrance of her tenth wedding anniversary. Bending over the water-filled basin, she saw the reflection of an old woman, her face lined with care, staring back at her.

Eula dipped her hand into the clean depths, her fingers splashing away the image. She would never look upon that wom-an again. She patted her face with the water, but she couldn't tell if it was hot or cold. With her hands dripping, she smoothed her hair and tugged the wrinkles out of her dress. She gave the knife only a quick glimpse as she picked it up and aimed its point at the fleshy part of her finger. Like everything else this morning, and for the rest of her life, she couldn't feel its sharp point jab into her flesh. When the bubble of blood oozed to the surface, she took her finger and smeared its redness across both cheeks. She pulled open a bottom drawer of her dresser and took out the hand mirror that she'd never seen a need to use. She checked her cheeks in its glassiness. The care-lined old woman was gone.

She was ready. With the lead from her shoes and stockings quickly disappearing, Eula walked through her parlor, past her kitchen, out through the now unhinged porch door, and over to her buckboard in the barn. She must ready her horse for a trip to Fedora's. It was time to redeem herself. When she sees her sis-ter-in-law, of course she will act as though nothing unusual has happened in the McNaughton household these last ten months.

Her fainting spell was just part of the change of life. Fedora will recognize that. All in all, she will act as though she understands everything and knows nothing. She will be the good Southern wife. After all, that is the only thing that Alex has ever loved about her.

CHAPTER TWENTY-EIGHT

"Cairo. Cairo, Illinois." The porter walked down the aisle of the just-stopped Illinois Central train.

Sitting bolt upright in the stiff seat, Annalaura looked out the window into the lamp-lit dimness of the railway station. A few passengers from the car just ahead walked the platform, puffing on cigarettes. The letters, C-A-I-R-O, stared back at her from the sign suspended just over the round-faced brass clock that showed ten p.m. But she read only A-L-E-X.

Annalaura, the children, Becky, and John had boarded that first train fourteen hours earlier in Clarksville, and after a three-hour layover in some Kentucky town too small to notice, John had settled them all into the dusty, colored-only coach bound for Chicago. Now, the porter, in his white railroad jacket, paused briefly beside Annalaura's seat. The man give her a slight wink as he pretended to check the destination on her ticket.

"Chicago, Illinois. Land o' Lincoln." He let a slight smile play across his lips.

Did he want to make sure she understood that he had just announced her arrival into the Promised Land? But was it?

Annalaura looked down at Lottie, lying beside her, deep in sleep, her little girl braids resting heavy against Annalaura's shoulder. Doug and Henry sat across the aisle with Aunt Becky, all three sound asleep—Henry curled up on his great aunt's lap. Annalaura started to whisper to Rebecca that freedom had come to her for real this time. They had crossed over into the North, where a colored person's life was supposed to be easier.

She glanced over at Henry's still body, dreaming his little boy dreams of drums and shoes that didn't pinch. Staring out of the window into the darkness as the colored porter pulled up the portable steps, Annalaura spotted Becky's wavering reflection in the window. Her aunt sat with her chin on her chest, her mouth open. The unfamiliar feel of a tiny smile played across Annalaura's lips, the first since the beating John had laid on her three days ago. If she could believe her husband, Alex still lived. She let her shoulders sink into the seat back.

It would be midnight in another two hours, and the porter had already announced that Chicago was eight hours away. Dawn would come soon enough, and with it, her own uncertain future. As the railroad man made his way out of their train car, clanging the heavy connecting door behind him, Annalaura caught a glimpse of movement across the aisle and four rows up. John carefully stepped over a sleeping Cleveland and swayed his way down the aisle. Before she could let the full fright take hold in her brain, her hand clutched the shawl covering baby Dolly. The husband she had betrayed walked toward her, his face bathed in flickering shadows.

Since this morning, when he had stormed into the cabin before Becky could get the old blunderbuss off its fireplace hook and ordered them all to come with him "right now," he hadn't said more than a dozen words to her. When she scooted her sore and bruised body to the far side of the bed, fierce to let no harm fall on Dolly, John let his words come out as cold as the barrel of Becky's gun.

"McNaughton ain't dead...yet," he'd said, "and if you wants to keep it that way, you'd best be comin' with me."

Annalaura couldn't recall much more about that moment, only that her brain felt like it was pushing her eyes right out of her head. Little Dolly's gasping cries brought her back to herself in the train car. She searched in her head for the right questions to ask her husband the why of it. She remembered that John had swooped her and the baby into his arms and shoved past a flabbergasted Becky. Even when he laid the two into the back of a wagon already crowded with Doug, Henry, and a shivering Lottie, Annalaura couldn't muster a word. Was it a trick? Had John killed Alex after all? Before the night riders caught up with them, was John driving her to take a final tormenting look at Alex's lifeless body? In the wagon, she'd clung tight to the swaddled infant as she grabbed at Doug's foot, resting in the small of her back.

"Cleveland?" had been the only sound she'd managed.

"Up top with Papa and Aunt Becky," Doug had whispered back.

Annalaura felt Lottie wrap her skinny arms around her mother's drawn-up knees. Why was John taking his own children to see a dead man? Even in her bewilderment, she'd felt the tears forming.

Under Becky's blanket, and a pile of old burlap that still smelled of last year's husked corn, Annalaura stretched out a hand to pat Henry's face, now snuggled hard into Doug's chest. Where was her husband taking them?

With Doug's shoe putting fresh bruises on her back, Annalaura tried to reach for Lottie as the wagon jolted to a wobbly stop. She remembered croaking something at Doug about covering little Henry's eyes. She would stop her children from seeing the sight of white-hooded men, stout trees, and knotted ropes, for as long as she could. She shut her own eyes tight, clung to Dolly, and let the darkness swoon over her.

The feel of rough hands, and the sharp stab of daylight, brought her back to the world. Annalaura worked Lottie's head and shoulders between her knees and rolled her own body on top of the newborn. But, it was too late. Before she could blink, she felt John take her in his arms and toss the blanket over her and the baby. She turned her face into his chest. She didn't want to see where he was carrying her as the hissing sound of steam beat into her ears.

By the time John set her down on the second of the train steps, Annalaura already knew that her husband had taken her to the Clarksville railroad station. With her eyes blinking in the light of the early morning sun, she looked up to see a stern-faced Cleveland grab for her arm. As John gave her a final boost, she turned to look out at the platform. Other than her husband handing up Lottie and Henry, and the four or five other people boarding the cars ahead, she didn't see a white-hooded man in sight.

As John boarded the train with Becky and Doug trailing him, Annalaura tried to pick the words out of her confusion. Her husband brushed right past her and settled next to Cleveland. As the porter called out his "All Aboard," John turned his face to the window. Only Aunt Becky had words for her, "Gal, thank yo' Jesus fo' this day."

"They say Chicago's three or fo' times bigger'n Nashville." John stood over her in the train aisle of the Chicago-bound train. "Lots mo' people livin' up there, but ain't many of them colored." John looked through the window at the Cairo sign.

Annalaura's shoulders shuddered at her husband's ramblings. What did he want?

"Too easy to find colored folks livin' up there." In the semi-darkness of the train car, John shifted his eyes to the top of her head. "Like pickin' out raisins in a bowl of milk."

Annalaura tucked the shawl tighter around Dolly, and eased the baby closer to her breast.

"This night air..." John pushed a hand toward the shawl.

The move sent a sudden shiver through Annalaura. Could she believe her husband? Did Alex still live?

John lifted his head. His eyes roamed across Annalaura's face. She watched him work his lips but no words came. A burst of steam belched from underneath the train. She heard her husband's loud swallow as he aimed a finger toward the shawl-wrapped bundle.

"Night air can be bad for little ones, the old folks say." He stared down at his spread fingers.

Annalaura stared back at him. Something was new. His eyes swam with eye-brimming water. "Night air bad," she managed.

The bulge in her husband's throat bobbed up and down. His nostrils flared.

"She all right?" He whispered as he looked at the shawl.

"She's just fine." Annalaura kept her eyes on John.

"Annalaura..." The word came out strained. "I'm not wantin' Chicago... but... if you think it be best fo' you and the chil'ren, then I...I mean that I won't...be stoppin' you." He parceled out the words.

Annalaura shook her head. What was her husband saying?

"McNaughton...If he took a notion to look..." John thrust a hand in his pant pocket and pulled out a balled-up wad of paper. "If you got yo' mind set on Chicago, then I reckon there's not much I can do to change it. But I wants you to know..." he shifted his eyes to Dolly, "I ain't never leavin' you again, Annalaura...not lessen you tells me to go." John pushed the wad between the folds of the shawl. "Becky says you callin' her Dolly." He settled his eyes somewhere between Annalaura's neck and chin. "Dolly...Dolly Welles. That'll set just fine with me."

John jumped to his feet, took a step toward the front of the railcar, stopped, and stared straight ahead just as the train began its slow roll forward. "Becky let me know who pulled that baby out of you. Snatched you away from the angel of death, she say." He started to move. John called over his shoulder as he began his way up the aisle. "You pick."

Annalaura shook her head in confusion. Her hand fingered the wadded paper. She smoothed out the wrinkles just as Lottie stirred. Annalaura stroked her daughter's shoulder, and offered up a silent prayer that her firstborn girl would never know the pain of being torn in two. She let her eyes rest on the paper. Her husband had given her the train schedule.

She stared at the printed sheet now lying open on Dolly's shawl. On the creased paper, she saw the names of unfamiliar towns lining the state of Illinois from Cairo, all the way north, to the end of the line. John had put a pencil scratch through the black letters of the last town listed—Chicago. Annalaura raised the shawl and stared down at her sleeping youngest daughter. Had her ears heard right? Did John tell her to pick? Pick what?

"Raisins in a bowl of milk." She murmured out loud. She let her fingers travel down the schedule, touching the strange names—Carbondale, Urbana, Danville, Bloomington. Strange towns. Unknown towns. If Alex cared to search for her, and in her heart, she knew he would, he would think only Chicago. Never Urbana. Never Bloomington.

Annalaura patted Lottie's shoulder. Across the aisle, deep in sleep, his head resting against the hard armrest of his seat, Doug smiled like he was dreaming of books with more words than pictures. Henry, Lottie, Cleveland—she owed them all the promise of hopes and dreams. And John. Annalaura let her eyes travel to the front of the train car. The head of the man she'd promised to love and obey 'til death parted them rose over the seat back, rigid, like he was waiting for something important to be settled before he could allow himself to drift into his own sleep.

The Land of Lincoln, the Land of Promise. She had promised John. She had promised Alex. Choose one, and all her yesterdays with the other had to be forgotten. Pick an anonymous name on a train schedule, and her new life would begin with John. He would take Dolly as his own. Love her as his own flesh. Choose Chicago, and become a raisin in a bowl of milk. A raisin waiting for Alex to knock on her door—to claim her as his own.

The train lurched around a curve. Annalaura felt Lottie's body burrow deeper into her aching chest.

Choose, John had made it clear. Two towns. Two men. A shaft of moonlight so bright that it won out against the gaslight in the coach car, bounced off the window, and settled across the back of her hand. She stared at her arm. A slight movement across the aisle drew her gaze to Becky. She shifted her eyes from the old Cherokee to her hand cradling Dolly, and back again. For the first time, she realized that she didn't need her aunt's second sight to give her the strength to do what she must.

Annalaura bent down to the shawl-covered bundle and kissed her daughter on the forehead. Choose, John had said. I forgive you. She took in a gulp of air and stared long seconds at her hand. Though the errant speckles from the moonlight had slipped away, her fingers still showed golden. The ache in her head that had held fast since John left her a year back slipped away. The velvet night outside the train window sparkled as clear as her mind felt. Annalaura looked up the aisle toward her husband. Bless him for his love, but she needed no forgiving. She had done no sin against her God, nor against her husband. Her eyes went to Dolly. Alex, trapped in his own world, had tried, like John, to force a choice out of her. But how could any choice belong to her when it was someone else who laid out only what he knew?

Her free hand fumbled over the thin, wrinkled slip of paper John had thrust at her. She caught her breath as she let the fingers that had caressed Alex's naked body play across each of the lined-over letters that spelled out CHICAGO. She lowered her eyelids to block out all sight in the train car. Her hand began a slow slide down the page. A raised place in the paper stopped her. She eased her eyes open and stared down at the letters on the smoothed-out sheet. Her answer had lain there all along. The pain in her heart eased. Choose, said John. Choose me, Alex had said. But she had a choice neither man had given her. Annalaura stroked Lottie's arm and settled into sleep, her mind at peace. All of her tomorrows belonged in only one set of hands—her own.

ACKNOWLEDGMENTS

Page has been a story demanding a voice for almost
one hundred years. Thank you, Teresa LeYung Ryan
(author of *Love Made of Heart*), for being the first to let
me believe that I could pull one woman's story out of
the dark world of secrecy and into the light. Bless the
California Writers' Club—Berkeley Critique Group/
David Baker and Anne Fox—for forcing the tools into
my hands to allow me to put thoughts to paper. To that
first batch of brave readers—Tootsie, Gloria, Juanda,
Dora Jean, and Rozelle—I owe you an immeasurable
debt of gratitude for wading through my sea of words.
And just when I thought *Page* would forever languish
on a bookshelf for my eyes only, Gilles, you gave me
the encouragement for that final push.

I will always be in awe of whatever force directed
Terry Goodman, senior acquisitions editor at Amazon-
Encore, to choose *Page* from all the manuscripts

submitted to him. Terry's input, encouragement, and support have been incredible. A special acknowledgment to the entire team at AmazonEncore. They've made this an experience of a lifetime.

I thank my family, Hank and Doug, for putting up with me these past six years. But, most of all, Grandma, this is for you.

HICKMANS